WARCHILD

DOCTOR WHO – THE NEW ADVENTURES

Also available:

TIMEWYRM: GENESYS by John Peel
TIMEWYRM: EXODUS by Terrance Dicks
TIMEWYRM: APOCALYPSE by Nigel Robinson
TIMEWYRM: REVELATION by Paul Cornell
CAT'S CRADLE: TIME'S CRUCIBLE by Marc Platt
CAT'S CRADLE: WARHEAD by Andrew Cartmel
CAT'S CRADLE: WITCH MARK by Andrew Hunt
NIGHTSHADE by Mark Gatiss
LOVE AND WAR by Paul Cornell
TRANSIT by Ben Aaronovitch
THE HIGHEST SCIENCE by Gareth Roberts
THE PIT by Neil Penswick
DECEIT by Peter Darvill-Evans
LUCIFER RISING by Jim Mortimore and Andy Lane
WHITE DARKNESS by David A. McIntee
SHADOWMIND by Christopher Bulis
BIRTHRIGHT by Nigel Robinson
ICEBERG by David Banks
BLOOD HEAT by Jim Mortimore
THE DIMENSION RIDERS by Daniel Blythe
THE LEFT-HANDED HUMMINGBIRD by Kate Orman
CONUNDRUM by Steve Lyons
NO FUTURE by Paul Cornell
TRAGEDY DAY by Gareth Roberts
LEGACY by Gary Russell
THEATRE OF WAR by Justin Richards
ALL-CONSUMING FIRE by Andy Lane
BLOOD HARVEST by Terrance Dicks
STRANGE ENGLAND by Simon Messingham
FIRST FRONTIER by David A. McIntee
ST ANTHONY'S FIRE by Mark Gatiss
FALLS THE SHADOW by Daniel O'Mahony
PARASITE by Jim Mortimore
WARLOCK by Andrew Cartmel
SET PIECE by Kate Orman
INFINITE REQUIEM by Daniel Blythe
SANCTUARY by David A. McIntee
HUMAN NATURE by Paul Cornell
ORIGINAL SIN by Andy Lane
SKY PIRATES! by Dave Stone
ZAMPER by Gareth Roberts
TOY SOLDIERS by Paul Leonard
HEAD GAMES by Steve Lyons
THE ALSO PEOPLE by Ben Aaronovitch
SHAKEDOWN by Terrance Dicks
JUST WAR by Lance Parkin

THE NEW DOCTOR WHO ADVENTURES

WARCHILD

Andrew Cartmel

First published in Great Britain in 1996 by
Doctor Who Books
an imprint of Virgin Publishing Ltd
332 Ladbroke Grove
London W10 5AH

Copyright © Andrew Cartmel 1996

The right of Andrew Cartmel to be identified as the Author of this Work has been asserted by him in accordance with the Copyright, Designs and Patents Act 1988.

'Doctor Who' series copyright © British Broadcasting Corporation 1996

Cover illustration by Jeff Cummins

ISBN 0 426 20464 6

Typeset by Galleon Typesetting, Ipswich
Printed and bound in Great Britain by
Mackays of Chatham PLC

All characters in this publication are fictitious and any resemblance to real persons, living or dead, is purely coincidental.

This book is sold subject to the condition that it shall not, by way of trade or otherwise, be lent, resold, hired out or otherwise circulated without the publisher's prior written consent in any form of binding or cover other than that in which it is published and without a similar condition including this condition being imposed on the subsequent purchaser.

For Chuck Cartmel

Chapter 1

Creed was rising up towards the light.

His head broke the surface and instantly noise rushed in at him from all sides. The sound of splashing water and the clamour and laughter of children echoed loudly off tiled surfaces. It was a hot day and the swimming pool was full.

Creed slipped onto his back and paddled slowly past the tall windows. The bored lifeguards sat in their high-chairs in day-glo shorts, occasionally shrilling their whistles at the antics of the kids.

Above them fibre optic image systems prowled like angular insects on the ceiling and, elsewhere in the sports centre, smart software watched for the pattern of images which would signal a swimmer in distress.

Creed swam placidly through panel after bright panel of sunshine. The daylight shone through the big windows and heaved and gleamed on the gently moving water. He rolled over onto his chest and began a slow crawl. Where was Eve?

He turned lazily in the water and saw her.

'Stay close, Eve,' he called.

'Yes, daddy,' piped Eve shrilly. His four-year-old daughter was paddling determinedly across the pool, her bright yellow inflatable armbands keeping her afloat. She was wearing a pair of blue rubber goggles that made her look like a miniature version of a 1930s aviation heroine.

As older kids swept past Eve their turbulence caused her to bob up and down momentarily, but she doggedly retrieved her course.

Creed rolled over and floated on his back so he could keep an eye on her. When he was sure she wasn't about to drift into any kind of trouble he turned away and swam another length.

He'd been in the pool long enough but he knew better than to try to hurry Eve when she was set on a course of action. She had inherited his stubbornness, along with a good measure of her mother's.

In the crowded men's changing-room he stood Eve on a bench and towelled her down, dressed her, then dressed himself. She took Creed's hand and followed him out, a tiny girl navigating through a forest of hairy, male legs.

They went up the stairs together, holding hands and out into the long branching corridors of the gym complex. Creed felt good after the swim, limber and fit.

Just past the restaurant and bar he bumped into his teenage son Ricky and a group of his friends.

'Hi, Mr McIlveen,' said the boys. Ricky muttered a greeting, not meeting his father's eye.

'What are you guys doing here?' Creed grinned at them. 'I can't imagine a bunch of losers like you indulging in a programme of physical fitness.'

The boys smiled back. 'You're right there, Mr McIlveen,' said one.

'We're only here for the girl-watching.' Another boy slapped Ricky on the back. 'For some reason this ugly bastard has a knack for attracting girls. It's like a magic trick. You go anywhere with him and he can find them.'

'It's not like he finds them. It's like he draws them to him.'

'It's no challenge in here,' said another boy, trying not to stare as a couple of lycra-clad gymnasts sauntered past. 'But it works anywhere. In the most unlikely places. He has the knack. He just draws them.'

'Like bees to honey.'

'Like flies to sh—' said one of the other boys, suddenly noticing Creed's four-year-old daughter and stopping from saying the word just in time.

Creed appreciated the effort but frankly Eve had heard most of the scatalogical catalogue of the English language from him; usually while he was skinning his knuckles on a wrench during various DIY projects at home.

As if sensing that she had suddenly become the unspoken object of attention, Eve squirmed uncomfortably and tugged on her father's hand. 'Well, I'd better be going,' said Creed. 'Good luck with your noble quest.'

'Yeah, we'll find the girls all right,' said one of the boys. 'Not that we're going to say hello to them or anything. We wouldn't do that. We're geeks and the geeks union doesn't allow it.'

Creed laughed and the boys laughed too. All except Ricky.

That was the problem, Creed realized. He got along fine with his son's friends. He just didn't get along with his son.

He said goodbye and turned away, leading Eve through the sports centre. Creed brooded briefly about Ricky. Had he screwed up as a father?

But it was hard to worry about that when his youngest daughter was holding his hand, feet skipping happily along the floor, weightless, a small balloon of love floating along beside him.

They had now reached the area of the sports complex containing the sauna and the weight-training rooms. A tall broad-shouldered man was emerging from the free-weight room, his back to them. He had a thick, bristling brush-cut and he was covered with sweat. Even before he turned around Creed had recognized him as Buddy Stanmer from the office.

'Hi Creed.' Stanmer was dressed in a pair of cut-off denim shorts with a white towel draped over his powerful shoulders. He took the towel and wiped it vigorously across his chunky red face as he squatted down, muscular thighs bulging, and crouched beside Eve. 'Hi, honey.'

'Hello, Mr Stanmer.' Eve winced as Stanmer rubbed his hand roughly through her damp hair. 'Been swimming with the old man, eh?' Stanmer straightened up and grinned at Creed. 'You should try weight-lifting if you want exercise.'

Creed made a polite, non-committal noise.

'Got to watch that midlife inertia,' Buddy Stanmer continued brightly. 'When a guy gets to a certain age it's real easy to just let things slide.'

Creed did some mental arithmetic while Stanmer was rambling. His age minus Stanmer's. He was shocked to conclude that the other man was about twelve years younger.

Creed tended not to think in terms of age. It didn't seem a particularly useful way of categorizing people. He pigeonholed people, all right. But by different criteria. Stanmer, for instance, he'd sized up accurately within a few hours of their first meeting.

'You don't notice it at first,' Stanmer was saying. 'But before you know it the waist starts thickening and the reflexes slow down and you get breathless just walking up the stairs. Don't get me wrong. At a certain time in his life a guy's entitled to take it easy. For most desk jockeys it wouldn't matter.' Stanmer dropped his voice conspiratorially as two teenage girls walked past in tennis skirts. 'But in our line of work things aren't so simple, huh?'

The girls glanced back curiously at the two men holding a whispered conversation. Creed felt his face getting hot. Stanmer was an idiot. The sports centre was private but the Agency was only one of its clients. They had to share the facilities with the employees of several large local businesses; you did indeed have to be careful what you said. But Stanmer was just attracting attention with his clumsy cloak-and-dagger act.

Eve tugged impatiently at her father's hand but Stanmer wasn't finished with them yet. 'I haven't seen you on the pistol range much lately, Creed.'

'I guess I'm shooting targets when you're not there.'

'I sure hope so. If you don't put in your required number of hours by the end of December they'll make you train up again and re-qualify.'

'That's right,' said Creed brightly. He was getting as bored as Eve.

'You should come out when I'm practising some time and we can run a few targets together. Blast a few bad guys. Maybe even put a side-bet down to sharpen our interest.'

'Sure, let's do that,' Creed lied. Stanmer was the better shot and he knew it – at least on the target range.

'And after a spell on the range I'll get you lifting weights,' Stanmer rubbed his blunt stubby fingers through his sweaty crew-cut. 'Fight that old middle-aged spread.'

Eve was tugging at Creed's hand again. 'Well, we'd better be going.'

'You're lucky,' said Stanmer. 'Having the whole weekend to take it easy. Personally, I'm going to get some steam then it's back in the weight-room. No rest for the wicked, I guess,' he chuckled. 'You'll see what it's like when I start you on a training programme.' He jabbed a playful punch at Creed. His heavy muscular fist crashed into Creed's bicep hard enough to raise a bruise.

'You're not starting me on anything,' said Creed, smiling a dangerously fixed smile. 'I don't lift weights. Number one: free weights are dangerous. One awkward lift can wreck your spine for life. It's a stupid form of exercise. The pattern of movement is all wrong. It's artificial. You never see an animal doing anything that stupid. Number two: I find it boring. All that endless repetitive movement just bores the hell out of me.'

'Sure. Artificial. Boring.' Stanmer nodded. 'I guess there's always excuses if you're looking for them.' He aimed another punch at Creed's arm, but Creed had run out of patience now.

He let his body slip into a defence stance, stepped inside the punch and caught Stanmer's fist in mid-air. He moved with such speed that he saw a flash of frightened surprise in Stanmer's eyes. Creed felt a hot stab of satisfaction. He'd had enough of this little prick standing here condescending to him, treating him like a middle-aged has-been while his daughter danced from foot to foot with boredom.

So instead of letting go of Stanmer, he squeezed. The man's hard, chunky fist made an odd popping noise in Creed's hand. Creed had hardly begun to squeeze when he saw Stanmer's face go white with pain.

He let go instantly, regretting what he'd done. He moved to try to help the man but Stanmer jerked away from him.

Creed bit his lip. He'd gone too far. Stanmer was an oaf but he wasn't stupid. Come Monday he was going to have to go back to the office and work with this man. He watched Stanmer leaning against the wall, flexing his hand as colour slowly returned to his face.

He was stuck with Stanmer. And Stanmer could be very dangerous to Creed on a professional level.

And perhaps in other ways.

But it was too late now.

Stanmer smiled an insincere smile, holding his hand at an awkward angle. 'Well, I guess I'll be seeing you back at the office,' he said, his voice trembling slightly, barely under control.

'Yeah, take care,' said Creed, hearing the shaming insincerity ringing loudly in his own voice.

'And don't work too many late nights. But I forgot, you don't, do you?' Stanmer was grinning now, as if a pleasant thought had occurred to him. 'Except those nights when Amy is working,' he said.

Stanmer turned away, leaving Creed standing there, sick with rage.

'I'd like to see you do the trick out here.'

Ricky and his friends were sitting waiting for a bus in the baking heat of the August day. The bus-stop was situated across the highway, a kilometre from the sports centre, in the middle of a featureless concrete nowhere. Under the unrelenting glare of the sun it might have been a geometric landscape on some alien planet, implacably hostile to human life.

Either side of the wide road had been cleared of vegetation in readiness for some ambitious development project which had stalled, leaving the hectares of flat, red dust to be stripped by the wind. The sports complex was a small box in the distance and there was no sign of human life.

The boys were sick of waiting for the bus. Ricky knew that his dad would have given them a lift home but he didn't like the idea, so he hadn't even mentioned it to the others.

Now they were getting bored and restless in the heat. It hadn't taken long for one of them to suggest that Ricky do his trick.

'This will be a real challenge. If you can manage to conjure one up out here it will be the ultimate example of your skill.'

'Haven't you horny idiots ogled enough women for one day?'

'No.'

So eventually Ricky gave in. He concentrated and did the thing he did in his head. The thing that always caused girls to appear.

And nothing happened.

Ricky's friends gradually grew restless and, though nothing was said, Ricky knew they were disappointed with him. They squinted into the shimmering heat-haze but the flat concrete landscape around them remained devoid of beautiful women.

When their bus finally pulled up Ricky's friends had sunk into a glum, defeated silence. The last boy to climb on board turned back to Ricky and slapped him on the shoulder. 'We'll come over and help you work on the car later,' he said. Then he added in a low voice, 'Don't worry about it, man. Nothing works every time.'

Ricky remained sitting at the bus-stop. His friends waved to him from the wide back window of the bus, good-naturedly giving him the finger and making other obscene gestures. As he watched them go he felt a hollowness in the pit of his stomach. It was strange to no longer be catching the same bus as his friends. But Ricky didn't live in the same neighbourhood any more.

He wished his family hadn't moved. Ricky wished they were still living on the other side of town. His family had had a house by the river with cool shady trees when they'd lived on the other side of town. All his friends lived there.

Now he didn't have any friends. And he couldn't even work the one damned trick which made him an interesting guy.

The bus drew away, dwindling down the highway, glinting in the hot sunlight. It was almost out of sight when a car pulled in beside the bus-stop. It was a small yellow Fiat. The window hummed down and the driver smiled through it.

'Hello, Ricky,' said the driver. 'You don't know me, but I work with your dad. I'm looking for him.'

Ricky smiled back at the driver, his spirits lifting. She was blonde and very beautiful, with eyes of a bright indeterminate colour, somewhere between blue and green.

'Have you seen him anywhere?' she said.

'Is this the way to the car park, daddy?'

'Yes it is,' said Creed. But it wasn't. His encounter with Stanmer had left him so angry he was still a little disorientated, like some enraged animal blundering blindly through the jungle undergrowth.

Creed took another turn through the sports complex and brushed through a crowd of giggling towel-wrapped teenage girls as they emerged from the sauna in a cloud of moist steam and clean shampoo smells. 'Is this the way?'

'Yes, it is,' said Creed as he led Eve towards the wide glass doors opening on to the car park.

'Where are we going now, daddy?'

'School.'

'School! But school doesn't start till next week.' Although she was still too young to go herself, Eve regarded the idea of school with a mixture of fascination and horror. She knew in a year's time she would have to begin going. Not kindergarten any more, thought Creed. Real school. Grade one.

'Then the gloves'll be off,' murmured Eve.

'What?' Creed grinned. Eve said the oddest things. 'You'll love school, baby. You'll be so excited you won't want to come home. It's an adventure.'

'I'll always want to come home.'

'Until one day, dear, until one day,' said Creed quietly.

Eve looked up at her father. He was a tall man with dark hair and deeply carved smile-lines in his angular face. He had the high cheek-bones and dark eyes of a Cherokee Indian. Eve didn't like it when her father sounded sad. Like he did now, or when he'd hurt the nasty man's hand. But he smiled at her then and Eve knew everything was all right again in her small warm world. She looked happily away from her daddy, down at her small feet, toes of shoes cleverly walking, as she strolled along beside him.

They walked across the wide sunlit parking lot, father and daughter.

Creed unlocked the car and Eve scrambled in. He bent down to buckle her into the passenger seat. That was when he saw the yellow Fiat cruising past in an adjacent lane of the car park.

Creed swiftly sealed Eve's belt and slid into his own seat, flattening himself so that at the angle of approach the driver of the Fiat wouldn't see him.

The yellow car eased past and continued around a corner into the next sector of the parking lot. As it went, Creed saw a flash of short blonde hair and a glint of silver earring as the girl driving checked her mirror. Then she was gone.

Creed let out a long sigh and realized he'd been holding his breath. He started the engine, released the handbrake and rolled forward.

'Daddy?' Eve's voice piped up from the back seat.

'Yes, honey?' Creed was squinting as brilliant afternoon sunlight slanted into the car. He polarized the windscreen and slid out into the traffic flow.

'Why are you hiding from Amy?' said his daughter.

Concentrating on getting into his lane for a right turn, Creed didn't reply.

'She's nice,' said Eve.

'Yes she is, honey.'

There was silence as he found his exit and joined the traffic flow moving sluggishly down-town.

'Is she too nice, daddy?'

Creed put the radio on, found a classical station and turned it up loud.

Chapter 2

There was something strange about the two women in first class.

Jessica Morrell pondered the matter while she finished collecting the supper trays and, with the help of the Scottish girl, pushed the trolley back into its niche in the stewardesses' station. They were due to land in London in an hour and a half and there were no more meals to be served, no more tea or coffee. The hardened alcoholics in Club Class were bound to demand a few more drinks, but on the whole Jessica's shift was over. She would let the new girl do the landing announcement and seat-belt check.

Now she sat down in the small semi-private space allotted for the cabin crew tucked in beside the first class toilets. She eased in behind the curtain, sat on the folding seat, slipped her shoes off and relaxed.

Jessica massaged her aching feet and pondered the matter of the two women in first class. They'd taken the aisle seats on either side of row C and spent most of the flight in low intense conversation, leaning out over the aisle so that their heads were almost touching, easing back in whenever a stewardess passed.

They'd accepted the minimum of hospitality; no drinks, a couple of coffees. The white woman had only eaten one meal, the black woman nothing at all.

They had an odd, slightly hard look to them which deterred Jessica from being too friendly. The black woman in particular had an unwavering no-nonsense gaze. When you met her eyes it snuffed out any attempt at small talk. So Jessica had just poured them coffee and left them to it, leaning out in the aisles, elbows over the edge of their seats, heads almost touching, the serious subdued flow of their conversation ceasing whenever one of the cabin crew walked past. The women would reluctantly bob apart, then back together again. There was a strange kind of intimacy between them. It crossed Jessica's mind that they might be lesbians.

She finished massaging her feet and quickly slipped her shoes back on as a passenger, a fat Belgian man carrying a folded newspaper, wedged his way through the narrow passage towards the toilets. It wouldn't do for a member of the cabin crew to be caught relaxed and barefoot. Jessica sighed and stood up, helping the Scots girl scrape the last of the food trays into the recycling container.

'I hope he isn't planning on doing the crossword in there,' said the Scots girl. She nodded to the toilet stall where the Belgian had vanished with his newspaper. 'We're going to need them all back in their seats soon.' The girl's name was Fiona, Fee for short, and this was her first time on the Budapest–London run.

'Don't worry, we've got nearly an hour,' said Jessica. 'What do you think of the two women in C?'

Fee scraped the last tray and dropped it through the hatch before leaning casually around the curtain to peer back into the cabin. 'Where?' she said. 'Either side of the aisle there?'

'That's them.'

'Hmm. Yes, a bit odd perhaps.' Fee got her computer out of her pocket and punched up the passenger list. 'Bernice Summerfield and Roslyn Forrester,' she said, reading the names off the tiny folding screen.

'I think they're lesbians,' confided Jessica.

'Fine, if that's what turns them on,' said the Scots girl. 'Good lick to them.' Then she realized what she'd said and instantly began to blush furiously. 'I mean, good *luck* to them.'

Jessica managed not to laugh until Fee had blundered hastily out of the cubicle to answer a drink request from club class, her face still a scorching bright pink under her freckles. The Belgian came out of the toilet to find Jessica gasping and biting a knuckle, howling silently into her closed fist. He frowned and headed back to his seat, rattling his newspaper.

Jessica managed to calm herself down. If she got the giggles she was lost. She wiped her eyes. Steady now. A fit of giggles in first class just wouldn't do. Deep breaths. There. That's better.

Half of this job was maintaining the proper façade, the unflappable smiling public face. You had to be calm and helpful even when you wanted to kill the passengers.

Roy had told her that, in later life, airline stewardesses developed terrible etched lines on their faces from all that fake smiling. 'That's nice to hear,' she said, lying in bed beside him. 'Will you still love me if I have a face like a corrugated roof?'

'No,' said Roy. 'But I'll pay for a face-lift.'

Now Jessica felt herself becoming lost in thoughts of Roy. She remembered the fight. They had never had one like that before. Oh, they'd argued. But never anything like this.

Scooter, their huge cowardly Alsatian, had lived up to his name and scooted at the first sound of their angry voices. He hid under the sofa in the front room, making helpless, small, lost-doggy pleas for peace as the argument between his beloved owners escalated towards violence.

They say that the kitchen is the scene of more domestic killings than any other location. Jessica wasn't surprised.

She'd been standing there on the tiled floor, facing Roy, and they'd both run out of vicious things to say to each other. That was when Jessica saw something gleaming out of the corner of her eye and she'd lunged for it and just let her rage explode.

Thank God, it hadn't been a knife. Just that row of glass bottles that she and Roy had filled with pasta and pulses. It had been the final thing they'd bought for their kitchen, which was the final room in the house that they'd decorated. She had remembered their shared excitement when they'd found the handsome old bottles lurking under a layer of dust in an antiques shop. Old blue Victorian medicine bottles. They had got them so cheap it was like stealing. They cleaned them up and gave them pride of place in the kitchen. It was the finishing touch. It seemed to set the seal on their moving in together.

While Roy watched, Jessica swept the glass jars on to the tiled floor. They exploded in a dancing jagged tangle of blue glass, lentils, dried peas, noodles. It sounded like a bomb going off and next door Scooter howled and fled with his tail between his legs.

Roy had just looked at her with level hatred in his eyes and said, 'I wish I'd thought of doing that.'

Then he turned and walked out.

She stared at the wreckage on the floor and wondered what she'd done. She began to cry. None of this would have happened if Roy hadn't been so vicious, so unrelenting in the course of their argument.

Of course, knowing what she did about Roy now, she understood why it had happened. Knowing what had been running through his mind at the time, it was no wonder.

It had all been revealed at the airport that morning before she left for Budapest. Jessica sat there in the cabin crew's cubicle and thought about that morning.

She had forgotten about getting the giggles, and about Fee blushing, and about the strange women in row C.

'I don't think the stewardesses like us,' said Benny.

'Why do you say that?' Roz leaned into the aisle so she could hear what her friend was saying.

'Well, did you see that one that just rushed by?'

Roz grinned. 'The one that was blushing like a stoplight?'

'Yes. Am I imagining things or did she give us the oddest look as she went past?'

'I shouldn't lose any sleep over it,' said Roz. 'Anyway, I don't intend to.' She moved away from Benny and settled back in her seat. 'Wake me when we're ready to land at Heathrow.' She closed her eyes and in a moment her tall body had relaxed bonelessly and she was sound asleep in her uncomfortable airline seat.

Jessica sat in the stewardesses' cubicle as the big jet rumbled through the sky, moving on its slow vector towards Heathrow in West London. In row C Jessica saw that the black woman was asleep. The white woman was staring across the aisle, watching her. It certainly wasn't a look of love or passion or even affection. So much for the lesbian theory. But it was an odd look. Almost one of fear.

Jessica forgot about it, lost in thoughts of Roy and that moment at the airport.

She'd turned up for work that morning looking like death.

She hadn't slept at all the night before, lying there in bed replaying the argument in her head. Her big gentle dog Scooter lay at the foot of the bed whining softly, sharing her sadness. The fragments of blue glass and the hundreds of tiny dry beans and pasta pieces still lay on the cold floor of the kitchen.

When the first pale rays of dawn showed in the bedroom window she forced herself to rise and clean up the mess. By the time she finished she just had time for a quick shower before she caught a taxi to Heathrow to start her shift. She was moving like an automaton. Everything was sluggish and slow. The world seemed colourless and dead. All the way to the airport she thought about Roy and how she'd never see him again.

He was waiting for her at the departure gate.

He was holding the biggest bunch of red roses she'd ever seen in her life.

He got down on his knees right there in front of the air crew, and asked her to marry him. Later, as she was rocking in the safety of his arms, feeling weightless, ignoring the third call from the cabin crew that it was time to go, Roy explained that this was why he'd been so tense, so unbearable to live with the last few days.

He'd made up his mind to propose to her but, to his astonishment, he'd found that he was paralysed with fear. What if Jessica said no? The more he'd thought about it, the more the possibility had swelled in his mind until finally, instead of proposing, he'd ended up picking a fight.

Poor bloke. He'd been terrified. Jessica didn't blame him. It was a big decision. She felt a little terrified herself, but the feeling was more than outweighed by the delicious excitement Roy had sparked off in her stomach when she saw him waiting for her with the roses. He had taken her in his arms and said the words to her. And he'd bought a ring, in secret, a week ago. A simple platinum band. Now the roses were in the cargo hold, on ice, and the ring was on her finger.

Jessica looked up from her engagement ring and down the aisle of the plane. Fee, the Scottish girl, was coming back towards her. The pink flush of embarrassment had faded from her cheeks. She made her way briskly up the aisle, a confident professional air hostess. She walked past the two women in C, for whom Jessica was now weaving new biographies.

Fee joined her in the cubicle. She saw Jessica studying the pale ring on her finger. 'Good on you,' said the Scots girl warmly. Jessica smiled up at her. 'The best bit will be seeing my mum's face when I tell her the news.'

'She'll be pleased.'

'Pleased? With a bit of luck the shock will finish the old bag off.' Jessica chuckled. Even thinking about her mother couldn't spoil the warm rush of pleasure she got every time she thought of Roy. She couldn't believe it. Love had finally worked. It was like being at sea for years, thrown here and there by the rough waves of storms, then finally coming into a safe harbour.

Jessica smiled at Fee and leant back, listening to the most familiar sound in the world. So familiar that it had faded to silence in her mind years ago.

The faint background roar of the four giant engines that carried these hundreds of fragile lives and these tons of metal safely through the night sky. Carrying her back to London, Roy and love.

'At last,' she whispered.

That was when the plane hit the turbulence.

They knew right away it was a bad one. They started getting ready.

As the turbulence grew more severe Fee and Jessica left their cubicle, moving quickly but without betraying haste. They had to appear calm themselves as they calmed the passengers down.

It worked. The people in first class seemed reassured by their efforts and as the turbulence gradually eased things returned to normal.

But then the second surge hit the plane, like a storm wave smashing into a small boat.

And then the engines stopped.

Chapter 3

Creed squinted out through his windscreen at the bright Saturday afternoon traffic. The residue of chlorine on his face made his skin feel tight.

'Why do they put chlorine in swimming pools, daddy?' said Eve from the back seat. Creed explained about disinfectant and public health as he navigated through the traffic. Since they'd left the sports centre it had steadily thickened and Creed found himself devoting more and more of his time to double checking the car's computerized decisions about speed, position and distance from other vehicles. The truth was, he couldn't get used to half this automatic crap. He liked a hands-on approach to machinery. He even preferred a manual transmission.

Eve fell quiet in the back seat, sensing her father's concentration and not wanting to disturb it.

As they neared the school traffic thinned out again and Creed tried to concentrate on his son Ricky and the problem that lay ahead. For the thousandth time he felt that peculiar parental exasperation. Why did his children have to complicate his life? Couldn't they just live with him in simplicity and peace until they grew up and found highly paid jobs to support him in his dotage?

No chance. It seemed that every time one domestic problem was solved, two more sprang up. And this one with Ricky was intractable and tenacious and profoundly baffling.

Creed remembered one summer when he and Ricky had gone on vacation, just the two of them. Justine had been pregnant with Eve. The weather was hot and she was feeling heavy and sensitive and moody. She suggested that Creed take off with Ricky for a few weeks while she stayed at home with

Cynthia. Creed took his son on a short plane ride north across the Canadian border. They landed in a small town called Kenora and rented a ramshackle cabin by a lake.

The plan was to do some fishing. Standard father-and-son bonding holiday. But after a few days of going out on the water, Creed had to admit that he had as little enthusiasm for the sport as his son. So they reeled in their lines and emptied the small jar of salted minnows over the side of the boat.

The rest of their holiday they spent lazing around. Ricky met some other kids his age and started hanging out in town with them. Creed went swimming in the milky green lake and came out with glistening black leeches on his skin. You couldn't just pull the leeches off because their mouth-parts remained attached to you and would become infected. But when the burning end of a cigarette was held near the leech the small parasite curled up and rolled off.

One day when Creed was sitting on the wooden dock drinking beer, and considering whether he wanted to go swimming in Leech Lake, Ricky got into some kind of trouble in town. He and the other boys were brought back in a police car. They dropped Ricky at the cabin before carrying on to deliver the rest of the disgraced children to their respective parents. The cops had paused to talk politely with Creed before getting on. They had seemed more amused by the incident than anything else.

From what Creed could piece together, the boys had wandered into a bar in a rough part of town. There was still considerable racial tension here between the native Canadians and the descendants of the white settlers. There were some bars that were definitely Indian bars and no white man who wanted to remain in one piece set foot in one of these. It had been into just such a bar that Ricky had led his group of new friends.

But there had been no ensuing violence. No race riot. The under-age white boys had emerged from the bar untouched. What exactly had happened was unclear. All Creed could glean was that someone had panicked and called the police, who duly escorted the boys home from their adventure on the wrong side of the tracks.

And that would have been the end of it, except the next day an old man came to visit Creed at the cabin.

He was an Indian. In fact, he was what might best be described as the local shaman. He didn't possess any of the traditional attributes of the witch-doctor or medicine-man. He wore jeans, an old check shirt, and drove a pick-up. Creed guessed his age at upward of 60 but the shaman was full of wiry muscular vigour. His long grey hair was fastened in a pony-tail with a turquoise and silver comb. His seamed face looked like a lizard's, Creed thought. The shaman removed the comb, shook out his hair and re-tied it as he sat on the porch of the cabin and talked with Creed.

Ricky was out on the water in the boat, forbidden to go into town and fishing for his penance. As Creed and the shaman talked their eyes kept returning to the simple shape of the boat sitting on the sky-filled lake. A boy sitting in it with his fishing pole angled towards its own reflection.

They talked about the Grateful Dead and some recent sporting events they'd both seen on satellite television. They talked and talked but the old lizard never let on why he'd really come to visit. But he took a long careful look at Creed when he thought Creed wasn't paying attention. And every time his gaze settled on Ricky the shaman got a distant, thoughtful look in his eyes.

He drove off without ever stating his business, shaking hands with Creed and thanking him for the beer. But as he climbed into the cab of his pick-up he looked back out at the lake one last time, towards the boy in the boat.

Now Ricky was fifteen, lanky, stoop-shouldered and a bit shy. An intelligent kid who somehow never seemed to fit in at school. In fact, despite a good record of academic achievement, he had been asked to leave the last three schools he'd attended.

The first time this happened it was a baffling shock to Creed and Justine. The second time, exasperating, and by the third merely a routine nuisance, calling for some logistical nimbleness.

The worst part was that none of the school principals and none of Ricky's teachers seemed to be able to give a concrete reason for the problem. It wasn't as though Ricky was dealing drugs in the playground or beating kids up. 'If only,' muttered Creed.

'What did you say, daddy?'

'Nothing honey.'

'It's OK,' said Eve from the back of the car. 'Ricky will be OK.'

Creed felt a strange little chill as he glanced at his daughter in the rear-view mirror. Maybe Ricky wasn't the only one of his kids who was a little odd.

Creed looked back at the road, trying to concentrate on the driving and the problem of Ricky. All they could get out of the schools was that Ricky 'didn't fit in'. While not actually being a trouble-maker, he was nonetheless some kind of disruptive influence in the classroom and his educators were uniformly glad to see the last of him.

As he drove, Creed found his thoughts straying from his son and returning to the encounter outside the sports centre. Returning to the cowardly way he'd hid in his car, waiting for the blonde to drive past.

Returning to Amy Cowan.

Amy was Creed's personal assistant at the Agency. Up until a year ago that role had been filled by a carrot-haired kid with an angular face called Casey Brennan.

When Brennan left to take up a better job on the west coast Creed set about surfing the data-bases and renewing contacts on the phone, wheeling and dealing and networking throughout the Agency, searching for a permanent replacement for Brennan. In the end the short-list had been a tense compromise between himself and the Washington office, and after a final round of negotiations only one candidate looked good enough to Creed. He actioned the transfer and Brennan's old desk was cleared of the layer of clutter it had acquired in the last few months, when it had stood empty and become a dumping ground for everyone else's low priority paperwork and empty coffee cups. Getting ready for his new assistant, Creed said goodbye to the temps, shortened his own working hours, restructured the work-flow, and heaved a sigh of relief.

But as soon as Amy Cowan arrived he knew she was trouble.

Chapter 4

Even as the plane began to fall from the sky Jessica kept the smile on her face.

The mechanical airline stewardess smile. She was fooling no one, but she kept smiling and moving quickly along the aisles offering empty reassurance to the passengers. It was her job.

A jet-plane is heavier than air. Its shape and the thrust of its engines enable it to fend off gravity, but inevitably this is a losing battle. Gravity will always win in the end. Usually passenger jets end their days on a runway somewhere, quietly taken out of commission and dismantled at the end of a long service life. When you unfasten components from the carcass of the plane the sheared-off heads of the old bolts fall to the ground to roll off the tarmac and vanish in the weeds beside the airstrip. Gravity wins.

But at other times gravity wins before an airliner grows old and retires. Sometimes it happens in the middle of a flight.

It's a fact of life. You learn to live with it. To accept the thought of dropping out of the sky.

You just hope it won't happen on your shift.

Now it was happening on Jessica's shift.

She moved down the long aisle of first class, reassuring the passengers. Smiling. She walked past the women sitting on either side of aisle C. They looked oddly calm. They were the only two passengers talking. Throughout the rest of the cabin there was a silence of deep respect and intense concentration, like you might get in a church full of devoted parishioners waiting for a vital word from the pulpit.

No one was looking at anyone else. Every passenger seemed intensely focused on their own inner world as the plane lurched earthward with sickening speed. It was a terrible silence. The kind you hope never to hear on an aircraft, because such a silence can only happen in the absence of that most familiar and reassuring of sounds. The sound of the engines.

The engines had stopped. No one was talking. The plane was falling out of the sky. The silence was worse than if they were all screaming. Jessica smiled at the passengers and thanked God for the two women in row C who kept stubbornly talking.

'It's called a windshear,' said the white woman matter-of-factly. 'The plane flies into an area of extreme turbulence, usually caused by a descending column of cool air hitting the ground.'

'Hits the ground and spreads outward in a circular pattern, right?' said the black woman.

'Right. Think of a ball-bearing dropped in oil. Same splash pattern. A circular fan of intense wind.'

'That was the turbulence we felt.'

'Yes,' said Benny. 'We hit a sudden headwind entering the circle of disturbance. But then when we were leaving the circle, the wind was going the other way.'

'Oh, Christ,' said Roz.

'Yes. We hit a sudden tailwind. The combination of violent winds in two different directions cut our airspeed.'

'And consequently caused a sudden loss of lift.' The cabin was completely silent around them. You could have heard a pin drop. Everyone was listening to them as the plane dropped out of the sky.

'It's called a windshear,' repeated Benny.

'Isn't there anything we can do?'

'Yes,' said Benny. 'Stewardess!'

The woman came at once. 'Stewardess,' said Benny, 'can you bring us a bottle of your best champagne?'

Jessica was galvanized into action. She moved along the aisles cracking open bottles of champagne. Why not? It was as good a way of spending her last few moments as any she could think of. Some of the passengers took the drinks eagerly, as grateful for distraction as she was. Others ignored her. Jessica pushed the trolley along the aisle, Fee the Scottish girl helping. Jessica was only concerned that she would do her job properly; that she would manage to serve everybody before they hit. Plenty of champagne in the trolley but still six more rows to go. Would she make it in time? She opened a bottle and cursed as her arm jerked and the champagne splashed everywhere. She would never finish her appointed task if the plane was shaking like this, shaking as the wings twisted and the engines roared.

The engines.

The engines were working again.

Everybody realized it at the same moment. Jessica saw a wave of smiles sweep across first class and never in her life had she seen so many human faces suddenly rendered beautiful by sheer joy.

The plane shuddered and began to recover altitude. Nobody cheered. Nobody said anything. But plenty of champagne was spilled as shaking hands lifted glasses to trembling lips. All of first class was drinking champagne in a ragged toast to being alive.

Jessica hauled the drinks trolley back into the alcove. She realized that she hadn't thought of Roy at all when the plane had been dropping. Was that normal? Was it a bad sign? Would the marriage work?

But Jessica had no doubt that the marriage would work when she felt the wave of love and happiness that swept into her as soon as she thought of him.

Fee came back into the alcove and they just stared at each other.

'I'm going to change jobs,' said the Scots girl.

'That's what I say, every time.'

'Any of that champagne left?'

'Certainly.' She glanced around the curtain as she poured them both a glass. 'You know I've changed my mind about the lesbians in row C. They didn't even flinch during that turbulence. I've decided that they're not lesbians at all. They're spies. You know, returning from a secret mission. Accustomed to facing danger.'

'You're out of your tiny mind,' said Fee. 'Here, drink some champagne.'

'Why is it my bag is always the last one off the plane?' said Benny. She stood anxiously watching the luggage rotate on the big carousel at Heathrow Terminal Five. Every so often another suit-case would come slithering out of the chute, slide on to the big segmented belt and glide slowly past them. It was never Benny's. She was beginning to wonder if this time the morons at the airport had finally lost it. Sent it on a flight to the Himalayas or something. She looked at Roz, standing waiting patiently beside her. They hadn't lost Roz's bag. It was the first one off the plane.

'Did you really think it was all over?' she said.

'What do you mean?'

'On the plane. You're the windshear expert. Did you really think we were going to die?' Roz was rubbing her neck where the passport control guy had touched her with the scanner.

'Well, there's a certain number of crashes every year. It's a statistical certainty.'

'That's kind of my job,' said Roz. 'Trying to avoid ending up as a statistical certainty.' She rubbed her neck. 'You know, air travel must have been more dignified back in the days when they had real passports instead of implants. I always feel like some kind of animal being inspected when they stick that thing on me.'

But Benny wasn't listening. 'Here it is!' she squealed, scrambling for her bag.

'God,' said Roz. 'You should see the look of relief on your face. It's pathetic in a grown woman.'

They were walking towards customs when the plump old lady detached herself from the crowd and came barging up to them. She was dressed in a combination of expensive but hideously tasteless clothes which looked like they'd been bought at random from second-hand shops in posh neighbourhoods. The overall effect was of a well-heeled bag-lady.

'Hello, darlings,' she said.

Roz just gave her a cold drop-dead look and kept moving, as if the old woman was some time-waster or lunatic. But Benny hesitated and stopped, recognition flickering in her eyes as she tried to place this strange old woman who stood grinning at her, her teeth discoloured and unforgivably crooked in this age of cosmetic surgery.

'Do you know each other?' said Roz.

'Yes,' said Benny feeling sudden pleasure as the name popped into her mind. 'Mrs Woodcott!'

'Took you a moment, though, didn't it, dear?' said the old woman. 'And I'm the one who's supposed to be having Alzheimer therapy.' She cackled, a little saliva gathering on her whiskery chin. Roz gave Benny an odd look. But then Mrs Woodcott swivelled her watery old gaze directly at Roz.

Roz felt herself caught in the searchlight beam of a formidable intelligence. Mrs Woodcott scrutinized her for a moment and then turned to Benny. 'Who is your friend with the fascinating eyes?'

'Oh, I'm sorry. Mrs Woodcott, this is Roslyn Forrester. Roz for short.'

'Enchanted,' said Mrs Woodcott, seizing Roz's hand in one bony old claw and squeezing it as though she was buying livestock. Roz couldn't help comparing her own firm brown flesh with the gnarled blue veins and pale liver-spotted skin of Mrs Woodcott's ancient hand. Heavy silver rings cut into the old flesh over her swollen bony knuckles.

'How odd to run into you,' said Benny. 'I was just thinking about Creed the other day.'

'Odd?' said Mrs Woodcott. 'Don't talk to me about odd, dear. I could write a book about odd. If this is what passes for odd in your experience you must lead a jolly normal life.' She was still holding Roz's hand and Roz was increasingly drawn to the notion of simply yanking it back. But suddenly the old woman shrugged and turned away. 'See you later dears,' she said. She waggled her hideous gnarled fingers and chuckled as she walked off.

Benny watched her go, then turned and hurried after Roz. As she caught up with her she saw two of the stewardesses from their flight standing beyond the sliding glass doors. One stewardess was holding a large bunch of roses.

'There are your spies,' said Fee. Jessica turned listlessly and peered over the bouquet of roses she was holding. She looked through the glass security doors and saw the black and white woman from row C. They had cleared immigration and were heading for the customs area.

Jessica nodded, trying to pretend interest. She kept her head down so as not to meet Fee's gaze. She couldn't stand the look of concern and compassion in the Scottish girl's eyes. Instead she shifted the bundle of roses and looked at her watch for the thousandth time. As she did so she couldn't help seeing the ring on her finger. The ring she'd only been wearing for a day.

'It's all right,' said Fee.

'How do you know?' muttered Jessica.

'There must be some explanation. Maybe he got the times mixed up.'

'He has a copy of my rota. He knew when I was landing. He promised to be here.'

'Maybe he's just been delayed. Traffic on the M25 can be terrible.'

'I tried the phone in the car. I also tried his portable. I also tried the house and the office. He's not there. He's not anywhere.'

'Well, there must be some explanation,' said Fee. But the comforting tone of voice wavered for a moment and Jessica knew that Fee had just thought of the same explanation which had occurred to her.

Roy hadn't forgotten when she was landing. And he certainly hadn't forgotten about their engagement. He just didn't want to meet her.

'He's changed his mind,' she said softly.

'Hush there now,' said Fee. But Jessica knew that she was thinking the same thing.

Roz glanced through the glass doors at the girl holding the roses. Their stewardess. She didn't look happy. The girl's obvious distress reminded Roz of something. Roz turned and looked at the white woman beside her. 'Benny?'

Benny didn't hear her for a moment. She was biting her lip with anxiety. The tight worried expression on her face pissed Roz off. Benny was basically OK; she was utterly reliable in a dangerous situation and there were few people whom Roz would rather have at her side. But beside being brave Benny was also highly intelligent, maybe too intelligent. And definitely too imaginative.

Roz knew the type. Tormented by their own intellects. They couldn't just accept things or let sleeping dogs lie. Their sweeping intelligences could always come up with something to worry about.

Benny was like that.

If Benny didn't watch out she'd turn into a jumpy old spinster.

Now Roz looked at Benny. Benny was biting her lip and frowning, clearly worried about something. 'What's wrong?' said Roz, against her better judgement.

'I don't know if I should go through the green lane or red lane.'

Roz stared at the airport customs area ahead. It was divided into two corridors, GOODS TO DECLARE and NOTHING TO DECLARE, the floors marked with red and green arrows.

'Well, have you got anything to declare?'

'My garlic and paprika is agricultural produce. Don't they have to check that for plant viruses?'

'I don't think you need to worry,' said Roz.

Benny frowned, her forehead wrinkling. 'I don't know, better safe than sorry. I think I'll take it through the red lane.'

Roz sighed with disgust. 'Suit yourself.' She'd been right. In a few years Benny would be a neurotic old maid jumping at her own shadow. Roz turned away and headed towards the green lane. 'I'll see you back at the house in Kent.'

She left Benny wandering hesitantly down the red lane.

Roz took a deep breath. It felt good to be on her own. She strode through the NOTHING TO DECLARE channel, customs personnel watching her without interest. Roz knew that she had nothing to worry about.

She had dropped the gun into the river in Budapest and she wasn't carrying anything else incriminating.

She was striding through customs, past anxious looking tourists opening their suit-cases for inspection. Ahead of her was the glass sliding door leading to the arrivals area.

Roz had almost reached it when she heard a voice.

'Excuse me, Miss.'

Roz kept moving.

'Excuse me.' The voice was sharper now. Roz looked up and saw two uniformed guards blocking her way. Both of them were armed.

'Would you mind coming with us, Miss?'

'Not at all, but there's really no need –'

'This way please, Miss.'

One of the guards took Roz's suit-case and the other led

her through a door behind the customs counter. People were staring at her.

The guard led Roz into an office with a couch, three chairs and a small desk. The guard carrying Roz's suit-case followed them into the office.

Sitting there at the small desk was an oddly dressed old woman. Roz felt a jolt of surprise. It was Mrs Woodcott. She looked up as Roz came in.

'That's her,' said Mrs Woodcott. 'Bring her in and lock her up.'

Fee sat there beside Jessica, keeping her company for as long as she could. They sat there together in the arrivals area for another half an hour. But then the Scottish stewardess had to leave and hurry into town to meet her own date.

So Jessica was left alone with the depressing anonymous furniture and steady flow of total strangers that only an airport can provide. She decided to give Roy another ten minutes. She tried all the phone numbers one more time. Then she gave him another five minutes, then another five. Then a final five, to bring it around to exactly the half hour.

Then Jessica made herself stand up. She felt oddly heavy, as if she'd just climbed out of a swimming pool. She stared dully at the flowers at her feet. She hardly recognized them. Jessica forced herself to pick them up. It was like picking up something filthy. She could feel an ugly anger rising in her heart. She didn't let herself think about Roy. She walked past the information stalls and the car-hire desks. Past people she knew well. As though sensing her need to be left alone, they didn't even look at her.

As she walked through the terminal Jessica up-ended the beautiful bouquet of roses. On her way out she jammed them into the nearest garbage can.

She could have caught a tube-train from the airport. She could have taken a taxi or waited for a lift from one of the other flight attendants coming off shift. That would have been the safe or sensible thing to do.

But Jessica didn't feel like being sensible or safe.

She cut back through a corridor restricted to flight personnel and opened a door onto the runways. She walked out of the concrete building into the grey slanting evening rain.

Night was falling swiftly over the great airport.

Jessica walked back towards Terminal One, walking airside in the rain with the thunder of the big jets coming in all around her. When she got to Terminal One she walked down a long slip-road. The occasional goods vehicle rumbled past but there was no one else on foot. With good reason. This whole area was forbidden to pedestrians.

Jessica didn't care. She walked along the exit-road in the rain until she came to the motorway approach lane. It was totally dark now. The rain was getting heavier. Jessica sheltered by a big concrete motorway support that rose to the dark road above. Headlights flashed by.

Jessica stuck out her thumb, squinting into the rain.

'I suppose you're rather angry at me,' said Mrs Woodcott. She was peering in at Roz through the opening in the low steel ceiling. Roz said nothing.

'Aren't you speaking to me?'

Roz said nothing.

'I thought those airport security guards were rather decent about the whole thing. Nobody's hurt you. Nobody's mistreated you.'

'Nobody's told me what the hell is going on,' said Roz.

'This really is a remarkable vehicle,' said Mrs Woodcott, pretending to take a sudden interest in the rubber lip of the roof-hatch. 'Why do they call it an APC?'

'Armoured Personnel Carrier,' said Roz. She had recognized the vehicle as soon as they'd walked round the corner of the airport building and she'd seen it parked there. Squat and blunt-nosed, built for armoured security under fire as well as speed. It was sheltered from the rain under a makeshift tarpaulin on the runway outside the airport's smallest terminal. 'You didn't answer my question,' said Roz. 'Why have I been arrested and put in this thing?' It was hot in the armoured personnel carrier and she was sweating.

'For heaven's sake,' said Mrs Woodcott. 'You have not been arrested. Stop dramatizing. You've been press-ganged. It's quite different.'

'Press-ganged?'

'It's an historical term,' said Mrs Woodcott. 'You may not recognize it.'

'Well, what does it mean?'

'Oh, dear,' said Mrs Woodcott, staring at something. She looked back into the hatch and waved at Roz. 'Sorry, dear. No time. Your colleague is here so I'd best be going.' She disappeared from sight but Roz could feel the vehicle shift on its suspension as the old woman climbed down from it. Then another shift in weight as someone else climbed up on to the APC.

A dark shape appeared in the open hatch above her and Roz moved back quickly to make room as a man dropped into the vehicle beside her.

The man wore a military style uniform, grey camouflage, but with no rank or insignia on it. He turned to Roz and looked at her for a long cautious moment before nodding a greeting. 'My name's Redmond,' he said. His face was thin, with a small ginger moustache. There was something tentative about his pale blue eyes but Roz couldn't detect any fear in them. A good sign. His voice was soft, with a trace of an Irish accent.

Redmond turned away and moved to the cockpit of the vehicle, contorting his body to climb into the driving seat.

Roz came forward and joined him. Sliding past the bulkhead which bulged with control panels she sat down in the shotgun seat. Redmond was busy with the computer, programming their route, but he glanced up from the illuminated map and gave her a surprised appreciative look as she sat down.

'You know how to move in here. Have you been in one of these things before?'

'I used to drive something similar.'

'Well, you're not driving this one,' he said pleasantly. He looked over at her and his deeply lined face creased as he smiled. Roz decided she liked his smile.

'So, what do you know about all this?' said Redmond, raising his voice as he started the big engine for its pre-drive warm up, the vibration so strong through the metal bulkhead that it rattled their teeth. He switched it off again after the statutory thirty seconds.

'I got the old bat's press-gang speech,' said Roz in the sudden silence. 'That's all.'

'So did that clear matters up?'

'Not really, since I don't know what a press-gang is.'

'Well,' said Redmond, playing with the catch on his seat-belt, 'in the bad old days of the Royal Navy, back when they were in wooden ships and using sails and that, they had a manpower crisis. No one wanted to join, not surprising since it was such an unpleasant job. Away for years on end and dreadful conditions and so on. So they sent out gangs to force men to join. To kidnap them, if you like. They'd go into pubs and grab unlucky "volunteers" and drag them off to spend years at sea.'

'And those were the press-gangs.'

'Right.'

'And now I've been press-ganged.'

'Well, don't feel too bad about it,' said Redmond. 'So have I.'

'What do you mean?'

'Same as you. I was coming through Heathrow last week, picking up a connecting flight, Aer Lingus to Belfast. But I never made it. They lifted me.' He shrugged and smiled again. 'And here I am.'

'But why did they choose you? Why me?'

'They're picking up anyone with combat or policing experience. If they ran you through a computer would they pick up anything like that in your personal history?'

'I guess so,' said Roz. 'So what does the bag-lady have to do with it?'

'Mrs Woodcott? She prepares the short-list of candidates as they come through passport-control.'

'Prepares it how?'

'Well,' Redmond hesitated. 'They say she's psychic.' He smiled an apologetic smile.

'Bullshit.'

'No, really. Like a water diviner, except instead of water she detects likely candidates. She gets paid a bounty for every warm body she provides.'

'Provides for what?'

Redmond turned away for a moment and typed commands into the computer. He listened carefully to the change in engine note as he checked system-status graphics on the screen. 'Well,' he said. 'You might say it's in a state of emergency.'

'What is?'

'London.'

'You mean the whole city?' said Roz.

'Just the city at the moment, but there are rumours that it's spreading into the surrounding countryside.' Redmond's face had a strained, sour expression. Roz got the strange feeling that he was trying not to look frightened. 'I hope those rumours aren't true,' he said. 'I hope we can at least contain it here. I'd hate to think of it spreading into the countryside.'

'What spreading? Contain what?'

'You're going to have to see for yourself.'

'I'm getting very sick of this,' said Roz. 'If there is a state of emergency why haven't I heard anything about it? Why isn't the news full of it?'

'Because it's a secret. The government's keeping it under wraps.'

'Why?'

'Because they're scared,' said Redmond.

Chapter 5

As soon as Amy Cowan had joined the Agency, Creed knew she was trouble.

Not that she failed to measure up in terms of her abilities. If anything, she exceeded his expectations, handling the work with confidence and savage glee at solving a difficult problem. This should have gladdened Creed's heart. Amy was very good at the job. Smart and young, with the initiative to sort out complications almost before they happened. She soon got a feel for her duties and organized a routine for handling them that put her predecessor in the shade.

But Creed knew she was trouble from the first moment he'd seen her.

It had been a bright winter day with a beautiful endless blue sky extending above an undisturbed mantle of fresh snow that spread across the farmland surrounding the Agency building.

Amy was half an hour late. It was her first morning and Creed was trying to decide whether this was sloppiness, a genuinely laid back attitude, or an enraging challenge to his personal authority, when Amy came barging in through the glass doors of the office.

She was panting, breath still steaming. She was so flustered at being late that she sat down at Creed's desk without taking off her arctic survival parka. Snow melted on it as they talked and a gradually growing puddle formed on the carpet under her.

The thing that Creed remembered most vividly from that first meeting was the way her eyelashes retained a delicate coating of ice from the sub-zero temperatures outside. Her lashes were still frozen when she first sat down. In the midst of the delicate nest of white lashes her eyes were a startling vivid blue-green. They regarded Creed curiously over high feline cheek-bones as she looked up from loosening her snow-caked ski-boots. For a moment she seemed too nervous to speak.

'My ancestors were Magyars,' she blurted out after a moment's silence. 'Sir,' she added.

'That's nice,' said Creed.

'They were apparently very tough, very resourceful people,' said Amy. 'That's a family legend, sir.'

'Don't call me "sir" again. It makes me nervous. What the hell are you rambling on about, Cowan.'

'What I'm trying to explain, Mr McIlveen, is why I'm late here on my first morning. It's completely unfair, Mr McIlveen. I know that's a completely wimpish thing to say. But it is unfair, when you consider that I set off at the crack of dawn, deliberately, to get into the office early. So I could make a good impression. I was going to be early. Two hours early, Mr McIlveen. Not late.'

'OK, your technique is gradually working,' sighed Creed. 'Forget Mr McIlveen too. Hearing you repeat it that way is like having my teeth drilled. You can call me Creed.'

'The stupid thing is, if I hadn't been trying so hard, trying to be early, none of this would have happened – Creed.'

'What exactly did happen?'

'If I hadn't set off two hours early I wouldn't have been on that particular stretch of road at that particular moment.'

'Would you like some coffee, Cowan? Sugar? You look like you need it. What particular stretch of road?'

'Through Gaines Woods.' It was a belt of thick forest about twenty miles away, separated from the Agency by a wide expanse of fields now buried under snow, huge adjacent hectares of unworked farm land.

'I know the place,' said Creed.

'I'd never driven through there before. It's full of trees.'

'That's why they call it Gaines Woods, I guess,' observed Creed unhelpfully.

'One of them fell on my car.'

'What?'

'One of the trees fell on my car. Totalled my cellular phone. I couldn't call anyone to come out and pick me up.

The highway was too far to walk and in the wrong direction anyhow.'

'Wrong direction?'

Amy still had her heavy parka on and in the central heating of the office she'd practically begun to melt inside it. The glaze of ice was gone from her lashes and her cheeks were bright red. She struggled with the zip of the parka then looked up at Creed. There was a sudden set of fierce determination on her clear, sweat-glazed face. 'I got up early this morning,' said Amy Cowan, 'because I wanted to come to work. And I didn't intend to let anything stop me.' There was a glint of steel in those eyes.

'Magyar blood, huh?' said Creed.

'I guess so. I was determined. So I set off across country.'

'You came all the way from Gaines Woods on foot?'

'In a manner of speaking.'

'In two hours?'

'Well, actually I used skis.'

'I'm impressed,' said Creed. 'Lucky you had some skis in the car.'

'I didn't, actually.'

'You didn't?'

'I had to make them. From branches.'

'Branches?'

'You know, like on a tree? Fortunately there were plenty of trees. The place was full of them. That's why they call it Gaines Woods, I guess.'

She looked up at Creed, frank eyes full of rude merriment. He grinned at her like a wolf over his coffee cup. 'I guess,' he said.

'They weren't really very good skis. Kind of a primitive lashed-together sort of rig. But the best you could expect using a Swiss Army knife.'

'So you managed to get here after the tree fell on your car, travelling across country on home-made skis, and you're only half an hour late.'

'That's why I mentioned my family. The Magyar blood. They're tough, resourceful people. It's thanks to those tough, resourceful genes of theirs that I'm only half an hour late.'

'Well, Agent Cowan,' said Creed, taking a deep breath. 'Just don't let it happen again.' He smiled at her. 'You'd better get cleaned up and catch your breath.'

'Thank you, sir.' Amy Cowan got up from her chair and noticed the puddle of melted snow on the carpet. She turned to flee in embarrassment.

'Oh, one last thing,' said Creed.

She turned back and looked at him expectantly.

'Do you always go through the Magyar routine on the first day at a new job?' said Creed.

Amy Cowan's face lit up with a spectacular smile. 'Sure,' she said. 'But I don't usually go as far as the handmade skis.'

Amy Cowan had blonde hair. Short blonde hair. Your fingers graze the short bristles near the roots, tracing the delicate contours of that graceful skull so full of intelligence and notions, and dreams.

Then your fingers move on, slip through her hair on to the sudden smoothness of her face and against her clean flawless skin, drifting down to encircle her high cheek-bones. They touch the lashes of the startling greenish blue eyes, which are gazing levelly into your own. Then your hand moves down her face, down that smooth skin to the oval bud of flesh under her nose and then down to her red lips, so firm and lush they almost seem swollen. And you caress them with the back of your hand, feeling them graze the skin there in an inadvertent kiss of contact, cool and slightly moist. Then you turn your hand over so that the more sensitive skin of your fingertips can touch those red lips.

And they are as smooth as the petals of a flower, but now you've got lipstick all over your fingers, like a stain that won't come out. And there's someone who mustn't see this stain. But all thought of that is being lost now because you're looking at Amy.

Amy's lips look heavier and fuller because of the smeared lipstick at the corners. And as her level jade eyes look into yours, you stretch out your finger as if you're pointing. And you put your finger gently between her lips and let their delicate pressure kiss it for a moment. Then you push your finger and her lips yield as you press deeper into her mouth. Now she smiles, opening her lips slightly and your finger slides all the way in, slipping with a warm moist shock into her soft mouth.

And you wake up with your heart ricocheting in your chest.

You're soaked with sweat and disorientated. The pulse is slamming in your skull, sending dream fragments throbbing through your mind.

A dream.

Only a dream. And dreams don't mean anything and dreams certainly can't harm you. Can't harm anyone.

You tell yourself this a few times and then you turn and look down at Justine.

You look at your wife, curled up asleep beside you.

Chapter 6

The Doctor was waiting for Benny when she arrived at the house. 'Good evening,' he called as she got out of the car. He was standing in a patch of moonlight near the front steps. He walked towards her, his feet crunching on the gravel. 'Where's Roz?'

'She said something about meeting us back here later.' Benny still felt vaguely ashamed of abandoning Roz at the airport. 'Why don't we have a stroll in the garden before supper?' The Doctor held out his arm in a courtly, old-fashioned gesture and Benny took it. The moon was high and yellow over the dark garden as they walked up the steps that led through the hedge on to the big lawn behind the house. After her hours on the plane the fresh country air was like nectar.

'The garden smells wonderful.'

'Doesn't it just?'

Benny found herself wondering for the hundredth time whether the Doctor experienced sensations in the way she did. When he smelled blossoms on a ripe late summer evening, for instance. Did he breathe the same rich fragrance that she did?

She looked over at the Doctor strolling beside her in the moonlight. His wrinkled, almost simian, face was abstracted and thoughtful. He held his head at an odd angle as though listening. But there was nothing to hear. Just the silence of a warm, summer night. They walked down the gently sloping lawn towards the shadows of the apple trees. Benny glanced at the Doctor again. He was clearly listening to something.

Benny strained her ears but all she could hear was their feet moving softly on the grass, now and then a stirring of wind or the gentle creaking of a branch in the orchard.

The Doctor frowned thoughtfully as he listened. She tried to read the expression in his eyes.

'What is it, Doctor?'

'What?' He turned to look at her, luminous crescents in his eyes from the moonlight. Then, as if aware of how disconcerting those eyes could be, he made some subtle change in his posture and the angle of his head altered. Now his eyes were safely hidden in the shadow of his hatbrim. He smiled at her.

'You looked like you were listening to something,' said Benny. Or maybe listening *for* something, she thought.

'Oh, it was nothing. At least, nothing to worry about.' Benny still couldn't see his eyes. 'You haven't asked me what's for supper,' he said.

'What's for supper?'

'Things you like. Peasant cooking.'

'Garlic?'

'In abundance.'

'And red wine?'

'Most certainly.' The Doctor smiled.

'Don't let Chris drink all of it this time.' They had reached the bottom of the lawn now and stood on the edge of the dark orchard. She could smell apple blossom and the green, nose-tickling aroma of weeds which had been baking all day under a hot sun.

'I'm afraid Chris won't be joining us,' said the Doctor. They turned around and walked slowly back up the lawn towards the house. Benny's arm was still linked with the Doctor's. 'I had to send him on an errand,' he said.

Benny felt her heart begin to accelerate in her chest. She'd known for days that something was up. But the Doctor sending Chris Cwej off confirmed it.

'What is this errand?' said Benny.

'He may be gone for some time,' said the Doctor.

'Will he enjoy himself?'

'Well, I certainly hope so,' said the Doctor. 'Because he didn't enjoy shaving his head very much.'

The Doctor left Benny sitting in the garden drinking a brandy and soda while he went to cook supper. She sat sipping her drink in the late summer moonlight. Delicious cooking smells drifted out to her from the small kitchen window. Benny kicked her shoes off and wriggled her toes in the dark dew-damp grass. She concentrated on the oily aromatic taste of the brandy, the small chunky music of ice in her glass. The warm country night surrounding her.

She looked at the dark weaving shadows of ivy leaves on the old house that rose above her. She listened to the stillness and silence of the night.

Then she heard it.

A distant, lonely sound.

It came from far off, beyond the trees at the foot of the orchard, rising in the night like the whistle of a late train thundering past in the night.

It made the hairs on the back of her neck stand up.

The sound rose and fell, seeming to change position, as if coming from different parts of the country. Rising and falling, dying away in one area and then starting up in another. High, raggedly mournful and chillingly lonesome, the sound rose up around her from every compass point of the dark Kentish night.

Benny found herself standing up, the lawn chair lying behind her in the grass where it had fallen. The glass in her hand was empty and she was vaguely aware of the ice cubes at her feet, as the brandy and soda drained away in the grass.

It couldn't be, she thought. The sound couldn't be coming from every direction like that. As though it was synchronized. As though it was everywhere. All the disparate parts of the sprawling countryside had come alive in the darkness and they seemed to share a common purpose. It made Benny feel like she was surrounded.

She turned away and hurried into the house.

There was a big enamelled pot on the stove, steam hissing from its lid, fragrant with the smell of garlic, herbs and wine. The cooking utensils were still lying scattered on the counter but the Doctor was nowhere to be seen. Benny's first reaction on finding that she was alone was a surprisingly strong sense of panic.

Benny repressed the urge to call out to him, to shout at the top of her lungs. The Doctor had evidently left the kitchen some time ago. The casserole was beginning to steam violently, rocking on the surface of the stove. Benny went over to it and turned the gas flame down until it was a delicate blue star, barely visible. Then she left the kitchen, going deeper into the house.

She finally found the Doctor upstairs in the library, staring at a computer screen. The computer was an old fashioned Apple Mac stacked anachronistically on a pile of leather-bound books on an antique desk.

The library was a mess. Floor to ceiling, shelves were stacked with books. Learned treatises bound with antique leather, lurid paperbacks, highly technical science texts and children's picture books lay randomly heaped on the dusty carpeted floor and on every available surface.

There was a billiard-table in here but Benny couldn't remember it ever being clear enough to play on. The old battered silk Biedermyer sofa had, also, long since been buried so deep in books that you couldn't sit on it. There were two fat floral arm-chairs, both succumbing slowly to the book cancer but still usable. The only piece of furniture which remained free of reading matter was an odd glass cylinder.

The cylinder was huge, perhaps two metres tall and as big in diameter as a bicycle tyre. It was seated on a black metal oblong with a few simple analogue controls and a green LED display. A faint electrical buzz could be heard if you put your ear against the cool glass. The sound of motors turning as they slowly stirred the green liquid in the cylinder. In its murky depths you could intermittently see the shape of a pot-bellied, naked, middle-aged man.

Benny tried not to look at the man in the glass cylinder as she hurried into the library, over to the old desk where the Doctor sat.

He glanced up from the computer screen and smiled at her. Immediately Benny began to feel less spooked. She always took comfort in the Doctor's presence. If ever there was someone you could turn to when weird shit happened, it was the Doctor. The strange howling she'd heard outside began to diminish in her memory. Had she really heard it?

'Is something wrong?' said the Doctor. 'You look a little out of breath.'

'Had to run into the kitchen. Supper was about to burn,' she said. 'I had to turn it down.'

'Oh, dear,' said the Doctor, looking up from the computer screen. 'I'd forgotten all about it.' He rubbed his eyes. 'I'm afraid I've become quite absorbed. Was it ruined?'

'No. I caught it in time. Absorbed in what?'

The smile faded from the Doctor's face. 'Look Benny, you've had a long flight. Why don't we talk in the morning?'

'I know that tone of voice,' said Benny. 'Something's wrong.'

'Well, it's something that's been brewing for some time,' said the Doctor. 'I've had to keep my eye on it, like the watched pot. Hoping it would never reach boiling point. But unfortunately, now it has.' The Doctor looked at her, his dark eyes serious. 'The pot is boiling and I've been forced to intervene.'

'Is that why you've sent Chris off?'

'Yes. He's gone under cover to try and contain the situation. But I can see all this talk is worrying you. Why don't we go and have supper? There's plenty of time to talk later. You look tired.'

'I'll be OK,' said Benny. But in fact she felt a sudden rush of exhaustion. She put a hand out to support herself. But instead of gripping the dusty bookshelf she expected, her fingers brushed across smooth, cool glass.

Benny looked up and saw the tall cylinder full of green liquid. In it the pale body of the big man floated. Some stirring of the slowly circulating current had pressed his face against the curved glass. His fat cheek was bunched in a sneering one-sided smile and one of his eyes was pinched shut while the other was open, staring fixedly at Benny. The general effect was of a drooling lunatic winking salaciously at her.

Benny heard herself giggle.

'By the way,' said the Doctor. 'Why did you come running up here? You seemed very excited about something.'

Benny had to think for a moment before she remembered the thing that had happened in the garden. Then she remembered the howling that had risen out of the dark, summer night. As she remembered, the fear returned. And with unpleasant synchronous precision, the noise began again.

It came vibrating through the antique leaded window-panes of the library, rising in the night. Coming from every corner of the dark countryside.

'Oh, that,' said the Doctor.

Chapter 7

'Watch out for the exit, daddy,' said Eve.

'Everything's fine, dear,' said Creed, frowning through the windscreen. It was true, though. He always missed the damned turning for the school. This time he was determined to anticipate it, getting across the traffic flow and into the exit lane without hurrying, as they turned into the road and drove up to the school.

Creed eased the car into a slot, parking with fatuous precision between painted lines in the wide, empty lot. 'Will you be OK in the car, baby?'

'Yes, daddy. Can I play the radio?'

'Sure,' said Creed, adjusting the voice-actuated controls on the car so that they'd respond to Eve's commands. 'You know what to do if someone comes along and you don't know them, and they maybe try to get in the car?'

'Lock all the doors and call mummy on the car phone,' Eve recited in a bored, singsong voice.

'Good girl.'

Creed left the car and went up the steps into the school. After the hammering heat of the car park the corridors were shadowy and cool. He felt a familiar, slightly guilty thrill of pleasure. It was nice knowing he never had to set foot inside this place if he didn't want to. He'd grown up. Escaped. Left school behind. But even after all these years it still exerted a strange power over him. The smell of the long corridors brought back memories of his own high-school years. Like the time when –

'Hey, dad.'

Cynthia was standing in the doorway of a classroom. Actually, as he moved closer Creed saw that it wasn't an ordinary classroom. Carpeted floor stretched away from the door in a gentle gradient; rows of empty seats were aimed up at a small open stage with a large, white screen. 'Have you been watching movies?'

'Sort of. Mr Retour was showing me some videos.'

'Who's Mr Retour?' For some reason Creed was instantly suspicious of the foreign sounding name. 'What sort of videos?'

'Old newsreels. All black and white and 2-D, and the sound was real primitive, but they were great.' Cynthia had that look of absorption she got when she found a book or a television show that captured her imagination. 'Mr Retour is going to be teaching me history.'

'What period?'

'Twentieth century.'

'That's a pretty big subject.'

'With a special focus on the role of charisma in the rise to power of Hitler and Mussolini,' recited Cynthia.

'Special focus, huh?' said Creed, grinning.

Cynthia instantly went on the defensive. 'Mr Retour says that the angle of Mussolini's chin was responsible for the fascist dominance in Italy during World War Two.'

'Well, I'm glad to know our tax-dollars are funding Mr Retour's salary.'

Just then a tall young man came hurrying down the corridor, clutching a heavy armload of school books. He was dressed incongruously in a long orange robe, which flapped around his legs as he walked, and he wore a small knitted cap on his head. He tugged at the cap in greeting and smiled shyly as he hurried past Creed and Cynthia.

'Was that Mr Retour?'

'No,' laughed his daughter. 'Mr Retour wears a tweed jacket and has these incredible, mad-scientist eyebrows. That's just some Buddhist monk who teaches Comparative Anthropology.'

'Tell you what, Cynthia. Why don't you go out and wait in the car with your little sister?'

'Why? Where are you going?'

'I just have one or two things to do in here first.'

'Is this to do with Ricky's problem?' said Cynthia, her voice suddenly dropping low and her eyes hungrily open for scandal.

'Just go wait in the car, Cynthia.'

'You don't have to get mad at me.'

'I'm not getting mad. Go wait in the car.'

'It's not my fault my brother's a spaz,' muttered Cynthia, as she strode away down the corridor. Creed shook his head and stood, watching her for a moment. Cynthia had already acquired the liquid rolling stroll of her mother's which had driven Creed crazy when they first met.

With a wrench of nostalgia he remembered the first night he'd spent with Justine in London. Walking up the steps in Pall Mall, Creed deliberately dropping back for a moment so he could watch her sweet ass in those black culottes; all insouciant sway of ripening hips, like a bountiful basket being carried with negligent grace.

Now, a lifetime later, Creed saw the same programmed pattern of movement in his daughter, like a beautiful intricate symphony someone had recorded on a tape and casually played back. He watched Cynthia go, heading for the car park with her feet tripping out a staccato message of petulance and teenage spite. And Creed felt all the familiar family-stalemate feelings of inarticulate love and exasperated rage. He sighed and turned away, going deeper into the building.

The school was built in the shape of a hollow square, with the administrative offices along the inside walls, looking out through smoked glass on to a flourishing central patch of flower-beds, green lawn and plantings. Creed wandered into the administrative section, past empty desks. It was like being in the Agency out of normal office hours, empty and tranquil on a holiday weekend. Creed was looking for the office of the school's principal and he reflected that, despite all the supposed democratizing influence of the open-plan office, it was still always possible to find where the king monkey sat. There was invariably something special about the boss's cubicle.

In fact, it turned out that the principal had an old-fashioned enclosed office all his own. An unheard of luxury these days. Beyond a secretarial bull-pen Creed found a door with a sign which read 'D. H. Pangbourne'. He knocked and, after waiting a moment, went inside.

The office was empty, the computer on the man's desk

switched off and a clutter of papers had been left stacked beside a brimming ash-tray. The nearest window was open, bringing in a cool breeze and the whispering of sprinklers. Creed shrugged. He couldn't blame the guy for deserting his post on this beautiful day.

He turned and left the office. He'd promised Justine that he'd come in and talk about Ricky, but he hadn't really been looking forward to it. As he left the office Creed began to feel a bit guilty about giving up so easily. Outside the smoked windows he could see the school gardener, a pot-bellied, middle-aged man, cursing and wrestling with a hose.

On impulse, Creed went out and gave him a hand. Together they struggled with it. The hose was twisting like a malicious living thing; wet writhing sine curves of green plastic. 'Careful,' said the gardener. 'This crap is so expensive you wouldn't believe it but it busts real easy.'

They straightened it out and suddenly simple fluid mechanics took over. The hose lay motionless and obedient, as a series of sprinklers slowly came to wet, spinning life.

'Thanks,' said the gardener. He was a burly monkey-like man with his skin burned nut-brown by years of outdoor life. 'Very nice of you to pop in specially to help me sort out the irrigation of our fertile little valley here.' He smiled proudly at the lovingly tended garden.

'Actually, I came in to try and see Mr Pangbourne.'

'Oh, yeah?' The gardener's face suddenly lost some of its cheerful glow. Creed liked the man. Now he found himself watching him carefully.

'So, what's he like, this Pangbourne?' he said. He had a sudden intuition that the gardener might tell him something worth hearing.

'Pangbourne? The principal?'

'Yeah,' said Creed. 'People say he's a little odd.'

'Well, it's a damned odd school, Mister.'

'Odd?'

'Designed to handle specially talented kids and problem kids.'

'I reckon kids are just kids,' said Creed.

'Sounds like you've got a few of your own.'

'A few, yeah. All teenagers have the same problems regardless of whether they're all potential Einsteins.'

'Or potential Hitlers,' chuckled the gardener. He fished in his pocket and dug out a couple of fat, brown cigars. He lit one and offered the other to Creed.

'No thanks,' said Creed. 'Though maybe I'll take one for later, when I need to fumigate my loft.'

They both chuckled as the man lit up.

'You got kids at this school?' said the gardener.

'Well, my daughter starts here next week. And so does my son. Or at least they're supposed to.'

'Is there some kind of problem?'

'Not really. Well, not with Cynthia at least. She's going on this trip to Europe with a friend. My neighbour's taking them. I was kind of relying on the school-board to block it but it seems you can't count on anyone these days.'

'Well, culture is important too, you know, friend.'

'You sound just like the school-board.'

'Probably do the girl a power of good.'

'You've obviously never met my neighbour,' said Creed. 'That rich, scrawny, angular old bitch.'

'Quiet, friend,' murmured the gardener, his voice low and unhurried as he exhaled blue smoke. It dissolved on the warm August air as he gently waved his cigar in greeting. Creed turned and saw Mrs McCracken emerging from the school. She crossed the lush green lawn in an unhurried fashion and joined them.

Instead of her usual skin-tight jeans she was wearing red stretch-pants and a man's checked shirt, tied to form a halter over the finest pair of firm tanned breasts that rich widowhood and elective surgery could provide. Mrs McCracken's eyes were concealed behind wrap around sunglasses that gave her a sinister insect-like appearance. She nodded at the gardener. 'Hello, Creed,' she said. Creed tried to read her eyes but all he could see was his own reflection in the sunglasses.

Whenever Creed met Lesley McCracken at the inevitable round of summer parties on Concroft Avenue, she made no attempt to conceal her distaste for him. She evidently saw him as a blue-collar upstart who through some terrible misunderstanding had erupted from the underclasses and blundered into her neighbourhood, ending up living three houses down from her.

The school gardener had fallen silent at Mrs McCracken's arrival and the only sound was the hissing of the sprinklers. Creed found it a little unnerving and Mrs McCracken seemed to be enjoying his discomfort. Creed cleared his throat. 'I was just talking to this gentleman about the eccentric Mr Pangbourne.'

'Mr Pangbourne?'

'The principal, the headmaster, whatever you call the head-honcho in a dump like this.'

'Oh, I know who Mr Pangbourne is, Creed dear,' said Mrs McCracken. 'I just didn't quite hear what you said. What was that adjective you used?' She glanced at the gardener then back at Creed adding in a friendly, informative voice, 'An adjective is a word that describes –'

'I know what an adjective is,' said Creed. He could feel his face getting hot. 'I said he was eccentric.' You patronizing bitch, he added silently.

'Is that the impression you have of this Pangbourne person? An eccentric?'

'Yes,' said Creed, beginning to lose his temper. Mrs McCracken always had this effect on him, and she knew it. She enjoyed needling him and Creed somehow couldn't stop himself rising to it.

'Eccentric how?' drawled Mrs McCracken, the gardener watching her silently.

'Frothing at the mouth and howling at the moon,' blurted Creed. 'Slaughtering small infants. Having intimate relationships with amphibians. How the hell should I know?'

The gardener and Mrs McCracken exchanged a look.

'Creed, dear, I take it you haven't been formally introduced to Daniel Henry Pangbourne.' She gestured languidly towards the man Creed had assumed to be the gardener. Then Mrs McCracken turned away, smirking, and pulled down her sunglasses to survey the garden. 'New shrubs are looking lovely, Daniel,' she said, her eyes glinting with amusement. Then she strolled off in a leisurely fashion, giving Creed a friendly nod as she went.

Creed turned to the man. Pangbourne's eyes were unreadable.

'Look,' said Creed, 'if this is going to affect my son's chances –'

'You can come to see me on Monday about your son. During office hours. That's my office over there.'

'I know, I went in there looking for you, Mr Pangbourne.' Creed struggled to find the right words. 'Look, my wife and I are both very grateful that you're letting Ricky into your school. We know it's very last minute –'

'Hold it right there. I am not committing myself on this matter, not in any respect.'

'What do you mean?'

'I mean I haven't agreed that your son will be coming here.'

Creed felt himself flush with sweat. School started in a few days. There was nowhere else Ricky could go. Pangbourne had to accept him. 'Listen, I don't know if I should mention this,' began Creed, 'but I work at the –'

Pangbourne pre-empted him. 'Don't think that where you work makes a blind bit of difference. I know exactly what goes on up there in that white office building on the hill. Up there at the Agency. You lot are no better than the CIA.'

'Oh, come on, Mr Pangbourne. That's nasty and untrue.'

Pangbourne ground out his cigar. 'Well OK. You aren't corrupt power-crazed idiots. But what are you? You're not a police force. You're not the FBI. You don't like to dress up in funny uniforms, so you're sure as hell not the military. How would you describe yourselves?'

'As the good guys,' Creed found he was smiling despite himself.

'Very glib. But who do you answer to? Who controls you?'

'Well, personally, I have to deal with a guy in Washington whom I've never met except over the computer.'

Pangbourne sighed. 'The shallowness of your political awareness troubles me, sir. You seem an intelligent man. Who pulls on the puppet strings that operate you?'

'Perhaps I don't see myself as a puppet, Mr Pangbourne.'

'But you represent a powerful paramilitary force in this country. What if control of your Agency was to –'

'Fall into the wrong hands?'

'Don't laugh at me, young man. How can such issues not concern you? Indeed, obsess you?'

'I guess I just like to get on with the real work,' said Creed.

'I suppose you do. And I imagine you really do think you're the good guys. Some would see you as a wedge in our democratic process, one that potentially opens the way to a totalitarian state. Yet there you sit, in your white building on the hill, imagining yourselves as crime-fighting secret agents. Yes, you do. I know you do. Look at you! I can see it on your face, in that big self-satisfied grin.'

'Well, crime-fighting secret agent,' said Creed. 'You have to admit, it's a better job description than sewage-maintenance engineer.'

'But is it a better job? Working in a sewer is probably cleaner.'

Creed felt a sudden pulse of anger towards the older man. It was a dangerous feeling. Keep cool, he told himself. 'Look, Mr Pangbourne, I'd better be going.'

'Yes, you better,' said the man abruptly, turning to his plantings. He called out as Creed made his way back into the school. 'I'll see you on Monday.' It was a command.

Creed wandered back through the school. He couldn't believe it. Here he was, back walking between high-school lockers again, down the long polish-smelling corridors. And feeling the familiar dread, after all these years, of being summoned to see the principal.

Chapter 8

'Beautiful evening.' Roz smiled in the light from the screens. She forced herself to concentrate on the one big screen directly in front of her, the one that was shaped like a windscreen. She had to concentrate on things.

After all, she was driving.

The airport buildings flashed past. Roz could see the reflection of the big armoured vehicle in the dark windows as it raced by.

Her big armoured vehicle. She was in charge of it now. It had only taken her five minutes to nag Redmond into letting her drive. He still hadn't told her the exact nature of the state of emergency. Give it another ten minutes of nagging, thought Roz and she smiled.

'You've certainly cheered up,' said Redmond from the seat beside her.

'I'm always cheerful. I just didn't like being press-ganged.' He was right, though. Roz's spirits had lifted considerably since she had taken charge of the vehicle. She liked it: she felt both safe and excited here, in the belly of this big metal beast. This was the way tank crews must have felt in the last war.

'Maybe I was overdoing it when I compared it to being press-ganged,' said Redmond. 'It's more like being drafted.'

Rain lay black and slick on the airport tarmac and flowed in clouds past the windscreen, as the big wheels of the vehicles mashed it into spray. Roz pushed a button and somewhere on the hull a jet of air from a concealed hose cleared the camera lens.

'Being drafted is just as bad, if you're being drafted to fight in a war you don't believe in.'

'Oh, you'll believe in this war all right,' said Redmond. 'Turn left here.'

'What if I don't agree about the enemy? One man's enemy is another man's friend.' Roz cleared her throat and assumed her most annoying nagging tone of voice. 'And incidentally you still haven't told me the identity of our enemy.'

'Don't worry, love,' said Redmond grimly. 'We won't have any problem agreeing on who the enemy is. Sharp right here.'

Roz was happily steering the big vehicle at dangerously high speed through the curving maze of exit-roads which encircled the airport. Road signs popped out of nowhere, suddenly shining in the headlights of the big vehicle. There was almost no traffic, and no sign of other human life.

So, it was something of a shock for Roz when she saw the stewardess. She brought the big vehicle thundering down an incline and swept into the shadow under a bridge and there it was, a face looming out of the darkness. A woman's face.

She was hitch-hiking. Standing under the bridge at the perimeter of the exit-road, sheltering from the rain. She had one small suit-case beside her. It was the stewardess from Roz's flight all right. What the hell was she doing out here?

'Sorry we can't give you a lift, love,' said Redmond, craning his head to catch a final glimpse of her in the rear screen. She had nice legs. 'But we've got business.'

The stewardess disappeared on the rear cameras in a flash of rain-spray.

Lesbians, thought Jessica Morrell. Lesbians are on the airwaves tonight for some reason.

She had been getting thoroughly depressed with hitching. She'd been standing under that bridge for half an hour and it was so miserable that the great waves of emotion slopping around inside her began to settle down a little.

So what if she had got engaged and then jilted in less than 24 hours? If there's one thing that's worse than that, it's standing on a grim motorway exit-road outside Heathrow Airport with water in your shoes, waiting for a lift.

Jessica began to feel silly. She'd only decided to hitch out of some bizarre sulky sense of rage. But who was she punishing? They were her feet standing in a growing puddle of oily water. Her toes that were cold and wet, not Roy's.

The bastard. How could he do it? She felt a pain in her

stomach when she thought of Roy. Had he been lying? Had he been planning this? To build her up by proposing and then to smash her down by abandoning her? No, that wasn't like Roy.

He must have meant it. Meant it when he proposed and then changed his mind. She remembered the bouquet of roses he'd brought all the way out to the airport and presented to her on his knees. The same roses she'd jammed head-first into a waste receptacle when she finally realized that he'd stood her up.

My God, they talked about women changing their minds, being unstable, blown around helplessly by their emotions. Look at Roy.

Jessica was growing increasingly miserable under the motorway bridge. Above her passenger jets rose into the sky, jewelled with red and green lights. Big, warm planes where friends and co-workers were pushing trolleys up and down nice dry aisles, with soft warm carpets under their feet. Jessica sighed out loud but the sound was lost in the grumble of the ascending jet.

Then a big military vehicle came roaring down the exit-road behind her. The bridge echoed with the engine of the armoured car, and Jessica instinctively stood further back from the side of the road to let the big vehicle pass. But she didn't move far enough because the vehicle slashed through a deep puddle and sprayed rain water all over her.

That would have been the last straw. Jessica was ready to break into tears. But it was just a minute later when another car came down the road behind her, a battered old white Mercedes.

What the hell. Even soaking, miserable and furious, Jessica was no quitter.

As the headlights of the Mercedes splashed her shadow against the concrete pillars, lurching, black and monstrous, she stuck out her thumb.

Now Jessica sneaked a glance at the driver sitting beside her. Lesbians, she thought. They're on my mind tonight. Maybe it's just sexual insecurity, the broken engagement and all that. The Mercedes passed under a street-lamp and amber light filled the car for a moment. Jessica scrutinized the old woman behind the steering-wheel. Definitely an old bull-dyke, thought Jessica. That's what I thought the first time I saw her hanging around the airport and that's what all the other stewardesses think, too. Old bull-dyke in tweeds.

'Penny for your thoughts,' said Mrs Woodcott, glancing away from her driving for a moment to smile at Jessica. She wasn't wearing tweeds today. She was wearing some sort of hideous floral creation. It was hard to see now that the street-light had passed.

'Oh, nothing,' said Jessica hastily.

The light in the car was dead. 'You'll have to forgive the mysterious appearance,' the old woman had said when Jessica climbed in. She had introduced herself as Mrs Woodcott as they pulled away.

Jessica knew her by sight but not, until then, by name. One of the other stewardesses had told her that Mrs Woodcott was something to do with airport security. This was a reassuring thought, somewhat ameliorating the sinister-dyke vibe Jessica detected from her.

'Thanks for picking me up,' said Jessica.

'You should never have been hitch-hiking,' said Mrs Woodcott crossly. 'Because of certain recent events, girls should be very careful about travelling on their own.'

'What recent events?'

Mrs Woodcott glanced across at Jessica, her face hardly visible in the faint moonlight through the windscreen. Her eyes were unreadable. Her voice was absent, offhand, as though her mind was on other matters. 'It's like Kenya,' she said. And she began to speak in her vague, distracted voice.

Jessica was hardly listening, peering out of the windscreen of the Mercedes as it sped along through the night. She was lost in thoughts of Roy. She stopped herself and made a conscious effort to forget Roy. No point worrying about that now. Just think about getting home and getting your feet dry. Cup of tea then a big brandy in a proper brandy glass to put that familiar silky fire in her stomach. Curl up on the big old comfortable sofa with her big old comfortable dog, and get slowly sozzled. Feel sorry for herself, listen to Dave Brubeck and hug Scooter, enduring his atrocious doggy breath as he panted ecstatically in her face.

Just get me home, thought Jessica. Luckily she was too

exhausted to be frightened, because the old woman beside her seemed to be getting weirder and weirder.

'They call this a state of emergency,' Mrs Woodcott was saying. It was as if she was musing to herself. 'Funny, because in many ways it reminds me of what they called the Emergency in Kenya. You're not old enough to have heard about it. It took place in the 1950s. How time flies.'

Jessica let the old bat ramble on. She tuned out, absorbing herself in fears of the future. What was she going to do? Why had Roy left her? Would she be able to find someone else? Was she too old?

She drifted into thinking about the times she and Roy had spent together. She remembered one wet day in Greenwich. They spent a charcoal-grey winter afternoon happily poking around in funny old junk shops, looking for blue antique bottles. Then they bundled into a warm pub afterwards to sit by the fire and have a drink. There they opened their bags and unwrapped their discoveries, their treasures.

She remembered the prize of their collection. It was a Victorian medicine bottle in the shape of a skull with the admonitory word 'poison' carved in the blue glass forehead. She had put flowers in it and set it on top of the shelves in the kitchen.

It had been one of the first to get smashed on the night of their argument.

Jessica didn't want to think about that night. When she did she felt the sting of tears in her eyes.

'Of course, the white settlers in Kenya had come to accept these social conditions as normal,' continued Mrs Woodcott. 'Even families with a tiny income could live in a kind of luxury, providing they were white. They had household servants to help with all their domestic tasks.'

The car sped steadily along, engine buzzing and tyres hissing as they traversed a motorway, shiny and black as oil. The road surface was still wet but the rain had stopped now.

'These servants were accepted, trusted, taken for granted. They were so familiar that, like wallpaper, they faded into the background of everyday life.'

The moon was shining in a high cold sky, pale neutral light coming through the windscreen. Jessica watched Mrs Woodcott's face in the moonlight. Concentrating on the road, not looking at Jessica, the old woman continued to talk, like someone speaking in a trance.

'Just think about it,' she said. 'Those courteous, obedient eyes. Eyes which you can't read. Teeth flashing in smiles. But who knows what those smiles really portend? What thoughts really go on in those alien skulls?'

Now, Mrs Woodcott did look up from her driving for a moment. Her dark eyes glittered at Jessica. She looked like an old school mistress fervently hoping her pupil will give her the right answer.

'Many things have the power to frighten us, but we reserve a particular dread for invasions from within. A disease you catch may be awful, but how much more awful the disease that comes from within your own body, traitor cells in the self. You do see what I'm getting at, dear?'

Jessica grunted something. How much more of this crap did she have to listen to? Never mind. She could endure it. Nice comfortable car and the rain's stopped; almost home now.

'So it was for the good white people of Kenya with their servants on the inside. Trusted, taken for granted, ignored. Imagine the horror when these trusted servants suddenly rose up to butcher their masters.'

Jessica counted the street-lamps as Mrs Woodcott went on about the Mau Mau uprising, telling horror stories of blood and torture, and bestial ceremonies called oathings.

She seemed to take pleasure in relating the gory details, glancing over at Jessica from time to time to watch the expression on her face. Telling of children murdered while sleeping between clean sheets, by the hands which had so recently laundered those sheets.

Jessica was hardly listening. She nodded her head at what seemed to be suitable intervals, only speaking when it became necessary to give Mrs Woodcott directions. Finally they pulled off the motorway and into the sprawling council estate where Jessica lived.

The Mercedes pulled up outside her house and Jessica thanked Mrs Woodcott and opened the door. As she got out, Mrs Woodcott said, 'Don't forget what I've been telling you, dear. Be careful.'

'I will, good night.' She heaved a sigh of relief as the

Mercedes pulled away. Then she took out her keys and turned to face it.

Home.

It was a small pretty maisonette with a rose-bush trailing up the brickwork. Jessica took a deep breath of cool night air.

Despite all the things that had happened, despite what Roy had done to her, Jessica found that she was delighted to be back. The moon was high. It was a clear cold night here, on the London orbital road, and there was surprisingly little traffic.

She walked up the concrete ramp that led to her garden gate. At the bottom of the ramp she resolved not to think about Roy again for a few days. But halfway up the ramp Jessica already found herself glumly wondering what fatal flaw in her personality had caused him to dump her.

She paused outside her front door, and took another deep breath. She had to prepare herself. Her little house might look the same in the moonlight, but it had been subtly altered. Everything had changed since she went away.

She stood hesitating with the key in the lock. This would be her first time stepping over this particular threshold. She was going inside to a new life. A life without Roy.

Jessica squared her shoulders, turned the key and strode across the threshold. Her first impression on entering the small house was of total silence. It immediately confirmed her worst fear, and she realized that in some tiny corner of her heart she'd been harbouring the hope that this was all some kind of mistake, that Roy would be here, waiting for her.

Roy wasn't here.

No one was here.

She stepped into the hot, quiet house, locking the door behind her. Her second impression was that someone had failed to take the waste-bin out of the kitchen. An over-ripe smell hung, faintly detectable, in the warm stale air. But Jessica knew she had emptied the kitchen bin. She'd done it just before she left.

She pushed through into the kitchen.

White and blue. That is how the kitchen had looked to her during that terrible night. She had been clearing up endless fragments of blue glass from the bright white tiles of the floor. And that was the image of the kitchen that had remained locked in her mind since she left. Bright blue scattered on the stainless white.

But now, in some kind of nightmare reversal, the clean white kitchen tiles were splashed with red.

Bright jagged slashes and splashes of red, her spotless kitchen floor transformed into a giant canvas in some ruthlessly modern art gallery; snow-white background with monstrous angular splashes of intense red.

A network of jagged red splashes, and there at the centre of them –

'Roy.'

Jessica felt a dire caving-in of emotions in some central portion of herself. She looked at the shape on the floor and, despite everything, she immediately recognized it as Roy. And following on that recognition came a flickering instant of intense joy and relief.

Because this explained why Roy hadn't turned up at the airport. He hadn't abandoned her at all. He just couldn't make it.

And swifter still, flooding into her mind to drown that joy and relief, came an agonizing shock of animal pain and loss.

Jessica made a small sighing sound and fell to her knees, banging them painfully on the cold white tiled floor. She didn't feel it. She reached out to touch Roy and then drew her hand back and studied the sticky patch of blood it had suddenly acquired.

How could this have happened?

She looked away from the torn body. Who could have done this to Roy? She was standing up again, getting to her feet and even going to the sink and washing her hand. Moving like a life-sized mechanical doll dressed as an airline stewardess.

Jessica's mind slowly began to function again. Something about a phone. Something she had to do. Something one always had to do in situations like this.

Use the phone. She had to use the phone. Jessica carefully dried her hands and went back out to the hall. She was numb, as if she'd shrunk into a tiny replica of herself, lost deep in her body and forced to operate her own limbs by remote control.

She stepped into the hallway, closed the kitchen door with one long distant arm, turned on her tall remote legs, walked a few steps.

Her bag was on the floor by the front door where she'd dropped it. Where she always dropped it, with a sigh of relief, when she first got home.

She bent over, moving very carefully, in case her head might come loose and roll off her shoulders. She bent over to pick up her bag and get the phone out of it, so she could call the hospital, call the police, call whoever one called in situations like this.

It was as she was bending over that Jessica suddenly realized something else was wrong.

The silence as she had stepped through the front door. Something was wrong. Not just Roy. Something else was missing.

As Jessica reached for the phone she remembered the old woman in the car. Mrs Woodcott's face in the moonlight as she went on and on, talking about the invisible enemy. The trusted servant. Taken for granted. Ignored. The killer within.

Jessica had the phone in her hand now, but she wasn't even aware of it. She had realized what else was missing and she was turning to look up at the dark staircase above her. Turning to look even before she heard the scraping of nails on floorboards.

Even before she saw the shape coming swiftly down out of the shadows at her. Moving with great speed but no haste. Moving through darkness.

Almost invisible in the shadows except for the glint of eye, gleam of fang.

Chapter 9

Creed emerged from the air-conditioned coolness of the school into the sledge-hammer sunlight of the parking lot, feeling dazed. He wasn't looking forward to going home. He was replaying the encounter with Pangbourne in his mind, rehearsing what he would say to his wife, when he looked up across the empty parking lot and saw there, in the late afternoon glare, the yellow Fiat pulling in off the road.

It was Amy Cowan's car. For a moment he tried to make himself see someone else at the wheel. But it was unquestionably Amy. She smiled and waved at him. Despite his best efforts Creed found himself smiling too.

He watched her through the bright glare that slid across her windscreen. The girl with short blonde hair and silver earrings. She always wore silver. It looked good on her, against the honey tan of her skin.

Amy steered the Fiat in a lazy half-circle and came to a halt just a few spaces from the only other car parked outside the school. Creed's Audi, with his two daughters sitting patiently in it, waiting for him.

Creed stood there in the parking lot for an idiotic indecisive moment. He felt exposed, like the last chess piece left on the board. He didn't want to bump into Amy, but there was nowhere to hide. And she'd seen him now. Creed saw her bending over to open the door of the car, and he thought for an instant of snow melting on an office carpet and delicate ice crystals on blonde eyelashes. The oceanic blue-green of her eyes. Eyes he could hardly bear to look into because he thought he might lose himself in them. Go down in their depths and never come back up.

He felt the eyes of his daughters on him as he walked towards Amy. There was no avoiding her now. Blonde hair, sea-blue eyes. Silver earrings. Wide, dazzling smile.

'Finally decided to get an education, eh?' Creed nodded towards the school building. It looked cool and dark, silent except for the snapping of the Stars and Stripes at the flag-pole on the roof.

'In a manner of speaking, yes,' said Amy. 'I've got to do some research and there's a guy who works here who's an expert in the field. His name's Retour.'

'He's my daughter's history teacher,' said Creed.

'You sound like you hate the guy.'

'I never met him. Shouldn't you be doing something?'

'Doing something?'

'It's Saturday. You remember, Cowan, the weekend? A young woman like you should be doing something. Not working.'

'It gets worse. I'm going back to the office after this. I'll be there most of the evening.'

Amy looked at him and they were both silent. Creed became uncomfortably aware that he was wearing a wide grin of vacuous stupidity. Amy broke the silence. 'I thought you might like to drop in.'

'Well, listen –'

'We could pull a couple of case-files. Crack some unsolved crimes together.'

'I'd like to, but you know.' Creed shrugged and nodded towards the car with his two daughters in it. 'I have this whole circus to attend to.' He thought guiltily of Justine. 'What I laughingly call my life.' Creed shrugged again, apologetically, and moved towards his car.

'Well, if you change your mind, drive out and see me,' said Amy. 'I'll take a break. If we can't crack any unsolved crimes perhaps we can crack a few beers together.'

'Beers?'

'Sure; I bet I can drink more than you.'

'You can probably drink me under the table,' said Creed. Then he instantly wondered if this sounded like some kind of sexual double-entendre.

Amy laughed and waved as she walked towards the school. She didn't look back again. Creed's initial sense of triumph began to melt away. He'd said no to Amy. He'd managed to stay away from her one more time. He'd done a good job.

So why did he feel this pang of disappointment?

Creed felt as if he was sitting in a placid tropical lagoon, and Amy was like a fresh warm current sweeping in from the sea. But Creed was comfortable sitting in the tepid water of his old life. So he'd built a dam of sand to keep the warm, new current out.

Creed watched Amy disappear into the school. The flagpole made its metallic lashing noise. The parking lot baked in the sun. Creed sighed, got into his car and started the engine.

All the way home he felt the heavy silence of his daughters in the back seat.

Chapter 10

'Who are you?' said the woman's voice. 'I wanted to speak to the police.'

'Just let me ask the questions, please,' said Roz. She shifted in her seat and adjusted the microphone. She was sitting at the communications console in the rear of the armoured personnel carrier. Redmond had only let her drive while they were on the orbital road. He took over as soon as they passed a sign that said: CENTRAL LONDON 8KM.

'Please. Who am I talking to?' the woman's voice had an edge of growing hysteria, reproduced authentically by the speaker in the roof of the armoured car.

'Just listen, please,' said Roz. To tell the truth, she was just as glad that Redmond had taken over the driving. She doubted she could match his skill at navigating the maze of streets that led into the heart of London.

'Are you the police? Who are you?' begged the woman.

Roz took pity on her. She forced herself to explain patiently. 'No, we're not the police, but we are working with them during the state of emergency.'

'I dialled 999 and I asked for the police.'

'Yes, but –'

'And I was talking to the police but then something happened.'

'Yes,' said Roz, biting back the urge to shout at the woman, to tell her to just shut up and listen.

'Then I was suddenly talking to you.'

'Yes,' said Roz. 'As soon as you said a certain word it was detected by a computer which recognized it and automatically transferred your call to the nearest unit in your area. In other words, they put you through to me.'

'Automatically did what? What word?'

'Dog,' said Roz.

The speaker above her was silent for a moment.

'Are you there?' said Roz.

'Dog,' said the woman. There was an ugly chuckling note in her voice as if she was about to begin laughing. Roz had no desire to find out what that laughter might sound like.

'Take it easy,' she said. 'Take a deep breath.'

But instead of laughing the woman began to cry. 'Dog,' she said, sobbing. Then: 'I came home, and I walked in, and I saw Roy dead in the kitchen.'

Roz covered the microphone. 'It's already killed one of the occupiers,' she called. At the front of the armoured car Redmond nodded silently as he concentrated on the driving.

'I saw Roy,' said the woman's voice on the speaker. 'And then I walked into the hall to get my phone. And then it came down the stairs.' The voice was shaking. 'He came down the stairs. Scooter.' Roz could hear that she was hanging on to her self-control by a thread. 'My dog,' she said. 'Our dog.'

'Don't worry. Hang on. We're on our way.'

'He was moving very quickly.' The woman sounded like a child now, like a little girl reciting a story.

'I got into the bedroom just in time,' confided the childish voice. 'It's safe in the bedroom. He can't get through the door.'

'We'll be with you soon,' said Roz.

'He's outside the door. He wants to come in but I won't let him.'

'Tell her I'm driving as fast as I can,' shouted Redmond from the front of the vehicle.

'Scooter's outside the door,' said the horribly childish voice. 'But I won't let him in.'

Scooter was outside the door.

But it was a good, strong, sturdy door. Roy had put it up, hanging it on the hinges himself.

The people they'd bought the house from had ripped out all the original fittings and replaced them with inferior modern designs. But over the course of many months Roy and Jessica had haunted the estate's communal recycling area and salvaged a full set of original doors.

With her help Roy had painstakingly replaced them. It was

their pet project, restoring the little house. The bedroom door had been the last one and Roy had put it up on his own, obstinately working late one Sunday night.

There was a sound outside the door.

Jessica concentrated on thoughts of that night. Thoughts of how strong the door was and what a good job Roy had done. She had made fun of him at the time. Lying in bed and telling him to forget it and leave it. Leave it until morning. To come to bed. To climb into the big bed with her.

Their bed. Jessica turned around in the darkened bedroom. She walked over to the bed and sat in a patch of pale light, hands folded on tightly squeezed-together knees. Picture of air stewardess in moonlight, she thought. Portrait of anxious flight-attendant on bed.

Jessica invented titles for the picture in her head. She didn't want to think about the door.

Scooter was outside the door.

Jessica realized she was still clutching the phone. She put it down on the bed beside her. She listened carefully but there was no sound outside the door. Maybe he was gone. Maybe he'd wandered downstairs and gone into the kitchen. No, not the kitchen. She'd closed the kitchen after she left it. After she saw what had happened to Roy in there.

Don't think about Roy.

Jessica sat on the bed carefully not thinking about Roy. She sat quite still. More than anything else in the world she wanted to get up and cross the moonlit bedroom. Go to that door and listen.

But no. She mustn't. She had to stay put.

That's what the voices on the telephone had told her. Stay exactly where she was until they came to get her. They would come and rescue her. She just had to stay where she was.

Sit here quietly on the bed. That wasn't so hard to do, was it? Sit here and feel the breeze stir across your face from the bedroom window.

It wasn't so bad. In fact it was very peaceful, sitting here with the breeze on her face in the night-time silence. Silence.

Scooter had gone.

He wasn't outside the door. He couldn't be. She would be able to hear him if he was. Jessica was sure she would. Once again she repressed the urge to get up and go to the door. Stay put, they'd told her. We'll be with you soon. But Jessica felt the persistent urge to get up and cross the dark bedroom and listen.

Listen at the door and perhaps open it just a crack.

Jessica was certain that Scooter wasn't outside any more. He'd gone downstairs. Perhaps through the sitting room, through the French windows and right out into the garden.

It was stupid for her to be shut up in this bedroom when she could be down the stairs and safely out the front door in about three seconds flat. Scooter could never reach her in that time. He was in the sitting room, or perhaps right down the far end of the garden by now.

Hell, she could do it in two and a half seconds. Out of the bedroom, down the stairs, past the kitchen and out the door.

She would see Scooter if he was anywhere on her route. Anywhere between here and the front door. He couldn't be hiding in the kitchen, waiting to pounce. He couldn't be in there because the kitchen door was shut. She had shut it herself, after seeing Roy.

Don't think about Roy.

Jessica forced herself not to think about Roy. But as she concentrated on doing that she found herself standing up. Getting off the bed and going to the bedroom door.

The door drew her to it with its promise of escape.

She had to get out of here. Roy was dead in the kitchen downstairs, and she had to get out of here before her head exploded with the unbearable pictures of what she'd seen.

Scooter wasn't outside anyway. He was downstairs. In the garden. She would hear him if he was outside the door.

Jessica placed her ear against the cool smooth wood of the bedroom door. She held her breath and listened.

All she heard was a deep buzzing silence, the faint vibration of something electrical in the house, transmitted by the wood of the door. Beyond that was the tiny echo of her own blood beating.

Beyond that, total silence.

Scooter wasn't out there.

Jessica put her hand on the doorknob. She twisted it and opened the door, just a crack. Just enough to peer out.

Scooter surged up at her from the shadowy carpet outside the bedroom, snarling as he drove his muzzle into the gap between the open door and the door-frame. He shook his head savagely, forcing his narrow skull forward like a battering-ram.

Jessica threw her weight against the door desperately trying to wedge it shut again.

But Scooter's head remained jutting through the opening, lips bared over thick, yellow teeth. His wet muzzle strained, so near Jessica could smell it.

The dog's hot foul breath fanned her face. She gave a moan of effort as she tried to drive the door shut, to crush that narrow skull, to force it back into the hallway.

Scooter made his own small grunt of effort and shook his lanky body with all his wiry strength. His long neck strained forward and suddenly his head was inside the bedroom. Inside far enough to get his jaws open. As soon as Jessica saw that she jerked back, inadvertently loosening her hold on the door and Scooter managed to get his shoulders into the room. His front paws were still stuck outside, trapped against his belly, rigidly flexing as they strained to slash and rend.

With his shoulders through the door Scooter was almost inside. He strained at Jessica, yellow teeth flashing. Saliva sprayed in her face as he barked. Jessica was already off-balance. Now as she tried to avoid the snapping teeth she found herself falling.

She landed on her shoulder on the bedroom floor but somehow managed to keep one hand on the door, gripping the knob.

As soon as she went down, Scooter saw his chance. He reared back to get momentum for the kill. As soon as he drew back, Jessica tried to slam the door in his face.

Scooter was moving too fast for that. His muzzle came jabbing back through the opening.

But Jessica was slamming the door with all her strength. The hard wooden edge of it chopped into Scooter like a guillotine, smashing against his teeth, grinding his head against the door-frame. There was an audible crunching sound and a moan as one of the strong yellow teeth came free of its socket.

Gelid ribbons of blood and saliva shivered down on Jessica's face as Scooter desperately shook and twisted his muzzle, pulling it back to free it.

As soon as he pulled it back, Jessica slammed the door and latched it again.

Jessica got up and tried to wipe herself off. Her knees were trembling as she walked to the dressing-table to grab a handful of Kleenex. She sat there, shaking. She wiped her face. Some of the saliva had got on her face. In her eyes. She prayed that Scooter wasn't rabid.

But what else could explain the terrifying change in his behaviour?

In a minute, when she got her strength back, Jessica would go and sit on the bed in the moonlight.

Sit on the bed quietly like a good girl and wait for help to arrive. It had been crazy of her to try opening the door. It had been a mistake. Almost the last mistake she ever made. Jessica stared at the bedroom door.

Beyond it the house was still and quiet.

Perhaps Scooter had gone downstairs.

Chapter 11

Creed's house was located in Concroft Avenue, a long quiet street shaded by tall old trees. Broad green lawns swept back from the clean sidewalks to the expensive white homes of doctors, lawyers, software engineers.

And secret agents, thought Creed, pulling into his drive. Crime-fighting secret agents. He smiled as he steered the Audi up the familiar gradient of his driveway. He coasted past Justine's battered old station-wagon, into the cool welcome shadows of his garage.

He often wondered what his neighbours would think of him if they knew what he really did for a living. The official story was that Creed was a long-term forward-planning financial analyst under contract to the government. This was a useful cover story; his job sounded so boring that no one ever bothered to ask him about it.

So Creed sometimes wondered what they would say if they knew the truth. That he wasn't just some number-crunching sadsack with a government sinecure. That he worked for the Agency. That he waged a secret war against crime.

What would they say then? What about that old hag McCracken? It would probably blow her mind.

Creed turned off the car and went into the house. The big building was empty, its rooms airy and silent, windows open to catch the summer breeze.

With a family of three children the place was never normally this quiet. To Creed the silence seemed almost religious, magical. He savoured it as it held for a wondrous moment before being rudely broken by the sound of Cynthia and Eve clattering into the kitchen arguing about a jar of peanut butter. Then there was a volley of shouts from the back yard.

Creed looked out of the window and saw Ricky, and two of his teenage friends, working on the vintage Ford Mustang they'd been painstakingly restoring all summer. The boys had spotted the car at a police auction two months ago. They'd taken one look at it and then raced home to borrow the maximum they could raise from parents, big brothers and sisters.

Creed had gently, but firmly, said no. He wanted Ricky to get his problem at school sorted out before he began to reward his son. And a first car, even one shared with two raggedy friends, was quite a reward for a fifteen-year-old boy.

But when he'd refused the money to Ricky, Justine had simply dug out her purse and offered her own credit card.

It had enraged him. As parents they were supposed to be a united front and something had to be done about Ricky. Justine was the first to say as much, so why the hell was she undermining his authority?

But, right now, Creed was willing to forgive her that. Because Justine had been washing the car with the boys and this had obviously degenerated into a water-fight. Someone had dumped a bucket of water on Justine, and now she was chasing Ricky and his friends around the car with a hose.

Creed came out of the kitchen, stood on his lawn, and watched his wife.

She was running around the car, shouting with laughter as her feet skidded on the wet grass. She was wearing a T-shirt and no bra. Watching her breasts bounce Creed felt a stupid grin forming on his face. Even after all these years of snot, diapers, madness and children she still turned him on.

In addition to that clinging soaked T-shirt, she had on a pair of skin-tight, cut-off black jeans. Creed remembered walking up those stone steps in London with Justine. The night they met, all those years ago. And then later, in that old musty patrician bedroom, snapping her bra off and discarding it in the darkness.

Now, he watched her racing around the car, whooping and throwing water, barefoot and brown and wild. She paused, panting and leant against the side of the car. She picked up a can of beer that was resting on the Mustang's roof and took a swig, half-sitting on the hood of the car, bare feet dug deep in the grass to feel the cool moisture on her toes.

All thoughts of Amy Cowan vanished from Creed's mind. Suddenly he was doing some lightning calculations.

Ricky and his friends would go out tonight, like they did every Saturday. Cynthia would spend the evening over with Lysette McCracken, probably helping her mother slay a black ram at the centre of a pentagram, or stick pins in wax effigies.

Which left Eve to be accounted for, but if Creed could get a baby-sitter at short notice that would free up the entire evening. He would tell Justine to get her glad rags on, then he'd take her out to a very classy bar, then an even classier restaurant and then to a very sleazy motel.

To a very sleazy motel bedroom. The kind with mirrors on the ceiling.

And afterwards Creed would drive a warm, tousled Justine home, nodding off to sleep on his shoulder. And he'd spill her into bed and drive the baby-sitter home. Then he'd return to his sleeping house, step through the door and savour the silence. He'd turn off the lights and do a quick inventory, to make sure none of the children had been decapitated or kidnapped. Then he'd slip back into the master-bedroom to wrap his arms around a sleepy, grinning Justine and see if they could re-enact that evening's motel visit, with improvements.

It would blow a hell of a hole in this month's budget, but this evening Creed was in no mood for economy measures. Occasionally he and Justine needed this. They needed to blow off steam. And she always loved it. Creed imagined the delight he'd see on her face when he suggested it.

Just then Justine finished her beer and suddenly scooped up the hose again. She pounced. Ricky and his friends hollered as Justine nailed them with the hose, a spray of water refracting in a rainbow over her head. Creed heard her laughter over the laughter of the kids, and he quickened his pace.

Something in Ricky's manner changed. His friends suddenly stopped running around the car. They'd sensed Creed's arrival. Still holding the dribbling hose, Justine was chuckling but she stopped when she saw Creed.

She turned and set the hose down, but in the instant before she turned away Creed caught a hot flash of rage from her eyes.

He just got that one look but it was enough.

Suddenly he knew that sex was the last thing Justine had in mind for him this evening.

Chapter 12

Jessica flinched at a sudden, small sound. She looked at the bedroom door, but it was solid and safely shut. Scooter was outside but he couldn't get in. She was safe.

Then the sound came again and Jessica realized that it wasn't the dog. It couldn't be. It hadn't come from the door at all. It had come from the window.

The sound came a third time. A delicate clattering.

Jessica went to the window and looked down. There in the moonlit garden, like a figure in a dream, stood Mrs Woodcott clutching an improbably large and ugly handbag in one hand.

She had a pebble in her other hand, ready to throw at the window, but when she saw Jessica she let it drop back on to the dark lawn.

'Hello, dear,' she called up in a loud whisper. 'Are you all right?'

'What are you doing here?' said Jessica. Her voice sounded hoarse and childish, and quite strange even to herself.

'Well, I turned on the car radio as soon as you got out. Official radio, special frequency to keep us updated about the emergency, dear,' Mrs Woodcott explained. 'I'd hardly driven any distance at all when I heard an emergency call being patched through. It took me a minute, but I worked out it was the address I'd just left. It was you.'

Jessica heard a quizzical guttural sound outside the door. With his keen ears Scooter had heard the old woman's voice.

'Mrs Woodcott –' said Jessica.

'They were patching you through to the armoured car units.'

'The French windows,' said Jessica desperately. She could hear Scooter pounding down the stairs.

Mrs Woodcott smiled up at her, not listening, intent on finishing her anecdote. Scooter would be down the stairs now. 'But they said anyone in the vicinity should help. And I was very much in the vicinity.'

'Close the French windows!' said Jessica. Nightmarishly, her voice seemed to have sunk to a hoarse whisper. Could Mrs Woodcott hear her? Scooter would be down the stairs and halfway across the sitting room by now. Halfway to the French windows, sharp teeth ready.

'What's that?'

Halfway to Mrs Woodcott.

'Close the French windows.' Jessica was leaning out of the window. She was straining but her voice had sunk to a harsh, barely audible mutter.

'The French what, dear? Oh look, the doggy's coming!' Mrs Woodcott stepped towards the house. She reached into the open French window, grabbed the nearest glass panel and slid it briskly.

Jessica could hear the whisper of the French windows sliding neatly shut below her, followed immediately by the sound of Scooter's blunt skull bouncing off the reinforced, burglar-proof glass.

This painful sound was followed by a long liquid growl of rage and frustration.

'Not a very nice doggy, though,' said Mrs Woodcott, peering through the glass, shaking her finger. She leant forward, wagging her finger in a reprimand at the snarling muzzle hovering just beyond the glass. 'Until your manners improve you can just stay in the sitting room.' Jessica could hear the insane snarling as Scooter began butting the glass repeatedly, trying to get at Mrs Woodcott.

She didn't seem at all worried. She looked up at Jessica. 'We need to get you out of there, dear,' she said. 'I don't suppose there's a ladder in that shed?'

The armoured car rolled towards the council estate in the moonlight. Redmond had cut the engine as soon as they came off the main road. Now they were rolling silently, drawn by gravity down the small entrance road that curved around the estate.

'This thing has a bayonet attachment,' said Roz.

'You don't see many of those,' said Redmond. He selected a staging point and let the computer take over, steering the armoured car the last 50 metres and parking it in the designated spot. He unstrapped his seat-belt as the armoured car rode up on to a wide concrete podium.

All around them were small clusters of low houses with small private gardens, grouped into an estate by concrete walls and access lanes. Redmond left his seat at the control panel as the computer slowly braked the vehicle to a halt and began the parking manoeuvre.

'What are we doing?'

'Parking,' said Redmond in his mild Irish accent. 'The fire-power in this vehicle is concentrated at the nose of the thing. It's clever enough that when it parks, it points the nose towards the area of maximum threat.'

Redmond came down the narrow aisle and joined her in the small cubicle that served as the vehicle's armoury. Overhead compartments, like those on an airliner, held a variety of small arms and anti-personnel weapons. Roz looked up at him, her face smooth in the pale blue armoury light, her eyes dark.

'And where is the area of maximum threat?' She handed him the weapon she'd chosen. A Styer AUG designed for civil disturbance and house-to-house combat in urban areas. It did indeed have a bayonet fixed, a lethal thin tongue of metal jutting out from under the barrel.

'Over there,' said Redmond, pointing out a small house on the far side of the wide flat podium. It was lost in a dark cluster of buildings, but electronically generated cross hairs singled it out on the front windscreen. 'Private dwelling, owned 99 years leasehold, 98 remaining, by Sutton, R. and Morrell, J.' Redmond squinted at the luminous read-out on a small corner screen. 'J for Jessica. Profession: airline stewardess. Jessica would seem to be our caller. R is for Roy and he sounds like the unlucky fellow in the kitchen.'

'How many animals in the house?'

'Just the one.'

'Piece of cake,' said Roz. She put a night-sighting helmet on. 'I go in, get J. Morrell and shoot the dog if it rears its pointy head.' She adjusted the bayonet on her gun. 'Seems like excessive fire-power, actually.'

'Don't be so certain,' said Redmond.

'All this for one dog?'

'Others may turn up.'

'Others?' Roz laughed.

'In fact, on reflection,' said Redmond, 'I think you should stay with the vehicle and let me go in and do the business.'

Roz stared at him. He was serious. He had his hand on her shoulder. She shook it off. 'No way, Redmond.'

He turned away and swore, rubbing his lean face. He slumped back into the command-chair and looked at her. 'I'd come with you but one of us has to stay with the vehicle. Those are strict orders.'

'Nothing we can do about that then.' Roz smiled and winked at Redmond. Her eyes and teeth were bright in the faint combat-ready light. Redmond watched her as she clambered out of the roof-hatch.

'Go down on to the street and enter by the front door,' he yelled after her.

She turned and looked at the armoured car. Redmond's head popped up out of the hatch in the roof. 'And be careful!'

'Any more concrete advice?' asked Roz.

'Yes, don't offer it any dog biscuits.'

Roz turned and marched away towards the houses.

The moon was high. The light from it was cold and clinical, giving good visibility except where inky patches of shadow lay. Roz could hear her own footsteps echoing off the surrounding walls as she marched across the concrete apron.

She followed Redmond's advice about going in by the front door. The only rear access to the dwellings was through a maze of small, walled gardens. A shadowy labyrinth which would be perfect for an ambush.

So she listened to Redmond and came trotting up the front path, opened the small gate and went on up to the front door.

Repressing a ridiculous urge to knock, she kicked the door in and went spilling into the narrow hallway, gun ready.

The vision enhancement on the helmet immediately showed body warmth in the next room, so she went through the hallway into a small sitting room.

The dog registered on the thermal display as a blaze of energy, a jagged red flame.

The flame twisted and surged abruptly, knifing towards her out of the darkness, barking madly.

But there wasn't a problem, because Roz had the Styer AUG ready and it was on semi-automatic fire, and she got it sighted and locked on to the dog as it jumped towards her.

But then Roz saw something out of the corner of her eye and suddenly there was a problem.

Because on the helmet's display there were now two other sources of body heat, only registering a pale pink, but definitely human-shaped. Standing upright, and moving around.

Two people, alive, in the garden outside, standing beside a ladder. Only the thin glass between them and the sitting room. They were right in the line of fire. Even if every bullet hit the dog dead-centre, they'd still have enough residual velocity to go through the glass, into the garden, and slaughter the people outside.

Roz realized this as the dog was still in mid-air. Her mind pulsed swiftly with alternatives for a fraction of a second. No way could she shoot.

So she dropped to the ground in a kneeling stance, and braced the stock of the gun against the side of her combat boot. The wicked bayonet of the weapon was pointing in the air at a steep angle.

This was the way African warriors had once hunted lions, Roz knew. A braced spear with a crossbar on it, so that the lion can't fight its way up the length of the spear and slay, in turn, the warrior who has just slain it.

There was no crossbar on the Styer AUG, but its magazine stuck out of the side of the gun at an angle and it was this that stopped the dog. He was still slashing at the air with his fangs, jaws working in a mad fury, when his shattered ribs finally locked against the magazine of the gun.

The dog's momentum stalled and his wildly cutting teeth gradually stilled as the gleam faded from his eye.

When she was sure he was dead Roz stood up, struggling against the weight of the impaled dog. She shook the gun, working the lifeless body free of the bayonet with her foot.

The dog's corpse slammed on to the floor with a heavy wet sound. Roz walked forward into the sitting room, keyed up and ready for anything. Beyond the French windows she could see the people in the garden. They were quite clear; the image system in the helmet was working on light intensification now and the moonlight was enough to render the figures unmistakable.

Roz felt the hair stir on the back of her neck. She was looking at two women, both of whom she knew. It was the stewardess from her flight, and the creepy Woodcott woman who had press-ganged her at the airport. She was banging on the window and waving at Roz.

'Nice to see you again, dear,' Mrs Woodcott smiled. 'What a good job you're doing.'

Roz didn't reply. There was a voice speaking in her left ear, on the tiny headphones fitted in the helmet. Redmond's voice.

'Roz, get out of there immediately.'

'Redmond, I've found them. Survivors. Two of them.'

'Bring them with you, then.' His voice was terse and urgent. 'But in any case, get out now.'

Roz slid the French window open and gestured for the stewardess and Mrs Woodcott to come in. 'What's wrong?' she said, activating the helmet microphone as she led the women quickly up the hallway.

'Never mind what it is,' said Redmond's voice. 'Don't think, just haul arse.'

'I can think and haul arse at the same time,' snapped Roz. 'Update me on the situation.' As she ushered the women out of the front door she heard Redmond sigh.

'The surveillance computers have locked on now,' he said in her ear. 'I'm getting readings from the buildings all around you, Roz.'

She led the women into the street. 'And what?' said Roz.

'They all read negative for human life.'

Roz guided the women off the pavement and towards the narrow alleyway that led between the clusters of small houses. Once they were through that they'd be on the open concrete of the podium. Exposed but close to their vehicle.

'They're empty?'

'I said they read negative for human life,' said Redmond. His voice was tense. 'I did not say they were empty.'

Chapter 13

They were going to have an argument. Not just an average argument, but one of those major explosions which occasionally erupted into their marriage like a tropical storm. After all these years together Creed recognized the signs. His spirits sank.

Standing in his backyard he suddenly felt the whole hot weight of the day sinking on to his shoulders. It had been a luminously beautiful summer's Saturday and he'd been the guy taking his daughter for a swim. But now he felt the day being redefined. Suddenly it was a sweltering Saturday in the dog-days of August, and he was the poor schmuck who was about to get chewed out by his wife. The obedient little suburban husband.

Creed's resignation began to change into a smouldering hostility towards Justine.

She had been smiling and laughing with the kids, happy and carefree a second ago. Now, like throwing a switch, she'd turned off the smile and the laughter. She'd deliberately ditched her good mood as soon as he strolled in.

Justine was obviously spoiling for a fight.

Well, if she wants a fight . . . thought Creed.

Justine strode past him, catching his eye. 'Got a second?' she said in that over-polite tone she always took when she was seriously pissed off with him. Creed shrugged and followed her into the house.

Justine chased the girls outside and they stood alone in the kitchen. They opened beers in a tense silence. They could hear the girls in the backyard running over to the car, annoying the boys.

'So, what did you want to talk about?' said Creed. He knew he should take a moderating tone, but to hell with that.

'Did you go to the school to talk about Ricky?'

Creed began to relax. At least he now knew what the argument was about. He realized that he'd been dreading something else. Justine accusing him of –

Creed had a momentary incandescent memory of ice crystals on blonde eyelashes. He repressed the thought and concentrated on what Justine was saying.

'Did you speak to the principal?'

'Sure.'

'You spoke to him yourself? You're sure it was Mr Pangbourne?'

Creed felt a flash of irritation. 'You think I might have got the wrong guy?'

'Well, according to Mrs McCracken you mistook the principal for the school gardener.'

Creed rubbed his forehead. It was starting to throb painfully. That bitch. 'What else did she say?'

'That someone else was there.'

Creed's anger suddenly changed to a hot guilty flush. 'Who?' he said.

'Amy Cowan.'

'Amy?' said Creed innocently. But he knew immediately that he'd made the wrong move.

'Mrs McCracken says she left the two of you at the school together.'

'Gee. How unlike Mrs McCracken to stir up trouble between a man and his wife.'

'In this case she doesn't have to do much stirring. I've seen how you look at that girl.'

'What do you mean?'

'Oh, come off it Creed. You just about have to winch your tongue back in your mouth every time she walks past you.'

Creed laughed. 'You're imagining things. She's a nice kid.'

'Don't take that stomach-turning paternal tone when you talk to me.'

Creed felt himself losing his temper. He fought to retain it, taking deep breaths. 'You know, this really is a shame. Because before you waded into me I was just about to suggest that we call a baby-sitter and take the evening off. Hit a restaurant and then hit the sack in some low establishment.

Make it good. Make it nice between us.'

Justine looked at him. 'Am I supposed to be grateful? You want a roll in bed, Creed? You feel an itch and you want to spend it on me and I'm supposed to be grateful? All because you got worked up talking to a young piece of ass in the school parking lot.'

Creed's thoughts blazed with rage then went dangerously cool. He grinned a predatory grin. He opened his mouth. He didn't know what he was about to say but nothing on earth was going to stop him saying it.

'And when you were washing the car? Dancing around with your tits bouncing? Out there in front of Ricky and his friends? I'm sure inciting a teenage erection was the furthest thing from your mind.'

Justine stared at him for a long, cool moment. Finally, she said, 'You're disgusting.' Her tone was calm and measured. 'You're a disgusting old man. Why don't you complete the picture?' Creed saw her eyes suddenly grow bright. 'Middle-aged and pathetic. Go and screw your brainless little office girl.' Then Justine sobbed and Creed realized her eyes had gone bright with tears.

She spun away from him even as he was reaching out to touch her and surged out of the kitchen, running up the stairs. Creed knew where she was going. Into the bedroom to slam the door and throw herself on the bed before the tears broke loose.

Creed automatically moved to follow her but halfway across the kitchen he paused; the game dictated that he now go up the stairs and comfort her. This was the way it always went. This was always the point where he went up to the bedroom and comforted her. And after she was finished crying they'd make love.

But suddenly, a strange new thought had crept into his head.

Why bother?

Why bother to explain anything to her? She'd already made up her mind. The placid suburban husband had strayed beyond his appointed pastures. He had transgressed and now he had to account for himself.

To hell with her.

Creed felt a surge of pure anger. To hell with her little

tribunal. He had done nothing wrong. She had blamed him even though he'd done nothing.

So he might as well do something.

Creed shook himself like a dog shaking off drops of water. What was he thinking? This was Justine. This was his marriage. This was his life. He couldn't just throw it away like that.

He let any thought of Amy Cowan drift out of his mind. He concentrated on the task at hand. Playing the game. Going upstairs to comfort Justine. Creed felt himself relax and he realized he'd been holding his breath. He felt a little shaken by the thought of what he'd almost done. His mind filled with thoughts of Justine upstairs, on the bed, waiting.

Creed was turning towards the staircase when he heard a sound behind him in the kitchen. He turned and saw a figure in the doorway. The figure had the bright summer evening at his back and stood in shadow and for a moment Creed didn't recognize the man who'd come into his kitchen.

But then he realized it wasn't a man. It was a boy, his son Ricky.

'What are you doing?' said the boy.

'How do you mean,' said Creed. He was annoyed and he knew it showed in his voice, but he couldn't help it. He wanted to be upstairs with Justine.

'What are you doing to mom? Are you beating her up?' Ricky looked up at his father, but instead of looking directly at him he stole a furtive glance. The poor kid was so damned tense and nervous that sometimes it broke Creed's heart.

But other times it just made Creed angry. Frustrated and pissed off. You just wanted to shake the kid till his teeth rattled. He was so shy and uptight that it made you uptight yourself.

What drove Creed crazy was the strictly unnecessary nature of it. Because he couldn't get rid of the notion that Ricky liked being the way he was. That it wasn't so much shyness as slyness. As if Ricky enjoyed making other people feel uncomfortable. It was like saying, if I have to suffer then I'm going to make you suffer too.

And that's what broke Creed's heart. He knew that it wasn't easy growing up. He vividly remembered his own painful teenage years. The shyness and scalding self-consciousness.

He sometimes wished he could just communicate with his teenage self. Reach back in time and tell himself that there was no need to take things so seriously. Everything would be all right. There was no need to suffer. If only he could communicate this message to that skinny kid over all these lost years.

Fat chance. He couldn't even communicate it to his own teenage son who stood before him now.

Ricky came all the way into the kitchen. He was wearing khakis and a T-shirt, standing in that stoop-shouldered fashion that made him look fatter than he was.

Ricky wasn't fat but he was soft. To Creed he had a maddening larval look. Not just soft but somehow uncommitted, undecided. Unfinished. He was a big kid with a sharp mind kept carefully hidden behind a vague nervous manner. He looked slow and plodding. On first meeting some people even thought he might be somewhat backward – until they got a glimpse of those eyes.

Now Ricky was looking up at his father in that nervous way of his, shy or sly. Sneaking glances at him.

Creed took a deep breath, trying to sort out the confusion of anger and love his son awoke in him. 'Look, Ricky,' he said patiently, 'your mother and I are having a discussion. Don't get in my way. And don't give me any crap about raising a hand against her. You know I never have and I never would, and you only said it because you thought it would make me angry.'

'You always know everything, don't you?'

'I know you. I know how your mind works. You're my son.'

'You're so smug, aren't you?' For a moment Creed was gratified to see a glint of anger in his son's shifty eyes.

He wished Ricky would, just once, lose his temper. If he could just fight back, blow off steam, shout at his dad. It would be a lot healthier than wandering around looking tormented all the time.

Creed grinned, maybe tonight would be the night.

'I don't mean to be smug, but yeah, I can read you like a comic book. You know that I'd never hit your mom.' As he thought of Justine he felt a sudden surge of impatience. He half turned away from his son. 'Excuse me,' he said, heading for the staircase. Heading for Justine. But Ricky called after him and something in his tone of voice made Creed stop.

'You're right. I only said it to make you angry. I thought you'd flip.' Ricky smiled a crooked smile. 'But it didn't work. So I guess I'll have to say something else to make you flip.'

Suddenly Ricky's piercing eyes were looking into Creed's. Those eyes were full of a strange blend of pain and anger. Creed realized he'd underestimated how upset his son was.

He began to come back into the kitchen, but then Ricky said, 'But I don't know why I should even bother.' His blazing eyes flicked nervously away from Creed, back into hiding. When he spoke again he was so quiet Creed wasn't sure for a moment what he said.

'You're not even my real dad.'

There was a sudden silence in the big house. Even the sound of the girls' voices, laughing outside with Ricky's friends, had lagged and stopped.

Creed couldn't quite believe what he'd heard. 'What did you say?'

'You're not my real dad.'

Creed's voice was icy now. 'Who told you that?'

'Mom did. She said my real dad was a guy called Vincent.'

Upstairs Justine lay on the bed. She had stopped sobbing and was listening carefully. She'd heard the low murmur of Ricky and Creed talking in the kitchen and a shocking thought had occurred to her.

What if her son said something?

What if he said something about Vincent?

Chapter 14

Roz looked at the dark houses all around her. The moonlight rendered them in stark contours of black and white. If she let her imagination really begin to work she could see those shadows moving, writhing with dark shapes.

She moved to switch on the helmet again, get some night vision and make certain. But she stopped herself. Don't worry about it. Just keep moving.

Fear began to lift under her ribs like a bird spreading its wings.

But it was all right. They were halfway along the alley now, Roz in the lead, Mrs Woodcott and the stewardess straggling behind, and they were past the patch of deepest shadow.

The remaining length of the alley was in bright moonlight and it was a clear run all the way on to the podium. She could see the armoured car waiting for them.

'Step on it,' said Redmond in her ear.

'Nearly there,' said Roz.

'OK, I'm opening the hatch now. Don't linger in the open.'

'Affirmative.' Roz started running. She was just about to emerge from the mouth of the alley when she heard a voice behind her.

'Wait a minute, dear,' it called breathlessly. Roz spun around to see Mrs Woodcott standing a few metres back up the alley. She looked slightly winded, but on the whole remarkably fit for a woman of advanced years who'd just run for her life.

'It's our chum,' said Mrs Woodcott, panting and clutching her big ugly handbag. She jerked her thumb back over her shoulder, in the direction she'd come. Roz stared back up the alley, waiting for Jessica, the stewardess, to emerge from the patch of shadow. But she did not appear.

'Where is she?'

'That's what I'm trying to explain if you'd just listen. She turned back.'

'Come on!' shouted Redmond's voice in Roz's ear. 'Get out of there.' The Irishman had been attempting to hide how close he was to losing his cool. Now he no longer bothered to conceal it. His voice had a raw ugly edge of panic that communicated itself to Roz.

'What the hell are you talking about?' she said, ignoring Redmond, trying to concentrate on Mrs Woodcott.

'Our chum, Jessica, suddenly turned around. She said she had to go back for something.'

'Go back for something?' Roz couldn't believe what she was hearing. 'She's gone back to the house?'

'Yes, I'm afraid so.'

Roz said nothing. She had been sweating heavily in the helmet before, but now perspiration flowed down her forehead in a smooth constant stream. The enormity of it was almost too much to comprehend. They were nearly out of the danger zone and the girl had turned around and deliberately gone back into it.

And of course she'd taken Roz back in with her.

Roz turned and jogged back into the alley. 'Roz, what are you doing?' said Redmond in her ear.

'I'm going back.' She was in the patch of shadow now, halfway up the alley again.

'Going back?'

'I have to fetch Jessica out again.'

'You have to what? Oh, Christ.'

'I'll be as quick as I can.'

'Roz, don't do it.'

'Almost there.' Roz was out of the alley and running up the pavement now, back towards Jessica's house.

'Roz, come back. Please.'

Through the garden gate. Front door still open the way they'd left it.

'Roz!'

Into the hallway, into the kitchen. Body on the floor. The boyfriend.

Roz stood looking down at the torn remnants of what had once been a human being. In her line of work Roz had often been confronted with sudden death. This had been a particularly nasty way to go. She wondered if he had at least died quickly.

She imagined the way it must have been, the sharp teeth coming at him in the moonlight. Coming at him unstoppably.

Roz was imagining what it must have been like when she heard something.

A tiny sound.

It hadn't come from the radio. Redmond had fallen silent. It came from outside the kitchen. Roz turned away from the body and moved silently back towards the kitchen door.

She carefully switched her night-vision helmet back on and stepped into the darkened hallway, the Styer AUG held high.

Roz turned to the left, looking down the short hallway towards the front door. Nothing.

She turned to the right and saw a tall glowing shape move towards her. The night-vision helmet made it look like a living flame.

'Roz.'

Roz took her finger off the trigger. It was Jessica, clutching something in her hand. A square. A picture. A small metal-framed picture. The glass and metal showed up as a cold blue on Roz's visor.

'I'm sorry,' said Jessica. 'I realized that I could never come back to this place.' She held up the picture. 'I wanted to take this with me.'

Image enhancement on Roz's helmet showed her the picture in the frame. A photograph. Jessica and the dead boyfriend, together on some forever-lost summer afternoon. The image system zoomed in relentlessly, gleaning further detail. There in the background of the picture was the dog, happily snapping at a frisbee in mid-air.

'I'm sorry,' repeated Jessica.

'Forget it,' said Roz. She realized that two of the figures in the photograph were dead. Roy and the dog, both were right now lying lifeless in this house. The thought made her queasy. 'Let's go.' She led Jessica back out into the empty street. The cool air felt good on her face. She started moving rapidly along the pavement.

'On our way, Redmond,' she announced into the helmet mike. She was moving quickly, anxious to be past the danger zone of the alley. Once she had nothing but open space between her and the armoured car she would be happier.

Still no response from Redmond. Roz felt a stab of alarm. She remembered the open hatch on the armoured car. What if he hadn't sealed it again? What if something had slipped inside? She started running towards the alley. 'Redmond, are you there?'

'It's too late, Roz.' His voice was a tired sigh in her ear.

'What?'

'They've cut you off.'

'They? Who? I don't see any of them.'

'They're all around you. Get back into the house again.'

'No, we can make it to the vehicle.'

'You can't. They're closing in, Roz. Better collect the old lady and get all three of you back inside.'

Roz stopped running and stood frozen on the pavement. Ahead of her she could see Mrs Woodcott standing in the mouth of the alley. She was waving at Roz.

'I'll drive around the front and pick you up,' said Redmond in her ear.

'OK,' said Roz. She beckoned impatiently for Mrs Woodcott to come and join her. As the woman began to move out of the alley Roz heard the engine of the armoured car start up. 'By the way,' she said into the helmet mike, 'don't forget to secure the hatch, Redmond.' Then she turned around to intercept Jessica.

Jessica was coming from the direction of the house, jogging shakily towards Roz. Roz tried to imagine what the stewardess had been through this evening and her mind flinched away from the thought. She held up her hand, gesturing for the girl to stop. She realized she wasn't getting any response from the vehicle. 'Redmond,' she said into the helmet mike.

Back up the pavement Jessica had duly stopped. But Roz had the strangest feeling that it had nothing to do with her. Jessica stood on the pavement, the small framed picture in her hand. She looked like someone who had stopped because she'd seen something. Something so startling that it rooted her to the spot.

'Redmond,' said Roz into the mike again. All she was getting on the helmet headphones was static. She shook her head furiously as though that would clear the static. Too many things were happening at once.

Mrs Woodcott was trotting from the alley to join her. But what about Jessica?

Roz turned to check on her. Jessica was still standing motionless on the pavement, staring up at a cluster of dark branches hanging above a nearby garden wall. From beyond the wall Roz could hear the distant grumble of the approaching armoured car.

For some reason the engine didn't sound right.

Roz activated the microphone on her helmet. 'Redmond!'

As if in reply to her call, the static on Roz's headphones suddenly gave way to a blast of sound. Roz hit the cut-off button and killed the headphone before it deafened her. Her brain slowly compensated for the extreme volume and she gradually identified the sound.

A huge, booming snarl.

As if a fanged muzzle had been at point-blank range, almost engulfing the microphone.

Then a movement caught her eye and Roz saw what Jessica was staring at on the garden wall.

Roz raised and fired the Styer AUG on full automatic.

She blasted away as the dark shapes came off the wall. They were moving with frightening speed. The shadows separated and Roz realized there were three of them. She sprayed the air with bullets but she only hit two. She just had time to see the third slam into Jessica, smashing her to the ground.

Then Roz had to spin and look the other way because there was gunfire behind her.

As she turned she saw Mrs Woodcott coming towards her. The old woman was holding a silver revolver she'd evidently fished out of her capacious handbag.

She was backing towards Roz, keeping her face towards the alley. Roz could see why.

A flood of angular dark shapes were emerging from the

alley, moving low along the ground. Mrs Woodcott backed away from them, pistol in her hand, taking aim and firing with deliberation.

Together Roz and Mrs Woodcott fought their way back to Jessica's house.

There was nothing they could do for Jessica. Roz had blasted away the dark shape that was crouching on her chest but that didn't help the stewardess. She was instantly buried under a mass of dogs who descended from the wall. Others were pouring out of a garden gate towards Roz and Mrs Woodcott.

Roz realized that nothing could save the stewardess now. She concentrated on saving her own life, and Mrs Woodcott's. They fired into the mass of approaching dogs, causing them to howl and back away momentarily as several of the pack dropped dead.

Roz and Mrs Woodcott retreated slowly. As they backed away along the pavement, Roz put her foot down on something and heard a crunch and then a tinkle of breaking glass. She didn't look down but she knew what it was.

The picture. The one Jessica had gone back for. Everyone in the picture was dead now. The thought flashed through Roz's mind as she backed through the garden gate and up to the front door of the house.

Mrs Woodcott was with her every inch of the way, occasionally loosing a well-aimed shot from her heavy silver revolver. Roz fired short dense bursts from the Styer AUG. They both walked backwards, slowly and carefully because they knew if they stumbled and went over they were through.

They backed slowly towards the safety of the house, along the garden path and up the front steps.

The pack followed them.

A thousand glittering eyes, ten thousand wet teeth. Flowing forward whenever it saw an opportunity or sensed a weakness. Retreating with howls and snarls as bullets lashed at its fringes. The night seemed to have taken on faces. All Roz could see was a solid wall of these furred inhuman faces. Damp snapping muzzles, hungry for her blood.

Roz and Mrs Woodcott inched their way up the steps and through the front door of Jessica's house. Roz fired a final wide burst on full automatic, and then they slammed the front door.

Outside the house the pack did not retreat. It remained standing, as if waiting for something.

Then, as if at a signal, they began to howl.

Chapter 15

Justine remembered surgical instruments. She remembered the light gleaming on them, and the cool dry touch of a hand in a surgical glove as it touched the inside of her thigh, and spread her open. She remembered the smell of beer and the flash of blue eyes above a surgical mask as the man prepared to kill her baby.

To kill Ricky.

Justine had been pregnant when she met Creed.

She had been pregnant with Ricky. Her belly fertile and swelling. And then Paulie Keaton had decreed that her baby must be aborted. Dry surgical hands on her inside thigh. Smell of beer. Flash of surgical instruments.

But Creed had rescued her. He had saved her baby's life. He had saved Ricky.

She hadn't told Ricky that.

She wished she hadn't told him anything.

In her most unhappy moments with Creed, Justine sometimes cynically wondered about the way they'd met. Her romantic saviour. She had fallen for him like a ton of bricks. But as the years passed she'd come to wonder how much of that had been love and how much just the hormonal surge of pregnancy.

But she'd been happy enough with Creed all these years. She'd never regretted leaving Vincent and after the statutory two year waiting period she'd signed her divorce papers without a qualm. Ricky had become Creed's son by then.

He'd never met his real father. In fact, he had no idea that he existed.

Until a few hours ago, that is. When Mrs McCracken had told her about seeing Creed in the parking lot of the school. Talking to that little blonde.

* * *

Now Justine lay on her bed, feeling her heart pumping with fear. She'd been angry. That's why she'd done it. For months now Ricky had been nagging at her. He knew there was some half-buried family secret that concerned him and he pursued it like a pig rooting after truffles.

Creed and Justine had an unspoken agreement not to tell the kids about her earlier marriage. But after Mrs McCracken's visit she had been so angry with her husband that she'd been looking for a way to lash out at him.

Then Ricky and his friends came round to wash the car and she'd joined in. When she'd gone into the kitchen with Ricky to fetch Cokes and he'd brought up the subject of the family secret she'd seen her opportunity to hurt Creed.

So, she simply told her son the truth. But she shouldn't have.

She should have spoken to Creed first. She'd dropped a bombshell on their family life and she hadn't even consulted him. And what if Ricky gave the game away?

He wouldn't. He wouldn't be that stupid, would he?

Creed would be furious. Justine had no idea what he might do.

But Ricky wouldn't tell him. He'd promised.

Now Justine could hear Ricky's voice, quiet in the kitchen below, then Creed's voice, even quieter. Then Ricky again, then the sound of the front door slamming.

She got up off the bed and ran to the window. She saw the car reverse out of the garage into the driveway, Creed at the wheel. He backed the car swiftly into the street, gunned the engine and took off, heading west.

Justine felt her heart sink as she watched the car disappear.

The sun was going down. The shadows were falling long and angular through the trees in Gaines Woods. Creed had driven this route a thousand times, and even without engaging the car's computer he could do it with hardly any conscious thought. Now, while he drove, automatically making turns, speeding up and slowing down, his mind was on other things. His mind was on Amy Cowan.

For months he'd been resisting her. He'd been building sand-castles in a tropical lagoon to keep the tide out. Now in his mind he let the sand-castles melt away. Now that warm tide began rushing in, sweeping away the barriers, sweeping away his resistance.

The car phone began to ring.

Creed switched it off.

He stepped hard on the accelerator, and the car sped through the deepening shadows of the woods as the sun went down.

He relaxed behind the wheel of the car. Racing through this August evening towards the Agency offices, he let Amy come flowing in towards him on an inexorable warm tide.

Chapter 16

'It's starting up again,' said Benny.

Her arms were covered with goose-bumps. She leant against the library window, peering out into the night, the Doctor beside her. They stood together, staring out through the old, leaded-glass pane. Outside in the Kentish night the noise rose and fell in eerie shimmers. It had been coming and going for hours.

Benny shuddered. She couldn't read the expression on the Doctor's face as he stared out.

'Yes,' he murmured. 'Yes, it appears to be getting nearer.'

'That's not exactly what I wanted to hear.' Benny could feel the sound getting to her, the way it had earlier. She had felt so vulnerable out in the garden that she virtually had to run indoors. Now the same spiralling fear rose in her with each swelling of the noise. Benny fought the fear. She forced herself to say something.

'What is it?'

'I don't know,' said the Doctor.

'It gets to me. I mean, I find it quite . . .'

'Frightening.'

'Yes, in a quick-panic kind of way. I mean, there's no thought involved. My mind is trying to tell me that there's nothing to worry about, but my body tells me to run and hide.'

'Maybe your body knows something your mind's forgotten.'

The howling rose and fell beyond the window, drifting eerily in the night air above the thick, rich orchards.

'You mean the sound triggers a response in me? On a physical level?'

'Yes. It touches on some ancient atavistic fear in you. Something deep in the communal human psyche.'

'You're talking about a race memory,' said Benny, feeling the fear ebb as her mind locked on to the discussion. 'And race memories are a load of cobblers. Sub-Jungian nonsense. You can't actually carry memories in your genes.'

'No,' said the Doctor. 'But the human body still retains the same structures it had millions of years ago. And so does the mind.'

Despite the eerie sound outside Benny found herself smiling. 'We're not going to get into the old mind-body argument, are we?'

'Mind exists as a function of brain activity,' said the Doctor. 'Like software running on a computer, to use a paradigm you'll understand. And the brain inherits the physical equivalent of hard-wired software.'

Benny nodded. 'Like the theory that we must have grammatical structures inside our heads because we learn language so quickly.' She remembered what Chomsky had said.

'Yes,' said the Doctor. 'A predisposition to certain patterns of thought, if you like. Electrochemical behaviour which is the precursor to true thought.'

'You mean like in a new-born baby?'

'Exactly.' The Doctor was warming to his topic. 'It was once believed that children were born with minds like clean slates. But even a new-born baby will imitate gestures that you show it, replicating them as best it can with its new muscles. That means that even a new-born human has a way of mapping an external stimulus on to its internal nervous system.'

'And that they can recognize a human being, and in some way know that they are human, too.'

'At the very least,' said the Doctor, 'there is a class of external stimuli which corresponds with pre-programmed internal behaviour.'

'Which is what you meant by race memory.'

'Yes.'

'So I've had this fear programmed into me by evolution.'

'Possibly.'

'And evolution usually knows what it's doing.' Talking to the Doctor had initially calmed Benny down. But now she felt like shuddering again.

The Doctor seemed perfectly happy to go on having a

discussion despite the unearthly cries rising and falling in the night outside. They didn't distract him in the least. What did eventually distract him was the thudding sound.

At first Benny thought it must be her ears playing tricks on her. The new sound was in time with the howling outside. At the end of each eerie chorus the heavy sound came in like the beating of a big, soft drum. Just one blow, as if to acknowledge the wailing. But each blow seemed also to be the impetus for the next sharply rising chorus of howls, as if it triggered them.

At first Benny thought she was hearing the pounding of blood in her ears. But then she saw the Doctor's eyes flicker in time to the sound, and she realized it was outside her head.

She made herself listen carefully to another descending eerie wail followed by the fat thudding noise. She tried to imagine what it might be out there in the night that could make such a sound.

She was relieved that the Doctor heard it, too. At least she wasn't imagining things. But this relief was short lived. Because Benny gradually realized that whatever was making the wet pounding sound wasn't outside in the night.

It was right here, inside. A thudding sound that was coming from somewhere in the darkened library behind them.

A steady thick wet sound, heavy and remorseless.

It took them a moment to find the source of it.

Benny watched as the Doctor took out a large linen handkerchief and wiped the glass. It seemed ridiculous that a two-metre-high cylinder with a middle-aged man floating in it could blend into the background like any other piece of furniture. But Benny had grown accustomed to the cylinder in its library alcove as time passed. There had, indeed, been occasions when she had forgotten about its paunchy naked occupant floating in the soupy broth, and had simply seen it as an object. Decorative, almost.

This was not one of those occasions.

'Jack!' said the Doctor excitedly. Benny suddenly felt guilty; she'd forgotten the name of the man in the cylinder; forgotten that he even had a name.

Not the Doctor. Now he stopped wiping the glass and

stuffed his handkerchief into his pocket. 'This is wonderful.' He crouched and read the LED read-outs in the cylinder's metal base. As he did so the howling outside the window reached another crescendo and in the cylinder there was immediately a sluggish movement.

Through turbulent swirls of cloudy liquid, Benny saw the pale bloated head turn towards her. Eyes squeezed shut, mouth slack, the big pale face jerked back. Then, long hair streaming in slow-motion behind it, the head lunged forward and slammed against the glass with a blunt ugly sound.

That was the sound she'd been hearing following on each chorus of howls. But suddenly Benny had the oddest feeling that it hadn't been following the howls. It had been preceeding them.

As if the howls were in response to the movements of the man. Benny stared at the face in the liquid.

'He's alive, then?' she asked.

'Of course he's alive,' said the Doctor testily. He was kneeling on the floor, punching buttons at the base of the cylinder. 'It's a life-support tank. He's always been alive.' The Doctor frowned at the control panel then, satisfied with his adjustments, scrambled nimbly to his feet. He smiled at Benny, excitement showing in his eyes. Then he turned and patted the glass, his hand just above the pale face.

'Jack was always alive,' said the Doctor. 'He just wasn't . . . here.'

'And now he's back?'

The Doctor leant closer and peered into the thick liquid of the tank, as if meeting the blind idiot stare of its occupant.

'I think he's on his way.'

Chapter 17

Creed parked his car in the wide empty lot outside the Agency and sat for a moment looking up at the big white building. He sensed that he was about to set out on a course of action which would change his life.

Reaching to open the car door he hesitated, his hand pausing in mid-air. Thoughts of Justine and the kids began to surface in his mind. Then thoughts of his son, Ricky.

But of course Ricky wasn't really his son. And Ricky knew that now. Thanks to Justine.

Hot steady hatred flowed into Creed's heart as he thought of Justine. Then all thoughts of her faded from his mind. He opened the car and got out. He walked through the parking lot, past a disgusted-looking kid in overalls. The kid was getting plumbing equipment out of the back of a van. Creed thought he was probably pissed off about being called out for a repair job on Saturday night. Who could blame him?

Besides the van there wasn't another vehicle in sight.

The sensors in the lobby read Creed's pheromone signature while the computer checked the bar-code on his identity card. Then the doors opened automatically, and let him into the big area in front of the elevators. He walked across the Agency logo set in the cool marble floor, past the empty desk where the security guard sat during the week, and stepped into the elevator.

As he rose he checked the computer in the elevator. There was a skeleton maintenance staff and a few other eager-beavers working the weekend shift. But up on their floor, he and Amy would be quite alone.

He hoped she would be waiting for him when he stepped out of the elevator. But when he got there the carpeted corridor was quiet.

He hurried along it and through the glass doors into his office. He remembered Amy pushing through those same doors on her first morning, with melting snow on her parka.

He walked through the maze of low walls that separated the desks in the big open office. The place was quiet, dim, empty. Beyond the tall narrow windows the sky was fading to the magnificent bruised purple of a summer night. Light glowed in a distant corner of the office.

Amy was sitting there in front of a computer with the pale screen-light shining on her face. He saw her dark eyes locked on to the screen, shadows over her high cheek-bones, the corner of her tongue straying out of her mouth as she squinted at the computer. She looked like a child lost in concentration and Creed's heart turned over.

He realized that he didn't know what he was going to say to her. But then she turned and saw him and he saw the look of startled delight on her face and he knew it didn't matter what he said.

'You came,' she said. Then, 'I can't believe it.'

'Well, you promised me free beer,' said Creed. 'Who wouldn't come?'

'There's one in the fridge,' said Amy, jumping up eagerly to get it. As she rose out of her chair she smashed her knee against the corner of the desk and winced with pain.

'Ow.'

'That was clever.' Creed reached out and touched her leg where she'd hit it.

She looked at him, her eyes dark and steady. 'Are you going to rub it and make it better?' she said.

'Where does it hurt?'

'There.' She moved her hand on to his and guided it across the warm curve of her leg. Creed's chest felt hollow, as if all his breath had somehow leaked out of him. He touched her leg, gently rubbing it in small, warm circles. Then he drew his hand away. It was as if his hand was magnetically drawn to her. Ceasing to touch her was one of the hardest things he'd ever done.

He moved his hand away slowly and deliberately. It felt numb, drugged by the warmth of her body. His heart was speeding in his chest, a swift muscular rippling. Amy was saying something. Creed forced himself to listen, to connect up the meaning of her words.

'I don't usually bump into furniture,' she said. Was her voice a little shaky? It was a low, warm voice. He heard it every day at work, talking on the phone at the desk next to his, gnawing away at the edge of his consciousness. The soft rise and swell of her words as she spoke to law-enforcement agencies all over the map, striking deals, doing business and playing politics, protecting Creed. Covering his back.

When he spoke his own voice sounded thin and tense. 'Yeah. Where's the superb coordination I read about in your files?'

'Maybe it's deserted me.' She was looking into his eyes, their gazes locked together. 'Or maybe the file was full of lies. Maybe it was all a trick and you should never have hired me.'

'Too late now,' said Creed and he reached out for her.

She came to him willingly and suddenly they were clutching each other in the darkening office, tangled together so it was hard to tell which hand belonged to whom as they grabbed and stroked each other and kissed, mouths locked and yearning.

Creed felt his consciousness spiralling away in dizzying excitement. Her body felt so different to his wife's. It was like discovering a new world.

'Here?' she whispered. 'On the desk?' He kissed her hot throat and he eased her up on to the desktop and she moaned, strong legs wrapping around his waist as if she would never let him go. He fumbled her shirt open. He slipped his hand under the elastic of her bra to feel the hard nub of her breast, nipple stingingly taut against the palm of his hand. He eased his hand out and slid it up her warm soft thigh.

He was removing her panties when the alarm went off.

It took a moment for the sound to break into his consciousness and be recognized. He looked down at Amy and saw that she was having similar problems shifting her mental gears. The awareness behind her eyes came swimming back slowly from some distant dreamy place. Her gaze sharpened and steadied as he eased his weight off her. 'What is it?' she said, hastily buttoning her shirt.

Creed was staring at the computer screen on the desk

behind her. There was a brightly coloured bar flashing on it, with the words 'Intruder alert' in high intensity white.

'Someone's on the third floor,' said Creed.

Creed eased along the corridor with a gun in one hand, his mouth dry. He'd checked two weapons out of the office arsenal, giving the other to Amy. She was coming up to the third floor via the staircase, having taken the elevator down to the second. Creed was also using the stairs, but he was descending from the fourth.

Their plan was to sandwich the third floor between them. Move in from above and below and catch the intruder.

At least, that was the plan until Creed came into the third-floor office, gun held ready in the Agency's regulation two-handed stance, only to find Buddy Stanmer sitting there with his feet up on the desk.

Buddy ran a hand casually through his greasy black crew-cut and smiled up at Creed.

'Are you going to rub it and make it better?' he said in a high falsetto voice.

Creed lowered his gun. The initial wave of relief at finding Stanmer was already beginning to give way to irritation. 'I got an intruder alert.'

'I know,' said Buddy Stanmer. 'I sent it. Only kidding. A little joke. Strictly against Agency rules.' He looked at Creed. 'But then I imagine so is screwing employees on a desk.'

Suddenly Creed registered what Stanmer had said earlier. About rubbing it and making it better. That was what Amy had said to him.

'You were there. You were watching us.'

'Hey, sorry,' said Stanmer. 'It was an accident. I was going to pick up some papers. But I barged in on the beginning of your touching little scene. Don't worry, I didn't stay long.' Stanmer smiled. 'As soon as I saw what was afoot I came down here and triggered the alarm.' He looked at Creed with an expression of comical innocence. 'I hope I didn't interrupt anything.'

'Are you out of your mind?' said Creed quietly. He turned away from Stanmer and set his gun on a desk. Then he took out a cellular phone and punched a number.

'What are you doing?'

'Amy's still wandering around, armed, believing there's a major security alert,' said Creed. Then Amy answered the phone.

'Are you all right?' she said.

'I'm fine. Listen carefully. There is no intruder, it was just a false alarm.'

Amy's voice was low. 'Are you OK? Has someone got a gun to your head? If they're forcing you to say that, just say everything is fine again.'

Creed laughed. Clever girl. 'No,' he said. 'It really is a false alarm.'

'What caused it?'

'Buddy Stanmer being an asshole.'

'I can get rid of this hand-gun, then?'

'Yeah,' said Creed. 'Ditch it and go back up to the seventh floor. I'll meet you back there as soon as I've finished dealing with Stanmer.'

'OK,' said Amy. 'See you in a sec.'

'OK.' Creed hung up, repressing the ridiculous impulse to blow Amy a kiss.

Stanmer was standing there, watching him. Waiting. 'Deal with me, huh?' he said.

'You don't like the sound of that?'

Stanmer winked at Creed. 'I didn't much go for that asshole remark either.'

Creed shrugged. 'Too bad. Now shut up and listen –'

'No, you shut up and listen, Creed. I've just about had enough of you. I've spent my entire career taking orders from half-wits and nonentities and I've had enough. You're the final straw. Look at you. Middle management in its ultimate incarnation.'

Creed said nothing. He stood there grinning, waiting for Stanmer to finish.

'You're dangerously incompetent,' Stanmer continued. 'You shouldn't be holding down your job.'

'Look,' said Creed, 'I'm sorry about the incident at the swimming pool.'

'What are you talking about?'

'About cracking your hand like that. It was a stupid thing to do and I unreservedly apologize.'

'Oh, don't worry about that.' Stanmer smiled. 'My hand hurt me for a couple of hours. This is going to hurt you for a lot longer.'

'Like I say,' said Creed, 'I was out of line at the swimming pool, but that doesn't excuse what you just did. Sending a false alarm is a serious breech of protocol and I'm going to have to report it.'

'I'll bet you are.'

'And you're going down for it, Buddy. I don't know if it's just going to be a written warning this time or a formal suspension. But either way I suggest you apply for a transfer to another division because I don't think things are working out for you here.'

'That would suit you down to the ground, wouldn't it?' said Stanmer. 'If I just up and left. But I'm not going to.'

Creed sighed. 'Then I'll have to recommend your transfer or your dismissal. Whichever you prefer.'

'I'll tell you what I prefer.' Buddy Stanmer smiled. 'I prefer a pay-rise and a desk by the window. Just for a start. Otherwise . . .'

'What?'

'Otherwise your wife hears about you and Amy butter-wouldn't-melt-in-the-crack-of-her-ass Cowan. About you screwing your personal assistant on your desk.'

Creed was silent for a moment. 'You know, I think maybe you really are out of your mind,' he said.

'You wish,' said Stanmer. 'You want to know —' but then he abruptly stopped talking. He was looking at something on his desk. 'Oh shit,' he said.

'What is it?' said Creed, stepping around the desk so he could see what Stanmer was looking at.

Stanmer was hunched over his computer, his face pale. He looked up at Creed. 'Security alert,' he said quietly. 'It's for real this time. Someone's broken in.'

'Where?' said Creed.

'The seventh floor. No immediate threat.'

No immediate threat, thought Creed as he ran down the corridor and threw himself into the elevator. Rebounding off one mirrored wall, he spun around and jabbed the button.

Seventh floor.

Amy.

Chapter 18

'He's about three years older than Ricky,' Creed said.

Amy put her hand on his shoulder and gently rubbed his back. Creed realized he was trembling.

'You had to do it,' she said.

'I know I had to do it,' snapped Creed. 'That doesn't make me feel any better about it. He was just a kid.'

The kid was lying on the floor between two desks. He had long hair and it streamed out on the pale carpet above his head like a flow of black ink. He was wearing white overalls that had been clean before. Now they had two small red patches just below his collar, where Creed had shot him. He was about nineteen. He was just a kid.

Creed remembered seeing him in the parking lot when he'd driven in. The kid had been unloading stuff from his plumbing van. The kid had looked disgusted about having to work on Saturday.

'He looked pissed off about his job,' said Creed.

'What?' said Amy.

'I saw him downstairs when I arrived. He looked pissed off about having to do his job. I thought his job was being a plumber. But I guess it was actually to break in here. Anyway, he seemed pissed off with it.'

Creed wondered if he was still trembling. It was difficult to tell because Amy was holding him so close, hugging him so hard.

'What happened? Jesus Christ.' They turned to see Stanmer coming through the glass doors. He had his sidearm in one hand but was already returning it to his holster. He kneeled beside the dead kid and studied the gun that lay beside the kid's outstretched left hand.

He was left-handed, thought Creed, staring down at the

dead body over Amy's shoulder. Kneeling on the carpet Buddy Stanmer looked up at them. Amy was still holding Creed and neither of them made any effort to hide the fact from Stanmer.

'What happened?' said Stanmer again.

'He was coming out of the communications room.'

'He was coming out and he saw me,' said Amy. 'He saw me and he pulled his gun. I was unarmed. I'd just put my weapon back in the armoury.' Amy winced at the memory. 'I was standing there unarmed and he drew on me and he was about to shoot me.'

'We're not sure of that,' said Creed.

'I'm sure of it. But before he could fire Creed came in and shot him.'

'Nice going,' said Stanmer. He bent over and picked up the kid's gun, kicking the kid's hand aside, as though there was some danger of residual activity.

'I killed him,' said Creed.

'You sure did,' said Stanmer. 'Nice shooting.'

'You had to kill him,' said Amy. She hugged him fiercely. 'You saved my life,' she said.

'And I was worrying about you getting enough practice on the target range,' said Stanmer. He shook his head, smiling.

'I haven't shot anyone in years,' said Creed. 'I'd forgotten what it felt like.'

'Don't waste any tears on this little bag of shit,' said Stanmer, stepping over the dead kid. 'You should be worrying about us.' He put the gun on a desk and looked around. 'He was coming out of the communications room, eh?' Stanmer shook his head woefully. 'This should never have happened. This is very bad news. If the opposition has penetrated us this easily, our security is seriously compromised.'

He walked over to the open door of the communications room. 'What did he do in here?'

'I don't know,' said Creed. 'We haven't had a chance to look.' He and Amy followed Stanmer into the communications room.

Inside the small concrete cubicle were five computers. They were unusual in that none of them were networked. Being connected to the network inevitably left a computer open to intrusion from outside. These computers talked to the outside world along a single land-line, connected to a single destination.

Stanmer moved deeper into the room to make room for Creed and Amy.

Four of the computers extended to other Agency communications centres spread across America. The fifth took messages off an international grid.

These were among the most secure computers on the planet.

All of the screens were blank or displayed routine messages, except for the international link.

There on the screen of the supposedly unhackable computer, ignoring all normal communication protocols, was a simply worded message:
Creed.
Need your help urgently.
Come at once.
The Doctor.

It was midnight by the time the intrusion team arrived. Violation of an Agency office called for a major security investigation. Amy had to act as cooperating local officer because Creed was busy arranging for an Agency chopper to jump him to the nearest international airport with an early scheduled flight to London.

The Doctor had used the word 'urgently'.

Stanmer was writing the report for the intrusion team and he got Creed's statement before he left. The senior investigating officer and Amy both sanctioned Creed's departure after confirmation from Washington and the SIO sanctioned Creed notifying his wife.

Justine had been worried sick since Creed had stormed out. But his phone-call didn't do much to reassure her. All he could say was that there had been violent action, that he was all right, and that he had been called away on immediate assignment.

'Can you tell me where?'

'England.'

'Is it something to do with the Doctor?' said Justine. Creed looked over at the SIO, who was listening on a headphone link. He looked at Creed and shook his head.

'I can't tell you that,' said Creed.

'Can I see you before you go?'

'If you can get here before the chopper arrives. It will be landing to pick me up on the field behind the main building.'

'I'll come. I'll bring the kids.'

Creed was on the verge of telling her not to. But she seemed to think it was important, so he let it ride. Who knows what sort of thoughts had been running through her head? He'd just walked out on her and then she hadn't heard from him in hours. What did she think had happened?

What would have happened if there had been no break-in, wondered Creed. What if there had been no Stanmer? No kid with a gun?

Creed found himself staring at the desk where Amy had been sitting when he'd come in. Where he'd kissed her and begun to undress her. He stared at the desk and then he sensed someone else's attention on him and he looked up.

Amy had been helping one of the intrusion officers plot the dead kid's movements across the carpet. They were marking his route with masking tape. But Amy had paused to gaze across the office and Creed realized that she had been staring thoughtfully at the desk, exactly as he had, at exactly the same moment.

Their eyes met and Amy looked away, her cheeks flushed with colour.

As it happened, Creed didn't get to say goodbye to Justine. Not properly.

The helicopter came buzzing in, out of the grey dawn, sweeping low across the tops of the pines in Gaines Woods. The SIO and Amy walked Creed out to the field behind the agency building. The SIO handed Creed an envelope full of faxed documents and initialled the fire-arms release as he gave Creed a weapon. Then he went back inside to join the investigation and left them waiting for the chopper.

Amy stood beside Creed, shivering in the early morning air. He wanted to put his arms around her but suddenly the helicopter was looming in the sky above them, the rising sun glinting off its bubbled hull, the pilot raising his hand in greeting.

Creed ran to the helicopter as its slowly sweeping blades

whipped dew off the grass. Creed was soaked to the ankles by the time he scrambled on board.

He shook hands with the pilot as he strapped himself in and the engine throttled up. The blades above them spun more quickly and suddenly Creed was watching the ground drop away. He looked down at Amy as they rose into the air. She waved and then wrapped her arms around her breasts, hugging herself against the cold. Her head suddenly angled away as she turned to look at something.

Creed followed her gaze and saw his old battered station-wagon roll on to the field, coming from the access-road that led to the car park. Justine was at the wheel. The kids were in the back.

They coasted to a halt and got out, all of them looking up at the helicopter. They were about the size of dolls. Justine, Cynthia and Eve.

Ricky wasn't there but Creed had the distinct impression that he was in the station-wagon. Sitting sulkily, having been dragged here by his mother.

Creed saw his wife turn to look at Amy, and Amy return the look.

But then the helicopter accelerated and speed and distance erased all detail from the scene as they banked and flew away, heading into the rising sun.

Chapter 19

Roz looked out of the window and was surprised to see that the stewardess's body was gone.

It had evidently been dragged away from the pavement outside by the dogs. Roz wondered how many dogs it had taken to do that. A lot.

But then, there was no shortage of them. They were all around the small house, their shadows writhing in the dark gardens of the estate nearby.

'Redmond, can you hear me?' Roz whispered urgently into the helmet mike.

'You don't have to whisper, dear. I think they know we're in here.' Mrs Woodcott was peering out from the lace curtains that covered the kitchen window.

There was no reply from the armoured car. Roz left the kitchen, stepping over the body of the stewardess's boyfriend. Mrs Woodcott let the curtains drop and followed her.

They went into the small hallway and checked on the front door. Despite having been kicked in by Roz earlier, the latch seemed to be solid and intact. The door was securely shut.

They walked into the sitting room where the corpse of the dog lay, its broken body sprawled heavily on a dark stain which had spread across the pastel carpet. Roz couldn't help glancing at her bayonet with a certain measure of martial pride.

Mrs Woodcott settled herself on a fat floral sofa. She picked up a frilled cushion and inspected it. 'I always imagined the House of the Dead as having nicer furniture.' She sighed and opened her handbag.

Roz saw bullets glitter in the moonlight. The rings on Mrs Woodcott's knuckly old hands glittered above them as she reloaded her revolver. The old silver gun was heavy and solid looking. Reassuring.

It was ridiculous, but Roz standing there with her state of the art Styer AUG slung over her shoulder found Mrs Woodcott's antique six-shot pistol reassuring.

'What are you doing over there?' enquired the old woman, as she clicked the pistol shut again.

Roz was standing by the window at the far end of the sitting room. The wall behind her was virtually all glass. French windows ran for two-thirds of its length. The rest was waist-high windows and Roz was carefully sliding one of these open.

Outside, the moonlit garden was silent except for the sound of the armoured car engine. The rattling echo was coming from the concrete podium beyond the garden wall.

'I was listening for that. The armoured car,' said Roz. 'Listening for Redmond. He –'

Roz stopped talking. Suddenly there was a shape in the window. A long black dog was surging in from the night outside, moving with unbelievable swiftness. It was coming through the window in such utter silence that its presence seemed unreal to Roz.

Equally unreal was the way in which Mrs Woodcott simply looked up from the sofa, raised her revolver, and pulled the trigger. The bullet hit the dog bluntly and squarely in the middle of its skull and it toppled back out of the window with almost comical promptness.

Roz quickly slammed the window shut.

The whole incident had lasted a fraction of a second. It had been like a well-rehearsed comedy act. For one surreal second Roz imagined herself touring the country. Playing the role of the magician's beautiful assistant. Standing on stage opening a window so a superbly rehearsed dog could promptly leap through it, and Mrs Woodcott could shoot it in the head. The dog would topple back out and Roz would neatly shut the window to thunderous applause.

She snapped out of the thought as another dark shape bounced up in the garden and slammed against the window. It hit the pane of reinforced glass hard enough to shake it in its frame. A grey dog with a wildly rolling eye pressed its muzzle to the pane, baring its long yellow teeth. It sank out of sight, snarling, leaving a heavy smear of saliva on the glass.

'They would seem to be in the back garden as well,' said Mrs Woodcott. 'Now what's this about the armoured car, dear?'

'I think Redmond's dead. I heard something growling into the microphone.'

'But the armoured car is moving. We heard it.'

'But I don't think anybody is driving it,' said Roz.

'Well, then we're not getting out of here,' said Mrs Woodcott matter-of-factly. She opened the revolver and reloaded the single spent cartridge. 'Dinner-time for Rover, I'm afraid.'

'Not necessarily,' said Roz. 'Like I said, I think the armoured car is in motion with no one driving it. But I think it's out of control and its headed –'

Mrs Woodcott held up her hand, motioning her urgently to silence.

'What is it?' said Roz.

'Quiet, dear. To the front door. Quick.'

Mrs Woodcott darted out of the sitting room. Roz followed her into the small hallway that led first to the kitchen then to the front door. Mrs Woodcott stood by the door, listening.

'What is it?'

'I don't know,' said the old woman. 'But there's something going on out front. I can't see anything through the peep-hole here. Go and look through the kitchen window, would you, dear?'

Roz went into the kitchen where Roy's brutalized corpse still lay on the floor. Roz was looking at it and thinking that they should cover it up when the kitchen window exploded inward.

The floral curtains were swept aside in a spray of broken glass as three lean dark shapes hurtled through into the kitchen.

Roz snapped the Styer AUG on to automatic and swept the room with it.

The floor of the kitchen was ceramic tile and created a potential for richochets so Roz kept the riot-gun at waist level and swept the bullets out in an arc.

The descending bodies of the three dogs entered the arc of bullets one after the other. And one after the other the dogs writhed and died. All three were dead by the time they hit the floor.

A fourth dog was scrambling over the sill of the shattered window, but before she could do anything about it she heard a blunt crashing explosion behind her and she recognized the sound of Mrs Woodcott's revolver.

The dog spun around, its big ears flopping as the bullet took the top of its head away. It dropped back outside the house with an audible thud. There was silence outside and nothing else came through the window.

Fragments of glass tinkled musically into the sink.

'Thank you,' said Roz.

'You would have got him if I hadn't, dear,' said Mrs Woodcott modestly.

Roz looked around. The kitchen was a mess. The bullets which hadn't hit the dogs had torn the place to pieces. Expensive metal cookware had been battered into strange angular shapes.

On the floor the three bodies of the dogs lay beside Roy. The tiles were slick with blood. It looked like the work-floor of a busy abbatoire.

'I know what you were going to say, dear,' said Mrs Woodcott. She said it in a conversational tone as though they were two ladies sharing a cup of tea at the vicarage picnic.

'What are you talking about?' Roz was concentrating on listening for sound through the open window. Their security had been broken with the window. Could they repair it? It might be possible to mount a successful siege action in this small house providing they could just repair that window.

'We were discussing the armoured car,' said Mrs Woodcott. 'Just before we were so rudely interrupted. And I believe I know what you were going to say.'

'What?' Maybe they could use the cupboard doors. Take them off their hinges and nail the plywood over the breached window. But where would they find a hammer and nails?

'I believe you were going to say that the armoured car was headed in this direction.'

'I was wrong,' said Roz bluntly. 'Even without Redmond driving it I was hoping it might come rolling across the podium and into the back wall of this garden.'

'Yes, if it hit the wall it would crash right through it. Then we could dash out into the garden and scramble aboard.' Mrs Woodcott's eyes gleamed. 'We'd be home and dry.'

113

'It's a nice thought,' said Roz. She kept an eye on the kitchen window but nothing seemed to be moving outside. 'But I was wrong. If the armoured car was coming it would have been here by now.'

That was when they heard the knock at the front door.

That was what it sounded like. Someone knocking. They looked at each other.

Roz was the first to speak. 'Could a dog make that noise?'

'Exactly what I was wondering, dear.' Mrs Woodcott leant out of the kitchen and peered down the short hallway towards the front door. She held her gun ready.

There was nothing to see. Just the front door in darkness, moonlight slanting in through the strips of pebbled glass that looked out on to the street.

Roz peered into the kitchen. Nothing stirred outside the window. Maybe the dogs had gone away. Roz opened her mouth to say as much but at that instant there was another knock on the door.

'Who's there?' called Mrs Woodcott brightly. There was no reply.

The hallway was silent. Roz forced herself to look back into the kitchen again, to keep her eye on the gaping window.

'Is someone out there?' called Mrs Woodcott. 'Yoo-hoo.'

In reply there was the knock again.'

Mrs Woodcott looked at Roz. 'I don't like this at all,' dear.'

'I'm going to see who's out there.'

'I don't think you should, dear.'

'You keep an eye on the kitchen window.'

'Don't go, Roz.'

'It could be help. Reinforcements. The police.'

'Then why don't they reply,' hissed Mrs Woodcott. Then she bellowed, 'Oi, you out there! Say something! You at the door!'

There was silence, then the knocking again.

'I'm going to see who's there,' said Roz.

'Don't. For God's sake.'

'It could be the police.'

'I never heard of a policeman who couldn't talk.'

'I never heard of a dog who could knock on a door,' said Roz, and started down the hallway.

'Careful, dear.'

'Keep an eye on the kitchen window.'

Roz was at the door now. The small windows set in the wood were pebbled glass, deliberately opaque. All Roz could see through them were amorphous patterns of shadow and moonlight.

But in the centre of the door there was a peep-hole, an old-fashioned lens on a cylindrical barrel, drilled through the wood.

She put her eye to it.

The lens distorted the world outside in order to give the maximum image. In the moonlight everything was clear despite the circular distortion of the fish-eye effect. Roz stared out and saw it on the door step.

The white dog.

The rest of the pack seemed to have fallen back to make a path for the dog. She could still see the route the animal had followed as it approached the front door. Now it kneeled panting on the front steps staring up at Roz.

Roz realized that the dog was white because it was old. It had a starved angular look to it, bones seeming to jut from its skinny body. It was the oldest dog Roz had ever seen, a walking skeleton, almost.

But there was still stringy muscle under the pale fur. And behind the shaggy white fur of the muzzle the dog's eyes blazed like coals.

The dog stared up at Roz. She had the disquieting feeling that it knew she was there. The dog shook himself and raised his trembling furry muzzle in the air.

All the other dogs seemed to be watching him. The old white animal raised his nose as if smelling the air. Then his throat pulsed and he gave a short, harsh bark, barely audible to Roz through the wood of the front door.

Immediately, as if in reply, Mrs Woodcot began shouting in the kitchen.

'Bastards. Get out.'

Roz was already running back into the kitchen when she heard Mrs Woodcott begin to fire her gun.

As Roz came in, the window was swarming with dark wriggling shapes. Mrs Woodcott was blasting away and Roz realized that she had been counting the shots without even knowing it because as soon as Mrs Woodcott fired the sixth and final round she stepped forward and took over, firing the Styer AUG in a long burst.

For a moment the window was swept clear but then more dogs began to force their way in, pushing past the corpses of their companions. Roz kept firing, killing them, but they kept coming.

In the background of her attention Roz was aware of Mrs Woodcott reloading her revolver, spilling the spent cartridges on the tiled floor, then reaching out to touch Roz on the shoulder.

'I think it's time for a tactical withdrawal, dear.'

'So do I.'

The kitchen window was momentarily free of intruders because the bodies of the dogs had formed a solid wall, plugging it shut. But already the obscene blockage was beginning to wriggle and shift as others pressed in from the outside.

Roz and Mrs Woodcott ducked out of the kitchen as the wall of corpses came down, slithering and tumbling into the sink and across the clean white counters as living dogs began pouring through in a flood of dark shapes.

Roz slammed the kitchen door behind them and was looking for something to block it with when Mrs Woodcott came through from the sitting room dragging an arm-chair. Roz was amazed at the old woman's strength.

'This should be all right if you can endure the hideous sub-William Morris fabric, dear.' She helped Roz wedge the kitchen door with the fat arm-chair. On the other side they could hear excited panting and snuffling and the click and slither of claws on the tiled floor. The dogs had taken the kitchen and they were triumphant.

Roz jolted with shock. The knocking had begun at the front door again, louder than before.

'Into the sitting room, I think.'

Mrs Woodcott and Roz began backing down the hallway. The arm-chair that wedged the kitchen door shut was trembling with the impact of blows as the dogs threw themselves wildly at the barrier. The front door was rattling in its frame too, as the knocks turned into ugly pounding sounds, and came louder and faster.

'If they get in we stand back to back,' said Roz. She had to shout to make herself heard.

'Agreed, dear,' yelled Mrs Woodcott.

Then Roz realized why they were shouting. It wasn't the noise of the dogs battering at the doors.

They were shouting to make themselves heard over the noise of the engine.

The armoured car engine.

Roz and Mrs Woodcott turned around in time to see the armoured car come rolling into the back wall of the garden. For a moment the low brick wall held; then it began to slowly crumble and topple, chunks of brick like broken teeth snapping under the weight of the vehicle as it ground inexorably forward.

That was when Roz knew that Redmond must be dead.

The vehicle was creeping forward in low gear, obviously out of control. Only luck had brought it here to them.

Small cement statues crumbled and toppled into an ornamental pond. Stone flower-pots shattered as the armoured car lumbered into the garden, dragging chunks of the wall with it. Shadows flowed out of the garden as the dogs retreated at the approach of this huge metal beast.

The big armoured vehicle had never looked so good to Roz. Sturdy and invulnerable, armour gleaming in the moonlight.

'We'll be safe once we're on board,' said Roz. 'Come on.' She reached for the French windows and slid the nearest panel open. The thunderous rattling of the engine came into the sitting room on a warm night breeze smelling of diesel.

'Our chariot awaits,' said Mrs Woodcott, grinning at the big vehicle rolling towards them.

Then the front door caved in behind them.

The first wave of dogs knocked the wedged arm-chair aside, unplugging the kitchen doors. A wild scrambling horde of dogs joined those already streaming into the hallway through the front door.

Roz and Mrs Woodcott turned to face them. Mrs Woodcott's revolver was empty within seconds and she began to reload, fumbling in her handbag for ammunition. Roz kept firing, but she knew it was hopeless.

Because the dogs just kept coming and she had the Styer AUG on rapid fire, spraying the hallway with bullets as fast as she could to stop them getting into the sitting room. But in a few seconds she would be out of ammunition and she would have to reload and the six bullets now in Mrs Woodcott's gun wouldn't buy them enough time to do that. The dogs would begin getting through.

So when the Styer AUG was empty, that was it.

Time for the bayonet.

But then the sound of the armoured car became deafening and there was a great rippling shearing noise as tall panels of glass snapped and shattered behind her. A rumbling crunch as masonry and plaster gave way.

Roz didn't dare look round; she had to concentrate on the dogs charging towards her. But she heard the screech of tearing timber as the armoured car ploughed through the sitting room wall and on into the sitting room itself. She fired a final burst at the hallway then risked a quick glance round.

The armoured car was snouting blindly forward across the wreckage of the small sitting room. The Persian carpet vanished under its churning wheels. A coffee-table with a family of ceramic elephants marching across it disappeared under the big vehicle with a crunching sound. A crystal chandelier was jammed against the ceiling by the high roof of the vehicle, and dragged shrieking until it shattered.

Roz heard Mrs Woodcott's pistol and she turned back to join in the holding action, only using single shots now, to preserve ammunition. The dogs were breaking through from the hallway, running across the bodies of their fallen comrades. Single shots weren't fast enough to nail them all. They were starting to slip through into the sitting room.

But it didn't matter because the smell of diesel was intoxicatingly heavy. Suddenly Roz could feel the slow-moving vehicle like a big gentle beast behind her, pressing warmly at the back of her legs.

With Mrs Woodcott beside her she scrambled over the bumper and up on to the sloping blunt face of the armoured car, as it crawled slowly forward into the sitting room.

The dogs had been hesitating, clearly frightened of the big metal beast they saw rolling massively towards them. But as soon as they observed Roz and Mrs Woodcott climb aboard their hostility overcame their fear.

They launched themselves at the two women clinging to

the front of the armoured car. Roz shot one and then the Styer AUG clicked, empty.

Mrs Woodcott shot one and then her revolver clicked.

Three more dogs threw themselves snarling into the air.

Behind them came three more.

They were all blown out of the air by a sustained burst from one of the machine guns mounted on the roof of the armoured car. The second machine gun swivelled on its angled pivot and swept a stream of flame up and down the hallway, slaughtering the shadowed mass still trying to press into the sitting room.

Roz looked up at the blasting machine guns pivoting above her, and that was when she knew that Redmond must be alive.

The engine note changed and the armoured car began to back out of the sitting room. Small chips of masonry and clouds of dust rained down on them as the vehicle rolled back out through the hole it had made. Suddenly they were outside in the cool night air.

'This is a bit more like it,' howled Mrs Woodcott jubilantly over the machine gun noise. She'd begun reloading her revolver as soon as the machine gun started and now she fired one final defiant shot at the retreating mass of dogs.

Roz took a last look back into the sitting room as they backed away. Through a savage gash in the wall she could see the total wreckage of the stewardess's small, tidy home.

Moonlight shone in through the gaping hole. Dogs of every size, shape and breed lay scattered and broken in the ruins. A few twitched and limped, but most of them lay still.

There was a messy slopping sound as one of the armoured car's tyres wallowed through what had once been an ornamental pond, and then the vehicle was back through the hole in the brick wall. The engine note changed as the vehicle began reversing out of the garden across the reverberant bare concrete of the podium.

'Come on, let's get inside,' yelled Roz. But Mrs Woodcott needed no urging; she had already climbed up on to the roof of the armoured car and was holding the hatch open.

She slithered into the vehicle and Roz was following her when she heard a cry from inside, then a gunshot. Roz threw herself over the lip of the hatch.

She landed on her feet inside, lifting the Styer AUG into a bayonet-ready position.

But it was all over. Mrs Woodcott was helping Redmond squirm out from under the corpse of the dog she'd just shot. There was blood all over the dog and all over Redmond and all over the interior of the armoured car.

'My god, what happened?' said Roz. But she realized that Redmond couldn't speak. He was holding his hand over some kind of wound in his throat. Roz immediately punched open the first-aid locker and dug out a combat dressing.

Mrs Woodcott got out of her way as she moved into the front of the vehicle.

'Secure the hatch,' Roz said as she stripped the sterile wrapping off the dressing. 'We don't want any more unofficial passengers getting in.' She could see that Redmond was going to be all right and with the rush of relief came a feeling of irritation. It had been careless to let a dog get into the armoured car.

As Mrs Woodcott secured the hatch, Roz applied the dressing to Redmond's throat. He gasped with relief as the pressure-dressing sealed the wound. Roz gave him a shot and handed him a pad of disinfectant so he could clean himself up; then she settled herself into the driver's seat.

On the main screen she could see the trail of destruction the armoured car had left on its path across the council estate.

'Lousy driving, Redmond,' she said.

'You try driving this thing with a bloody dog chewing on one arm while you're trying to stick a knife between his ribs with the other, in between trying to stop yourself bleeding to death.'

Chapter 20

It felt very weird to be in school but not be part of the activity.

Ricky shifted uncomfortably on the bench. He was sitting in the corridor outside the principal's office. This bench was generally used by those who'd been summoned to see the principal for disciplinary reasons, so no great thought had been given to the users' comfort. It was a plain hard wooden bench set in a recess between two long banks of lockers.

Ricky looked up as his mother came back down the corridor, looking sweaty and angry in her best summer suit. She was leading his little sister, Eve, by her hand.

'Thanks for all your help,' she said to Ricky as she walked past. She said it in a tight, angry, sarcastic voice.

'Oh, come on, mom.'

'Oh, come on?' Justine was walking towards the principal's office, but now she did a sudden U-turn and stalked towards the bench where Ricky sat.

Ricky looked hastily around. Luckily this corner of the school was quiet. Although it was the lunch hour he'd seen few kids and most of the passers-by were harassed-looking teachers hurrying to take refuge in the staffroom.

Fortunately there was no one at all around at the moment. No one to hear him have an argument with his mother. Ricky squirmed with embarrassment on the bench as Justine stood over him, eyes blazing.

'I am here begging with this man to get you a place in this school,' she hissed, 'and you can't even be bothered to help me out.'

'How could I, mom?' Ricky pleaded.

'What do you mean, how could you? All I asked you to do

was take your little sister to the bathroom. Is that so difficult?'

Absolutely impossible, thought Ricky. If any other kids saw him taking his little sister to the can he would never live it down at this school. He was going to have to come to this dump every day. If they accepted him. He was going to have to try and fit in with these kids. And that was going to be hard enough as it was.

Wisely, Ricky didn't say any of this. He just sat with his head down, looking at his feet and the grey stone floor, as Justine stood over him with her eyes blazing.

After a moment she made a sound of disgust and strode off, tugging Eve along with her. She stepped back into Mr Pangbourne's office, marching past his secretary, the fat bitch who could have helped her by taking Eve to the bathroom for her, but who had politely declined to assist. Justine went on into Pangbourne's office, leaving Eve sitting out with the secretary.

With a bit of luck she might drive the old lard-bucket crazy.

'Sorry about that,' she said, sitting down opposite Pangbourne's desk again. The small office smelled of cigarette smoke and there was a big glass ash-tray on the principal's desk with a fine residue of ash in it.

'No problem,' said Pangbourne. He was reading a hardcopy of Ricky's school records.

'This is a special school, Mrs McIlveen, for special children.' Pangbourne looked up at her with sceptical, pale blue eyes. 'Specially bright children. Geniuses and prodigies. Specially difficult children. The discipline problems.'

He smiled at Justine. 'Why do you want your son to come here?'

Justine took a deep breath. Pangbourne was clearly a decent, intelligent, compassionate man.

She was going to have to lie to him.

Outside Ricky sat waiting on the bench.

He sighed.

The corridor was empty in both directions. His initial relief at being in a quiet part of the school had been replaced by boredom.

He hadn't brought a book with him. There was nothing

around to read, not even a poster on the wall. Nothing except for a small plaque displaying the rules for operating the fire-extinguisher. Ricky had already memorized these.

Ricky wished something would happen.

His mother seemed to have been talking to Mr Pangbourne forever. He sighed again. He could hear kids in the playground outside. Occasionally an unseen door would open around the corner and he would hear the clatter of lunch trays in the canteen.

Ricky wanted something to happen.

Ricky decided he'd make something happen.

Justine nodded at the papers on the principal's desk. 'My son is a discipline problem. You can see that there.'

'Sure, I can see that he's changed school more often than a lot of my kids change their underwear, if you'll excuse a down-to-earth parallel.' He looked at Ricky's attendance record. 'But I don't think that's the full story.'

He pressed a button on his desk and after a moment a skinny teenage boy came into the office.

'This is Clement,' said the principal. The skinny kid nodded shyly at Justine. 'Clement is our resident computer wizard.' Pangbourne got up so the kid could sit at his desk. Clement hunched forward over the computer and began typing swiftly, obviously uncomfortable about sitting in the principal's chair. Pangbourne smiled at Justine. 'I got him to do a little digging for us.'

'Digging?' said Justine, her heart sinking.

'Into your son's background.'

The skinny kid got up from the computer and hurried out from behind the desk. Pangbourne returned to his chair, frowning as he studied the screen. He looked at Justine. 'It seems that your son just can't stay in a school. Yet there's nothing wrong with his scholastic record. His grades are excellent and, what's far stranger, there's no official record of any disciplinary offences, at least not on any data-base we can get into. Whatever this boy's problem is, it looks like no one wants to talk about it.'

'Maybe he doesn't have a problem,' said Justine.

'We've all got problems,' said Mr Pangbourne.

* * *

In the corridor outside Ricky was looking at the floor between his feet. At first he watched the toes of his running-shoes, which were moving in small slow orbits of boredom.

But then he began to concentrate on the smooth grey floor below his feet. The floor was concrete with some kind of glossy plastic paint on it. The colour was mostly grey but there were specks of red, black and white in it.

Ricky sat and concentrated on the colours of the floor. After a while the specks of red and white and black began to float against the background like planets floating in a strange grey void. A weird galaxy in some distant dimension. He could almost hear the strange music of these alien spheres.

Ricky relaxed and slowly closed his eyes. He was almost ready.

He sat unmoving on the bench with his eyes shut, listening to the sounds of the school all around him.

Every institution has its own identity, detectable in many ways. The sound of a building full of people develops its own distinctive signature. The subdued depressed mutter of an office on Monday morning. The buoyant boozy optimism of the same place Friday, after lunch.

Ricky sat and listened to the school, letting its characteristic rhythms sink into his consciousness. He was getting to know the school.

Ricky concentrated for a moment more and then he pressed. That's what it felt like. It was as if he'd applied pressure with his mind.

He wasn't certain exactly what it was he did, but it reminded him of pressing on one end of a water bed and watching the mattress bulge at the other.

Ricky pressed with his mind and then he opened his eyes.

All around him the corridor was full of girls.

The girls looked at each other strangely and stared around, as if they had been summoned here but they were uncertain who or what had done the summoning. The girls were vital, distinctive, vividly pretty. Some of them had brought boyfriends along with them, hand in hand.

Their usual wanderings around the school had suddenly brought them here, but now that they'd arrived none of them quite knew why they were standing in this corridor.

None of them noticed the boy on the bench who sat quietly, smiling.

Then, cutting through the girls, came an older kid wearing a leather jacket. Trailing after him came a small group of teenage boys. A certain frightened silence among the girls followed their passage. On the back of the kid's leather jacket was an image of a wolf, evidently hand painted by someone. Ricky couldn't imagine that the kid had painted it himself. He looked like the only way he could use a paint-brush was as an offensive weapon, reversed in a thuggish fist and jabbed into his opponent's eye.

Ricky sat on his bench and watched the arrival of the thug and his followers.

Everyone was stepping back as they walked slowly past. The thug strode down the corridor ahead of the others. He glanced at Ricky but his gaze moved on without pausing, dismissing the boy on the bench as not worthy of his attention.

On the bench Ricky felt a flash of triumph. It was a strange wordless emotion, but if he could have put it into words he would have said, 'I've fooled them again.'

The thug in the leather jacket came striding back past Ricky. He didn't even bother glancing at the nondescript kid on the bench this time. Ricky kept his head hanging down to conceal a smile of victory. He'd done it again. Fooled them all.

He stole a look at the girls standing nearby. He knew that these girls represented the elite, the aristocracy in the school's pecking order. Now they stood in the corridor, not quite knowing why they were here.

But Ricky knew why they were here.

The painted wolf folded and flexed on the back of the thug's leather jacket. Ricky watched him move among the girls.

If the girls were the school's velvet glove, he was its iron fist.

The thug stood for a moment in puzzlement and frustration and the other kids seemed to be holding their breath.

Ricky knew that the kid in the leather jacket was the local bully. The true power structure of the school. Sitting shut up in his office Mr Pangbourne might believe that he ran this place, but Ricky knew what the truth was.

The thug was the uncrowned king of the playground and classrooms. This kid with his gang of cronies who didn't even know why they were here.

Ricky knew why they were here.

The small crowd in the corridor was beginning to look anxious. They'd obviously seen this look in the thug's eyes before and they regarded it as dangerous. Ricky watched the kid in the leather jacket, but circumspectly, so as not to draw his attention. He had learnt long ago that people seemed to become aware of his gaze very quickly and they would look around, trying to make eye contact with him.

Ricky dreaded eye contact. So he'd learnt a trick for watching people. He'd kind of look at them indirectly, out of the corner of his eye. And this seemed to stop them becoming aware of his attention.

Ricky sat watching the thug out of the corner of his eye.

The kid had an odd look on his face. It was a look consisting of rage and frustration. Ricky understood. He was frustrated because he didn't know what was going on. What was he doing in this corridor full of girls?

As unofficial king of the school he had a feeling for this place. Without even being aware of it he sensed the changing emotional currents that flowed through these familiar rooms and hallways. This was his territory and he sensed the mood of it.

Now, he had picked up a sense of commotion in his domain. And it was not a commotion he'd brought into being.

He didn't know what had caused it. But he did know that his position in the school's pecking order had been threatened. He could feel it in his guts.

Now he was getting angry and the kids around him were reacting. They were alarmed by his anger.

So Ricky let go of him.

He let go of all of them.

The mood of the small crowd in the corridor instantly changed. It was like a crowd on a street suddenly losing interest in some minor spectacle; a traffic accident that had proved disappointingly routine. So the crowd broke up and began to drift off, fragmenting into bored twos and threes, wandering aimlessly back towards the classrooms.

* * *

'Ricky is just a normal teenager like any other,' said Justine. 'He's just had a run of bad luck.'

'Bad luck, you say?'

'Don't get sarcastic with me,' said Justine. She was losing her temper. The strain of worrying about Creed was telling on her.

'Look, Mrs McIlveen, it's obvious that you're a lady with a lot of troubles at the moment.'

'Obvious?'

'Don't misunderstand me,' said Pangbourne, smiling. 'I'm not inviting you to behave snappishly with me. I won't sit still for disrespectful behaviour from anyone.' He was still smiling but his blue eyes were steely. 'I'm just saying that any fool can see that you've been served more than a fair share of worries on your plate at the moment.'

Justine opened her mouth to make some angry reply and to her astonishment found that she was on the verge of crying. The tears were welling up in her. She closed her mouth and put a hand over her face.

Pangbourne leant forward and wordlessly dug a clean white linen handkerchief out of his jacket pocket and handed it to her. Justine accepted it gratefully. She hesitated for a moment, reluctant to soil the beautiful handkerchief, then she blew her nose noisily into it.

'I'm sorry,' she said. 'I have some problems at home. And then on top of that I have this problem here with you.'

'I wouldn't say we had a problem,' said Pangbourne mildly.

'Really? Well I packed my daughter off to her first day of school this morning but my son had to stay home. Because he doesn't have a school to go to. Because I've been unable to get a decision out of you. That sounds like a problem to me.'

'Hold your horses, Mrs McIlveen. That account sounds rather like I'm to blame.'

'Well, who else is refusing to let Ricky come to this school and begin his studies?'

'Now let's not overstate the case,' said Pangbourne. 'I have not categorically refused to admit your son.'

'Then why isn't he sitting in a classroom with the other kids right now?'

'Nobody's sitting in a classroom right now, Mrs McIlveen. It's lunchtime. But the reason that your son is not in my school is because I am still waiting for some straight answers.'

'From whom?'

'From you.'

'Me? What do you want me to tell you?'

Pangbourne suddenly looked weary. He straightened the pile of papers on his desk. He switched off his computer and looked up at Justine. 'I've pulled every document and report that I can find on your son. And I'm still none the wiser.'

'Maybe there's nothing to be wise about.'

'Oh, I think there is.'

'You sound angry, Mr Pangbourne.'

'I'm angry because there is clearly more to your son's problem than meets the eye. And that's because someone is making damned certain that no useful information is in danger of meeting my eye. I'm talking about a cover-up.'

'A cover-up?'

'Yes. I sense the hand of the government in this.'

'I think you're paranoid, Mr Pangbourne.'

'Well, your husband thinks I'm a gardener.' Pangbourne leant forward. 'But I am not some naive hick. I do know what your husband does for a living.'

Pangbourne must have seen the spasm of alarm that crossed Justine's face. His manner immediately softened. 'That was tactless of me. I'm sorry. You're clearly worried about your husband now. It must be difficult being married to a man whose job involves those kinds of ... demands and hazards.'

'I can't talk about any of that.'

'Of course not. But forgive me for bringing up your husband's job at what is obviously a sensitive time. It's just that I have this fundamental sense of outrage. I am legally entitled to look at your son's school records.' Pangbourne's hard blue eyes had softened. Now they were almost imploring. 'Damn it, it's my job. I need to know about this boy and his problems in a school environment. But the Agency has blanked all that from his records.'

'I honestly don't think they have,' said Justine. 'That's what I meant about you being paranoid.'

'Well, why is there so obviously some kind of discipline problem with Ricky but no information at all on what the problem is?'

'Because none of the schools wanted to go on the record with what they saw.'

'Why?'

Justine hesitated. 'I'd appreciate your frankness,' said Pangbourne.

'Frankly,' replied Justine, 'because I think they were spooked.'

'Spooked?'

'They didn't want to look silly so they didn't describe what they saw.'

'And what did they see?'

Justine shrugged. 'Ricky's problem.'

Pangbourne almost moaned with frustration. 'But what exactly is his problem? Does he extort money from other kids at knife-point? Does he wet himself in class? Does he expose himself in the playground? Forgive me, but I've had all of those in the past.'

Justine was giggling. 'God no. It's nothing like that.'

'What is it then?'

Justine frowned. 'It's kind of hard to put into words. But Ricky just seems to draw trouble.'

'He would hardly be the first trouble-maker I've been saddled with.'

'I didn't say he makes trouble. He draws it. Like a lightning-rod. But not just trouble. He draws all kinds of things.'

'What do you mean?'

'I don't know. Events. Things. Things just have a knack of happening around Ricky.'

'You mean he becomes the centre of attention?'

'Sort of. There's just sort of a vibe about him.'

'Which draws the attention of the other children?'

'And the teachers,' said Justine.

'That's not necessarily a bad thing,' said Pangbourne.

'No, not necessarily. But most of the time, for Ricky, it seems to be. He draws a lot of hostility.'

'The other kids dislike him.' Pangbourne took a pen out of his pocket and began making notes in a small calfskin book.

'It's not even a straightforward dislike,' said Justine. 'The kids just all seem to become irritated with him.'

'Irritation versus dislike? We're splitting hairs, aren't we?' Pangbourne smiled.

'No, when I say irritate I mean irritate,' said Justine. She hadn't meant to confide in Pangbourne but the words were pouring out of her. 'Irritate like an itch. The other kids become intensely aware of Ricky. And it makes them uneasy. And then uneasiness turns to hostility.' Justine realized that she was sweating profusely. She looked up at Pangbourne and saw that he was listening with great attention.

'I see,' he said, when it became evident that Justine had nothing else to add. 'I must say that after all this it really doesn't sound so bad.'

'Well, you wouldn't believe what a relief it is to talk to someone about it.'

'You seem almost ashamed.'

'It's just a bit weird, that's all,' said Justine.

Pangbourne smiled. 'I'm used to weird kids.'

'That's probably what they thought at all of Ricky's other schools.'

'Scopes High School is not like other schools,' said Pangbourne. There was suddenly enthusiasm in his voice. 'We pride ourselves on achieving miracles with even the most demanding teenagers. I'm not saying that their heads rotate and they spew green bile, but we have seen some fairly startling behavioural disorders. Ricky may even find that he's put in the shade by some of our current students.'

'You mean you're accepting him?' said Justine.

'He can start tomorrow if you like.'

'That's fantastic.'

'I'm sure we can handle anything Ricky can throw at us,' said Pangbourne.

'I'm sure you can, too,' lied Justine.

Ricky watched the crowd begin to fall apart and drift off. Unfortunately the thug and his cronies showed no inclination to leave. Instead they'd suddenly become fascinated by the lockers nearest the principal's office. They stood together in a whispering group, snorting with restrained mirth as they formulated a plan.

Then they formed a loose semi-circle and one of them jumped up and smashed at a locker with an impressive karate kick. The other kids made admiring noises but the thug grimaced and shook his head sadly. He gestured for the others to stand aside. He took a few steps back, so he was almost on the other side of the corridor, his back against the opposite bank of lockers.

The girls who hadn't already wandered off had now turned and were watching with full attention. Some of the girls who'd wandered off drifted back.

The thug carefully measured the distance then ran across the corridor, launching himself in the air in a perfectly executed martial arts manoeuvre that brought his feet up high towards the approaching locker. He hit the metal door of the locker at head-height with a powerful lashing kick.

The noise was instant and thunderous, making everyone jump. The thug landed nimbly on his feet and disdainfully turned away as his followers clustered around the locker to admire the results.

The earlier karate kick had left a detectable mark on the locker, but the thug's one had resulted in a substantial dent which looked like it had buckled the locker beyond repair.

One or two of the girls were still staring in shock but most of them were fashioning frosty or drop-dead expressions of some kind, radiating disapproval of the thug. The thug evidently wasn't bothered. He was completely satisfied with his action, which after all had restored him to the centre of attention where he belonged.

Just then the door to the principal's office popped open and Mr Pangbourne's fat secretary peered out, scowling.

Most of the kids in the corridor chose this moment to depart, slipping away as discreetly as they could, but the thug remained calmly standing in the corridor. He had cleverly positioned himself in front of the damaged locker so that the secretary couldn't see it.

The thug's chief crony, a chunky red-haired kid with a wispy goatee, came scooting over and quickly stood beside him, so as to hide the small mark made by the karate kick. Between them they completely camouflaged any sign of vandalism as they lounged against the lockers. Their buddies were grinning at the slyness of the move.

The secretary looked at them, knowing that something was going on, but not sure what.

'What was that noise?' she said. She looked at Ricky sitting on his bench but Ricky did the thing where he let his eyes go dreamy and vague. That usually caused people to ignore him and it worked perfectly now. The secretary's gaze moved on and latched on to the thug and his red-haired friend.

'Well?' she said. 'Wally Saddler. What are you grinning about?'

'Nothing, ma'am,' said the red-head politely. He had an angelic expression on his chunky face that caused his friends to writhe with silent laughter.

'You're not fooling anyone, Saddler.'

'If you say so, Miss Marcroft.'

The secretary shifted her gaze to the thug. 'What caused that noise I heard?'

The thug pretended he didn't hear her.

'Christian Leemark, I'm addressing you.'

The happy expression faded from the thug's face. He looked at the fat secretary standing in the open doorway and then he started walking towards her. Red-haired Wally Saddler glanced anxiously at the damaged locker that stood exposed as the thug called Leemark strode forward. But the secretary didn't notice it. She was too busy watching Leemark close in menacingly on her.

Everyone else in the corridor was watching him, too.

Everyone except Ricky. In crowd situations, when the group's attention was all focused on the same place, Ricky made a habit of looking somewhere else. You never knew what you might discover.

Ricky spied the girls watching the action, their eyes hungry for the drama. He heard the thug's voice speaking softly. 'Listen carefully Miss Marcroft because I'm only going to say this once.'

'Don't use that tone with me.'

'Shut up and listen.' His voice was soft and low and everybody was listening. 'You call me Wolf Leemark. Or Mr Leemark. Or just plain son of a bitch.'

'Don't you dare use that sort of language.'

'Just don't ever call me that other name,' said Wolf quietly.

He stood facing the woman, dangerously polite. The other kids stood watching, waiting.

'You'd better be getting to your classes now.' The secretary sounded calm and not at all spooked but Ricky could see the sheen of sweat on her fat face.

Wolf didn't budge. 'Did you hear me?'

'I'll call you by any name I want to, young man.'

'Oh, no, Miss Marcroft. That's just the point,' said Wolf. 'That's the point I'm trying to make.'

'What's in a name?' said a voice.

Everybody looked around to see a strangely dressed man. The man had evidently emerged from the staffroom and come down the corridor without anyone hearing his approach. This wasn't surprising since his feet were bare except for loose fitting black slippers.

He was a tall, athletic-looking young man who might have been a gym teacher. Except his sole item of clothing was a flowing saffron robe which seemed to be held together by a couple of casual folds. No self-respecting gym teacher would have been seen dead in such a foreign-looking, sissy garment. And then there was the young man's head.

'Hey,' said Wolf, grinning delightedly at the stranger's appearance. 'Hey, look at this!' He turned away from Miss Marcroft, forgetting all about his conflict of a moment ago with the fat woman. Ricky saw her struggling with mixed emotions. She was greatly relieved to have Wolf's menacing presence directed away from her. But at the same time some part of her was annoyed about no longer being the centre of attention.

Now Wolf stood in the middle of the corridor smiling up at the tall, young man. The young man smiled affably back.

'Hey, baldy!' said Wolf admiringly. Because the young man was indeed bald. Or, rather, his head had been carefully shaved quite recently.

'Fashion statement,' said Wolf, circling the tall young man to fully inspect his bare skull and orange robe. Ricky noticed that the young man didn't turn warily to keep his eye on Wolf. Most people would have been very apprehensive about having the thug behind them, but the young man was apparently unconcerned. He seemed to be pleasantly free of any kind of anxiety; serene and at peace with himself. It was this attitude that led Ricky to suddenly realize what the stranger was.

Some of the members of Wolf's gang had begun to chuckle at his clownish inspection of the young man. They wanted to join in the game. 'He's a skinhead, Wolf!' said the chubby red-head.

'No, I'm not,' said the young man affably.

'No, he's not, Wally,' said Wolf. He turned to the young man. 'How do you get it so shiny? Your head. Do you have to shave it every day?'

'Most days. I usually shave first thing.'

'And then what? Turtle Wax?' Wolf's cronies chortled at this witticism and the young man smiled appreciatively.

'Not really,' he said. 'Just occasionally some talcum powder.'

'Well if you're not a skinhead, what are you?'

'He's a Buddhist monk,' said Ricky. He didn't mean to say it out loud. It just popped out. He cursed himself and for one hot terrible moment it seemed as if everyone in the corridor was going to turn and stare at him. But luck was on Ricky's side. Before the other kids devoted all their attention to him they first looked at Wolf to check on his reaction to Ricky's outburst. Wolf was the dominant male and the crowd was taking its cue from his reactions.

And Wolf responded by simply nodding his head and absorbing the Buddhist monk information as if it came to him through the thin air rather than from any human agent. He took it silently on board but ignored its source. So everyone else ignored Ricky, too, and went back to looking at Wolf.

Ricky heaved a sigh of relief.

'That's right,' said the young man. 'I am a Buddhist monk. You can call me Young Master if you like.'

'Young master-bater,' said Wally Saddler and several of the other boys laughed, but the monk ignored the insult.

'So, what are you doing here?' said Wolf. 'Delivering a Chinese take-away?'

'Hey, can I have some hot and sour shrimp?' wise-cracked Wally Saddler.

'No, I'm teaching Comparative Anthropology,' said the monk.

'And who the hell do you think is going to attend a turkey of a course like that?'

'You for one, Wolf Leemark,' said the young man, smiling. 'My course is compulsory and you'll begin attending tomorrow.' He nodded politely and walked off before the speechless Wolf could think of a response.

An electric bell began to ring, echoing down the school corridors, signalling the end of the lunch-hour. Miss Marcroft returned to her office.

Wolf Leemark shrugged and turned away. Along with the other kids he set off for his first afternoon class. While Ricky watched him go his mother came out of the principal's office. She was leading Eve by the hand and her face was glowing with happiness so Ricky knew right away that she'd been successful.

'So when do I start?'

'Tomorrow, smart-ass,' she said as they walked out to their car. 'What was all that noise in the hall earlier?'

'Just getting to know my classmates,' said Ricky.

Chapter 21

Usually Creed remained awake on planes, even on long flights, but just before his jet began its descent to Heathrow he slipped into a jangled, confused sleep. He woke with a start as the plane hit the runway, bouncing gently on its landing-gear and coasted slowly towards the international arrivals terminal. He'd been dreaming in a fragmented way about Amy and Justine and, oddly, his son Ricky.

Creed rummaged in the overhead locker while he waited for the slow-moving crowd of passengers to exit the plane. He didn't have any luggage except for his one carry-on bag and the small packet he'd left with the steward when he'd boarded the flight.

He collected the packet as he left the plane. A waterproof grey pouch which was surprisingly heavy for its size. It contained Creed's hand-gun and his Agency permit under diplomatic seals. The steward said nothing as he handed it back but Creed could tell that he'd guessed what was inside.

With no luggage to collect Creed went straight to passport control where he was waved straight through as soon as the bar-code reader identified him.

He thought that the small waterproofed parcel might create some problems in customs, and he'd foreseen a delay while the local authorities examined the weapon and scrutinized his documentation.

What he didn't foresee was Mrs Woodcott.

'Creed, darling!'

Creed turned around in the crowded customs area to see a strange-looking old woman closing in on him. But even before he recognized her face there was something about her that triggered memories for him.

And suddenly he was remembering the sights and smells

of London. How odd that he'd flown across the world to this destination, this huge city, but only now did it become real to him.

London. Creed was flooded with memories of the place. Memories of searching for Justine in this big, dark city. Of knowing he had to save her and save Ricky who was growing in her belly.

London's warlord of crime for a decade had been Paulie Keaton. Justine had made the mistake of getting Paulie Keaton angry. Paulie was a man who savoured revenge and he'd planned to put Justine to work as a slave in one of his whorehouses. But first he was going to terminate the baby she carried.

Creed got to them in time. He saved them. Saved Justine and Ricky.

But the search had been a strange one. He remembered his feet echoing in the endless night of this great city as he followed his heart-beat and his instinct.

He remembered a Japanese girl wearing Justine's jacket, reaching for a gun. Creed was too fast for her, getting to his own gun first and pressing it against her leg under the table. No one else in the restaurant even knew what was going on.

Well, maybe one person.

'Creed, what a marvellous surprise this is. I mean running into you like this. What a marvellous surprise – especially for you.'

'You think so?' said Creed. Mrs Woodcott had already taken his arm and was walking beside him like some doting, dotty old aunt.

A pretty stewardess walking past gave them a strange look.

'How is Justine?' said Mrs Woodcott.

'Just fine. Great. She's lovely.'

'Is that why you winced at the mere mention of her name?'

'I did not wince,' said Creed. His sinuses had been blocked since landing in England, but now they cleared with anger.

'Perhaps flinch would be a better word. Sorry if I touched a sore spot.'

'Forget it,' said Creed, forcing himself to relax. 'What have you been up to all these years?'

'Oh, you know. Making ends meet. Earning a crust.'

'Doing what?'

'Well, just recently,' said Mrs Woodcott, 'by selling old friends down the river.'

'Down the river?'

'It's just an expression,' said Mrs Woodcott as she led him over to the doorway where the two brawny security officers were waiting.

'I can't do this,' said Creed.

'You are doing it,' said the woman in the camouflage jacket. She turned away from him and gave her full attention to the rubber seal of the roof-hatch.

'I can't be here,' said Creed. He began backing away from the armoured car.

'You are here. And you're not going anywhere.' The woman looked up. 'Redmond's inside and he's watching you on the screen.' She went back to working on the hatch. It had a rubber seal like a fat collar running all around the rim to cushion the metal door when it shut, and guarantee a tight seal. Or at least that was the intention.

But the once smooth rubber seal was now ragged and torn and the woman appeared to be mending it with some kind of puncture repair kit. 'I don't want to sound like I'm threatening you but there's all kinds of fire-power on this vehicle and Redmond has his finger on the button.'

'What are you trying to say?'

The woman put the puncture repair kit aside. 'Don't try wandering off unless you want five-hundred rounds of high calibre tracers through you.'

'Considering that's not a threat it's pretty effective,' said Creed.

A voice behind him said, 'Making friends, are we?' Creed turned to see Mrs Woodcott standing in front of the airport building which seemed to be the headquarters for the armoured car crews.

'Look, I don't have time for this,' said Creed. 'I'm on urgent business.'

'So was I,' said the woman, emerging from the hatch and climbing down from the armoured car. She was black, hard-looking but quite pretty. For a moment, when he first saw her she'd reminded him of Anna, an old girlfriend of his on the police-force who had died in the line of duty. But the resemblance had been an illusion, dissipated as soon as this woman opened her mouth.

Her name was Roz. She scrambled down from the armoured car, nodded at Mrs Woodcott and then looked at Creed. 'I was also on urgent business when they grabbed me.'

'So was I,' said a soft rasping voice. A man appeared in the hatch of the armoured car. 'Hello, I'm Redmond.'

'Hello,' said Creed. 'Look, if you're in charge there's been some mistake here.'

'Oh, I'm not in charge. I just thought I'd come up and say hello face to face, instead of being a disembodied voice muttering the occasional comment past Roz's bony arse in the hatch.'

'Watch the abusive language,' said Roz dangerously. 'And my arse is not bony.'

'If anyone's in charge, it's her,' said Redmond, nodding at Roz. Now Creed could see why his voice had that rasping note to it. His throat was heavily bandaged.

'But I'm involved in official security work,' said Creed.

'Well of course you are, dear,' said Mrs Woodcott. 'That's why I nabbed you. Because you have experience with violence and mayhem, and covert operations. That's why I apprehended all three of you.'

'You see?' said Redmond. 'We are just as much the unwilling conscripts as you.'

'When you get on board,' said Roz, 'we can have a nice historical discussion about press-gangs and the draft.'

'My goodness,' sighed Mrs Woodcott. 'Look at all of you fine young people standing beside that great armoured vehicle. You look like hardened combat veterans. Well, Creed doesn't, but that's only because he's still holding his suit-case. I wish I had a photograph of the three of you. I feel so proud. Like a mother.'

'Mothers don't traditionally get paid a bounty for forcibly enlisting their offspring in the security forces,' said Roz. A passenger jet rumbled overhead, climbing up into the air on the first leg of its intercontinental journey.

'One must move with the times,' said Mrs Woodcott.

'What about them? What about the security services?' said

Creed. 'The police and the army. Why can't they deal with this?'

'Because the state of emergency has swamped them. They need all the help they can get. Just imagine it's been a long hot summer in London, and everything is as dry as tinder. Brush fires are breaking out on every piece of open ground and the fire service is stretched beyond its resources dealing with them.'

Mrs Woodcott absent-mindedly squeezed the large handbag under her arm as though checking that something was still inside it. 'When I speak of brush fires, Creed, you understand that I am speaking metaphorically of the nature of this emergency.'

'Well what is the nature of this emergency when you're speaking non-metaphorically?'

'Probably best not to tell you at this stage.'

'I want to know what is going on,' said Creed. 'Don't give me this hush-hush bullshit.'

'He sounds just like you,' said Redmond fondly to Roz.

'You all right there, Creed?'

'Fine,' said Creed from behind the steering-wheel.

'He seems to be getting the hang of it,' said Roz dryly. It had taken her much nagging to get command of the vehicle from Redmond on their first ride together. But Creed had been in the driver's seat before they even left the airport. Redmond had seemed perfectly happy to let him drive. Hadn't even put up a fight. Maybe it was some gender-based, male-loyalty thing.

Or maybe nearly having his throat torn out had caused Redmond to mellow.

'You're lucky you weren't killed.'

'I was indeed lucky,' said Redmond. 'Very lucky, thank God.'

'If you were more organized you wouldn't need to rely on luck so much.'

'Look, for Christ's sake,' said Redmond hotly. 'For the last time, I did not leave the hatch open.'

'Well who opened it, then?'

'They did.'

'They?' said Creed from the driver's seat. The big screen

in front of him showed concrete bridges flashing overhead as they swept out of the airport.

Roz and Redmond ignored him. 'You saw how they chewed away at the rubber seal,' said Redmond. 'You repaired it, so I know you saw.'

Roz shook her head unhappily. 'Still,' she said, 'it's hard to believe they could open it.'

'Hard or just frightening?'

'Frightening,' agreed Roz. 'I don't want to believe they're that intelligent.'

In the front of the vehicle Creed repressed the urge to ask who *they* were. He had a fleeting wish that the Doctor was here in the armoured car with him. Even after all these years the Doctor still impressed him as the guy you wanted in your corner when things started getting weird.

It would be nice if the Doctor was here.

In the back of the armoured car Roz was thinking exactly the same thing as she got the Styer AUG down from the arms locker, reloaded its spare magazine and began attaching the bayonet.

'Is that a bayonet?' said Creed, turning around in his chair.

'Keep your eyes on the road,' said Roz. She was still a little stung about Redmond letting Creed drive the armoured car so soon. 'Yes, it is a bayonet.'

'I thought they went out with the Crimean war.' Creed glanced at the screen but the traffic situation hadn't changed in the last few minutes. There weren't many cars on the road, and what few there were stayed well clear of the armoured juggernaut that was speeding into west London.

'Roz had good luck with a bayonet recently,' said Redmond from the navigator's chair where he was sprawled.

'Is that right?' said Creed.

'Only don't ask her about it or you'll get three hours of drivel on the subject of African lion-hunting spears.'

'You really are extremely rude,' said Roz, reversing the Styer AUG and slamming its butt on the floor to make sure the bayonet was firmly secured.

'Sorry, I didn't mean to be,' said Redmond. He leant forward and spoke confidentially to Creed. 'I'm actually a great fan of Roz's.'

'Ass-kisser,' said Roz.

'Seriously,' said Redmond. 'You and Mrs Woodcott both. You saved my life.' He scratched at the thick pad of bandages on his throat.

'None of that would have happened if you had secured the hatch properly,' said Roz.

'Hey. Quit arguing in the back,' said Creed from the steering-wheel. He said it with the authority of an experienced family man who had gone on long trips with children. Then he chuckled. 'So Mrs Woodcott saved your ass, did she?'

Redmond clambered up into the front of the armoured car to sit beside Creed. He was glad to get away from Roz. 'That's right,' he said. 'Well, my throat actually. I was fighting off this —'

'Dog,' said Creed.

'Oh no,' Redmond called back to Roz. 'Our new colleague has correctly guessed the mystery question.'

'That was quick,' said Roz, leaning forward to put her head on Redmond's shoulder. She hadn't really meant to nag him about the hatch. It's just that he'd nearly got himself killed and she couldn't bear the thought that he might have been careless. She wanted Redmond to come through this business in one piece. 'You must have given him too many clues.'

'No,' said Redmond. 'He just plucked the answer out of the blue.'

'Even assuming that dogs have suddenly become unpredictably vicious —'

'Oh, you can assume that, all right,' said Redmond tugging at his bandage.

'Vicious and well organized,' said Roz.

'Even assuming that, how can there be enough of them in London to create a civil emergency?' Creed was slowing the vehicle down and checking its location against the computer map. He glanced around at Roz. 'We're at the place where you wanted to stop.' He put on the brakes and the big vehicle slowly coasted to a halt.

'Good,' said Roz as she made her way to the back of the vehicle. She began to climb up towards the hatch.

Creed called after her. 'Don't think I've forgotten my question.'

'Here's someone who may be able to answer it,' said Roz, opening the hatch.

She climbed up the ladder until she was invisible above the waist. Redmond stared at her buttocks jutting just below the hatch and silently mouthed the words 'bony arse' at Creed.

Creed felt a shift in the armoured car's suspension as someone climbed on board. Roz said something which he couldn't hear. Then she began descending, her boots ringing on the metal rungs of the ladder as she came back through the hatch. There was the sound of someone following her.

'– need for an investigation,' Roz was saying, her voice sharp with irritation.

'Not an investigation, just an appraisal,' said the man who followed her into the armoured car. He climbed to the bottom of the ladder then stood blinking in the semi-darkness. He was a tall paunchy man with a small moustache. In one hand he carried what looked incongruously like a sports bag. He would have been more at home with a brief-case, thought Creed. This man shouldn't be carrying a sports bag; he looked the sort who was permanently behind a desk in an office.

Kind of like me, thought Creed wryly.

'I'm really not very happy about this either,' said the man.

Roz ignored him. She was smouldering with rage. The man looked like he might burst into tears. He seemed bewildered at finding himself in the small cabin of the armoured car with three strangers. He reminded Creed ludicrously of an overgrown infant on his first day at school, suddenly and inexplicably abandoned among strangers by his parents. He wouldn't let go of his bag and he didn't know where to sit down.

Redmond took pity on him. 'Our friend was just asking a question,' he said, nodding at Creed. 'He doesn't believe there can be enough dogs in London to create an emergency like this.'

Redmond's ploy worked. Confronted with a question in his field of expertise, the man immediately relaxed. In a seamless transition his nervousness was replaced by arrogance. He looked at them as if they were peasants.

'Clearly your friend has never seen the figures on urban

animal populations,' he said in a snotty tone. He folded himself like a big bird into the chair by the communications console. He set his bag carefully between his feet as if it might wander off if he didn't watch it closely. Then he took a small book out of his jacket pocket and began to read it in the dim light provided by the glowing control panels. He was ignoring the others completely.

'What's your name, pal?' said Redmond.

The question seemed to bewilder the man. He carefully folded his book shut again and looked at Redmond. 'I'm Peverell. Norman Peverell,' he said.

'I'm here to assess the situation,' he added, as if this might clarify matters.

'Yes, we know that,' said Redmond. 'You're the man from the ministry.'

Suddenly Roz's smouldering rage burst fully into flame. 'I don't know why we have to go through this,' she said. 'I don't know why you have to assess anything.'

'We are in a very weird situation, Ms Forrester. People are seeing strange things and saying even stranger things. Fear breeds weird stories and hysteria. Even from hardened combat veterans we are hearing reports of things that are quite unbelievable. Reports rather like yours.'

'Then why are you even here? Why are you taking me seriously at all?'

Norman Peverell frowned. He looked a little frightened again. 'Because it would appear that you've seen the White King.'

Chapter 22

The long rubber hose was surprisingly heavy and Benny was getting fed up with carrying it. 'I didn't know this thing would weigh so much,' she said.

'It doesn't,' said the Doctor. 'At least in terms of weight-per-metre. The problem is that there are so many metres of it.'

'You're telling me,' said Benny, helping the Doctor to haul the heavy coil of hose up the staircase. The Doctor was unwinding the hose and carefully playing it out behind them as they went, making sure that it didn't snag on the banisters.

'Where did you get this thing?'

'I had it stored in the cellar,' said the Doctor.

'I mean, what is it for?' said Benny. 'Why did you have it in the first place?' She glanced back at the winding green length of hose that curled like a monster snake, running back down the stairs to the ground floor. From there it ran past the sitting room and disappeared around the corner to the kitchen where the Doctor had anchored the other end of it under a heavy ceramic jar in the sink.

'Well, it was for the garden originally,' said the Doctor.

'The garden?'

'It was part of the sprinkler system.'

'Why have a sprinkler system in a jungle?' said Benny nastily. She was getting fed up lugging the heavy, rubber-stinking hose. The slimy length of it was smeared with a thick coating of dust, like so many things in this house, and this dust had begun to transfer itself to Benny's hands, face and blouse. She was going to need a shower and a change of clothes after this.

'Now, now, the garden wasn't always in the state you're familiar with. There was a time when it was beautifully tended. And even now it isn't really so bad. It's certainly not a jungle. I've been in jungles,' said the Doctor. 'And you couldn't get one to grow here in south-east Kent. Entirely the wrong climate, even these days.'

They were at the top of the stairs now and the Doctor waited patiently for Benny to stop panting before he turned and went along the hallway towards the library. The Doctor never really seemed to get winded, a fact which normally would have impressed Benny but now seemed merely annoying.

'I still think this is a pretty stupid idea,' she said. Her shoulder was aching from the weight of the hose and that rubber smell was beginning to give her a headache.

'You have a better one?' said the Doctor. It seemed it was now his turn to become irritable.

'Well, there must be an easier way,' said Benny. She set the big coil of hose down for a moment.

'The only alternative would be to move the cylinder itself down to the kitchen.' The Doctor paused thoughtfully. 'You know, I did seriously consider that. It's not as difficult as it sounds. We'd just have to lower it carefully on its side and roll it on to something which would be easy to slide. A rug, say.' The Doctor's eyes were gleaming as he worked out the problem in his mind. 'So long as we fixed handles of some kind to the rug we could manage to pull it,' he said. 'Like the travois system used by the native Americans.'

'The what?'

'Very clever people, but for some reason they never invented the wheel. Just didn't get around to it. No one in the American continents ever did. Or perhaps they lacked the perceptual structures that would have made it an inevitability. Instead they dragged their loads along behind their horses using a kind of sledge arrangement. Referred to as a travois.'

'Fascinating.'

The Doctor had also paused now, halfway along the upper hallway. 'You can drag remarkably heavy loads in that manner, you know.'

Benny could see that he was warming to the idea. 'Actually, maybe the hose –'

'And then,' said the Doctor, 'all we'd need is a secure

arrangement of ropes and we could slide the cylinder gently down the stairs.'

Benny's mind was immediately filled with an alarming image of herself assisting the Doctor as he used an elaborate system of ropes to lower a giant, fragile glass cylinder slopping with green fluid and containing a comatose naked man. Lowering it clumsily down the long staircase.

Benny winced as she imagined the ropes slipping, the cylinder sliding out of control, jolting down the steps to the hallway below. Smash. Glass, blood, green fluid.

'No, no, this is fine,' she said hastily, picking up the hose again. And then the Doctor grinned and she realized that he'd been teasing her. This made her feel angry, or at least feel that she ought to feel angry.

'Why, for God's sake, do we need to run the hose all the way to the kitchen?' she said, in a voice which she hoped would convey her displeasure.

'I thought I explained. We need to drain the fluid from the cylinder. That's why the other end of the hose is in the kitchen sink.' The Doctor sounded smug.

'Why not just run the hose out of the window? We could drain it into the garden and then we'd only need about three metres of it.'

'What? Drain the fluid into the rose-beds?'

'They're a mess anyway.'

'At least they're alive. We don't want to expose plants to the fluid from a life-support cylinder.'

'Why? What exactly is it?'

'Life-support cylinder fluid,' said the Doctor, unhelpfully.

Benny sighed and carried the hose towards the library, unspooling it as she went.

The Doctor popped the top off the cylinder using car tools. He had to stand on a pile of the *Encyclopaedia Britannica* to reach it.

When he got it open Benny passed him the end of the hose and he fed it into the murky green liquid. He whistled tunelessly as he worked. It sounded like something by Bach. He'd been in an odd mood ever since the man in the cylinder had begun to stir. Jubilant. Triumphant. Insufferable, thought Benny.

'Here, could you hold this for me, please?' Benny obediently held the hose for the Doctor as he trotted back down to the kitchen. She heard his footsteps on the stairs and then, a moment later, the sound of the small electric pump he'd brought in from the garage.

The hose made a startling slurping noise, like a glutton sucking soup. The fluid in the cylinder began to stir turbulently. Benny was tall enough to hold the hose over her head but it was starting to make her arms ache. She climbed up on to the pile of encyclopedias the Doctor had vacated. Now she could assume a more comfortable position, holding the hose at waist level, plus she could peer inside.

The pump continued chugging in the kitchen and the liquid pulsed in time with it. She peered over the lip of the cylinder and watched the thick green liquid bubble as it started to drain, passing up into the hose on its long journey to the kitchen.

Benny stared down into the murky depths. The stuff was draining with maddening slowness. But then there was a considerable amount of it in the tank. She tried to estimate the volume of the liquid as she stood over the open top of the cylinder. The Doctor had allowed a considerable length of slack on the hose and now she realized why. As the level of fluid dropped she had to lower the hose further into the tank to pursue it. It wasn't an exciting task. The green stuff descended centimetre by slow centimetre.

It smelled like petrol combined with another odour, almost herbaceous, that reminded Benny of something. After a while she decided that it was like fennel. Then she remembered what the Doctor had said about the liquid killing the roses and she decided it might be better not to inhale the fumes from the stuff, so she averted her face, staring at a mildewed set of Lewis Carroll on the nearest bookshelf.

Holding the hose was a boring task, at least until the dropping level of fluid began to reveal the man inside. At first just a few tangled strands of red hair, then the whole crown of his head, then the fish-white skin of his forehead. The cylinder's inhabitant began to emerge.

Benny had never known it – him – as anything other than an unconscious body floating in green fluid. She had to make an effort to remember that he was called Jack and that he had once had a life.

The liquid in the tank was down below the level of Jack's eyes now. Benny avoided looking at them. If they suddenly flew open she didn't want to meet their gaze. She had no desire to be staring directly into whatever strange emotions might have been bred by years of dreaming in the green liquid.

There were footsteps outside the library. Benny annoyed herself by jerking with alarm. It was just the Doctor, of course. The sound of the pump echoing from the kitchen had covered his approach.

He came into the library smiling. He was carrying a big roll of fabric folded over one of his shoulders. In his other hand he was balancing a silver tray, like a waiter. On the tray there were four objects. They appeared to be a syringe, a bottle of brandy, a ham sandwich and an air-pistol.

The Doctor inspected the descending level of fluid in the cylinder with satisfaction. 'That pump is working rather well, don't you think?' he said brightly.

Somewhat peeved at being left on her own for so long, Benny frowned at the Doctor and wagged the hose in the thick green liquid. 'If this stuff is so toxic don't you think it's irresponsible putting it down the drain?'

'It's going directly into the septic tank. It will break down harmlessly there.'

'I didn't even know we had a septic tank.'

'Oh yes, a huge one.' The Doctor went to the billiard-table and began to clear the accumulated books off it.

'Remind me not to hammer any more croquet-hoops into the lawn, I'd hate to strike a gusher.'

'Oh, it's far too deep for that,' said the Doctor. He was clearing the table with remarkable speed, stacking the books neatly on the floor. 'It consists of several interconnected cells or vaults which can be drained independently.'

'I'm not sure I need to know all the gory details.'

'Well, anyway, it's a superb construction,' said the Doctor. He set the roll of fabric and the silver tray down on the newly cleared billiard-table. 'It could have been made even larger but then it would have broken through to the wine cellar.'

Benny sighed. She didn't know that they had a wine cellar

either. 'All right,' she said. 'I give up. Tell me what that stuff is for.'

'What?' said the Doctor, following Benny's gaze to the billiard-table. 'The tarpaulin?'

'No, the stuff on the tray. The syringe I can guess. Something to help bring our friend back to life.' The hose suddenly slurped loudly, sucking air, and Benny realized that she'd let the level of fluid drop faster than the hose. She paid a few more centimetres of slack into the cylinder and the draining resumed smoothly. The liquid was down to Jack's shoulders now. His thin bearded face stared blindly up at her, gaunt with suffering, a Renaissance Christ in green goop.

'That's right,' said the Doctor, picking up the syringe and checking it. 'Just plain adrenaline. I'll inject it into his heart, unless you want to do the honours.'

'No thanks. Why didn't you do that years ago, if a shot of adrenaline is all it takes?'

'Oh, it requires a lot more than that to bring him back,' said the Doctor. 'We might conceivably have revived his body but that would have been pointless with no mind to inhabit it.'

Benny stared down into the cylinder, the blank haunted face staring back up at her, eyes squeezed shut, lank beard and hair slimed with the thick liquid. 'And you think his mind is back now?'

'I think it's coming,' said the Doctor tersely. Suddenly Benny wondered if he was less certain than he let on. Perhaps he was as dubious about Jack's recovery as she was. Maybe he was taking a big chance on this. If so, it was churlish of her to challenge him about it, to step on his optimism.

Benny changed the subject. 'What else have you got there? It looks like a bottle of brandy and a ham sandwich.'

'Correct. Armagnac and smoked Bavarian ham, to be exact.'

'Why?'

'In case he's hungry when he wakes up.'

'And he's definitely going to need a drink, right?'

'Right.' The Doctor smiled.

'What about the gun?' said Benny. She grunted with effort as she fed another length of hose into the cylinder. The process of draining seemed to be accelerating. The liquid was halfway down Jack's chest now, droplets of it clinging to the thick mat of copper hair between his nipples.

'Ah yes, the gun,' said the Doctor, his smile fading. He went over and picked it up. 'It's just an air-pistol.'

'I can see that,' said Benny. 'What's it loaded with?'

The Doctor broke the gun open and showed her the scarlet tail-feathers of a dart, chambered and ready to be fired. 'Anaesthetic,' he said. 'Very fast acting.'

'How come?'

'Just in case.'

'In case of what?'

'Psychotic behaviour. It's not uncommon when someone has spent a prolonged period in a life-support tank.'

'Brilliant,' said Benny. 'You don't want to give me a hand with this hose, do you?'

Chapter 23

'Grown-ups will always tell you that you should trust them. But take it from me, as a general rule you shouldn't trust any of the bastards further than a midget can throw a piano. Me included. Mind if I smoke?'

'No,' said Ricky, a little startled by the question. 'Go ahead.'

Mr Pangbourne smiled gratefully and began to rummage in the drawers of his desk. He dug out a crushed-looking pack of cigarettes, shook one out, put it between his lips and lit it. With the first inhalation of smoke he visibly relaxed. 'Ricky,' he said, 'you might think that the more important a man gets, the more privileges he acquires.' As he spoke, smoke spilled from his mouth in interesting shapes that drifted and changed as they dispersed in the small office. 'But in fact sometimes it's the other way around. I mean, look at me. Principal of Scopes High School. I'm the head-honcho here. I run the place.' He paused and wiped some fine particles of ash off the sleeve of his jacket. 'And therefore, you might think, I'm a man of importance. Yet, I can't even have a cigarette.' The heavy lines around his eyes wrinkled as he smiled at Ricky. 'Along with power comes responsibility. I'm supposed to set an example. Almost nobody smokes these damned things any more.' He tucked the cigarette packet back into his desk drawer. 'I've got some cigars in here, too,' he said. 'But I only smoke those out in the open air. I do have some compassion.'

Ricky didn't reply.

'High-school principals aren't meant to have bad habits,' continued Pangbourne. 'I can just about get away with having a quiet cigarette when I'm alone. But I could get in a whole lot of trouble smoking while you're in here with me.' He peered at Ricky through the haze of smoke. His eyes were shrewd, gleaming with intelligence. 'You might say that you're the one who wields the true power here. After all, if you wanted to report me, you could get me into some deep shit with the school-board. Forgive my blunt language but I'm talking to you man to man here.'

'I wouldn't report you,' said Ricky. He felt somewhat off-balance and dizzy and it wasn't just the nicotine in the air. He'd just come out of his last morning class, double-maths, when a trainee teacher stopped him in the hallway and handed him a slip of paper. Printed on the slip was a formal request for him to go and see the principal. The slip was initialled by Miss Marcroft, Pangbourne's fat secretary.

Luckily no one in the hallway noticed, otherwise Ricky might have begun to attract attention, something he tried to avoid at all cost. He'd hurried down the central stair-well, happily anonymous in the crowd of kids laughing and talking as they headed towards the lunch-room.

At least, most of them had been talking and laughing. Sitting on one of the landings reading a tattered paperback, apparently oblivious of the crowd pouring past her, had been the kid he'd started to think of as Sad Girl.

Sad Girl was about the same age as his sister, but obviously not the member of any of the trendy cliques which seemed to so readily embrace Cynthia. Sad Girl looked like she didn't have a friend in the world and she spent most of her time between classes sitting in the stair-well reading or staring into space. She seemed to be even more adept at avoiding eye contact than Ricky himself.

Ricky had gone to the principal's office thinking he knew what was waiting for him. The rules and routines of such an encounter were fairly rigid and formalized, and Ricky had plenty of experience in being called to see the principal.

Basically you could expect three things: a lecture, a pep talk, or a warning. But his encounter with Mr Pangbourne had not yielded any of these three so far. Indeed, it hadn't yielded anything recognizable from his extensive past experience.

He wasn't accustomed to a school principal who smoked cigarettes, said 'shit', or called him a man.

All in all, it had been a pleasant surprise, and therefore it was a bit of a disappointment when Mr Pangbourne finally buckled down to business and began to behave in a more familiar fashion.

He stubbed out his cigarette in the big glass ash-tray on his desk and looked at Ricky. 'Well, I guess I'd better tell you what this is all about. You're new here in my school. I could give you some crap about how I like to talk to all my new students when they start, to get to know them a little better. But you'd have to be pretty stupid to believe that – why?'

The question came out sharply and suddenly, taking Ricky by surprise. 'Why?' he repeated, playing for time.

'Yes. Why would you have to be stupid to believe that?'

'Because of the number of kids you have here,' said Ricky, quickly doing some calculations in his head. 'You must have hundreds of new kids every fall. Just talking to each one of them would take you a good part of the year. And that's assuming you didn't have anything else to do.'

'Exactly,' said Mr Pangbourne with satisfaction. 'And we both know that I have much more pressing things to occupy my time. Like smoking.' He pulled open his desk drawer and took out the packet of cigarettes again. 'Don't ask me why I insist on putting them back every time I light one up. Maybe this way I can fool myself into thinking I don't smoke so many.' He lit another cigarette, inhaled gratefully and stuffed the pack back in the drawer. 'Or maybe it's just a tidiness compulsion. Anyhow, I'd offer you one but if I did I'd really get into trouble with the school-board.'

'That's OK,' said Ricky. 'I don't smoke.'

'You know,' said Pangbourne, 'it's funny. I wasn't even tempted to offer your mother one.'

'She doesn't smoke either.'

'Please don't interrupt when I'm making a clumsy attempt to get down to business. I mentioned your mother because we had a long talk about you the other day.'

Pangbourne watched Ricky tense up at the mention of his mother. For the first time since he'd come into the office he shot a direct glance at the principal.

Pangbourne was startled by the burning intensity of those adolescent eyes. Like a lot of shy kids, and a lot of sullen ones, Ricky spent most of the time avoiding eye contact, staring down or away. But when those eyes finally came out of hiding, they had a piercing directness that was quite unsettling.

They made Pangbourne think of accounts he'd read of great leaders and charismatic holy men. The stare that looked into your soul. They said that Rasputin had eyes like that.

And Charlie Manson.

And Hitler.

'Your mom and I talked about what we called your problem. Do you think you have a problem, Ricky?'

'You want to know what my problem is?' Ricky wasn't sure what was happening to him. Suddenly his voice was shaking. He had the strangest impulse to trust this man. Pangbourne sat across the desk from him, waiting patiently, not trying to force an answer out of him.

So Ricky took a deep breath, and told the truth.

'I just want them all to stop looking at me.'

'Who?'

'You, them, everyone.'

'The other kids?'

'Everyone.'

'You want them to stop looking at you?'

'To leave me alone. Get their eyes off me. To pay attention to someone else, for Christ's sake.'

'You feel that everyone is always looking at you?'

'No, not always. Don't make it sound like I'm crazy. Paranoid or something.'

'I didn't bring up craziness or paranoia, son.'

'Maybe not, but I know what you were getting at.'

'Now, that does begin to sound paranoid.' Pangbourne's voice was smooth and ruthless, making Ricky more and more angry.

'Oh, just go to hell.'

'That's constructive.'

'Well, if you don't believe me, just come and watch sometime. See what it's like for me.'

'And what will I see if I do?'

'I didn't say everybody was looking at me all the time,' said Ricky hotly. 'Most of the time they don't even notice me. I work damn hard to make sure they don't. To make sure they leave me alone. It's a full-time job getting them to ignore me. But sometimes I forget and then the bastards all start staring with their hungry little eyes.'

'Really? And what are those eyes hungry for?'

'I don't know,' said Ricky. The anger was starting to drain out of him now, leaving him feeling exhausted. In contrast, Pangbourne seemed to have revived. 'It's like they expect me to have the answers or something,' said Ricky.

'What answers?'

'I don't know. The answers to whatever questions they have. Don't ask me. I don't know if they even know themselves. They're like a bunch of stupid sheep.'

'That sounds a rather unhealthy way of looking at your fellow human beings.'

'Then why don't they take their stupid sheep-eyes off me?' said Ricky venomously.

'Maybe you're imagining it.'

'Sure. And maybe you're imagining my school record.'

Pangbourne smiled. 'Good point, son.'

A long thoughtful silence settled over the smoky office. After a while the principal cleared his throat. 'Ricky, if I was to say that I thought you were a pretty smart kid, would you think it was just some kind of ass-kissing tactic?'

Ricky couldn't help smiling. 'Yes, sir,' he said.

'Well, maybe something can be a tactic and still be true. What do you think about that?'

'I think that's another tactic, sir.'

'Well, let's assume for a minute that you are smart. Now I'm going to ask you to use some of that intelligence on this situation here.'

At the mention of his situation Ricky's smile faded. 'I notice you didn't say problem.'

'More ass-kissing,' said Pangbourne lightly. 'I want you to try and guess why everyone pays so much attention to you. You said they want something from you. Well, what do they want?'

He could see Ricky beginning to shrug, to say he didn't have any idea, but Pangbourne held up a hand and stopped him. 'I'm just asking you to make a guess, son. Just try.'

There was another long silence in the small office. Finally Ricky shrugged and said, 'Maybe people have got an emptiness in them. Maybe they think I can fill it.'

Pangbourne nodded slowly, then glanced at his watch and frowned. 'Looks like I'd better let you go or you won't get a lunch-hour today.'

Their meeting was over. Ricky was surprised at the sudden plunging disappointment he felt.

Ricky went out quickly, leaving the door open. As soon as he left Miss Marcroft came hurrying over. Pangbourne knew what she was up to. The fat woman was going to shut his office door again.

But before she could do so, he beckoned her in. She entered reluctantly and stood well away from his desk, her nose twitching disgustedly. She looked like she was ready to sprint back out into the fresh air at any second.

Pangbourne was accustomed to this behaviour from his secretary. It was her not-so subtle way of registering disapproval of the lingering smell of cigarette smoke in his office. She probably imagined that she was getting nasal cancer just breathing in here. Whenever he called her in, Pangbourne felt guilty and amused in about equal measure.

'Miss Marcroft, I wonder if you could do something for me.'

'I'm going to have my lunch now.'

'Yes, well I know that. You have your lunch at the same time every day.' And the same lunch for that matter, thought Pangbourne who had seen the plastic containers of homemade fruit salad that Miss Marcroft religiously stashed in the staffroom refrigerator. He often thought that these dainty daily concoctions wouldn't provide enough calories to nourish a fieldmouse. On the basis of the fruit salad diet Miss Marcroft should be sylph-like. Yet her massive bulk remained the same. Day after day she kept bringing in these tiny lunches, but the fat just didn't budge. Maybe she secretly gorged every evening, thought Pangbourne. Or maybe it was some inescapable glandular condition. The poor thing.

'You can do me this favour on your way back from lunch, Miss Marcroft. Just visit the library for me.'

'The library?'

'Yes, I want any books we've got on certain subjects.'

'Which subjects?' said Miss Marcroft. Her voice was blunt, nearly rude, but her face assumed the dreamy expression that meant she was about to commit something to memory. And her memory hadn't failed Mr Pangbourne yet.

'Charisma, leadership and religious hysteria,' he said.

Miss Marcroft nodded, as if to say that any idiot could remember that. She also managed to give a little disapproving frown at the quirkiness of his request.

'Anything else?' she said sarcastically.

'Yes, pick me up a pack of cigarettes on the way back,' said Pangbourne.

'Just kidding,' he added, but not before he had the satisfaction of seeing a flash of disgust and horror in Miss Marcroft's eyes.

After she left, shutting the door rather harder than was necessary, Pangbourne remembered something. He was thinking about his conversation with Ricky.

He realized that the kid had called him sir. The thought gave him a quite disproportionate feeling of pride.

He felt so good he even postponed his next cigarette for ten minutes.

Chapter 24

By the time they reached the council estate the moon was up. Creed watched it complete its slow journey, rising above the low roofs and dark trees like a big white balloon.

The estate was quiet and very normal looking. The only odd thing was the lack of light in the windows of the houses. The place seemed ninety per cent deserted.

The only sign of the recent night's trouble was the collapsed garden wall which Creed could see on the far side of the podium.

The hatch clanged loudly behind him. He looked up as Roz and Norman Peverell climbed out of the armoured car. He and Roz were still arguing.

'I still think it's insulting that you won't just believe me,' said Roz.

Norman Peverell rubbed his small moustache. 'In my job I've heard lots of weird stories. We have no shortage of weird stories. What we're short of is verification. That is what I'm after tonight.' He stood and stared across the concrete podium at the clusters of small houses with their walled gardens. 'The great low-rise housing experiment,' he said.

'Where are the people?' said Creed. The question had been bothering him ever since they'd arrived.

'People?'

'The inhabitants.'

'Evacuated, mostly,' said Norman Peverell. He seemed a little surprised by the question, as though people weren't normally a factor in his thinking.

'Mostly?'

'Well, a few stubborn die-hards insisted on staying.' Norman Peverell gestured towards the scattered houses with lights still burning in their windows.

'And a few didn't make it,' said Redmond, appearing in the hatch of the armoured car. 'Like the stewardess and her boyfriend.'

'You stay inside while we reconnoitre,' said Roz. 'And don't forget to seal the hatch properly.'

But Redmond got out of the hatch and climbed down from the armoured car. He was wearing a combat helmet like Roz's, with night vision and communications hardware built in, and he had a gun slung over his shoulder.

'No. You stay inside the armoured car, Roz. I'm going to reconnoitre. I've always wanted to reconnoitre.'

Roz was too surprised to argue. She even unbuckled her helmet and began to climb back on to the vehicle when the civil servant cleared his throat.

'I'm afraid Ms Forrester has to come along. She was the one who saw the White King.'

'Well, I'm not going back on board.' Redmond rubbed the bandage on his throat, looking at the armoured car. 'It's not so bad when it's moving but I've had bad experiences in that thing when it's stationary.' He smiled a charming smile. 'I guess you might say I have a touch of claustrophobia.'

'Not ideal for somebody who has to work in an armoured car,' said Roz grouchily.

'Not ideal,' agreed Redmond. He turned to Creed. 'I'm afraid that just leaves you.'

'Leaves me?'

'To stay on board and keep an eye on things.'

Creed shrugged and climbed back on to the vehicle. The truth was that he didn't mind going back inside. There was something he wanted to do and he didn't want the others knowing about it.

'Oh, Creed –' said Roz.

'Don't worry, I'll secure the frigging hatch,' called Creed as he disappeared inside.

Redmond chuckled.

'I'm just security conscious, that's all,' said Roz, a little stung. 'There's nothing wrong with that.'

They turned and set off towards the small cluster of houses on the far side of the podium. Their shadows jogged along beside them, crisp and precise in the bright moonlight.

Roz was the first to break the silence. 'Why do they call it the White King?' she asked.

'Because it's white,' said Norman Peverell.

Roz sighed with disgust and didn't reply. Redmond didn't want her getting pissed off, so he interpreted the sigh for Norman Peverell.

'We know the dog's white,' he explained. 'Roz got a good look at him.'

'Good look?' said Roz. 'He was as near to me as you are now.' She remembered standing in the nightmare half-light in the hallway of the stewardess's house, staring through the peephole at the strange white dog who sat patiently on the steps.

Roz realized that they were approaching the place where she'd last seen Jessica's body. She held the Styer AUG ready, set to rapid fire and she was scanning the low-walled gardens on either side of them as they walked past. Whenever they came to tree branches that hung out over a wall they took a careful detour, walking in the middle of the road. Roz hadn't forgotten how the dark shapes had come flowing over a wall like this to bring the stewardess down.

Redmond was saying, 'I think what Roz meant was, why do they call it the king?'

Norman Peverell frowned. 'Interesting question,' he said.

'It just acquired the name as stories spread by word of mouth. This creature seems to have almost become some kind of urban myth. That's one reason the ministry is so reluctant to accept any unconfirmed sightings.'

'What do you mean, unconfirmed? I said I saw him and when you asked me I confirmed it.'

'With all due respect, Ms Forrester,' said Norman Peverell. 'We have to be rigorous about the White King. He has almost become –'

'He?'

'We assume it's a male.'

'Why?'

Norman Peverell paused to consider his words carefully. 'Do you know anything about population dynamics, the theory of the alpha male?'

'No.'

'Never mind. We don't have to refer to the animal as "he". For purposes of discussion by all means let's refer to it as an "it". Over the years it has almost become the subject of a cult. Reports were just beginning to be taken seriously in government circles when that article in the *Fortean Times* appeared and –'

Roz interrupted again. 'Did you say years?'

The paunchy man looked up in surprise. Roz and Redmond were both staring at him. With their weapons and helmets and camouflaged jackets they looked like a pair of fierce apparitions in the moonlight. Norman Peverell blinked at them. 'Sorry?'

'You said years,' said Redmond. 'You said that people have been seeing this thing for years.'

'Yes. Well, reports of strange behaviour among the dog population. Strange group behaviour, to be more specific. Just anecdotes initially. Small silly-season stories in the daily newspapers and so on. But gradually the sheer number of reports snowballed and the security services, that is to say, people like myself began to take notice. Of course, we served D-notices.'

'Bloody typical,' said Redmond.

'I don't get it,' said Roz. 'D-notices?'

'The Official Secrets Act,' explained Redmond. 'An English speciality. Supressing information. Muzzling the press.'

'It's not the press that needs muzzling,' said Roz. She was remembering jaws open wide in the moonlight, the jagged ivory of fangs.

'Well, the freedom of the press is a separate issue.'

'To you, maybe,' said Redmond.

'In any event, we stopped the newspaper reports so as not to alarm the public while we looked into the reports ourselves. And as we began to dig deeper there were these other stories, rather disturbing stories.'

'I'll bet they were disturbing,' said Roz.

Creed sat in the dim interior of the armoured car bent over the communications console, trying to puzzle out the computer manuals in the dim blue light. If he could familiarize himself with the operating system he'd be able to find a way around its security features and get a message to Amy. Failing that, he would try reaching the Doctor.

Creed was glad he'd been left alone by the others. If they'd seen him doing this they would have tried to stop him.

Contacting the Doctor might be easier and anyway he needed to get in touch with him. The Doctor had said the situation was urgent. He'd said he needed Creed's help. What sort of help? And what was the situation? Perhaps he was already knee deep in it.

Creed was wondering about that when the alarm went off.

He hurried back up the narrow aisle to the front screen. The thermal-imaging night-sight showed something on the far side of the podium, at the rear of the armoured car.

A glowing mass moving like lava, flowing towards him from the maze of dark houses and gardens. Creed felt a tingling in the pit of his stomach, a ticklish sensation halfway between fear and excitement. He zoomed in on the undifferentiated lava-like glow and gradually the screen began to reveal the shapes of individual dogs.

Dogs.

So they hadn't been kidding after all.

Creed quickly checked the status of the machine guns mounted on the rear of the armoured car. There were fewer than on the front, and they were of smaller calibre but Creed was confident they could cope with anything these animals could throw at him.

All the same, he was a little unnerved by the sheer number of the dogs. His eyes drifted back towards the screen that showed them coming towards him, wending their way between the shadowy houses in a slow, unending stream. They kept coming, in extraordinary numbers, and there seemed plenty more still behind them.

Creed watched for over a minute and despite himself he felt a prickling of awe. The hairs began stirring on the back of his neck.

It was an unpleasant sensation.

Creed forced himself to return to checking the machine guns. He remembered with some embarrassment his remark about there not being enough dogs in London to create an emergency.

The weapons computer beeped. The rear-mounted machine guns were powered up and ready for use. Creed spent a few seconds practising how to rotate and aim them. He could leave them on automatic, using motion sensors to choose their own targets and fire on them 'at will'; odd terminology to apply to a soul-less machine.

His eyes drifted back to the main screen and the endless molten flow of the dog pack. 'Not enough dogs,' he muttered to himself, with chagrin. The pack was leaving the shadows of the houses now and coming out on to the podium.

'Good,' said Creed. 'Good dogs. Keep coming. Give me a clean line of fire.'

The sound of his own voice reminded him that he had to send a transmission to Roz and Redmond. They needed to be notified of this development.

But Creed would never send that message.

Because he was reaching for the microphone when he looked up at the screen again and saw the woman.

Chapter 25

Ricky left Pangbourne's office and stepped into the corridor. He was making his way towards the lunch-room when he realized that, for the first time in his life, he found himself wishing that a visit to the principal's office could have lasted longer.

For some reason, this thought made him think of Creed. Ever since the confrontation in the kitchen on Saturday night he'd been trying to tell himself that he didn't have a father; that he had no idea who his real father was.

But the truth was that he still thought of Creed as his father. And no matter how hard he tried to sustain his feeling of rage and grievance, he couldn't even remember what their argument had been about. He just knew that his father was gone, supposedly on business, and his mother was miserable.

He remembered driving out to the Agency office on Sunday morning, his mother frantically packing them into the station-wagon so they could rush out to say goodbye to his dad before he left. Racing at a breakneck speed that had Ricky and his sisters uniquely silent in the back seat, as Justine sped along the long looping curves of the road through Gaines Woods.

And they still arrived too late, just in time to see the helicopter containing Creed disappear into the bright approaching cloud-front of the new day. Ricky remembered how he'd refused to get out of the car and wave goodbye.

Now he felt that he'd behaved like a sulky little prick. He wished he'd waved goodbye to his father. To Creed. Whatever you wanted to call him.

His 'real' father was supposed to be his genetic father. Some guy he'd never even met.

To hell with that, his real father was Creed.

Ricky was absorbed in these thoughts as he stepped into the warmth and food-smell of the lunch-room. The big room was full of the clamour of kids eating. Trays and cutlery crashed like percussion above the steady rumble of conversation, boy-laughter and girl-laughter rising from one table or another.

Ricky found a table where he could sit with a couple of kids from his maths class: Tommy Barretta and Phil Mendick. Neither of them were total geeks – the school geeks were established at a table nearby – but both were outsider-types, which was pretty much the way Ricky classified himself.

Tommy Barretta was an outsider because of the flaming acne that pockmarked what would otherwise have been a handsome and square-jawed face. Phil was ostracized purely on the basis of his last name. Ricky wondered what the hell kind of parents would send their kid to school with a name like Mendick. It virtually begged for penis and homosexuality jokes. Of course, maybe his parents were proud of the old family name and refused to change it just to silence the mockery of a stupid bunch of kids. But it was a shame that Phil had to suffer due to his parents' pride. And even Ricky thought it was a stupid-sounding name and could only be improved by being changed to virtually anything else.

Just thinking about it now made Ricky feel enraged on Phil's behalf. Phil was a pretty good athlete, but no amount of prowess in the gym or on the playing field would ever outweigh the stigma of those snickers every time the coach yelled out 'Mendick!' during Phys Ed. How could Phil's parents be so insensitive? To Ricky it was just one further example of the gulf of incomprehension between parents and their children. Nothing could get across that gulf.

After grabbing a chair with Phil and Tommy, and leaving his books on the table to save his place, he selected a tray and headed to join the line for hot meals.

The food at Scopes High was pretty good and Ricky felt his appetite growing as he stared at the bright colours behind the heated glass and breathed in the cooking smells. His stomach growled quietly with approval as he watched the white-clad kitchen staff spoon the neat portions on to his plate. Ricky chose a delicately spiced coconut curry; great-looking plump mushrooms deep-fried in batter; and some kind of freshly baked bread delicately marbled with red and green, revealing the herbs and tomatoes in it. And, just for the hell of it, onion rings and fries.

All he needed now to make this feast complete was a nice, cold drink.

He set his tray down at the cutlery station and headed over to the soft-drinks machine.

In some ways this was a dangerous thing to do, because the machine was against the wall right behind Wolf Leemark's table. Ricky hadn't forgotten his encounter with the school bully the other day. Leemark had been pissed off because someone was intruding on his turf. Admittedly, he didn't know the identity of that someone, but it was only a matter of time until he found out.

Leemark was holding court at his table with a group of thuggish jocks, including the plump red-haired clown called Wally Saddler, and a skinny sexy-looking girl with long suntanned arms and legs.

Ricky felt a surge of jealousy about the girl's presence on Wolf Leemark's table. What were the odds against such a girl ever sitting beside Ricky in the lunch-room? She wasn't exactly beautiful, but she had a cute kind of turned-up nose, a nice smile, and that great tan. There was just something about her that was exciting, that took your breath away in a sexy kind of way.

Then sexual interest began to give way to alarm. Some faint alarm bell was going off in Ricky's mind; he'd begun to feel anxious as he crossed the room. He knew he'd already made some bad mistake.

He realized too late that he was paying too much attention to Wolf Leemark's table.

The suntanned girl had become aware of him looking at her. Now she was looking back. And as a result Wally Saddler had noticed him, too.

Ricky could see a look of dumb hostility forming on the red-head's chubby face. That was bad. And if Wolf Leemark noticed him, it would be even worse.

But then one of the other thugs at the table said something, a joke, and everyone laughed and Wally Saddler was distracted. He forgot all about Ricky as he turned to his friends and said something else, another joke. Eager to get in on the act, eager to top everybody else.

When Ricky reached the far wall of the lunch-room he felt a wave of relief. He'd got away with it. His back was tingling with the awareness of Wolf Leemark's table right behind him. It was like having an unexploded bomb behind him. Ricky gave the drinks machine his order, paid for it and collected the cool can as it rolled out of the machine's refrigerated interior.

Drink in hand, he turned back to collect his tray. Moving slowly across the lunch-room he did his best to become unnoticeable, just one more anonymous kid in the crowd; and this time none of the boys at wolf's table even looked up as he crept past them.

The girl was still watching him, though. Out of the corner of her eye, trying not to be obvious about it. Dropping a paper napkin on the floor, and sneaking a glance at Ricky as she reached under the table to pick it up. He could feel her eyes on him as he set the soft-drink can on his tray and carried it back to join Tommy and Phil at their table.

Tommy and Phil were OK. They were outsiders but they welcomed Ricky's presence and he knew they'd soon be friends. Phil made some insulting remarks about Ricky's choice of lunch and Tommy made gruesome speculations about the origins of the protein in the curry, but it was only good-natured ribbing. Ricky felt relaxed and buoyant. Life wasn't going to be so bad at Scopes High. Maybe the trouble wouldn't start for a long time.

Maybe it wouldn't start at all.

Ricky set about eating with considerable gusto. He was thoroughly enjoying his curry, mopping up the golden sauce with thick chunks of bread, when he noticed the piece of paper sticking out from under his plate.

He knew immediately that it was a note. And he knew that someone must have stuck it on his tray while he was tiptoeing past Wolf Leemark's table to get to the soft-drinks machine. He also knew that he had to pull the note out and read it, but he didn't want to.

There was no way it could be anything good.

Ricky thought about it carefully. He continued to eat so that Tommy Barretta and Phil wouldn't notice anything. He shovelled the curry into his mouth but he couldn't taste it; his appetite was gone.

It was possible, he supposed, that the note was from some fantastic girl who had fallen in love with him at first sight. But the only girl he'd seen that he liked so far was the one at Wolf's table and she'd been in his view all the time. She couldn't have left the note. More likely it was from a social reject like Sad Girl.

More likely still, it wasn't from a girl at all. Probably from some jock who'd taken an instant dislike to Ricky, suggesting a time and place for a murderous bludgeoning in an after-school fight.

With a sinking feeling Ricky carefully worked the note out from under his plate so the other boys wouldn't see it. This way, if it turned out to be some humiliating insult, they wouldn't know about it.

Ricky unfolded the note.

It was a small, blue-lined piece of paper torn out of an exercise book. The uppermost side was blank but he could see writing on the other side. Ricky turned the note over.

It said: *'I know who your real father is.'*

The shock was like having cold water thrown over him.

Who could know about this? Who could know what was happening in his family? It was as if someone was reading his mind.

But the shock only lasted for an instant. Because almost as soon as he turned the note over and read those words, the PA system buzzed and an electrically amplified voice cut across the noise of the lunch-room.

'Richard McIlveen to the principal's office. Richard McIlveen to the office, please.'

Tommy Barretta and Phil Mendick shot Ricky a sympathetic look as he stood up from the table. His meal was only half finished but that didn't matter; he'd lost his appetite now. In any case, he couldn't afford to delay. When they called you to the principal's office they meant right away.

Ricky scooped up his books and walked across the lunchroom. The place had gone deadly quiet after the announcement and now every eye was on him. Being called to the principal was generally believed to signify imminent punishment, so some of the looks from the other kids were supportive or sympathetic. But most were just frankly curious.

The looks from the boys at Wolf Leemark's table were openly hostile.

All of Ricky's attempts at camouflage had proved futile. Now, very much against his will, he was the centre of attention. Half the school was looking at him. There was still the usual canteen noise of plates being scraped and food being consumed but all talking had stopped.

Ricky felt the gaze of his school-mates like hot sunlight on sunburnt skin. It only took fifteen or twenty seconds to cross from his table to the door but the walk seemed to last forever. A few whispers started as he neared the door of the canteen, some of them coming from Wolf Leemark's table. No one took their eyes off him. But, despite the whispers, there was none of the usual jeering or humorous shouted warnings one might expect in a situation like this. All the activity in the big room was suspended in a tense silence. And, somehow, Ricky knew this was his fault.

He wasn't scared, but he was deeply troubled. His mind was occupied with the contents of the strange note. There was simply no room left for worrying about something as mundane as being summoned to see the principal, or what the other kids might think of him.

So, instead of radiating fear, Ricky was communicating another emotion. And the other kids were picking up on it. Maybe it was something about the way he walked, or his posture, or the expression on his face. Perhaps all three. In any case, they felt his mood and it infected the whole room.

And they didn't like it.

In particular, Wolf Leemark and his cronies didn't like it. They were like spectators at a play who had been happily ignoring the action on stage, talking loudly among themselves, with their feet up on the seats in front of them. And then suddenly an actor had walked out on to the stage whom they couldn't ignore.

For years Ricky had been able to fool everyone, perhaps even himself, into believing he was just some shy geeky kid. It was a nice comfortable little niche that he could hide in. Sometimes his carefully fostered disguise would slip, and those were the times when he had to be careful. But now, his disguise seemed to have slipped so badly it was beyond repair.

In the past when he found himself being noticed by people he always managed to shed their attention, or at least break the spell somehow. Normally he would have tripped, or dropped his books, or just managed to look so damned awkward and uncomfortable that the other kids would have begun to snicker and make insulting remarks. And then they would laugh and dismiss him. Move on and notice something else, forget the frightened gawky kid walking to the principal's office.

But Ricky didn't walk like a frightened kid. He walked like a holy man summoned to see a king, or a general leading his troops into battle, not even bothering to glance over his shoulder to see if they were following him. He was lost in the seriousness of his thoughts, the crumpled note still wadded in his closed fist.

As he left the lunch-room he could feel Wolf Leemark staring at him. He knew that this was going to lead to trouble, but there was nothing he could do about it and all his concentration was focused elsewhere. He was caught up in the problem of the note. And the subsidiary problem of why Mr Pangbourne wanted to see him again so soon.

On the way out of the lunch-room he saw Sad Girl sitting near the foot of the central staircase. She looked up from her book. She'd obviously heard the PA announcement and now she was watching him as he climbed the stairs. Ricky looked back at her and for an instant their eyes met. It was as if Sad Girl had forgotten, for a moment, that she never looked anyone in the eye. But then she quickly looked away, dropping her gaze back to the tattered pages of her book.

Ricky climbed the long staircase, the tightly folded note now cutting into the palm of his hands. He watched his feet on the stone steps, not wanting to exchange stares with anyone else.

'Hello Ricky.'

Ricky looked up. He'd reached the ground floor now and was hurrying towards the principal's office, still staring at the floor of the corridor. So of course he hadn't noticed the woman. She was standing by the drinking fountain, in an alcove between two rows of lockers; standing there as if she was waiting for someone.

'Sorry to drag you out of the lunch-room like that,' said the woman. She was one of the teachers; Ricky knew that because he'd seen her coming out of the staffroom that morning. He could hardly help noticing her; she looked far too lovely to be a high-school teacher, and perhaps a little too young as well. She was carrying a canvas shoulder bag and wore a plaid skirt with a plain white blouse, but no ornamentation or jewellery except for the small silver earrings half concealed by her blonde hair. The silver looked nice against her tanned smooth skin.

Her blue-green eyes were looking directly into his.

'My name's Amy Cowan,' she said. 'I'd like to talk to you.'

Chapter 26

The woman was wearing an airline stewardess's uniform.

Creed watched her on the screen of the armoured car. She was moving through the moonlight like a sleep-walker. Or maybe like someone deep in shock, he thought. She walked among the mass of dogs that poured out from the houses, weaving a little from side to side.

At first Creed had the eerie impression that she was in command of the dogs, leading them like some kind of Pied Piper. It was a natural reaction. Seeing a human being among a mass of animals moving in a coordinated fashion it's natural to assume that the human being is in charge.

But, if anything, it seemed to be the other way around. The stewardess was moving in a dazed fashion, following the erratic path of someone who was falling-down drunk. The dogs were guiding her, nudging her ankles when she wandered off course, flowing around her to force her to walk in the right direction. It reminded Creed of the way sheepdogs worry and cajole a renegade sheep back to the flock.

The stewardess began to wander off at an angle and the dogs quickly and efficiently nudged her back where they wanted her. They were bringing her out on to the podium.

Towards the armoured car.

Creed cursed. He tore himself away from the screen and began typing away frantically at the computer. He had to change the weapons software. He'd programmed it so the guns would automatically blast anything that came near the armoured car.

That included the stewardess.

Creed glanced back at the screen. He zoomed in to see the woman's face. She might have been extremely pretty under normal circumstances but now there were bruises around her eyes and a dark smudge across her forehead. Her face had the puffy unhealthy look of extreme exhaustion. Now she was nearer he could see the stains and tears on her uniform. The stockings on her long shapely legs looked like they had been shredded.

She looked like she'd been through hell. With her dark bruised eyes she seemed waif-like and vulnerable in the moonlight.

'Target at fifty metres,' said the weapons computer.

Creed quickly went back to typing. He had to reprogram the weapons system so it would only aim and fire on the dogs, not on a human being. He cursed again as he typed. The military software he was wrestling with didn't make changes easy. He couldn't just tell it to kill dogs and spare human beings. He had to type in some kind of description of what a human being was – general size and weight – and a similar description of a dog. Then tell the computer to recognize one and shoot it, and recognize the other and avoid shooting it.

Creed was swearing steadily now, a non-stop stream of obscenities. Sweat was running freely down his sides as he typed. He glanced up at the screen again; he wasn't going to be able to make the changes in time.

'Target at twenty metres from firing distance,' said the computer as if confirmng his thoughts.

Creed stopped typing. 'Activate voice control,' he said.

'Password?' said the computer.

'Shit,' said Creed. He began to hunt frantically through the pile of manuals.

'Password not recognized,' said the computer. 'Target fifteen metres from firing distance.'

Creed tore through the manuals. Nothing. As he flipped frantically through the pages a loose piece of paper drifted out and floated lazily in the air.

'Target at ten metres,' said the computer. 'Preparing to fire.'

Creed snatched the piece of paper out of the air. On it, in large clear handwriting, it said: *Litre of milk, 100 grams cheddar cheese, med. cauliflower.*

'Target at five metres. All weapons ready,' said the computer.

Creed turned the piece of paper over. On the other side it said: *Password: Engagement.*

'Engagement!' yelled Creed.

'Voice control activated,' said the computer. 'Commencing firing pattern on all rear-mounted guns.'

'Stop! Don't shoot.' Creed's shouts were so loud they set up a painful ringing echo in the confined space of the armoured car.

'Firing sequence aborted,' said the computer mildy. 'Targets now inside firing zone.'

'Don't commence firing until I tell you,' said Creed. 'And fire only on targets that have substantially less body mass than that of a human being. Is that clear?' Creed wasn't sure it was even clear to him.

'Activating variable target option. Please specify new target parameters or use existing ones.'

'What are the existing ones?'

'To fire exclusively on targets approximating the size and shape of domesticated dogs found in western Europe,' explained the computer pedantically.

'Jesus Christ,' said Creed. 'That was exactly what I was trying to program you to do.'

'Please specify new target parameters or use existing ones,' repeated the computer.

'Activate existing parameters,' said Creed.

'Activated,' acknowledged the computer.

'Where are the targets now?'

'Ten metres inside the firing zone.'

'OK, now you can start firing,' said Creed. He jammed his fingers into his ears to protect them from the echoing thunder of the machine guns on the hull.

But nothing happened.

Creed cautiously took his fingers out of his ears. Nothing. Silence except for the faint hum of air-conditioning in the vehicle.

'Why aren't you firing?' he said.

'No targets that match parameters,' said the computer tersely.

Creed swore again and swung around to look at the screen. Sure enough, the stewardess was out there on the podium, walking slowly towards the armoured car. If anything, she was moving even more unsteadily now, practically staggering. That wasn't what got Creed's attention, though.

The stewardess was staggering by herself. The horde of dogs that had been following her, guiding her, had melted away. Not one of them was visible out in the big open space of the podium. They must have retreated to the cluster of houses at the edge of the concrete apron, Creed thought.

His first reaction on seeing the stewardess on her own was a surge of triumph. In the back of his mind he'd been wrestling with the problem of how to get her safely separated from the dogs. Now the problem seemed to have solved itself neatly.

Perhaps a little too neatly.

He kept watching the screen while he tried to decide what to do. The stewardess was moving in an increasingly erratic manner. It was as if the dogs had been keeping her upright. As Creed watched she stopped walking altogether, standing there in the moonlight. 'Standing' was perhaps the wrong word. She was swaying unsteadily on her feet and almost immediately she began to topple.

'Shit,' whispered Creed.

He watched helplessly as the stewardess fell forward on to the pavement, first on to her knees, then forward from the waist in a kind of clumsy shallow dive, flat on her face.

Creed winced as he watched her head connect with the concrete.

Then he was out of his seat and moving down the aisle of the armoured car, scooping up a first-aid kit as he went. He paused for an instant by the arms locker to grab the first two weapons that came to hand, a metal-hafted knife and some kind of automatic pistol.

Creed dropped the knife into his boot as he put his foot on the bottom rung of the metal ladder that led up to the hatch. The pistol had a clip of ammunition taped to its grip. He untaped the bullets and slammed them into the pistol as he climbed, unfastened the hatch, and clambered out into the night.

Creed paused for a moment as he moved down from the vehicle, scanning the housing estate for signs of activity. Everything was silent, still. But inside his head some kind of warning signal was going off. This was all too pat, too easy.

Still, he didn't see what else he could do. He had to make a move. The woman was lying there, just a few metres from the armoured car. She was in bad shape. He had to get her on board and it looked like the dogs had withdrawn from the area, for whatever reason. Who knew how long they'd be gone?

He had to act now, before they came back.

He had no choice, but still it felt all wrong. You didn't spend a lifetime in Creed's line of work without developing some instincts. Now those instincts were telling him this was some kind of trap. Every nerve in his body was shrieking. But Creed kept climbing down from the armoured car. He kept telling himself that the computer would automatically blast any dog that came near. He would be perfectly safe.

'Sure,' muttered Creed, a cold feeling growing in the pit of his stomach. He hit the ground and began to run. His blunt shadow bobbed ahead of him in the brilliant moonlight as he sprinted across the concrete.

He reached the stewardess and crouched beside her. She was lying face down on the podium, motionless. He touched the stained shoulder of her tunic and there was so little response he wondered for a moment if she was dead. Then he felt a weary shifting of muscles under his hand. The stewardess's head moved slightly, as if she wanted to lift it but was too exhausted. He reached under the tangle of long dark hair, gleaming in the moonlight, and cleared it from her face.

Up close the bruises and cuts looked much worse. Her eyes were squeezed shut as much by the damage to her face as by exhaustion. Her mouth was cut, the lips swollen.

Creed lifted her shoulders off the ground, rolling her at the same time, so her face lifted from the concrete. Her muscle tone was so slack it was like shifting a sack of potatoes. But as he turned her over she moved a little, settling into his arms like a sleepy child.

Creed held her with one arm. With his free hand he ripped open the velcro flap of the first-aid kit and shook its contents out. Fat wads of dressings. Rattling plastic containers full of pills. Glistening hypodermic ampoules. Creed fumbled with the ampoules, trying to read over the stewardess's shoulder in the moonlight. He managed to select one containing morphine.

He wondered what other medication he should give her immediately and what could wait until they were safely inside the armoured car. Definitely give her the morphine now. And some benzedrene. He was unwrapping the sterile seals from the ampoules when the stewardess opened one dark swollen eyelid to reveal a gleaming crescent of eye.

She looked at him for a moment, then opened her mouth.

'Roy?' she said. Her voice was thick, clotted with pain and fatigue.

'No, honey, it's me,' said Creed gently.

She didn't seem to hear his words. Or perhaps her mind was in some place where she couldn't understand them.

'Roy,' she said again. Her voice was clearing and you could detect the tone of it now, pick up the emotion behind it. The stewardess sounded sad.

'All the blue glass is broken,' she said.

Creed later thought it was as if her voice was a signal, because no sooner had she spoken than all hell broke loose.

Creed wasn't paying much attention to anything except the injured woman in his arms. He was listening but he wasn't watching his surroundings. He knew the defence system on the armoured car would spot anything that looked like a dog and scythe it down with machine-gun fire. So he let himself get careless; allowed all his attention to focus on the woman in his arms.

As he injected her, first with the morphine then with an ampoule of benzedrene, Creed was staring down into her face. The stewardess's skin was pale in the moonlight. The first warning he had of the thing's arrival was an inky patch of shadow falling across that pale skin.

Creed looked up and saw something that had come wobbling out of a nightmare. In fact, it was so preposterous it looked almost comical.

The flood of terror that hit Creed had nothing to do with the thing itself. It was the implication of the thing.

Creed let the stewardess slump out of his grasp as the thing reared towards him. The implication was intelligence, he thought. The stewardess's head slumped against his knee as he rose to his feet. Intelligence on the part of the enemy. Creed stood up slowly so the stewardess would hit the ground gently. The empty ampoules crunched under foot as he stood up to confront the approach of the enemy.

An enemy intelligent enough to know the armoured car would fire automatically on anything that looked like a dog.

Creed raised his gun. The thing was almost on top of him now. It certainly didn't look like a dog. It looked like a Heironymous Bosch creation, an obscene insult to nature.

It moved shakily because it wasn't one dog. It was two. The bottom of the thing was a Great Dane, a specimen so large it was probably at the limit of the armoured car's ability to recognize a dog. It moved slowly and painfully, blood flowing down its lean shoulders and flanks towards its paws. A trail of blood followed it as it closed in on Creed, staggering silently towards him, shaking. It was shaking with effort, because of the load it carried on its back.

Balanced there was a Bull Terrier, a brutal-looking, bullet-headed dog. The terrier was riding on the back of the larger animal. Blood flowed down from its firmly planted paws.

But it was the Great Dane's blood. Creed realized that wounds had been deliberately torn in the larger dog, chunks of his flesh bitten away so that the terrier could plant his feet deep in the wounds and ride more securely.

With the terrier on its back, the Great Dane was far too large and entirely the wrong shape to activate the computer in the armoured car. It had crossed the podium without a shot being fired, silently stealing up on Creed.

'Nice try guys,' said Creed. 'But no cigar.' His voice was steady; his fear was gone now. It was just one more situation to deal with, so he dealt with it.

Creed thumbed the safety off the automatic pistol, aimed and fired. He'd decided to deal with the Great Dane first; get rid of the larger animal and therefore the larger threat. It was a bad mistake.

The Great Dane was wounded and exhausted. But the terrier was fresh and ready for combat. As soon as Creed fired, it launched itself off the shoulders of the larger dog. The Great Dane went down, finished, but the terrier was in mid-air and before Creed could take aim it had crashed into him at chest level, knocking him off his feet.

With shocking swiftness the blunt head of the dog was stabbing forward, nuzzling between his shoulder and neck, like an obscene lover seeking a kiss. He felt its damp ticklish fur and the hot beating of its breath as it opened its jaws, fangs going for his jugular. Going for the kill.

Creed brought up one arm to block the move and jabbed his gun hand at the thing. He was hoping he would get the gun between those slicing jaws and blow the dog's head off.

He was half right.

The gun went between the dog's jaws, but at the wrong angle. The barrel jutted out of the other side of its mouth so, when Creed fired, the bullet went flying off harmlessly into the distance.

Then the dog's teeth clamped down on the gun and it snapped its head back, tearing the weapon from his hand. A second snap of the head and it sent the gun flying through the air to clatter down in the darkness somewhere. Then with an almost inaudible growl that blunt muzzle shot forward again, teeth bared as it stabbed towards Creed's face.

As soon as the dog had bitten down on the gun Creed knew he'd lost it. Even before the terrier tore it from his grasp he had begun to reach out with his other hand. Not towards the dog, but down towards his own foot.

As the dog shook its head and threw the gun away Creed already had his fingers inside his boot, wrapped around the metal haft of the knife he'd concealed there. He was pulling it free as the dog lunged towards him again. Creed rolled away so the dog couldn't get at his face or neck and raised his elbow in a blocking manoeuvre. The powerful jaws closed on his elbow, its six incisors sinking into the muscle of his arm.

The hot spasm of pain gave Creed fighting strength. He drove his free hand upwards. The moonlight made only the faintest ripple on the blue metal of the blade as the knife flashed. The terrier promptly released Creed's elbow and dodged the blade. Creed shifted position to get a second shot but the dog immediately ploughed forward, both front paws hitting his chest so hard it knocked the breath out of him.

He managed to retain his grip on the knife but the terrier was on top of him now, too close to get a decent shot. Its jaws were ripping at his chest, snapping buttons off his camouflaged combat jacket. Creed kept his chin tucked firmly down on his chest so his neck wasn't exposed. The dog darted forward, head at an angle, jagged line of fangs digging at his face in an attempt to take one of his eyes.

Creed twisted his face so the dog could only get at the hard bone of his skull. He felt its teeth score his forehead, slicing open a long flap of skin. Creed savagely butted at the dog, using his head as a weapon. He felt a vicious satisfaction as bone connected with bone; something delicate in the dog's head crunched and gave way. Saliva sprayed everywhere, mixing with blood, both his and the dog's. The terrier backed off, but only for an instant. It shoved his head back towards him and once again Creed forced his chin against his sternum to hide the vulnerable flesh of his throat. He held the knife firmly in one hand and grabbed the dog's head with the other. He needed to pull its head back far enough to reveal the animal's throat. Then, one quick cut and it would all be over.

The terrier was butting at him, chewing at his chin. The thing was trying exactly the same tactic. If it could get Creed's chin up and expose his throat it would be the winner.

Blood was running freely from Creed's scalp wound now, trickling into his eyes. While he could still see what he was doing, Creed stabbed for one of the dog's eyes. But it twisted its narrow skull and the blade slid off a hard ridge of occipital bone. Instantly the dog lunged for his knife hand; Creed pulled it back just in time to avoid those sharp teeth sinking into his wrist. Now the thick blood was running down either side of his nose in quantity, pooling in his eyes.

He blinked but his vision only cleared for an instant. He tried to shake his head but immediately the dog was digging for his throat. He knocked it away and held his head still, locking his chin down again. There was nothing else for it. He kept his head still, let the blood gather in his eyes and continued to fight blind.

He felt the hot rank breath of the dog as it kept twisting in the darkness, hunting for an opening so it could finish him. He groped for the dog's head with his free hand and grabbed it, trying to force it back. He needed to get the knife under its chin, that was the only sure way for a kill. But it was no good. The wound in his arm was telling on him now and he didn't have the strength to force the animal's head back.

Then suddenly, magically, the dog's head began to bend back. It was as if some other force was helping Creed lift it away. He couldn't see what was happening and the terrier seemed to be as puzzled as he was. It gave a bemused little whine as its muzzle was forced upwards. Creed sensed that he had enough of an opening now and he blindly drove the knife upwards, twisting it as it went in.

There was an immediate hot flood of liquid on his fist and down his arm, splashing into his face. The dog shivered and struggled but it was all over now. Creed kicked it off him and the terrier thrashed on the concrete, dying as Creed gouged his knuckles into his eyes, wiping his face clear.

When he got the blood out of his eyes the first thing he saw was the stewardess kneeling over the dead dog and he knew that she had helped him, grabbing the dog's head and forcing it back.

She'd saved his life. The woman turned to look at him; her pupils were pin-points in the moonlight as a result of the morphine. The drugs must have given her enough strength to pull herself together. Luckily for him. Lying sprawled on the concrete the terrier looked pathetically small and helpless in death. She looked at it for a moment then up at Creed.

'Scooter,' she said sadly as if remembering something.

'Whatever you say, darling,' said Creed.

'Perhaps Ms Forrester could show us where she saw the White King?'

'Oh, for God's sake, stop calling me Ms Forrester,' said Roz. 'My name is Roz.'

'Fine. Show me where you saw the White King, Roz.'

Norman Peverell followed Roz out of the sitting room and up the hallway. The stewardess's house was a surreal stage-set which went from war wreckage at one end to domestic normality at the other. They'd entered through the hole in the garden wall, a huge ragged gap fringed with shattered bricks and twisted metal reinforcing rods exposed by the armoured car's brutal entry. They'd picked their way across the desolate garden with its shattered urns and ceramic decorations. Cracks in the concrete had allowed the small pond to drain into the surrounding ground. It was now a bare, plastic lined cavity, dry and smooth, somehow disturbing.

Like an empty eye socket, thought Roz.

They'd come through the garden into the sitting room. Now they were in the hallway that led to the front of the house. They didn't pause by the kitchen. They kept going to the front door. Roz stopped and stood there, fragments of moonlight on her face from the small pebbled window.

'Here?' said Norman Peverell.

'Here.'

'What happened exactly?'

Roz sighed. 'I told you all that in my report.'

'Are you sure you didn't leave anything out?'

'Yes. No. I didn't leave anything out.'

'Forgive me, but this creature, who I might add is so elusive he's almost legendary, has only ever been observed fleetingly and unreliably, from a distance. He has been the subject of special investigation but has never even been photographed. No one has ever got close to him and survived to report it.'

'So?'

'So it seems a little extraordinary that he just casually reveals himself to you.'

Roz shrugged. 'What can I say? He was just sitting out there on the doorstep.'

'Just outside this door?'

'Just outside this door.'

She pulled the front door open to show him. The lock on the door was broken and it opened easily, swinging a little unevenly on its hinges.

Moonlight filled the hallway as she opened the door. It was remarkably intense and Roz's eyes were immediately drawn up towards the big white moon that was riding in the cloudless London sky.

That's why she didn't see it right away.

Norman Peverell was saying, 'It just seems strange that you had such an encounter –'

'A close encounter,' chuckled Redmond. He was coming up behind Norman Peverell, who stood behind Roz. Both of them screened the open front door from Redmond's sight.

'If you like,' said the civil servant. Redmond walked up to stand behind Roz. 'A close encounter. It just seems a little strange that you saw the White King and –'

'Lived to tell the tale,' said Redmond. He chuckled again but the sound died in his throat. He was close enough now to see out of the front door.

To see what Norman Peverell and Roz had already seen.

Outside the front door a narrow footpath led down to the low gate that separated the front garden of the house from the street.

The footpath, the front garden and the whole street were thick with dark shapes. What seemed like a million eyes glittered in the moonlight. And all those eyes were watching them.

Not one of the dogs made a sound. That was the worst thing. Their silence seemed to suggest a frightening level of intelligence and power, massed out there in the night. They were like an army of disciplined soldiers waiting for orders.

Even before Roz recovered from the first shock of recognition she realized that the dogs must have gathered very quickly. They had gathered in great numbers and total silence, moving in coordinated groups like well-drilled troops.

They sat patiently, pressing close to the house in untold numbers. Only where the footpath neared the house did the press of bodies lessen. The pack kept a respectful distance from the front steps.

Sitting on those steps, head angled so he could gaze up at Roz, was the strange white dog.

He waggled his head and bared his long teeth in what looked almost like a smile.

Chapter 27

'I thought I was supposed to see Mr Pangbourne,' said Ricky.

'Excuse me?'

'The announcement over the PA said I was supposed to go to the principal's office.'

'Well, that was what you might technically call a ruse,' said Amy Cowan. She smiled at him over her shoulder as she slipped her key-card through the electronic sensor. The lock on the door clicked open. She swung the door wide and led him into a small office situated across the hall from the school library.

The office was hardly bigger than a broom closet but it had a large window which occupied most of one wall and two comfortable arm-chairs crowded in beside the desk. Amy sat in one of the chairs and gestured for Ricky to take the other one. He settled into it gingerly, holding his books on his lap. They were sitting so close together their knees were almost touching and Ricky had to fight the impulse to stare at her smooth bare legs.

But it was her face that really got to him. There was something faintly familiar about it. Sea-green eyes and a soft mouth. Ricky wanted to see that mouth move, so he started talking.

'What do you mean by a ruse?' he said.

'I couldn't very well send a message over the PA saying "Ricky McIlveen, come to the guidance counsellor's office". Your friends might have wanted an explanation of that.'

'They're going to want an explanation anyway. Everybody starts gossiping when you're called to the principal.'

'Sure,' Amy smiled. 'But even being dragged to the

principal's office doesn't have quite the stigma of seeing the school guidance counsellor.'

'You mean because it's like going to see a shrink?' said Ricky.

'Well, it does have some of the same connotations. Although, of course, we're not fully trained psychiatrists.'

'I guess that's why you don't have a couch in your office,' said Ricky and then he blushed because, sitting in this small room so close to Amy Cowan, there suddenly seemed to be a sexual implication to the remark.

But Amy remained relaxed and friendly. 'What you might call my "shrink" duties, talking to the kids about personal problems and so on, that's only part of my job. I'm also here to give career advice and help students choose a suitable programme of higher education so they can maximize their natural abilities and talents.' She suddenly smiled at him, her eyes flashing. 'Does it sound like I just memorized that this morning?'

'No,' said Ricky. 'Not at all.'

'Well, I did.'

Amy turned and looked out the window. Her blonde hair swayed back and he could see the silver semi-circle of earring piercing the delicate pink flesh of her ear-lobe.

'I'm not really a guidance counsellor. I don't really work at Scopes High School.' She looked back at Ricky, her expression deadly serious now. 'I actually work at the Agency with your dad.'

And then Ricky knew why she looked familiar. He'd seen her on that windswept Sunday morning, standing on the field outside the Agency buildings as his dad rose up into the sky in a helicopter. Standing there staring at his mom, and his mom staring back at Amy with the oddest expression on her face. And now he remembered seeing her on other occasions too; in her yellow car, outside the sports centre, looking for his dad.

'You don't look too surprised,' said Amy.

'I guess I've got a lot on my mind at the moment.' Ricky remembered the note that had been slipped onto his lunch tray. The crumpled piece of paper was now jammed into the pocket of his jeans. 'It would take a lot to surprise me.'

'That's good, because I thought I was slipping. Like maybe

I should wear a badge saying "undercover agent".' Amy was trying to keep the conversation on a light-hearted level but Ricky could see a definite tension in her. He glanced down at the canvas shoulder bag she'd dumped on the floor. Now that he knew Amy worked for the Agency he knew that there was most likely a gun in it. She certainly couldn't be concealing one anywhere else.

'What are you doing here? Is this something my dad set up, for my protection?'

Amy looked relieved. 'That's it exactly,' she said. 'Creed was called away to England on some kind of emergency.'

'Some kind of?' said Ricky. 'That isn't too specific.'

'No, it's not. The Agency doesn't actually know much more than that. We received a distress signal from someone called the Doctor. Does that mean anything to you?'

'No.'

'You're sure you never heard your mom and dad talking about someone called the Doctor? Someone they used to know a long time ago, back when they first met in England?'

'Nope.'

'Well, don't worry. That's a side issue. The main thing is, I'm here to help in case you need anything.' Amy looked at him and Ricky realized that the interview was over.

Then a thought struck him. 'Why is the Agency making such a big deal of this? I mean, Dad's gone away before and they never bothered to give us personal bodyguards or anything.'

Amy looked at him for a moment. It was as if she was trying to decide whether to give him a straight answer.

'Good question. OK, I don't want to worry you or anything, but there does seem to be something going on, and your family are definitely the centre of some kind of attention.'

'What kind of attention?'

'Damn; I've got you worried after all,' said Amy. 'Are you all right?'

Ricky had been all right until she asked if he was all right. Now, to his horror and shame, the pressure of recent events came to a head. Ricky felt a shifting, liquid sensation behind his nose and eyes.

He was going to start crying. Like some snot-nosed little kid. Like a girl, like a sissy.

Ricky reared up from his chair and struggled blindly for the office door. He found the handle and tugged it open, but it was too late.

Amy scrambled out of her chair and put her arms around him, holding him tight, the soft pressure of her breasts against him, the fringe of her blonde hair ticklish against his face.

The smell of her perfume all around him.

'She really is a piece of ass,' said Wolf Leemark.

'So what's the plan?' asked Wally Saddler.

'Well, she's the guidance counsellor, right? So I go to her and get some guidance counselling.'

'Good plan.' Wally kept any hint of irony out of his voice.

'Like, I tell her all about my personal problems,' continued Wolf.

'Very good.'

'And she takes notes, crossing her legs and I get to look up her skirt and maybe see her beaver. That's phase one of the plan, anyway.'

'Sounds fine,' said Wally Saddler. They were walking back along the corridor that led from the lunch-room towards the school library. 'You going to pretend to be schizophrenic, or are you in two minds about it?'

A couple of members of the Wolf Pack laughed as they followed Wolf and Wally down the corridor. They got the joke. Most of the others didn't get it, but they laughed anyway, eager to be part of the group. Wolf didn't laugh. Wally figured that he got it, but the Wolf didn't like to laugh at any joke unless he told it himself. He continued talking, all serious.

'Listen, Wally. With my record I'm not going to have to pretend at all.'

Wally Saddler remained respectfully silent. He knew better than to interrupt Wolf when he was talking about his past.

'All I'm going to have to do is mention my family history and I'll be in there. Amy Cowan's going to start taking notes –'

'That's her name, huh?' said one of the Wolf Pack.

'What?' said Wolf. He stopped walking and turned around to face the boy who'd spoken, a new kid who'd just arrived at Scopes High this year. It was easy to see that Wolf's chain of thought had been disrupted and that this pissed him off.

Wolf shrugged his shoulders in his leather jacket, a gesture of impatience and imminent anger rather than uncertainty. It was as if he was limbering up for a fight, which indeed, quite often, he was. Wally had seen this mannerism of Wolf's countless times. It caused the wolf on the back of his jacket to twitch in an interesting way, as if the painted wolf was eager for blood, too.

Wolf stood staring at the new boy. The new boy began to sweat under his gaze. He obviously wished he'd never spoken; he just wanted Wolf to stop looking at him. But Wolf was waiting for an answer. When the boy finally replied it was in a frightened, tongue-tied voice.

'I just said, that's her name, huh?'

Still Wolf said nothing; still he stood there waiting.

'I mean,' said the kid, almost stuttering with fear now, 'you said Amy Cowan and, uh, I mean, is that her name or what?'

Wolf stood there, looking at him, silent. The kid realized to his terror that he wasn't off the hook yet. He kept on stuttering.

'I mean, the guidance counsellor, that's her name, right? The real piece of ass you –'

'Watch your mouth,' hissed Wolf.

'Sorry. Hey, I apologize. I don't know what I said. I just said what you said. I didn't mean nothing. You just said she was a piece of –'

'Don't you refer to Ms Cowan in that way,' said Wolf, deadly quiet and very dangerous now. Wally began to tense up, expecting Wolf to challenge the kid to a fight.

But instead Wolf just said, 'Keep a clean tongue in that dirty mouth of yours when you talk about Ms Cowan.' He turned away again, shrugging his big shoulders inside his leather jacket as if it wasn't quite large enough for him.

Wolf started walking down the corridor again and Wally and the others all followed.

The Pack was unusually silent as they strolled through their domain. It was a tense kind of silence and Wally decided to ease it with some light-hearted kidding. 'So, Wolf, you nervous? I mean, we're almost at the shrink's office.'

Wolf grunted a monosyllable.

Wally persisted. 'You just going to go up and knock on her door?'

'Yeah.'

'Then what? How are you going to break the ice? Give her some sexy answers to her ink-blot tests? "And what does this one look like, Wolf?" "Another gaping vagina, ma'am".'

'No,' said Wolf curtly. 'I figured I'd tell her about my father.'

Wally Saddler could have bitten his tongue. This was out of the frying pan into the fire. When Wolf got started about his old man there was no telling what he might do. Wally abandoned the idea of light-hearted kidding and let the tense silence return as they walked down the corridor, past the entrance to the gym, and turned the corner that led to the library.

Just past the library was Amy Cowan's office. And Amy was standing there, in the doorway. Wally hadn't got a good look at her before. Now his first reaction was a warm horny approval; from what he could see, she was every bit as attractive as Wolf had said.

His second reaction was shock. Because Amy was standing there hugging a man.

No, it wasn't a man. It was just a kid. Worse than that, it was that geeky kid from the lunch-room, the one Wally had spotted eyeing up the suntanned girl. The arrogant little bastard who had gone strutting out when he was called to the principal's office. Marching out of the lunch-room like he didn't know the meaning of fear. Like he owned the place.

Now here he was, in the arms of this hot gorgeous blonde. Wally stopped dead with surprise, as did the rest of the Wolf Pack. Wally knew it was dangerous, but after a second he risked a look at Wolf. He couldn't resist it. He had to know how he was reacting.

The expression on Wolf's face was priceless. Wally would have laughed out loud, except he knew he'd be endangering his life.

Wolf stared at the woman hugging the boy. His face showed an emotion that seemed utterly alien; Wolf's normal expressions seldom varied from arrogance and rage. But now he looked like an aggrieved infant. The way a baby might look if you whipped its bottle away while it was in the middle of sucking on it. Wolf just couldn't believe that life was doing this to him. The shock was total. You could see him forcing himself to piece his thoughts back together, like a jigsaw somebody had scrambled.

Wally had to admit that Wolf recovered pretty fast. He started walking again, moving quickly, swinging his long arms and legs in the rolling arrogant stride that was his trademark. His face composed itself again into an aloof, superior mask. The members of the Wolf Pack scrambled to catch up with him as he marched past the library and past Amy Cowan's office without even slowing down, as if he had never had any intention of stopping there.

But Wally was walking beside him and he saw the look on Wolf's face as he walked past Amy Cowan and the kid she was hugging. Wolf shot a look of pure venom at the kid. The kid didn't even see it; his head was buried in Amy's shoulder. Nose in her tits, no doubt, thought Wally Saddler with a pang of envy.

But Amy didn't miss Wolf's glance and she shot a look back at him, one of undiluted anger. Like she resented Wolf's intrusion at this highly personal moment.

For the second time in a minute Wally repressed the dangerous urge to laugh at Wolf. If his big buddy wanted to score with Amy Cowan he'd got started on completely the wrong foot.

Good luck, Wolf.

As they walked to the next corner and wheeled around it, walking fast to keep up with Wolf, Wally realized that their fearless leader was muttering something under his breath. As soon as they were around the corner Wolf spun around and faced them, his muttering turning into full volume speech.

'He's dead,' said Wolf. His voice was surprisingly cool and controlled. Wally knew that this was Wolf at his most dangerous, but he said nothing.

'He's dead,' repeated Wolf. Wally still didn't reply and neither did any of the other members of the Wolf Pack. Like Wally they were staring over Wolf's shoulder. Wolf didn't notice. He was too caught up in his icy fury.

'I'm going to kill him,' said Wolf simply. 'I'm going to kill the little prick.'

'Which little prick is that?'

Wolf spun around at the unexpected sound of the voice, and he saw what the others had already seen.

Mr Pangbourne was standing there behind him.

'Beg your pardon, sir?' said Wally, coming to the rescue. You could always count on Wally Saddler when you needed to pull the wool over the eyes over some dumb adult.

But Mr Pangbourne wasn't buying it.

He stood there facing the Wolf Pack and under his withering gaze the most dangerous individuals in Scopes High School suddenly began to feel like a bunch of dumb children.

They might scare the other kids but Pangbourne was way beyond the reach of their intimidation. There was a lean country toughness about the old man, a deep seen-everything cynicism. The principal frowned at them like he had found something unpleasant on the sidewalk.

'You said something about little pricks. A more vulgar and low-minded person might make the insulting observation that the only ones of those around here are likely to be inside your pants,' he said quietly. 'Now get to your class.'

As he said these words the bell rang, marking the first lesson of the afternoon. It went off as if Pangbourne had signalled it. Wally guessed that the principal had deliberately contrived the coincidence. The old bastard was clever that way. But the other members of the Wolf Pack reacted like a bunch of superstitious natives. They virtually scuttled away towards their classrooms. But Wally wasn't fooled.

And neither was Wolf.

He remained standing there in the corridor, looking at the old man defiantly. Finally he turned on his heel and began to saunter off casually, his every move an insult and a provocation.

But Pangbourne was way ahead of him. He spoiled Wolf's exit by calling him back.

'Just a minute, son.'

His firm voice didn't allow the possibility of disobedience and Wolf froze, then reluctantly wandered back.

'Wolf,' said the principal, 'there's something you ought to know.' Wally Saddler noticed that the old man didn't use Wolf's proper name, the way some of the other teachers did. Wolf hated being called Christian and the teachers often used this as a petty form of punishment. But Pangbourne never resorted to this tactic, and to Wally this was another example of the man's cleverness.

'Wolf, your father's coming to see me. He called this morning to arrange an appointment.'

Wally saw the flicker of surprise on Wolf's face before it was quickly concealed. 'So what?' said Wolf, his face a blank, arrogant mask again.

'So, I thought you might know what it's all about.'

Wolf faked a yawn. 'Nope.'

'You're sure?'

'If you want to know what it's all about, ask him.'

'I intend to,' said Mr Pangbourne. 'Anyhow, Wolf, I thought you'd better know he was coming in.'

Wolf shrugged as if he had no idea what Pangbourne was talking about. As if the man was senile. But Wally knew that Pangbourne was right, and that he was doing Wolf a favour. If Wolf's old man was on the warpath again, all kinds of shit could hit the fan. And some of it might end up on Wolf. Wally knew that for all his pretence of indifference and tough-guy cool, Wolf was just a frightened child where his father was concerned.

You'd never guess this from the insolent way the kid moved, though. Pangbourne watched Wolf swagger off, then he turned to look at Wally. 'What's the matter, Saddler? You decided that you're exempt from classes?'

'No sir,' whined Wally. 'But I've got this terrible headache. I think it's a migraine, sir. Can I go see the nurse and get something for it? I'm going to need some medication quick or I'm going to be seeing zig-zags and stumbling all over the place.'

'Don't yank my chain, Saddler. Migraine is a fascinating psychological affliction. You're not a sufficiently interesting individual to suffer from it.'

'That's a terrible thing to say, sir.'

'And anyhow, I've seen your medical record. You're as fit as a slave-trader's mule. Now get to your class or you're looking at a week of detention.'

Wally scooted off after Wolf, wondering if the old bastard was really familiar with his medical record. Weren't those things supposed to be confidential?

He caught up with Wolf just as he was striding up the staircase and on to the second floor. They walked into their next lesson together. The teacher was busy at the front of the room, drawing something on the board, his saffron robes flopping around his arms as he drew. His back was to the class and some of the kids were fooling around at their desks. The fooling around stopped the instant that Wolf walked in. If there was any undisciplined behaviour in Wolf's classes it was at his discretion. Otherwise, the kids would suffer punishments that scared them more than anything the teachers could ever dish out.

So, as Wolf walked in with Wally at his side, all the kids' faces swivelled anxiously towards him, seeking to gauge his mood and get his approval. All the faces except one.

The kids in the classroom relaxed. Because Wolf suddenly had a huge happy grin on his face. And Wally knew the reason why.

It was because of the one kid who hadn't looked up as they marched in. A dumb kid who sat looking at a text-book, absorbed in it.

The kid from the corridor. The kid from the lunch-room. The one who'd been hugging Amy Cowan. He must have come up the stairs on the other side of the library while they'd been busy with Mr Pangbourne.

Wolf looked at the kid and smiled.

Outside in the school parking lot Wolf's father was steering his old Chevrolet into a parking space. The first couple of times the car didn't go in right. Francis Leemark liked to get his vehicle neatly between the painted lines, so he kept backing out and steering in until he got it just right.

The process seemed to take a long time, and the longer it took the angrier the old man became.

Finally he was satisfied, and switched off the engine. In the sudden silence and brilliant sunlight, the heat seemed to close in on him in the car. Along with the heat he felt his rage brewing in him, steady and powerful.

They said there was a storm coming and when it broke it would clear the air. Francis Leemark hoped so.

He popped the glove compartment to make sure his gun was still in there.

It was, still snug in its regulation army holster. He closed the glove compartment again, feeling better about things. The rage was still there and the afternoon heat enwrapped him like a physical presence, but he felt better.

It was good to know there was a gun handy. A man never knew when he might need one.

Francis Leemark locked the car and went into the school.

Chapter 28

'Careful,' said the Doctor. 'Stand back.'

Benny moved away from the billiard table as the Doctor prepared the syringe.

The library was silent now; the chugging of the pump in the kitchen downstairs had ceased and the last of the liquid had been drained from the tall, glass cylinder.

Jack lay on top of the billiard table, sprawled out like a strange beached sea creature. The tarpaulin had been unrolled and spread underneath him to protect the green felt on the antique table. Small droplets of the liquid were scattered across the tarpaulin. It was gelid and slow to evaporate. Benny stared at the naked body, trying to stop her eyes fixing on the shrivelled tangle of Jack's genitals.

It had been a considerable struggle to get him out of the cylinder and on to the table. Somehow the Doctor had managed it without getting too dishevelled but Benny knew she was looking a wreck.

'Messy business,' said the Doctor sympathetically. 'Ace found that out when she had to revive someone from a life-support tank.'

Benny sniffed at the oily gunk which had soaked into her shirt. Definitely smelled like petrol and fennel, she thought. 'How did Ace manage it without ruining her entire wardrobe?'

'I believe she got undressed. And in any case, Ace never worried too much about her wardrobe.' The Doctor frowned thoughtfully. 'In fact, that was Vincent she was reviving. He seemed to spend half his existence in life-support tanks. Vincent, and now Jack.' He looked down at the body on the billiard table, green fluid slowly draining from it. 'Odd how patterns weave themselves. Vincent and Justine and Creed. Jack and Shell.'

The Doctor leant over the billiard table and injected Jack with the adrenaline. For a moment nothing happened, and then the man on the table abruptly spread his fingers, splaying them out in a convulsive, spastic fashion. Benny looked down and saw that his toes were curling too, the arch of his foot straining back painfully. After a moment the spasm subsided and Jack lay still again.

'Excellent,' said the Doctor.

'Is that it?' said Benny, who'd been expecting Jack to at least open his eyes.

'Don't you notice anything?'

Benny looked at the body on the billiard table. The naked man was lying sprawled and quite motionless except for the slight rise and fall of his chest. 'No,' she said.

'Look again.'

Benny scrutinized the man and found her eyes returning again and again to the shaggy mat of damp copper hair on his chest, and the tiny subtle movements as he breathed in and out.

Then she got it. 'He's breathing again.'

'He never really stopped. Or, at least, there was always some low level of respiration continuing while he was in the tank. But now, yes, he's breathing properly again. Breathing air.'

'So when will he wake up?'

'Oh, I'm afraid he has some way to go yet,' said the Doctor. He had half turned away from Benny and he was taking something out of his pocket.

'What's that?'

'Oh, nothing.' The Doctor turned to her and showed her the battered gold pocket-watch he was holding. 'Just checking on the time.' But he made no move to open the watch. Instead, he bent over and picked up the silver tray which he had perched on top of a pile of books. On it was the ham sandwich, the bottle of brandy and the air-pistol. 'You know, this may take longer than I expected.' He offered the tray to Benny.

'No thanks. I don't need a gun.'

The Doctor smiled. 'You really ought to eat this sandwich before it gets stale. I can make another one for Jack when he revives. And why not have a drop of Armagnac, too? You've earned it.'

'Don't try to distract me.' Benny ignored the tray. 'You're up to something. I can tell by the furtive way you were fishing around in your pocket.'

The Doctor shrugged forlornly and set the tray aside. 'Why is it that I have no gift for deception?'

'Don't come that with me, Doctor. Some would say that you're the prince of deception. Now let's see what you've really got hidden in your pocket.'

'It's not in my pocket, actually. It's hidden in here.' The Doctor pressed the fob on the gold watch and its lid clicked neatly open. 'I just wasn't sure how you would react to it.' He held the watch for Benny's inspection. Inside, pressed against its glass face, was a small, white tablet. There was nothing printed on it to disclose its identity but Benny knew exactly what the tablet was.

'Warlock,' she said.

'I'm afraid so. I know you had some disquieting experiences with this substance so I wasn't sure you'd welcome its presence.'

Benny could smell the heavy liquorice odour of the drug. Now that the pocket-watch was open the smell from the pill seemed to be filling the room. It brought back a rapid stream of memories. The apartment of the Mayan brothers in New York and a long afternoon of drinking and drugs as grey storm clouds had rolled across the sky outside. Creed had been there and they had all taken warlock. The drug had come into the room, into their minds like a living presence. It had presided over the strange seance during which a man had died.

Benny had watched him die and hadn't lifted a finger to help.

'It's all right,' she said. 'I'm just a little surprised. I didn't think you had any of the stuff. I didn't even know it still existed.'

Benny sniffed at the fumes from the life-support fluid that clung to her clothing. She realized she had made a mistake earlier. It wasn't fennel at all; it was the same oily cloying liquorice odour that emanated from the pill. Jack was steeped in the stuff. 'What did you do, put it in the tank with him?' Benny had an absurd vision of the Doctor sneaking into the library at night, taking the lid off the cylinder and sprinkling warlock into it as if he was feeding fish.

'No,' said the Doctor. 'That smell is just the residue of the drug in Jack's body.'

'After all these years?'

'Yes, you might say that warlock and Jack have been existing in symbiosis in the life-support tank. They've shared the long vigil together.'

'You mean it's been renewing itself in his body?'

'Sustaining itself, shall we say. But now he's in need of a booster dose.' The Doctor poured a glass of brandy then he took the white pill out of his watch and crushed it between his fingers, letting the coarse white powder sift down into the glass. Benny noticed that he was careful to wipe his fingers afterwards, using a handkerchief which he then wadded and discarded in a waste-paper basket. The liquorice smell in the room became much more intense after he crushed the pill. Benny felt herself becoming light-headed.

'Could you help me, please?' The Doctor gestured for Benny to join him at the end of the billiard table. She shook her head and made herself concentrate.

'What do you want me to do?'

'Just tilt his head up for a moment.'

Benny took Jack's heavy sleeping head in her hands and gently lifted it, her fingers deep in his damp unkempt hair. The petroleum smell of the life-support fluid was quite overwhelmed by the liquorice-reek of warlock. As she held his head the Doctor raised the brandy glass to his lips and carefully poured the contents between Jack's half-open lips. The redhaired man swallowed reflexively and as the last of the spiked brandy disappeared the smell in the room eased somewhat. But Benny didn't find the sudden change reassuring. It was as if the warlock had merely gone into hiding, taking up residence in Jack's body.

She lowered his head back down on to the billiard table, staring down into the pale face. Did it look somehow different now? Was there a hint of pink in his cheeks and pale lips that hadn't been there before?

There was definitely a change. She couldn't quite define what it was but the blank helpless expression seemed to be gone. Instead of that unformed, unborn look he now had the aspect of a man who was merely sleeping. Or maybe not even sleeping.

Maybe just pretending to be asleep.

Benny slid her fingers out of his hair, slowly, as if she was afraid she might disturb him. 'Are you sure we're not getting in over our heads here?'

'No,' said the Doctor. He picked up the air-pistol from the silver tray and handed it to Benny. 'Would you just keep an eye on him for me?'

'Where are you going?'

'I need to go and find a few essential items. It won't take long but I also need to get a vehicle from the garage.'

'A vehicle? Why?'

'We're all going for a little ride,' said the Doctor.

Chapter 29

Creed was searching the armoured car for the first-aid kit when the radio came to life. The stewardess was settled in the navigator's chair and she looked like she might fall asleep at any moment. Creed wanted to clean her wounds properly while she was still awake to cooperate.

But just as he'd found the medical locker a voice came over the ceiling speaker, causing them both to jump.

'Creed. Are you there? Over.'

It was Roz's voice, speaking in a low urgent hiss.

He sat down at the communications console and responded.

'Creed here. Are you all right?'

'Jesus. Where were you?'

'It's a long story, over.'

'Are you still in one piece?'

'Just about.'

'Is the armoured car operational?'

'Yes.'

'Then get over here. Right away.'

'Where are you exactly?' said Creed. The tension in Roz's voice was affecting him. His pulse-rate was climbing and the fatigue of a moment earlier had disappeared. Creed was ready for a fight.

'Do you know how to follow my radio signal? I'll transmit continuously.'

'Is that Roz?' said the stewardess, rising sleepily from her seat and coming forward.

'Who's that?' said Roz sharply. 'Did I hear someone with you?'

Creed shrugged and passed the microphone to the stewardess. 'Roz, it's me, Jessica,' she said.

There was a moment's shocked silence and then Roz said, 'Jessica?'

'Yes. It's me. I'm still alive, thanks to your friend.'

There was another pause and then Roz's voice came back, business-like again. 'Well, then you can show Creed where to go Jessica. We're upstairs in your house. Can you do that?'

'Sure.'

Creed was already in the driver's seat, starting the big vehicle. The engines came to life with a grumbling roar that rattled the armour around them.

'Come on up and sit beside me, honey,' he called, looking back at the stewardess, grinning.

'I'll drive you home.'

Roz kept thinking she could hear rain. But the constant hissing sound outside came from dried autumn leaves blowing around the empty concrete roadways of the housing estate, circulating in a steady night breeze.

Redmond was staring out of the bedroom window, holding his gun. 'They haven't moved,' he said. Roz came and looked; down below the ruined garden was still thick with dogs. They lay among the rubble, indistinct shapes in the darkness, silent and patient.

'What about the White King?' said Norman Peverell. He was pacing back and forth in the narrow confines of the room, occasionally sitting down on the bed that they'd jammed against the door, then after a moment rising and continuing his pacing.

He was driving Roz crazy with his constant movement. 'Are you all right, Norman?' she said, perhaps with rather more edge to her voice than she'd intended.

'Yes, perfectly all right,' said the civil servant without even attempting to sound sincere.

'Of course he's not,' said Redmond, still peering out of the window. 'He's dying to go to the loo.'

'He's what?' said Roz.

'Look at him,' Redmond nodded. 'He's dying for a slash. It's perfectly all right, Norman. It's perfectly normal.'

Roz turned to look at Norman Peverell and by the exquisitely embarrassed expression on his face she knew that Redmond was right.

'Especially in a combat situation like this,' Redmond was saying. 'Everybody's bladder goes funny. And this is your first time. There's nothing to be ashamed of. In fact, I'd say you've done very well so far. Wouldn't you say that, Roz?'

Roz just grinned. The thing she liked about Redmond was that you could count on him when things got rough; but when the pressure was off he could relax. And somehow he managed to make you relax, too. The end result was that when the fighting started again you were better able to cope with it. Constant stress was a killer, and Redmond prevented it setting in.

Now he stepped away from the window. 'You could go out there, if you like,' he said. 'Do it out there, I mean. Through there.' He jerked his thumb towards the window.

Norman Peverell was sitting down on the bed again, nervously tapping his feet on the floor, looking like a man who wished he was anywhere else in the world but here.

'I'm fine. I just wish you'd stop talking about it,' he said.

'We won't look, you know. I promise. And I'll make sure that Roz won't look. God knows what kind of loose morals that girl possesses.'

'I know you're trying to help,' said Norman Peverell.

Roz grinned at him. 'He's right, I won't look.'

'I know you're both trying to help, to cheer me up, but I wish you'd just drop the subject.'

'It's not going to go away,' said Redmond. 'Well, maybe it will go away for a little while but it's going to be worse when it comes back.'

'Go on,' urged Roz. 'He's right.'

'Look,' exploded Norman Peverell, 'I am not going to . . . do anything out of the window. All right?'

'Suit yourself,' said Redmond, 'but the only other option is to go out there.' He pointed his gun at the barricaded bedroom door. 'You could run along the hallway to the loo, but I doubt if you'd live long enough to get there.'

Roz silently agreed with him. She thought of their battle to get up the stairs.

She'd swung the front door open and her heart had seemed to stop for a moment. The White King had been sitting there on the steps, looking up at her with that strange smile and then he'd given some kind of signal; Roz didn't know what, but there must have been a signal, because all at once the massed force of dogs came surging in from the darkness, in through the broken kitchen window, through the shattered front door. They came flowing past the White King as he sat watching calmly, like a general observing his troops go into battle.

Roz realized later that what she should have done was shoot the White King. Kill him and perhaps the attack would have ended then and there.

There was no doubt in her mind that the White King was the leader of the pack. That somehow he was responsible for this whole nightmare. He certainly was something more than an ordinary dog, although she couldn't imagine what.

She didn't know what he was and she didn't care. Leave speculations about mysteries to the likes of the Doctor. Roz had no time for theories. She was hard-headed and practical. The Doctor would probably be fascinated by the White King and want to study him, measure him, maybe run an experiment. Extend the frontiers of knowledge. Not Roz. She just wanted to put a bullet in the White King's head and see what effect that had on the pack. That was her idea of a useful experiment.

She was willing to bet one well aimed bullet like that would instantly cause the pack to lose its discipline and order, send it falling back into chaos. Perhaps the dogs would begin tearing into each other, forgetting all about their common enemy.

She told Redmond that and he'd smiled and said, 'That's what they used to say about my country. They used to say we'd turn into savages if the foreign military pulled out.' But he agreed with Roz. The only thing he disagreed about was that he wanted to be the one to shoot the White King.

But they both missed their chance. They didn't even give it any thought at the time. Their only concern had been survival, as wave after wave of savage animals launched themselves into the hallway of the small house. They must have fired five-hundred rounds between them, the muzzle flashes of their automatic weapons lighting up the narrow hallway and staircase in bursts of flickering white light. They'd moved cautiously and calmly, making a slow retreat from the front door, up the stairs, along the upstairs hall and finally into the bedroom.

They'd pushed Norman Peverell along ahead of them, into

the safety of the room, slammed the door and shoved the bed against it.

After a while the frantic barking in the hallway had stopped.

'I really think you ought to use the window,' said Redmond.

'For the last time, no,' said Norman Peverell. 'As I told you, I'm fine.'

Redmond sighed, drawing the curtains aside. 'Shame,' he said, staring down at the silent masses in the dark garden.

'I was rather looking forward to the spectacle of you peeing on the enemy.' He glanced at Norman. 'You're sure you wouldn't like to?'

'Absolutely certain, thank you.'

'Ah well,' said Redmond, 'might as well do this then.' As he spoke he swept the curtains aside and opened the window.

'What are you doing?' said Roz. She hurried over to Redmond as he climbed on to the window-sill and stepped out of the window.

'Where are you going?' she hissed. Redmond smiled at her and ignored the question. She leant out of the window as he moved further away, feet searching carefully for the narrow outside edge of the window-sill. His hands were above him, out of sight. He winked down at Roz.

'It's perfectly safe,' he said. 'I've got my hands on the gutter. Runs along the edge of the roof.'

'For God's sake, Redmond. Get back inside.' In the garden below Roz could see the dogs. They were on their feet now, milling around excitedly. They were all staring up at Redmond, eager and silent, watching his every move. Waiting for him to slip. She leant further out. 'Get back before you break your neck.'

'You have so little faith in me it hurts.' Redmond's voice sounded distracted. He was preoccupied with finding handholds and footholds in the darkness. Roz looked up at the dark lip of the roof. He was inching along it, hands busy in the shadows. The aluminium guttering made a squealing, wrenching sound as it took his weight and Roz's stomach turned over.

'Don't do it. It won't hold you.'

'You're speaking to a man who climbed into more than

one room in Fort William Catholic Girls' School when he was young,' said Redmond. 'This is nothing.'

'Come back. I'll give you a hand.'

'Nonsense. I'm going up on to the roof. To look around a little.'

'Creed will be here any minute with the armoured car.'

'I suppose I just can't wait,' said Redmond apologetically.

And before Roz could stop him he was gone, climbing effortlessly up out of sight. She swore and pulled her head back into the bedroom.

Norman Peverell was staring at her.

'I don't know if I can wait, either,' he said miserably.

But Roz wasn't listening to him. A thought had suddenly occurred to her. 'Norman, you're familiar with the floor-plans of the houses on this estate aren't you?'

Norman Peverell nodded sadly.

'And this house shares a common roof with its neighhours on either side, doesn't it?'

'You're just trying to distract me. That's terribly kind of you, but –'

'Doesn't it?' snapped Roz. Norman Peverell blinked in surprise, his bladder forgotten for a moment.

'Yes,' he said. 'But why do you ask?'

Roz had crossed back to the window now and she was peering out. 'And those houses have both been evacuated.'

'Yes.'

'So there's nothing to stop the dogs getting into them and up on to the roof somehow?'

'Oh, my God,' said Norman Peverell.

But Roz was already climbing out of the window and up on to the drain-pipe, following Redmond.

Chapter 30

Comparative Anthropology, thought Wally Saddler, wasn't really a very good description for what this class was all about. As a matter of fact, it was kind of interesting. Some of it even chimed in with a few observations Wally had made through hanging around with Wolf.

Not that Wolf would have noticed. All his attention was fixed on the kid who sat in the first row, Ricky McIlveen.

All of Ricky's attention was on the teacher. Their teacher was the Buddhist monk, the shaven-headed freak who called himself the Young Master. He wandered down the aisle between the desks, his saffron robes flapping loosely around him, his flip-flops softly slapping the floor. He seemed lost in concentration, absent-mindedly rubbing one hand across the smooth contours of his shaved scalp. Several of the girls watched him with fascination, obviously taken with his exotic appearance.

'One of the first topics we'll address in these classes is religion and its importance to different human communities. But religion is a very abstract concept, a cold ideology divorced from the warm flesh and blood of human beings. So we'll focus on the subject of religious leaders such as Christ, Mohammed, and Buddha. When we discuss these remarkable individuals we tend to focus on their doctrines rather than the men themselves. The message rather than the messenger, if you like.'

The Young Master had wandered back to the front of the classroom. Now he gathered his orange robes around himself and perched on the corner of his desk, tucking his long legs under him in the lotus position.

'Now what I propose to do is reverse that emphasis. To set aside the message and talk about the messenger. What kind of men could create whole new belief systems, literally changing the minds of millions of people?'

At the back of the class Wolf Leemark shifted uneasily in his chair. He was beginning to feel distinctly uncomfortable about the direction this lesson was taking. All this talk of religion made him think about his old man. Wolf Leemark didn't like to think about his father. Wolf was virtually a man himself now, tall and strong. All day long he moved through this school where the fear and respect of the kids made him feel even taller and stronger. Most of the time Wolf was full of the pleasure of his life. Most of the time he could forget about his past.

Forget what it had been like to be a frightened child, powerless and utterly at the mercy of others.

At the front of the room, the bald monk was saying, 'In some fundamental sense, the great religious leaders were no different from other great leaders of men. A king, say, or a general.' He smoothed the contours of his silk robe around his folded knees. In the front row of the classroom, two of the girls were trying to see up his robe.

'Obviously a great prophet or a religious leader can make a more enduring or valuable contribution to humanity. A king may at best pass some enlightened laws and improve living conditions for his subjects. A general may at best lead his fellow men to their slaughter, for his own personal glory. But the prophet can, through his teachings, improve the entire human condition. He can lead his fellow men to their salvation.'

In the front row of the classroom one of the girls passed the other girl a note. On it, in back-slanting peacock-blue ink, it said: *'I don't think he's wearing any.'* The second girl blushed a deep scarlet and hid the folded note in her text-book. The young monk kept speaking, caught up in his topic, not paying any attention to them.

'Yet all these men, the great kings, generals and prophets, have in common their ability to inspire others to follow them. To believe in them and follow their commands. In a sense, such men define the reality of their fellow human beings.'

At the back of the classroom Wolf began to relax. The monk was drifting away from the topic of religion and he could ignore him now. He let himself drift off into vivid sexual fantasies about Amy Cowan. Wolf bending over her, Amy not wearing a stitch – but let's leave her shoes on, shall we? – as she lies naked on the desk in her office and Wolf applies himself sweatily to her.

But just as Wolf had begun to relax at the back, at the front of the classroom Ricky had begun to feel deeply uneasy about the direction the Young Master's lesson was taking.

'How can such a thing be?' said the monk. He seemed perfectly relaxed, sitting cross-legged on top of his desk. His composure seemed to make the kids pay attention. There was none of the fidgeting and whispering a novice teacher might expect from a class full of teenagers. 'How can ordinary people surrender control of their own lives? How can they allow someone else to define their beliefs and behaviour?' The monk suddenly swung his long muscular legs off the desk and stood up again. He flowed into motion with the smooth thoughtless grace of the athlete, the girls in the front row watching every move he made.

'Yet all over this huge planet, in wildly different cultures, over thousands of centuries of human development, this pattern emerges again and again. A leader will stand out from the masses. And those masses are willing to follow his lead.' The Young Master frowned thoughtfully, massaging the smooth skin of his forehead. 'It's as if all human beings are programmed with the need to respond to this kind of leadership. It isn't a voluntary thing. It's something built into human nature at a deep, unconscious level. This need, or vulnerability, is a kind of indentation in the behavioural carapace of the human mind. Like the pocket at the corner of a pool table. Only imagine that the pool table is steeply tilted towards that pocket. All you have to do is set a ball on the green felt of the table and it will go rolling straight into that pocket.'

The monk was patrolling the classroom again, wandering up and down the aisles, pausing now and then to make a point. He paused in front of Wally Saddler and Wolf Leemark at the rear of the classroom. Both of the boys were unusually silent. It was almost a respectful silence and it had no small impact on the other kids. If Wally and Wolf didn't dare disrupt this lesson then it must be something important.

Not that the boys were paying attention to the teacher.

Wolf was lost in a detailed sexual revery, concerning the school guidance counsellor, and Wally was simply phased-out with boredom.

The Young Master turned and smiled at the kids all around him. It was kind of a dreamy smile and Wally wondered idly if the guy had been smoking before class. Maybe he'd got high on Nepalese Temple ball or some other fantastic pot he'd brought back with him from some remote mountain fastness. Those Buddhist monks would need something to get them through those long cold winter nights besides the Yak-butter tea.

'The pocket on the pool table is like the human capacity for belief,' said the Young Master. 'The influence of a great leader is like the pool ball rolling inexorably into it.'

He began to walk back towards the front of the classroom again.

'I said before that all human beings had this behavioural indentation, this capacity for blind belief. But I wasn't telling you the truth. Not the whole truth. Most human beings possess this structure in their minds. The vast majority do. But there are a very few rare individuals who are different.'

The monk stopped at the front of the class again but this time he didn't sit on his desk. Instead he remained standing by the front row of kids.

The two girls sitting there were no longer watching his legs. They'd lost interest because a couple of minutes ago they'd begun to grow extremely uncomfortable. Up until that moment they'd both been relaxed and happy. A bit hot and giggly and comfortably horny, safe in the familiar fuzzy warmth of a school classroom with its powerful associations of boredom and security.

But for the last couple of minutes they'd been growing more and more uptight. Neither of them could have explained precisely why. But if you'd asked them they would both have told you that it had something to do with the kid sitting at the end of the row beside them. The new kid. The one called Ricky McIlveen.

Maybe it was something to do with the uncomfortable angle at which his body was twisted around, his torso turned away from them to face the monk. Maybe it was the tense way one hand gripped the side of his neck, like the kid was clutching at himself. His whole posture radiated anxiety. He was staring up at the Young Master, listening intently. It was as if he was terrified at what he was about to hear.

'Those individuals are the ones who set the ball rolling on the pool table. Instead of the need to believe they have the capacity to inspire belief. Instead of a behavioural vulnerability they have a gift for exploiting that vulnerability. We can see the same basic structures operating in animal populations. A single individual who dominates the actions of a whole group. In human beings the effect is more complex but the designation is the same. We call this kind of individual the alpha male.'

Mr Pangbourne stood at the open window of his office, looking out at the school garden he'd nurtured over the long hot summer. The honeysuckle had finally started to thrive and it was growing all over the wooden trellis he'd fixed to the wall around his office window. Pangbourne had cut the wood for the trellis himself, just like he'd drilled the holes in the wall for attaching it. Now, in the late afternoon and early evening, he could open his window and enjoy the rich wafting smell of the honeysuckle.

He'd be able to enjoy it even more if his sense of smell was a little keener. This was one argument for giving up smoking. Indeed, it was about the only argument Pangbourne could think of. He repressed the urge to dig the pack of cigarettes out of his desk drawer and light one. He had a visitor due for an appointment any moment now.

He took one last deep breath of the honeysuckle fragrance and shut the window. The office should have aired out by now, the smell of tobacco dissipated. Pangbourne didn't like to expose his visitors to the unpleasant side-effects of his addiction. Not unless they were old friends or he found himself particularly comfortable with them.

His next visitor didn't fall into either of these categories.

So Pangbourne picked up the heavy glass ash-tray from his desk and emptied it into his waste-paper basket. The ash-tray gleamed in the afternoon sunlight, its sharp angles transformed into prisms. It had been a gift from his third wife, a Swedish academic who had bought it for him from a glassworks near the small town where she'd grown up.

He emptied the ash-tray, taking care that the weightless flakes of ash wouldn't float back up into the room, and he thought about his third wife. Like a lot of Swedes she loved to smoke and it had been cigarettes that had first brought them together. They'd met in the darkness, two tiny bobbing orange flames, as they smoked outside a mutual friend's house during a faculty party. Cigarettes had united them in a world of non-smokers.

The marriage had been long and happy; despite their heavy consumption of tobacco they'd both remained healthy. Pangbourne had fallen into a pattern of believing that if he never worried about their health nothing bad could happen to either of them.

But then a routine scan had shown a dark patch on his wife's lung. The doctor wanted to talk to her about it and she'd raced over to his office in her car. Halfway there some maniac overshot a red light and hit her sideways, spinning her into the path of a big truck. They later told Pangbourne that the first impact would not have been fatal but after the second one there was no chance. She'd died on the way to hospital without recovering consciousness.

The dark patch on the lung scan had turned out to be a false alarm. A software error caused by an inexperienced technician.

In a sense, thought Pangbourne, you could argue that smoking had in fact killed her. If your taste ran to that kind of elaborate, convoluted logic. Pangbourne's taste didn't. For him the whole matter was considerably simpler: she was gone and he still felt a blunt pain every time he thought of her.

He sighed and looked at the heavy ash-tray in his hand. The weight of it seemed to him, for a moment, like the weight of memory. Best to let go of it.

He was putting it back on his desk when the door clicked open and Miss Marcroft's fat face looked into his office.

'He's here,' she said. Her voice had that pinched nasal tone which was a result of trying to speak and hold her breath at the same time. Miss Marcroft didn't want to inhale any of his poisoned carcinogenic air.

Pangbourne found himself smiling as she withdrew and closed the door. He sat down at his desk and glanced at the screen of his computer before switching it off. It wouldn't do to let his visitor see the information about himself that was displayed there.

Francis Anthony Leemark was Wolf Leemark's father. He was, in many ways, a similar man to Pangbourne; a widower, ex-soldier, ex-farmer who had grown up in a primitive agricultural backwater of America. But there all resemblances ended.

Francis Leemark was a religious fanatic of the kind who absorbed the dogma of Christianity without ever learning anything of kindness or forgiveness. He and his wife had beaten and mistreated Wolf on a regular basis until the boy was big enough to fight back.

Pangbourne felt a flicker of distaste which he repressed as the door opened again and his visitor came in. He wanted to maintain an open mind if that was possible. Nothing good would come of meeting this man if he couldn't see out over the parapet of his own prejudices.

But instead of the frail, wizened bigot he was expecting, the man who stepped into Pangbourne's office was young and strong. Far too young to be Wolf Leemark's father.

Pangbourne frowned as he recognized his visitor.

'Mr Retour,' he said.

'Mr Pangbourne,' said the visitor, settling into a chair without being invited.

'This isn't an ideal time. I have an appointment with a parent.'

'I know. I saw him waiting outside.'

Pangbourne felt a flush of anger. 'And you got by my secretary?'

Retour shrugged. 'She just let me in. Perhaps we should attribute it to great personal charm.'

'Perhaps we should attribute it to the fact that you're a bully and an extortionist.' Pangbourne didn't bother trying to stop the rising tide of rage. 'Perhaps we should attribute it to the fact that you work for a secret wing of the government which wields more power than is good in any democracy.' These feelings had been building up for weeks and the words just flowed out of him. 'Perhaps my secretary is as sick of you as I am and feels as helpless as I do. Maybe she's sick and tired of having you walk in here and order us around.'

'Oh, come on,' said Retour. 'We're a little more subtle than that.'

'Yes. You're so subtle your right hand doesn't know what your left is doing. I had a father in here the other day who works for your precious Agency and he didn't even seem aware of the operation you're running in my school.'

Retour smiled. 'Well, you know us cloak-and-dagger types.'

'All I know,' said Pangbourne hotly, 'is that I have members of staff who have been forced on me. How the hell am I supposed to run a school when it's staffed with spies instead of teachers?'

'Don't exaggerate, now. There's just two of us.'

'To my knowledge,' said Pangbourne.

'Don't get paranoid. Besides, I think that I'm a pretty good history teacher. The kids all seem to like me, anyway. And you won't have any complaints about Amy Cowan either.'

'I just want you people out of my hair. Whatever you're up to I know it isn't helping me educate my kids.'

'Well, if it's any consolation we won't be bothering you much longer,' said Retour. 'That's what I came to tell you. It looks like our operation is going to be over sooner than we thought.'

'And how am I supposed to replace two staff members in the middle of a semester?'

'I'm sure that's a problem you won't have to worry about.' The man called Retour smiled and rose from his chair. 'Oh, and by the way, apparently your secretary tried to borrow some books from the library for you.'

'Are you monitoring my reading-matter now?'

'Not at all. I was just going to say that I've got those books. I'm using them in preparing my classes but I'll be finished with them soon and then they're all yours.'

'Thank you kindly,' said Pangbourne with heavy sarcasm.

'Well, I just dropped in to touch base. I'd better let you see your visitor.'

Retour got up and left the office, leaving Pangbourne trying to control his anger. He wanted to achieve some peace of mind before he addressed the problem of Wolf's father. But it was too late. The door swung open again almost immediately and Francis Leemark stepped in.

'Mr Leemark –'

'That's right,' snapped his visitor. He was a fierce little gnome of a man, gnarled and bony. He came in and perched restlessly on the chair in front of Pangbourne's desk as if he might spring out of it at any second. 'Chair's still warm,' he muttered. He rubbed his deeply lined face and stared at the principal with hot dark eyes. He was, if anything, angrier than Pangbourne.

'That's right, Mr Leemark, I just wanted to apologize –'

'Seems to me you've got a lot of apologizing to do. I hope the rest of your afternoon is free because I figure it'll take you that long just to get started.'

Pangbourne bit back the sarcastic retorts that filled his mind. He forced himself to remain civil. 'I was going to say that I apologize for keeping you waiting. My last visitor was an unwanted intrusion. He just barged in here without an appointment.'

The little man stared steadily at Pangbourne. 'Probably another parent unhappy about the way his kid is being treated in this dump. Probably a man who doesn't like the sort of stuff you teach here. If you can call that teaching.'

Pangbourne took a deep breath. 'Well, in any event, I gather that's what you've come about.'

'I've come about my boy.'

Pangbourne nodded. It was hard to believe that a big tall kid like Wolf could have been fathered by this tiny man. Maybe the mother had been tall.

'It can't be easy raising a child on your own,' said Pangbourne, trying to strike up some kind of rapport with the man. The rising mood of hostility in the office wasn't going to benefit anyone.

'Wrong. It's dead simple raising a kid. A man just follows the tenets of the Bible and the principles of a free democracy.'

'There could be a lot of worse starting points,' said Pangbourne. 'I'd certainly agree with you about the free democracy.'

'Dead simple,' repeated the small man. He had that annoying tendency of some old people to simply ignore what you said and plough ahead with their own conversation. Talking to such people was less a dialogue than two monologues which wouldn't connect. 'What makes it not so simple is people at schools teaching godless heresies in an attempt to undermine morality.'

'We're not here to undermine anything, Mr Leemark. Scopes High School specializes in bright kids and problem kids. Some of them, like Wolf, are both.'

'Don't use that name for my son. He's called Christian. Christian Leemark.'

'I can't say it's a name he seems to relish,' said Pangbourne.

'You just shut up and listen,' said the old man squirming angrily in his chair. 'I understand you've got some kind of gook teaching in this school.'

Pangbourne's own anger was barely in control. He could feel the meeting spinning out of control. He forced a smile. 'Well I'm afraid you've been misinformed there. "Gook" is a corruption of a Japanese word for Korean people. And we're not lucky enough to have any Korean teachers on our staff at the moment.'

'Well who's this bald-headed monkey-man you've got working here?'

'The Buddhist monk, you mean?'

'That's right.'

'He's as American as you or I.'

'Speak for yourself. He may be as American as you but he's sure as hell not as American as me, sonny.'

Pangbourne found his artificial smile finally fading from his face.

'Swishing around your school dressed up in a woman's robe,' continued the old man. 'Is he some kind of fairy?'

'You seem to be drifting off the point here,' said Pangbourne. He spoke in a blunt tone of voice, no longer making any attempt to be civil. It was the first sincere thing he'd said since Wolf's father had begun to rave at him, and it seemed to grab the old man's attention.

'Eh?' he said. 'What's that?'

'Well, pappy. I just think you should make your mind up whether you're being xenophobic or homophobic.' Pangbourne grinned at him, his own country accent growing stronger now as he let his anger and contempt show. 'I can help you with the long words if you like, pappy.'

The old man stared at him, his dark eyes bright as a bird's.

'How are these for long words,' he said. 'Atheistic, godless, unpatriotic, corruptor of youth.' A small fleck of saliva had gathered at the corner of the old man's mouth. He wiped it away with his sleeve. 'Don't deny it. You are teaching foreign religions, false faiths.'

'Did you say something about corrupting youth?' asked Pangbourne calmly.

'That's right. Indoctrinating them with blasphemous heresies.'

'Well, how's this for corrupting youth?' Pangbourne opened his desk drawer and rummaged in it. He repressed the urge to grab a cigarette and instead removed a sheet of paper, a computer print-out.

Francis Leemark watched him closely as he drew the piece of paper out and read from it.

' "Numerous subcutaneous wounds and extensive bruising, difficult to detect visually because subject received repeated beatings with a large wire object, most likely a clothes hanger. Despite the obvious painful nature of the injuries the child denies that anything unusual has happened to him. He refuses to say who might be responsible for said injuries".'

Pangbourne put the paper back in his drawer and flicked a cool gaze up at the old man. 'That report was filed by a social worker over ten years ago. I guess Wolf would have been, what? Six and a half, seven years old?'

'My boy's not called Wolf. His proper name is Christian. Christian Leemark.'

Now Pangbourne met the old man's fierce dark gaze and held it. The two men looked into each other's eyes. Pangbourne's stare was unwavering and finally the old man looked away, twisting his mouth in an expression of disgust.

'Don't you have anything to say about that report I just read to you, Mr Leemark?'

There was a silence in the small office and then the old man said, 'Christian's mother was a God-fearing woman.'

Pangbourne shook his head, grinning. 'Nope, pappy. Christian's mother was a clinical psychopath who never should have been left alone with a child.'

'She was harsh but she was fair. That woman understood that there's a heaven and a hell.'

'In her case I hope so, Mr Leemark, because there'll be a special corner of hell reserved for people who hurt small children.'

'Christian was raised in a decent, compassionate home where respect for the Lord was paramount. Just as his name suggests.'

'Wolf was raised in a hell-hole, and the only reason you were ever allowed custody of him was because you could prove you were away playing soldiers while most of those wounds were inflicted.'

'You saying that I'm not fit to raise kids?'

'Mr Leemark, you're not fit to raise cotton.'

The old man's chin juddered as he ground his teeth with rage. Pangbourne wondered if any of those teeth were still his own. For a long moment Francis Leemark seemed to be too angry to speak. Then he forced his trembling lips apart and said, 'How dare you say that? You're the one teaching innocent kids un-Christian religion. Heathen lies.'

Pangbourne said, 'Listen up, pappy. When I was a little kid I sat in a one room schoolhouse. And this lady teacher used to tell us stories. Her old apple-cheeked face would light up with a beautiful inner light, and she'd sit there and tell this room full of helpless little kids stories of a man being tortured and nailed to a cross. How he had a crown of thorns that cut into his forehead and was given nothing to drink but vinegar from a sponge. And the wind howled around the room and we cried and we tried to cover our ears but we couldn't stop her. She was bigger than us. And after all, she was supposed to be our teacher. She'd been entrusted with us and she could do anything she liked to that room full of little kids.'

Pangbourne stared across his desk at Wolf Leemark's father.

'And I swore that if I ever had the responsibility of teaching children I'd never expose them to that sort of wicked nonsense. You should have seen that old woman, pappy; she made that horrible story come alive in every gruesome detail. And she may have thought she was doing good, but what she really relished was the look of shock on each little face. So what, if she believed she was spreading the good word, pappy? She scared every poor kid in that class until they wet their beds. I had nightmares for weeks afterwards. No, make that years.'

'Well, the lesson obviously didn't get through,' said Francis Leemark. And with the swiftness of a snake striking he scooped up the big glass ash-tray from Mr Pangbourne's desk and in one swift motion slammed it into Pangbourne's head and that felt so good that he slammed it again and after the man had dropped face down on to the desk he stood up and leant over and just kept on slamming it, with a wet heavy sound like a hatchet chunking into damp timber when you were chopping lengths of firewood on a clean rain-wet morning.

Old man Leemark's arm had the strength of a gnarled hickory branch. He kept raising and swinging tirelessly.

It was hard work, but he didn't mind. As he worked he lost himself in the memory of a long-gone autumn morning, smoky rural sky above and wet grass under foot as he breathed the clean outdoor air and chopped firewood in the farmyard, his arm swinging rhythmically as if he was wielding a hatchet. He felt the fine pleasant muscular ache of his God-given body doing honest labour. And it was only when the ache threatened to turn into a cramp that he stopped swinging, and returned from the memory of that damp smoky morning.

Francis Leemark blinked slowly and looked around. He was like a man awaking from a deep sleep, not quite sure where he was. He wasn't at the farm. He was indoors, in a small room. What was this place?

There was something he was holding in his hand, but Francis Leemark didn't want to look at that yet.

And there was a desk in front of him with something on it, something big and red and wet, but he didn't want to look at that, either. He knew these things would just distract him further. Instead he looked out of the window.

There was a window set in one wall and through it he could see flourishing greenery outside, but he wasn't out in the country. He wasn't at the farm. He hadn't been at the farm for years. His daddy's old farm. He hadn't been there for forty or fifty years.

Yet it had seemed so real, the smell of the long wet grass and the rhythmic damp chunking sound of hatchet biting into wood. But, where a moment ago there had been an endless smoky autumn sky, there were now white walls hemming him in. And instead of the long orchards of the farm, there was just a pissy little school garden beyond the window.

The school. That's where he was. At Christian's school. He'd come here to see the principal.

Francis Leemark squeezed his eyes shut to help himself concentrate, to get his bearings. A man had to get his bearings now and then, and what better way to do that than just shut your eyes for a peaceful moment or two? Shut out the busy world and all its gaudy distractions. That's why the Lord gave you eyelids. Sometimes, when he was driving these days, Francis would get a little confused. Especially in heavy traffic, or when he was driving along a familiar route and he discovered that the damned fools had changed it. Changed the roads. No wonder a man had to stop now and then in traffic to squeeze his eyes shut and get his bearings. Ignore those impatient idiots who started honking their horns at him, distracting him just when he was trying to concentrate.

One day he'd reach into the glove compartment to get the gun he carried there, the hand-gun he'd brought back from the Mexican wars. Then he'd teach those young bastards to honk at him. Then they'd be in for a surprise.

One day he'd reach into that glove compartment.

One day he'd do something that would show them all.

Francis Leemark opened his eyes and looked at the sticky ash-tray in his hands. He looked at the amazing bright red stains that had suddenly appeared on the clean white walls of this office. Then he looked at the mashed thing lying face down on the desk.

Slowly a smile formed on his lean, lined old face.

Mr Pangbourne wasn't saying anything clever now.

Mr Pangbourne wasn't saying much of anything at all now.

'And don't call me pappy,' said the old man. He dropped the ash-tray on to the carpet with a wet thud and left the office, carefully closing the door behind him.

He nodded to the big fat secretary as he went out. She obviously hadn't heard a thing. 'Mr Pangbourne says he ain't to be disturbed.'

The woman nodded curtly, as if he was saying something perfectly obvious. Big rude, fat girl.

Wolf's father went out of the school by the front entrance, striding out in his military way; there was absolutely no hurry. He went out to the parking lot and opened the car door.

The car was as hot as an oven after sitting unshaded in the parking lot. He popped open the glove compartment and reached into it, his hand disturbing the still, warm air.

Francis Leemark took out his gun, slammed the car door shut, and turned back towards the school.

Chapter 31

'Why are we going this way?' said the stewardess.

Creed frowned with concentration as he steered the armoured car off the concrete podium and down a sloping ramp. A second later they were on the horseshoe-shaped road that encircled the estate.

The big vehicle bumped as it eased off the curb on to the road surface and Creed slowed down for a moment to steer through a narrow stretch between a thick cluster of parked cars.

The twin rows of empty parked cars seemed eerie on the abandoned estate. Either their owners had fled without them or they hadn't managed to flee at all.

As Creed eased the armoured vehicle through into a clear stretch of road he relaxed and stepped on the accelerator. He glanced back at the stewardess, perched nervously in the navigator's chair, staring up at the big screens above the driver's seat. Finally he responded to the stewardess's question. 'What do you mean?' he said.

'Why didn't you drive straight across the podium? It would have been quicker than going all the way around by road.'

'We thought about that,' said Creed. 'But Roz wanted me to come around by the front of your house.'

'Why?'

'Because the White King is out the front.'

'And what are you going to do with the White King?'

'Corner him. That's what Roz asked us to do. Corner him and cut off his escape.'

'And then what?'

'Blow him to hell,' said Creed. He expected this to get some reaction from the stewardess, but she said nothing; she was leaning forward alertly, staring at one of the rear screens.

'This vehicle has a computerized defence system doesn't it?'

'Sure.' Creed was startled by the question but he was coming around the curve in the road that would bring them out in front of the stewardess's house. The big vehicle was moving at high speed and he had to concentrate; he hardly registered what the stewardess was saying.

'So it gives an alarm if anything comes close?' said the stewardess.

'Yes, assuming it's the size of a dog. Or a couple of dogs, since I reprogrammed it.'

'But would it give an alarm if we were getting close to something as big as a car?'

'No,' said Creed absently. 'Why do you ask?'

'Because – look out!'

Creed glanced up. Suddenly another vehicle had appeared on the main screen, cutting in from a concealed side entrance on to the road directly in front of the armoured car. It jumped out in front of them with breathtaking suddenness, shining in the moonlight. It was a long, gleaming black vehicle.

A stretch-limousine, thought Creed, as he hit both sets of brakes, causing the armoured car's tyres to give a tormented squeal as it slowed to an emergency stop. The stewardess shot forward in her seat, bouncing painfully off the dashboard. 'Put your seat-belt on,' snarled Creed, as annoyed at himself for forgetting it as he was at the stewardess.

On the main screen the long black limousine was fishtailing along the curving road ahead of them at high speed. Creed released the brakes now and the big vehicle rumbled forward again, the melted patches on its tyres smoking in the moonlight. He had just barely managed to avoid smashing into the back of the limousine. Going at this speed, with its massive weight and reinforced exterior, the armoured car would have crushed the other vehicle like an empty Coke can, killing everyone inside.

'They're in a hurry,' said the stewardess, rubbing her forehead where she'd slammed it against the dash. Creed was pleased to see that she seemed to be all right.

'Stupid bastards,' he said. They were gaining on the long black car now and he could see that there was something strange about it. He'd been wrong before. It wasn't a stretch-limo. The proportions were different. And the back of it was squared off.

There was something familiar about the strange shape of the shiny black vehicle. Then Creed noticed the curtains in its rear window and he realized what it was.

'It's a what-do-you-call-it,' said the stewardess.

'A hearse,' said Creed.

Roz eased herself up on to the roof slowly and carefully; even so she nearly got her head blown off.

'For Christ's sake, Roz, don't do that.' Redmond lowered his gun, staring across the rooftop at her in the moonlight. 'I thought you were one of them, coming up after me.'

'That's why I'm here. They could come up on either side of you.'

'Very true,' said Redmond, raising his gun again and looking from right to left with a swift nervous sweep of his head. 'So what are you doing here? Trying to put the wind up me?'

'No, I've come to watch your back.' Roz raised her own gun and strolled across the roof to the spot where Redmond stood.

'Very kind of you.'

'Isn't it just? Now, do you mind telling me why you came up here?'

Redmond hunkered down on his haunches and gestured for Roz to join him. She sank down and sat patiently on her heels, watching the rooftops on either side of them. 'I'll show you,' whispered Redmond, 'if you want to crawl to the edge of the roof with me.' He slipped down on to his arms and knees and lowered himself on to his belly.

'No, I'll wait back here and keep an eye on things. Just tell me what you're up to.'

'The White King,' whispered Redmond. 'He's in the front yard. I think I can get a clear shot at him.' He patted the side of his weapon affectionately. 'Night-scope and all that.'

'But Creed is coming in the armoured car. That's what I arranged. He's going to cover the front yard and pick off the White King if he can.'

'Sure, that's the plan,' said Redmond. 'But why should he

have all the fun? More to the point, why should he get all the glory?'

'Glory? I knew it. It's some kind of male competitive thing. Can't you keep your hormones under control?'

'I guess not,' said Redmond happily. 'It must be my time of the month.' He began crawling towards the edge of the roof, his gun cradled over his folded elbows.

As soon as he reached the lip of the roof he paused and checked his weapon, making sure that it was fully loaded and the sight was calibrated accurately. No mistakes, now. Only when he was satisfied with the gun did he allow himself to peer over the edge of the roof.

Down below in the front garden of the house the dogs were scattered in small groups, kneeling patiently, waiting. The White King was sitting on his own by the front steps of the house, all of the other animals keeping a respectful distance from him. The nearest cluster of dogs were three or four metres away; they sat watching the White King, quietly awaiting some action from him. Like courtiers, thought Redmond.

As he looked beyond the small front garden of the house he saw the innumerable other groups of dogs scattered across the roads and yards of the estate, until they vanished in the dark distance. Redmond had the dizzying feeling that if he could just see the position of the entire pack all at once it would form a pattern, a pattern of cosmic significance. A swirling mandala with the White King at its centre.

Now, this is no time to get imaginative, thought Redmond.

He raised his gun and took aim at the dog called the White King. The night-scope immediately brought it zooming into close, sharp detail.

The old dog shook itself wearily and slowly raised its head, its long ears trailing back on its wedge-shaped skull. It lifted its muzzle and peered up into the night. Redmond knew that it couldn't possibly see him but nonetheless he had the eerie feeling that the White King knew he was there.

It was staring up at him through the night-scope with a strange sort of awareness in its dark eyes. The dog peered unwaveringly up at Redmond as he switched his weapon to single fire and jacked a round silently into the chamber. It was as if the White King knew exactly what he was doing. Redmond suppressed a shudder.

But that couldn't be true. If the dog knew he was aiming a gun at it, surely it would try and escape? Get up and run. Summon its courtiers to help. Do something.

Wouldn't it?

The dark eyes of the dog stared up at Redmond, full of knowledge and resignation. And despair. Redmond squeezed his own eyes shut and silently cursed himself. This was worse than imaginative. He was going round the twist. All he could see below him was a gaunt animal, eyes an unreadable black in the processed moonlight of the telescopic sight. But he was reading a world-weariness and suicidal resignation into the eyes of the creature. He was reading intelligence there. It was as if the dog knew what he was doing, and that he was doing it a favour.

Sheer madness.

Well, there was one easy cure for it. Pull the trigger and be done with the whole thing.

Redmond saw some of the dogs sitting near the roadside begin to stir restlessly. He realized that for some moments now he'd been hearing a sound. His subconscious mind had already detected and identified it as the raw rattling noise of the armoured car's engine.

The big vehicle was approaching along the curved perimeter road of the estate. All the more reason to shoot the White King now. No telling what might happen when Creed arrived with the full fire-power of the armoured car.

It wasn't just a matter of glory. Certainly, it would be nice to be the man who bagged the White King and put an end to the terror in London. They'd probably give him the keys to the city. Not a bad result for a kid from the Divis Flats.

But it wasn't just the glory. Redmond wanted to get it over with because it was too good a chance to miss. He had a clean shot now and who knew when that might happen again? Who knew what might happen in the next few seconds?

The White King's narrow skull was perfectly framed in the computer-generated crosshairs of his night-sight. Its dark eyes stared at him with sad knowledge. Redmond began tightening his finger on the trigger.

That was when he heard the other sound. Another vehicle. Approaching from the same direction as the armoured car and moving fast.

Redmond hesitated for a second when he heard the sound. He wondered who might be coming in the other vehicle. The reinforcements Norman Peverell had promised? Had poor bladder-bursting Norman worked out a way to summon them?

Redmond speculated for a moment before he began to pull the trigger, and then it was too late.

Racing out of the night, sleek and gleaming under the street-lights, came a long black hearse. It was a gigantic vehicle with sweeping tail-fins that must have dated back to the 1950s.

Redmond froze with surprise. He failed to take his shot. And then events began to move too rapidly to be easily absorbed.

The armoured car appeared along the perimeter road following the hearse; it braked violently and swerved to a rubber-burning halt to avoid a collision with the hearse. The hearse had abruptly skidded to a halt beside the pavement, and now it sat there, parked sideways, blocking the road.

In the front of the hearse Redmond could just about make out a man and a woman. The man was swinging the front door of the hearse open even as the big armoured vehicle screeched to a halt behind him. He was apparently oblivious to the threat of the dog pack that was massed all around him.

The nearest groups of dogs had immediately leapt to their feet, turning to face the hearse, preparing to defend their leader.

But the White King had suddenly left his spot on the front steps. He was bounding up the garden path and out of the front gate with youthful vigour, loping towards the hearse.

The scores of dogs who had begun to close in on the long black vehicle hesitated. They'd seen the man jumping out of the hearse and they were obviously poised to attack, to close in fast and rip him to pieces.

But they made no move towards him. Instead they turned and watched the White King as he raced along the pavement towards the hearse.

The ancient withered dog was running with the speed and excitement of a puppy. The ranks of other dogs backed away to clear a path for him as he dashed towards the man who'd emerged from the hearse.

He was a small man in a pale jacket, wearing an incongrous straw hat which he clutched to his head, as if he was more worried about losing his hat than anything else.

'It's the Doctor.'

Redmond looked up to see that Roz had joined him at the edge of the roof. She stared down into the street. Redmond turned to follow her gaze and he was just in time to see the White King slow down and approach the Doctor; it moved unsteadily now on its frail legs, head shaking a little as it jabbed its muzzle up at the Doctor.

And began to lick his hand.

Chapter 32

Miss Marcroft was lost in thoughts of fruit salad when the nasty looking old man came back into her office.

It had only been a short time since lunch but Miss Marcroft could still distinctly taste every flavour of the tart, chilled fruit she'd consumed. She was lingering over these flavours when the old man came back in. Francis Leemark. He was Wolf's father. She had been willing to give him the benefit of the doubt, but the old man had proved to be, if anything, worse than his son. Even more rude. And more arrogant.

'I need some information,' Leemark announced, as he came marching back into her office.

Miss Marcroft ignored him and pretended to be busy on her computer. Let the old bastard wait.

But he wasn't going to wait. He leant over the desk, his musky body odour and the sour smell of his coffee-breath wafted at her and thoroughly destroyed the delicate memory of this lunch-time's fruit salad. Miss Marcroft hated people who drank coffee almost as much as she hated people who smoked. She frowned with concentration and began typing on her computer keyboard.

'You've got a fellow teaching here says he's a Buddhist monk?'

Miss Marcroft ignored him and kept on typing.

But Francis Leemark wasn't going to be ignored.

'I want to know what class he's teaching in, right now.' He was leaning across the desk, much too close to her.

'Why do you want to know?' She didn't look up from her computer.

'I just want to know. So just tell me.'

Miss Marcroft finally deigned to look at this rude intruder.

There was something strange about the way he was standing, one hand dug deep in the pocket of his old canvas work jacket. 'I'm not sure I should give out that information,' she said.

The old man began to shout. 'I have a son at this school. I have the right to know what goes on here.'

Miss Marcroft reached out for her telephone and pressed the button that activated the intercom in Mr Pangbourne's office. 'Mr Leemark is back,' she said. 'And he wants to know –'

She didn't get any further because the old man reached out with one hand and slapped it down on the phone, breaking the connection. She looked up at him with fury in her eyes that died as soon as she saw his other hand.

It had come out of his jacket pocket.

It was holding a gun.

He was pointing the gun at her.

'Mr Pangbourne ain't going to be answering any questions. Now tell me which classroom that bald-headed freak is in.'

The Young Master was sitting cross-legged on his desk at the front of the room again. He was reading from a large book open on his lap. Occasionally he'd alter his position slightly and his baggy orange robe would shift around his knees and the girls in the front row would repress giggles.

' "The crowd wants to wake the dreamer in their midst",' said the monk, reading aloud from the book. ' "For fear that otherwise they might prove to be figments of his dream".' He slapped the book shut and looked up at the class full of teenagers.

'Who wrote that book?' asked a pinched, studious-looking boy in the second row.

'You might call it a Zen text,' said the monk.

'Well, I've read a lot of Zen,' said the kid.

'Me too, but only now and Zen,' shouted Wally Saddler from the back of the class. And beside him Wolf Leemark grinned.

'Quiet please,' said the young monk and, oddly enough, Wally obeyed. The monk turned back to the kid in the second row. 'Now what were you saying?'

'Well, it just doesn't sound like any Zen proverbs that I've ever encountered.'

The Young Master smiled. 'That's not surprising, because in fact it was written by a friend of mine. Written especially for the lessons here in this school. But the point is, like those who fear the dreamer, we too are drawn to certain ones among us, drawn by their strange composure. This is what, for lack of a more adequate term, we call charisma. Some human beings possess this strange talent. For some it's like a thousand-watt light they can't switch off. When they walk through a crowd everyone notices them. The crowd doesn't know it but on a deep unconscious level they look to these individuals for subliminal signals. Instructions on how the pack should behave. Hence the alpha male.'

Sitting in the front row Ricky McIlveen looked pale and tense, the very picture of someone hearing something he didn't want to hear. All the kids sitting near him seemed to have picked up on his tension. But the mood had not quite communicated itself to the back of the room where Wolf Leemark held sway. As the other kids nearby watched with expressions ranging from hero-worship to disgust, Wolf suddenly slumped over in his chair, head limp and eyes closed. He made an extremely loud snoring noise.

At the front of the room the monk grinned good-naturedly at the noise and the laughter that followed it. He set his book aside and shook one of his voluminous sleeves aside so he could glance at his incongruously modern wrist-watch. 'I agree that it all sounds a little esoteric,' he said, climbing down from the desk. The girls in the front row bent low over their desks, taking one last look as he stood up. 'And next week we'll suggest some alternative paradigms to explain dominance in groups, as well as looking in further detail at the underlying mechanism. I want you all to read up on behavioural display in Skene and Lipsett, and write me a three-page essay on whether you think this is the key to alpha male dominance.'

At the mention of the three-page essay a disgusted groan arose from the kids, who were now standing up, gathering their books and noisily scraping chairs back under desks.

'OK, OK,' said the monk as the bell rang, signalling the

change of periods. 'That's three pages on my desk next Tuesday.'

At the back of the room Wolf grinned and said, 'OK, let's go.' He slipped out swiftly from behind his desk, taking Wally Saddler by surprise. Wally scrabbled to pick up his ratty old gym shorts and the one battered school-book he carried around, and followed.

'What's up?' he said, catching up to Wolf.

'We're going to nail him.'

'Nail who?'

'Who do you think, numb-nuts? Ricky McIlveen.'

'What, right now?' said Wally with a sinking feeling in his stomach.

'Sure. A little accident in the hallway between classes.' Wally shook his head, worried. Fights took place after school, they always had. That was normal; it was the way things worked. Wally was more shocked than he cared to admit by this break with tradition.

A pale, tense-looking Ricky McIlveen was standing at the front of the class now, talking to the Buddhist monk as the other kids filed out.

'He looks worried,' said Wally.

'He's got plenty of reason to be,' said Wolf. 'Come on. Let's wait outside and then we'll nail the little bastard.'

Wally followed Wolf out of the classroom into the mêlée of kids sweeping along the hallway. They stood waiting, their backs to a long bank of lockers, waiting for Ricky to come out.

But when he finally appeared he was still deep in conversation with the Young Master. The tall monk strolled along beside the boy like some exotic bodyguard as they walked past Wally and Wolf, heading down the hallway together.

'Damn,' said Wally, hiding his sudden rush of relief. 'Doesn't look like we'll get a shot at him.'

'Oh, I don't know,' said Wolf, pushing lazily away from the lockers and starting down the hall after the boy and the teacher.

'But Wolf, we can't do anything while the shine-head is with the kid.'

'You can't always have everything on a plate, Wally. Sometimes you've got to meet luck halfway. Let's just follow them a while and see what happens.'

Wally reluctantly set off down the hallway with Wolf, just close enough to Ricky and the Young Master to keep an eye on them in the crowd.

The mass of kids in the hallway was beginning to thin out as they disappeared into their appointed classrooms. As the crowd thinned Wally felt increasingly nervous. He and Wolf were nearing the location of their next class, which was Phys Ed, and Ricky and the monk were still deep in conversation.

'I don't think this is going to work out, Wolf,' he said.

'Don't be like that Wally. Think positive.' And Wolf smiled, because just then Ricky and the monk stopped walking.

'This is it,' said Wolf.

Sure enough, they had reached the point where the hallway forked in two different directions. Ricky nodded at the Young Master and then turned away to walk down the corridor towards the gym. The bald young man continued on his way towards the staffroom, his saffron robes flopping loosely around him.

'Right on,' said Wolf in a low, prayerful voice. 'OK, Wally. We grab him before he gets into the gym.' Wolf Leemark turned to Wally Saddler and grinned. 'Then we rush him down to the boiler-room, work on him for a couple of minutes then go in and change for gym like nothing happened. OK, Wally? Wally. What's the matter?'

Wally Saddler was staring down the branch of corridor that led towards the staffroom. The young monk had stopped walking and was staring at something. In the corridor in front of him the crowd of kids had thinned but there were still thirty or forty laggards who hadn't reached their classes yet. Now suddenly these kids had fallen silent. And they were moving, moving in a hasty panicky way.

What was apparently random motion swiftly assumed a pattern as it spread through the crowd. The kids were fleeing from the centre of the hallway, scattering towards the locker-covered walls. They were moving away from someone, making room for his passage.

Someone was coming down the corridor, towards the Young Master.

It was weird seeing the kids hastily making way like this. It reminded Wally of an old movie he had once seen;

one about Moses and the parting of the Red Sea. As he stared down the corridor, watching the strange phenomenon develop, Wally noticed Ricky McIlveen appear again. There was something about the kid; you always noticed him in a crowd.

Ricky was coming back from the direction of the gym. He had evidently sensed that something was wrong.

Standing beside Wally, Wolf Leemark was saying, 'What's happening? What is –'

And then he fell silent. Because the cluster of kids had finally cleared, pressed back against the lockers on either side of the hallway. And suddenly it was possible to see the figure that was coming, approaching the Young Master.

Then Wally saw who it was. He couldn't believe it for a second. Then he quickly stole a glance at Wolf's face, to see his reaction.

Because the man coming up the corridor was Wolf's dad. Old-man Leemark was walking towards the Buddhist monk with one arm outstretched and the most peculiar expression on his face. It was an expression of grim joy, unlike anything Wally had ever seen. Wally didn't even need to look at what was in old-man Leemark's outstretched hand.

It was obviously a gun.

'Hey, monkey-man!' called Wolf's father. 'I've got something here for you.' He stopped and raised the gun, turning his body in the classic pistol-fighter's stance, to minimize the target area of his own body, and took careful aim.

The gun was pointing straight at the monk's head. His poor bald head looked naked and terribly vulnerable. Wally Saddler felt a sickening dropping feeling in his stomach. He knew what was about to happen and there was nothing anybody could do to stop it.

Oddly, the strongest thought that flashed through Wally's mind was a powerful sympathy for Wolf. What was about to happen would mark him forever. All his life up to now he'd merely been the son of a crazy old coot. From this point on he would be the son of a murderer.

But then a voice called out along the corridor. There was a shocking power to the voice so that at first one didn't hear the words. One was just aware of the impact of the four sounds, like the sudden raw jolt of electricity applied directly to one's nerves. And then the meaning of the four words slowly penetrated the listeners' brains.

'Put that gun down.'

It was a voice of absolute authority. A voice so unquestioning in its command that any thought of disobedience was impossible. It was the primal father telling the child what to do. Everyone in the corridor responded to it. Even Wally found himself, for one idiot-second, trying to put down a gun when he wasn't even holding one.

Old-man Leemark, on the other hand, didn't lower his gun. But the voice bit into his mind and he couldn't ignore it. His finger had been tightening on the trigger but now he stopped, hesitating for a second.

And that was enough.

The Young Master threw himself forward in an elegant arcing martial arts kick that put Wolf, and every member of the Wolf Pack, to shame. He was still in mid-air when his foot connected with old-man Leemark's gun, and sent it flying to land with a clatter twenty metres down the corridor. Then he threw himself on the wiry old man and effortlessly drove him to the floor, locked in an unbreakable wrestling hold.

But no one noticed that.

Everyone was staring at the person who had spoken. The source of the voice which had commanded them all. The voice like fire burning into their minds.

Everyone was staring at Ricky McIlveen.

The crowd stood looking at Ricky and Ricky looked back at them.

Finally the monk had to shout from the floor of the corridor where he was writhing and wrestling with the desperate old man. 'Somebody help me. Somebody call the police!' His voice was strangely thin and ineffectual after Ricky's. A cheap imitation fashioned from inferior materials.

Several of the kids, jocks on their way to the gym, came out of their paralysis and rushed to help him. One of them scuttled down the corridor, bent down and gingerly picked up the fallen pistol as though it might be red hot. The other kids in the hallway kept right on staring at Ricky.

Except for Wally. He turned to stare at Wolf, and Wolf turned to meet his gaze.

As their eyes met Wally knew that things had changed forever. For him and for Wolf, and for the whole school.

Then suddenly he couldn't see anything more in Wolf's eyes, because Wolf turned and fled.

From the window of her office Amy could see the flashing blue lights of the ambulance and the police cars.

There had been three police cars, but one of them followed the ambulance as it shot away along the small service-road that led into the centre of the school complex. The vehicles hit the main highway and accelerated towards the hospital, their sirens keening as though in mourning for Daniel Pangbourne.

A second police car followed them a moment later, but this one was heading in the opposite direction, towards the police-station. Locked in the back, sitting ramrod straight, was Wolf's dad. Francis Leemark. The old man had his chin up, full of defiance.

The second police car had a bit of trouble getting started, slewing in the churned ocean of mud which an hour earlier had been carefully tended lawn and shrubbery.

'Thank God he can't see what they've done to his garden,' said Amy.

'Yes,' said the man called Retour. He was sitting in one of the arm-chairs that dominated her small office, his leg casually hitched over the side. Now he got up and joined her at the window. 'A crime scene does tend to get a lot of wear and tear.'

Outside only the third police car remained; the two officers assigned to it were inside the school, sitting in the gym behind some hastily arranged folding tables. They were trying to take coherent statements, one at a time, from dozens of semi-hysterical kids who sat waiting, bored or weeping, on the bleachers.

Retour looked out of the window and studied the intersecting morass of tyre tracks and footprints; he smiled. 'If the headwounds don't finish Pangbourne off, one glance at this mess will.'

Amy turned and stared at the man, her blue-green eyes suddenly alight with anger. 'This has all worked out according to plan for you, hasn't it?'

Retour turned and met her stare, quite unperturbed. He had a studious angular face, thin and carved with fine lines, like a pious monk obsessed with study. His eyebrows were bushy and dark, rising in jagged shapes over his eyes.

Looking at Amy he seemed distant and amused, no more than mildly curious about her or anything else.

'What do you mean?'

'You planned it. You expected Leemark to come in and kill Mr Pangbourne.'

'Kill him? According to those attentive young fellows from the ambulance, Mr Pangbourne is still very much alive, registering brain activity, and a whole host of other fascinating subtle metabolic signs.' Retour shrugged. 'And even if paramedics are, by definitions, people who weren't quite bright enough to be doctors, I don't think we should dismiss their opinions out of hand. They seemed like nice enough guys.'

'You know what I mean,' said Amy. 'This is exactly what you planned. Old-man Leemark comes in and goes berserk. And poor Dan Pangbourne takes the brunt of it.'

'On the contrary. I never planned on Mr Pangbourne getting hurt.'

'Do you expect me to believe that?' said Amy. She turned away from the window, intending to sit in one of the arm-chairs. But then she changed her mind because Retour might do the same and then they'd be jammed together in close proximity, knees touching.

Instead Amy sat behind her desk, using it as a barrier between herself and the man.

But Retour showed no inclination to move away from the window. 'I don't know why you shouldn't believe it,' he said. 'It's true. We primed Mr Leemark, all right. But he was supposed to be aimed at the school's resident Buddhist monk, not the school principal.'

Despite her best efforts, Amy felt a certain professional interest awakening in herself. 'And, by the way, how did you arrange that?'

Retour smiled. 'As you might imagine, Mr Leemark subscribes to some fairly interesting magazines of the super-patriot, vigilante, guns-are-good-for-us variety. We just made sure that he received some copies of an additional wacko publication, one we printed ourselves. It notified all right-thinking Christians of the presence of a shaven-headed heathen in their school, contaminating innocent children with blasphemous ideas.'

'All right-thinking Christians?'

'Well, just Leemark, actually. We only distributed one copy of the magazine. We just wanted to stir him up and get him to come in here.'

'Did you know he'd come carrying a gun?'

Amy's voice was sharp but Retour remained calm and unmoved. 'We knew it might be a possibility,' he said.

'What would you have done if he'd come in here and started shooting kids?'

'It wasn't kids he was after. And anyway, if it looked for an instant like he might threaten Ricky's life we would have intervened immediately. But I knew that it wouldn't go like that.' Retour smiled modestly. 'Although I couldn't have predicted how well it would go. Did you see the way Ricky handled the crowd? Did you see the way they responded to his voice?'

He looked at Amy and his angular face was suddenly transformed, glowing with what looked like pride. He stared at her, grinning, as if he expected her to smile back.

She looked at him coldy. 'Too bad Mr Pangbourne ended up the way he did.'

'As I said, that wasn't in the plan. It was just a side-effect.'

'But you don't seem too upset about it.'

'Well, I have to admit that it was a bonus.'

'That's nice. An elderly man is beaten half to death with a glass ash-tray and it's a bonus.'

Retour shrugged. 'Pangbourne was a pontential danger to this whole project. He was inquisitive and smart, and a trouble maker.'

'And he didn't like us working in his school,' sighed Amy. The afternoon light coming in through the window had taken on a gloomy pre-storm luminosity that made everything look strange. She was surrounded by the familiar objects of this small office, all of them carefully selected as set-dressing for her role as a compassionate and concerned high-school guidance counsellor.

She had personally chosen the objects. A graceful vase for fresh cut flowers. A couple of chunky coffee mugs in cheerful colours. A framed poster of a breathtaking Caribbean beachscape; white sand under a purple night sky. It had been fun choosing these things. Now, they looked alien and faintly menacing. Amy felt depressed and more than a little guilty. She had liked Pangbourne.

'Cheer up,' said Retour. 'Things are going better than we could ever have planned. We're going to be finished here very quickly.'

'Stop it with all this "we" business,' said Amy. 'This is your operation. You're in charge. I'm just one of the hired hands. And a disillusioned one.'

'That will change when you see the results we're achieving. Ricky is developing at a faster rate than I'd ever imagined possible.'

'Poor kid,' said Amy.

'Within a couple of days he's reached a point that I thought would take weeks of careful nurturing.' Retour came away from the window and sat at the arm-chair nearest Amy's desk. To face her he had to sit at an awkward angle and stare slightly upwards, with the bulk of the desk in between them. According to theory, this should have given Amy a definite feeling of being in charge.

It didn't. Retour smiled at her, his ravaged scholar's face gleaming with enthusiasm. 'This is the sort of incredible luck you read about. If you study the great scientific discoveries you realize that they weren't carefully planned endeavours at all. In fact they usually involve outrageous, fortuitous accidents. Some lab assistant accidentally puts some gunk in the wrong petri dish and you wind up with penicillin. It's as though a discovery has to happen. As though it's trying to break through into our awareness.'

Despite herself, Amy found that she was listening closely to what Retour was saying. She had experienced that feeling herself when she'd tried to be a hotshot scientist at Cornell. On those rare occasions when her research had been going well.

Retour, damn him, picked up on her sudden interest. 'You know what it's like,' he said. 'You work at a problem and work at it and then suddenly it's as if critical mass is achieved and a chain reaction begins. The revelations come rushing toward you by every available route.'

Amy faked a yawn. 'It all sounds a bit mystical to me.'

'Really? Well look at what happened today. Outrageous good fortune. I had no idea exactly when old-man Leemark would come bursting in. It could have occurred at any time. Yet it happens this afternoon. The perfect moment to reinforce and magnify the effect of what we already achieved in the lunch-room.'

'What exactly did happen in the lunch-room?'

'You mean you haven't seen the recordings? Well, never mind, you can study them this evening. Rest assured that you did your part perfectly. But the critical thing was to make Ricky the centre of attention and yet, at the same time, give him a shock so that he couldn't retreat into his usual defence postures. He usually becomes intensely self-conscious. He hates the attention of the other kids and he reacts like a porcupine. He becomes so uncomfortable that if you look at him you begin to feel uncomfortable yourself. His anxiety is infectious. It's like the spikes of the porcupine driving away unwanted attention.'

Amy was silent. Despite herself, she found that she was listening again, anxious to know what he would say next.

Retour was caught up in his story. 'All we needed to do was make sure Ricky was too shaken up. Too preoccupied with some small emergency to follow his usual pattern. So I made sure that the summons to the principal's office was timed to coincide with his reading of the note we planted for him. Bang.' Retour slammed a fist down on the arm-chair for emphasis. Dust rose in the strange light. 'He reads the note so he's off balance. And then, bang.' His fist came down again and dust lifted. 'The kids hear his name on the PA and they all turn to look at him. The timing was perfect.'

'I know all that,' said Amy, feigning indifference. 'I meant what exactly was that note? Who wrote it?'

'I did,' said Retour.

'And what did it say?'

' "I know who your real father is".'

Amy sat silently for a moment. Then she said, 'And do you?'

'Yes,' said Retour. He climbed out of the arm-chair and went back to the window. The strange light of the imminent storm glowed on his face.

'Yes,' he said. 'I certainly do.'

Chapter 33

'Norman, Norman, Norman. Listen to me. It's nothing to be ashamed of.'

Redmond set aside his cup of coffee. It wasn't easy finding a suitable surface to put it on. The stewardess's sitting room looked like a war zone. He finally selected a semi-intact coffee table and set it upright in front of the sofa.

These were the only pieces of furniture in sight that were both unbroken and the right way up; their normality contrasted strangely with the rest of the ravaged sitting room. The back wall of the room was open to the London dawn and a cool breeze was flowing in through it.

Redmond positioned the coffee table and sat down again beside Norman Peverell, on the sofa. The civil servant was wearing a ratty old dressing-gown which had once belonged to the stewardess's boyfriend. He sat glumly sipping from a cup of tea, staring down at his bony ankles, not looking up at Redmond.

'I knew a guy, said Redmond. 'His first time under fire he was so frightened he crapped himself.'

'It wasn't because I was frightened,' said Norman Peverell hotly. 'It was just because I couldn't get to the loo.'

'Exactly!' said Redmond.

'And I didn't, as you so delicately put it, "crap myself".'

'My point exactly. This guy lost it completely. We heard small-arms fire and we dropped to the floor. He crapped his pants and then, this is the worst part, he was so ashamed he stood up and ran.'

'My God.' said Norman Peverell. He was silent for a moment. 'Did they cut him down?'

'That's right. Small-arms fire, right? He got himself killed, right? Now, that is genuinely something to be ashamed of.

Getting yourself killed. You, on the other hand, should be proud of yourself Norman. You have survived. That is the primary objective in the combat zone. Therefore you count as one of the victors in this recent scuffle. You're a winner, Norman.'

The interest which had briefly animated Norman Peverell's face faded. He buried his nose in his tea-cup. 'I am not a winner. I am a grown man who has wet his trousers.'

'Yeah, but after all that waiting, your bladder hurting like hell, I bet it was a nice sensation.'

'A nice sensation?' Norman Peverell blinked up at Redmond, startled. 'What?'

'Letting go. Finally letting your bladder go after all that time. What a relief it must have been. I bet it was a lovely sensation.'

'What?' Norman Peverell was staring at Redmond like a man who couldn't believe what he was hearing. 'It must have been a what?'

'Just for the first ten seconds or so. You must have enjoyed it.'

'What are you suggesting here?' Norman Peverell blinked angrily, setting his tea-cup down. 'Are you suggesting that I'm some kind of pervert?'

Before Redmond could reply, there were footsteps in the hall and the stewardess came into the sitting room. She'd showered and changed her clothes, and looked amazingly good for a woman who had survived the ordeal of the last 24 hours.

'Hello Jessica,' said Norman. His eyes had lit up when he saw her come into the room. He hopped up off the sofa. 'Here, have a seat.'

'Thank you, Norman.'

'If you don't mind sitting beside Redmond, who was just insinuating that I was some kind of pervert who enjoyed wetting himself.'

'I wasn't insinuating anything of the kind,' said Redmond. 'I was just saying it must have been –'

'We'll have none of that talk now,' said Norman Peverell sternly. 'There's a lady present.'

The stewardess smiled at him. 'Your clothes are out of the washing-machine, Norman. I've put them into the drier.'

'Thank you, that's so kind of you. Can I get you a cup of tea?'

Norman Peverell was easing himself beside the stewardess now, sitting close beside her on the small sofa, and gazing up into her bruised, smiling face. He was able to sit beside her because Redmond had stood up. Neither the stewardess nor Norman Peverell had even noticed him get up. They only had eyes for each other.

They didn't notice Redmond leave the room, either.

He walked along the short corridor and out of the front door into the cool, blue morning.

Roz was sitting on the front steps beside her friend, the girl called Benny. They both had large mugs of coffee, steaming in the chilly air.

'That was the weirdest thing I've ever seen,' said Roz.

'Oh, I don't know, we've seen some weird stuff,' said Benny.

'What's that?' said Redmond, settling down beside them.

'The way the dogs all just left,' said Roz.

'The way they returned to normal, you mean,' said Benny. 'Like a spell had been broken.'

'So, what did I miss?' said Redmond.

'Well, it was like they had been in formation before,' said Roz. 'Every dog knowing where it had to go and what it had to do. Working together. A precision machine.'

'A nest of termites,' said Benny. 'There must have been thousands of them, their behaviour all meshing together. Then, all at once they ceased to be an organized group.'

'Yeah, the machine fell apart. The big doggy machine,' said Roz. 'One minute it was a pack, all the members working together, and then it was just a bunch of dogs.'

'A very large bunch of dogs.'

'It was like they were suddenly all looking around, wondering where they were. What they were doing here.'

'Like they were waking from a spell,' insisted Benny.

'All looking around, confused. And then they started to wander off. Going home, I suppose. All those dogs. All at once. There were a few fights that broke out amongst them. But only a few.'

'So for the most part they dispersed peacefully?' said Redmond, smiling.

'That's right. Thousands of dogs.'

'You know,' said Benny. 'We could even hear them howling in Kent. There must have been tens of thousands of them, all over the country. Hundreds of packs.'

'Or just one big pack.'

'All under the control of the White King.'

At the mention of the name all three of them looked up at the dog.

It was the only dog still in sight, frail and old, its long scrawny body sprawled on the pavement beside the hearse. It lay there limp and motionless. The only sign of life was the lazy twitching of his tail, sweeping back and forth in doggy contentment.

'He's been lying there since we arrived,' said Benny. 'Did you see him when he first went near the hearse?' Redmond shook his head. 'I've never seen a dog act like that. It was like he was going crazy with joy.'

The White King stirred lazily to make way for the Doctor as he stepped over him.

'He did, didn't he?'

Dawn sunlight was angling into the front of the hearse, showing the Doctor inside, bent over, evidently looking for something. The rear of the vehicle, however, remained shielded from view, with its dark curtains still tightly sealed.

Redmond nodded towards the hearse. 'What's in the back of it?' he said.

'No one you know,' said Benny.

The highly polished exterior of the hearse gleamed in the early morning light. The Doctor's legs protruded from the vehicle's open front door; they wiggled as he writhed around inside, looking for something.

'Do you want a hand?' said Creed.

'No,' said the Doctor's voice from inside. 'It's just this rather annoying glove compartment. It's stuck. I suppose the glove compartment doesn't get used much in a vehicle like this. Ah. There we go.' There was a clunking sound and the Doctor emerged from the front of the hearse, smiling.

He leant out, his hand extended, offering a small enamelled box to Creed.

Creed took it and examined it. The box was a chunky

hinged cube, surprisingly heavy, as if it was made of lead. The exterior of the box was lacquered a shiny black, with gold-coloured lettering cut into it.

The lettering was ridiculously elaborate and Creed doubted he would've been able to read it even if it had been in English.

But the lettering appeared to be Russian. What they call Cyrillic script. Creed hefted the small box. It was cool to the touch.

The Doctor slammed the glove compartment shut and scrambled back out of the hearse. Creed looked up as he came over.

'Is it made of lead?'

'No. Another metal similar in weight,' said the Doctor. 'Gold.'

Creed traced the antique Russian lettering with his fingers. 'What's inside?'

The Doctor drew a small gold key out of his pocket and waggled it. 'I could tell you,' he said, handing the key to Creed. 'But I won't need to. As soon as you open the box you'll know. Even before you see it, you'll know what's inside.'

Creed took the key. The Doctor was right. He knew what was in it as soon as he unlocked it and opened it the merest crack.

Because suddenly there was a strong liquorice aroma all around them, hanging on the clean morning air. Under the hearse the old white dog suddenly whined.

'Warlock,' said Creed. He opened the box the rest of the way and saw that the drug was in its unprocessed form: a couple of withered mushrooms; the distinctive yellow, green and purple splotches faded an almost uniform brown on the dried folds of the fungi.

'Yes, I'm afraid the past has come back to haunt us,' said the Doctor.

He took another key from his pocket, but this one was just an old-fashioned car key on a plastic Playboy rabbit-head keyfob. The Doctor went around to the curtained rear of the vehicle and unlocked the tail-gate. As he swung it open the White King was on his feet and leaping fluidly into the rear of the hearse.

Creed stared in surprise; the ancient dog had moved like an eager young pup. Now the Doctor was scrambling in after it.

After a moment's hesitation, Creed followed them.

The Doctor was pulling the curtains open, letting the steadily brightening sunlight into the back of the hearse. 'On the other hand,' he said, 'some might argue that is precisely the proper function of the past. To come back and haunt us.' As he scraped the curtains back and light swept into the gloomy interior Creed could see that the old dog had shoved itself in beside a long object on the floor of the hearse.

Creed had expected to see a coffin. But this was something quite different.

There was a body in the back all right, but it was lying in a transparent two-metre-high cylinder which was surrounded by piles of cushions.

Creed set down the box of warlock, which he was still carrying, and crawled forward to get a better look. The dog was close to him now and Creed was surprised that he could get near the thing without flinching. In recent hours dogs had come to represent the enemy, but this one gave no hint of menace. It seemed utterly harmless, old and frail, all its attention focused on the cylinder.

The huge cylinder was half buried under the cushions and pillows. There were dozens of them, tattered and dirty; a motley assortment which looked like they had been pillaged from sofas and beds in a run down English country house. The dog twitched beside him and sneezed. Creed sympathized. His own nose was tickling with the musty, dusty smell of the pillows and cushions.

But in a moment it was overpowered by the liquorice scent of the warlock which was wafting from the small box Creed had set down, filling the back of the hearse. He tried to ignore it and concentrate on the strange contents of the hearse.

The cushions and pillows were jammed in beside the big cylinder, wedging it into place. Creed realized that they were a good idea; the cylinder appeared to be made of glass and didn't look like it could take much bashing about.

The Doctor was kneeling on the other side of the cylinder. He nodded down at it. 'Do you recognize him, Creed?'

Creed stared down into the cylinder, at the face of the naked man lying inside it. The face was hauntingly familiar.

The memory tugged at him for a moment then slipped away.

The man had red hair plastered across his pale forehead, mashed down by the wide piece of elastic which someone had put on him like a headband. The headband secured a cluster of electrical components to the man's head.

Creed couldn't identify their function but they looked hastily assembled; jury-rigged. A long cable ran from them into the front of the hearse where they connected to a miniature TV-screen propped in the front seat.

'Been busy with the soldering iron, I see,' said Creed. He looked at the tangle of electrical components that rested on the man's head and then he noticed the beads of moisture in the man's hair around the fat rubber headband.

Creed realized that the man was sweating, and as he watched the man's eyes rolled back and forth under his closed lids, like a sleeper deep in REM.

'He's alive,' said Creed.

'Yes, he is. Do you remember his name?'

'Jack.' The name had suddenly popped into Creed's head, and the sensation was rather disturbing.

It was just the familiar sensation of one's memory suddenly retrieving a missing piece of information, but it felt a little odd to Creed. Almost as if someone else had put the name in his head.

The smell of warlock was growing thick and heavy in the back of the hearse even though the tail-gate was open. Creed felt the strange rush of the drug, still familiar after all these years. The blood pulsed in his head with a new precision and delicacy, like some precious molten metal transmitting strange electrical currents.

Creed scrambled back to the open tail-gate and sucked in lungfulls of the cold clean morning air. The sky above him was a deep beautiful blue, a tiny jet leaving a vapour trail across it like a white scar.

'Are you all right?' said the Doctor.

'Yeah,' said Creed, taking a final lungful of air, then crawling back into the hearse to join him. 'The smell of the warlock was starting to get to me, that's all.'

'Forgive me,' said the Doctor. 'I'd forgotten all about it. Could you give it to me please?'

Creed handed him the small enamelled box, leaning across

the glass cylinder with Jack inside it. 'Was this a life-support tank?'

'That's right. We just drained the fluid out of it. Jack isn't conscious but we still thought it would be reassuring for him.'

'Reassuring?'

'Yes, we had to bring him up to London with us. He was our guide. He enabled us to find you.'

'How?' said Creed, trying to concentrate. The heady liquorice smell of warlock was beginning to get to him again. He shook his head to clear it and the Doctor noticed.

'It's all right, Creed. I'll seal this box up properly in a moment and then the smell will be gone. Just let me do this first.'

He reached into the enamelled box and fished out a small fragment of dried mushroom.

'What are you doing?'

The Doctor leant over the glass cylinder. 'I'm going to feed this to our friend here.' Creed realized he meant the White King.

'Won't we have to mix it with some dog food or something?'

'Not with this dog.' The Doctor reached his hand out towards the White King, who lay panting on a pile of cushions beside the cylinder.

The old dog sniffed at the piece of mushroom in his hand and then suddenly caught it between his teeth, shook his head and gulped it down. The Doctor leant back and snapped the small enamelled box shut. He glanced up at Creed who was staring into the glass cylinder.

'Jack . . . Isn't he the guy we had to rescue from the animal experimentation lab?'

'Yes, it's all coming back to you now, isn't it?'

'Yeah. They'd dosed him with warlock and something very weird happened to his mind, didn't it.'

'Yes, he lost it.'

'Lost it?' said Creed.

'Yes. He lost his mind, but not in the conventional sense. When Jack lost his mind it went somewhere else.'

Creed looked up from the man in the glass cylinder. He stared at the Doctor, then he looked at the White King.

The dog was pressing its nose against the glass of the cylinder, peering lovingly at the man inside.

'You're kidding,' he said.

'No,' said the Doctor. He pulled out a handkerchief and wiped the cylinder where the dog's breath had fogged the glass, revealing the pale face inside. He stuffed the handkerchief back in his pocket and patted the dog on the head.

'Jack is coming back,' he said.

The sun was rising, lighting up the country lanes ahead of them as they drove south and east, following the small secondary and tertiary roads into Kent.

The hearse was a large vehicle with a spectacularly wide front seat, from an older and grander age of motoring. But it was still quite a squeeze with the five of them sitting up front. Oddly enough, no one wanted to sit in the back with Jack and the White King.

Benny found it annoying that no one would sit in the back. The truth was, they were scared. Well, perhaps scared was too strong a word. After all, there was indeed something strange about the unconscious man in the glass cylinder wedged in the back of the hearse, and about the dog which lay worshipfully across him.

It had the others spooked. Benny felt a little contemptuous. It was so ridiculous that none of them would sit in the back. They were all grown-ups.

Not that Benny wanted to sit in the back, herself.

The Doctor wouldn't have minded, of course. But he wasn't the problem. He was so small that he took up virtually no room in the front seat. It was Creed and Redmond who took up the room.

Roz had insisted on driving, so Benny ended up wedged between the two big men.

'Why did you insist on coming with us, anyway, Redmond?' she said. Benny realized that she sounded rather unfriendly, but being jammed in here like a sardine made her cross.

'Well, I was at a bit of a loose end,' said Redmond affably. 'What with the state of emergency suddenly being over and all. And you seemed like an interesting bunch of folk to visit for a little while. Since the Doctor was kind enough to invite me down to his house in Kent.'

'Well, couldn't you have caught the train? No, look I'm sorry. I didn't mean that. But shouldn't you have stayed with Norman Peverell and Jessica? Won't they need help?'

'They didn't look like they'd welcome anybody's help,' said Creed. 'Or anybody's company.'

'I thought Norman was supposed to be summoning reinforcements,' said Roz, squinting over the steering-wheel into the steep rays of early sunlight. Benny wished she'd lower the sun-visor. It wasn't safe driving like this.

'I'm sure he'll get around to it,' said Creed, and both he and Redmond chuckled.

'What do you mean?'

'Well, the emergency's over and all that,' said Redmond. 'There's no more danger. No hurry. Might as well take it easy.'

'I can't imagine Norman taking it easy. He's a stickler for rules and regulations.'

'Maybe he's loosening up a little.'

Creed and Redmond laughed again and Roz frowned at them. 'What is the joke?' she said.

'Well,' said Redmond. 'I suppose pissing your pants is one way to strike up a conversation with a pretty girl.'

'People have met under stranger circumstances,' said Creed. 'And ended up together.' He repressed an image of his wife; a flash of her in London on the day they'd met. Walking up that long stone staircase in St James. In his memory she was forever walking up that staircase in her black culottes and leather jacket, defiant and young and so beautiful.

'But do you really think he'll get his leg over?' said Redmond.

'Yes,' said Creed.

'Male bullshit,' said Roz.

'Maybe, but I still say they'll end up in bed.'

Roz turned and looked at the Doctor. Her normally caustic tone was tempered by her respect for him.

'What do you think?'

The Doctor pursed his lips. 'Oh, I think quite probably.'

'Does that mean yes?'

'Yes.'

'But her boyfriend's just been killed,' said Roz.

'And Norman's just pissed his pants,' added Redmond irreverently.

'Precisely,' said the Doctor. 'They're both extremely vulnerable. They need each other at this point and if they can help each other heal their wounds then that's good.'

'What do you think, Benny?'

'I think Roz should put the visor down so she isn't driving with the sun in her eyes.'

The old house on Allen Road looked warm and welcoming as they approached it, the tyres of the hearse crunching on the gravel drive. Benny had climbed out to shut the gate behind them and suddenly there was enough room in the front so everyone could relax, for the last half-minute of the journey anyway.

The hearse climbed the curved length of the drive and stopped in front of the big garage, which had once been stables designed for a dozen or more horses.

The house beside the garage was big, clean and simple in its lines; its bricks a warm rusty shade of red.

Creed was startled by the intensity of the memories it stirred in him. 'It's just the way I remember it,' he said.

'You can have the same bedroom upstairs if you like,' said the Doctor. Roz pulled the hearse to a halt outside the garage and they all climbed out, yawning and stretching.

They heard footsteps rattling on the loose gravel behind them and turned to see Benny sauntering up the driveway. She looked exhausted after wrestling with the rusty gates.

Creed shivered in the cool morning air as he followed the Doctor to the back door of the house. The Doctor paused to scoop up a bottle of milk, then he unlocked the door and held it open for Creed.

Creed stepped into the big farmhouse-style kitchen and froze on the spot.

'Are you all right?' said the Doctor.

'Yes, fine,' muttered Creed.

The truth was, he was experiencing a rush of memory so powerful it was almost incapacitating. It was in this room that, in a very real sense, he and Justine had come together.

They had made love already, of course. But Justine was still married to Vincent. And she was carrying his child. She and Creed had begun their affair under the intensity of danger. Their lives had been at risk and Justine had been unavoidably separated from her husband.

For all Creed knew at that point, she might have gone back to her husband. Perhaps for all that Justine knew, too.

It might have happened that way.

Justine had been hanging indecisively between the two men. Her husband and her lover. Fate had made up her mind for her; fate in the shape of a man called Harrigan who'd walked in carrying a gun. Walked into this same kitchen, all those years ago.

Justine had been sitting here between her husband and Creed, and Harrigan had walked in carrying his gun. He had come here to take Creed's life.

Afterwards, after they stopped him, Justine had run to Creed and put her arms around him and that had decided the matter. Justine had made her choice. She stayed with Creed, and so her husband turned away and walked out of their lives.

They never saw Vincent again.

The Doctor pulled out a rickety wooden stool and set it beside the kitchen counter. 'You look rather distracted,' he said, offering the stool to Creed.

Creed sat down on it and began to take his jacket off. 'Just thinking,' he said.

'Lost in the past?'

'Yeah.'

'I know what that's like,' said the Doctor. 'Let me make you some coffee. I'm sorry if that stool's uncomfortable but all the cushions are still in the hearse. I'll get Benny to unload them.'

He put the coffee on and wandered out of the back door again, leaving it open so that the cool early morning smell of the garden drifted in. Birds hopped in the patches of sunlight on the rough paving stones outside.

Creed hardly noticed. He was lost in thoughts of Justine. It was strange how fate had nudged them together, intervening at critical moments. They never would have ended up in bed if Paulie Keaton hadn't threatened to kill her baby and Creed hadn't come to her rescue. They never would have come together if Harrigan had not come stomping into this kitchen with his cowboy boots and his revolver.

The Doctor came back into the kitchen and began to rattle around in a cupboard, selecting mugs for the coffee which was beginning to pulse up hotly in the percolator. As soon as the jug was full he poured the first steaming aromatic cup for Creed and set it in front of him with a delicate Victorian bowl full of coloured crystal sugar and the milk bottle he'd just picked up outside. The delicate seal on the bottle was ruptured and the Doctor apologized. 'They've never been able to work out a way to stop the birds getting at it. I trust you don't begrudge a small bird a drop of milk.'

Creed smiled and shook his head. He stirred his coffee and reflected that, as strange as it was to remember how he and Justine had come together, it was even stranger to be back here now, with all those years of love, marriage and kids, stretching out behind him.

And to know that he might not be going back to her.

Creed was tired from the long night and the uncomfortable drive down to Kent. Never accept a lift in an overcrowded hearse, he thought.

In his mind he was telling the story of the ride in the hearse. Telling Amy, her sea-green eyes wide open and staring into his, as she listened to him, spellbound. Then Creed found himself sleepily slipping through the colour of those eyes into an erotic waking dream where he swam naked around the warm waters of a lagoon with an equally naked blonde girl, lithe and young, and tanned.

She flickered through the warm water in front of him, gold of hair and limbs against the blue-green water. And he was swimming with her, swimming in circles in the warm lagoon. Then he realized that they weren't swimming at all. They were being swept around by a swirling current, around and around in this tropical lagoon like a giant jacuzzi.

And then the warm vortex swept them together and she was in his arms, hot and wet, her lips tasting salty.

Suddenly outside the kitchen, someone started to scream and it ripped Creed awake.

It was Benny. She was screaming, out in the driveway. Quickly Creed was out of the back door and running past the garage.

The Doctor was running behind him, their feet spraying gravel up from the driveway.

The others were already there, beside the hearse with Benny. She'd stopped screaming. She was standing back now, moving away from the hearse. The tail-gate of the big black car was hanging open.

Benny backed away, a look of shock on her face. Redmond and Roz stood staring at her, looking a little uncertain. Then they both drew their guns at once and climbed into the back of the hearse.

A moment later Creed and the Doctor reached Benny. The Doctor went to her immediately and took her hand. Creed kept going towards the hearse. There was a fresh morning breeze stirring, and the sharp liquorice smell of warlock was swirling out from the back of the vehicle.

Redmond came backing out of the hearse, straightening up and lowering his gun. He had a disgusted, and slightly disappointed, expression on his face. He looked disdainfully at Benny who stood there with the Doctor holding her hand.

'It's nothing. It's just the old white dog in there. He's pegged it,' said Redmond. 'He's dead.'

Roz was backing out of the hearse now, also lowering her gun. Creed began to relax again. There was clearly no imminent danger here. Redmond was smiling at Creed. 'Just the dog,' he said. 'That's all it was.'

'No!' said Benny suddenly, angrily wrenching her hand free from the Doctor's comforting grip. 'That was not all it was. It was also –' Benny lurched to a halt.

'Also what?'

'Also me,' said a low, croaky voice.

A shudder went through everyone standing there. Everyone except the Doctor. They all turned around to stare at the rear of the open hearse.

A naked man with lank red hair was leaning on the tail-gate.

He was pale and gaunt enough to suggest a corpse which had recently crawled out of a coffin inside. But probably the most disturbing thing about his appearance was his face. One moment it would be hideously slack. Then the next, the muscles of his face would be in violent spasm.

After a moment Creed realized that the man was trying to smile at them.

The Doctor was the first to go over to him, and put a

reassuring hand on the man's shoulder. 'Welcome, back,' he said. 'Welcome home, Jack.'

The others approached hesitantly and stared down at the man; pale, gaunt, exhausted, but very much alive he lay shaking in the back of the hearse.

'He looks like shit.'

'Now, Redmond, that's rather insensitive when you consider that our friend is coming back from years of deep coma. Think of him as an intelligence coming back out of nothingness, like a space traveller descending through endless reaches of the black sky. Or imagine him surfacing from the mind's deepest oceans.' The Doctor patted Jack's shoulder, but now it was like he was slapping him with affectionate camaraderie. 'A traveller in strange places. What has he seen?' said the Doctor. 'What has he experienced?'

'Could you be a little more enigmatic?' said Redmond.

'What the Doctor's trying to say,' said Creed, 'is that Jack has spent a decade or two floating around in a life-support tank.'

The Doctor patted Jack on the back again. The gesture was strangely reminiscent of patting a baby reassuringly on the back. 'That's only half the problem,' he said. 'Jack's body may have spent those years floating in a tank, but his mind spent them inside the body of a dog.'

He nodded to the White King. The dog lay sprawled across the floor of the hearse, looking strangely shrivelled in death.

Redmond shook his head. 'What are you trying to tell me, Doctor? That Jack here was the White King?'

'Well, you might say he was *in* the White King.'

'In the dog?'

'His consciousness, yes. To put it simply, his mind was inside the dog's brain.'

'Well,' said Redmond. He didn't seem to have any trouble grasping the concepts the Doctor was presenting. Instead he seemed to be growing angry. 'Perhaps,' he said, 'Jack would like to tell us just what the hell his consciousness was doing creating a state of emergency by making every frigging dog in London run amok?'

Jack looked up at them from the tail-gate of the hearse. His facial muscles were under some kind of control now, only occasionally subsiding into spastic convulsions. 'I was trying to reach you,' he said in that deep, rough voice. It sounded like a rusty mechanism grinding back into action after years left idle.

He gulped and gagged painfully. 'Sorry,' he said. 'It hurts to talk.'

Redmond wasn't sympathetic. He was shaking with rage. 'I can't say that's much of an excuse for your behaviour. What do you mean you were trying to reach me?'

'Not you,' said Jack. 'The Doctor.'

Jack closed his eyes and lowered his head, as though the effort of talking had exhausted him. If not for his flushed pink colour he would have looked like the motionless figure in the glass tube again. The Doctor looked concerned. He eased the man back on to the floor of the hearse.

'Don't try to talk, Jack. Benny and Roz, take Creed inside the house. Someone find Jack some warm clothing and someone fix him some hot food. Nothing too hard to chew.'

As always, the Doctor took command effortlessly and no one thought of questioning his instructions. He looked up at Redmond after the others had left and said, 'I'll try and explain. Jack's behaviour with the dog packs was a cry for help. An attempt to attract my attention.' His face became grim. 'And I imagine that he also went a little mad after all those years trapped in a body that wasn't his own.'

'Why did he have to attract your attention?'

'Because I'm the only one who could help him.' The Doctor glanced down at Jack. The man was shaking himself awake again. He cleared his throat and after a momentary effort, he spoke again.

'I heard what you said, Doctor.' He smiled his horrible, face-writhing grin. 'I'm not mad.'

'I'm sorry I said that, Jack. I only meant that you'd undergone a shattering ordeal.'

'Not mad. Not me,' said Jack.

'Of course not. Try and relax. We'll carry you inside in a minute.'

But Jack kept doggedly talking, visibly fighting off sleep. 'It's not me.'

'Of course not,' said the Doctor.

He and Redmond looked up at the sudden crunch of gravel and saw Creed approaching with an armful of clothes. 'I think I've got every woollen garment in the house,' he said. 'The women folk are in the kitchen arguing about who's the expert at making toast. How's our friend?'

'He'll be all right. Help me get some of this clothing on to him before his core temperature begins to drop. Here, you take his arm Creed.'

On the tail-gate of the hearse Jack's eyes snapped open. 'Creed,' he said.

'That's me, tiger. Now try to put this sweater on.'

'Creed, you have to watch out.'

'I always do, friend.'

'You have to watch out. You're in terrible danger. I'm not mad.'

'Of course not.'

'I'm not the one who's mad.'

'That's it. Now see if you can stand up. Good. One step at a time.'

'It's not me. It's him. He's mad. Very mad.'

'Who's that, sport?' said Creed.

'Vincent.'

Chapter 34

'Vincent?'

There was no response. So she tried again. A little louder this time.

'Vincent. Hey Vincent.'

'What?'

'Nothing.' Amy kept her eyes on the traffic and concentrated on driving. She smiled blandly, concealing the sharp jolt of triumph she felt.

The man who called himself Retour was looking across at her from the passenger seat of her yellow Fiat. 'Oh, very cute,' he said after a moment. 'Very clever.'

'I thought so,' said Amy smugly.

'And you tested your theory.'

'Right.'

'You said the name Vincent to see if I'd respond to it.'

'Right.'

'And I did.'

'Right.'

'Look Amy –'

'Ms Cowan to you.'

'Look, Ms Cowan. I'm suitably –'

Amy interrupted him. 'Full name: Vincent Wheaton. Correct?'

'Correct.'

'Vincent Wheaton. So why are you calling yourself Retour?'

'Look. I'm suitably impressed with your computer snooping skills. You must be very clever at hacking into forbidden files if you've dug out my real name. But frankly, Ms Cowan, it doesn't change the bottom line.' He looked at her, his face tight with anger. 'And the bottom line is that you work for me. So just keep driving.'

'But why Retour?'

'Why not?'

'Because it's kind of clumsy and obvious. "Retour" is French for "return".'

'Is it?' said Vincent. 'How appropriate. You take a left here and it's Concroft Avenue.'

'I know where I'm going.'

'Yeah, I guess you do.'

They pulled up in the shade of the trees outside the McIlveens' big white house. A bright red sports car from an earlier epoch was parked in the driveway and a woman was just walking away from it, up the front steps of the house.

'That's the neighbour, Mrs McCracken. Widow. Look at that body. You can get a fair idea what killed the husband.'

Amy sighed disgustedly and didn't reply. Up on the porch Mrs McCracken reached for the doorbell then hesitated.

'She's not ringing it. She's coming back down off the porch.'

'Do you think she saw us?'

'No. She's just going around to the back of the house for some reason.'

'Why?'

'Who cares why. Ricky just stepped out of the front door.'

'OK. Drive slowly and let him get out of sight of the house before we pick him up.'

Ricky's faithful old sneakers, almost worn out and held together mostly by their laces now, scuffed along the sidewalk as he walked towards the bus stop. Ricky caught the bus to school everyday. Unlike his sister he didn't have any snobbery about using public transport. His sister was a princess who had to be picked up in a vintage sports car and chauffeured to school. Not that you'd call Mrs McCracken a chauffeur.

Ricky liked Mrs McCracken and she'd offered to give him a lift every day, too. But as much as he might like Mrs McCracken, the thought of being cooped up with his sister and her best friend was too much to bear.

And then there was the thought of arriving at the school in that distinctive shiny car. No way you could escape attention arriving in that. All the kids would be staring. Everybody's eyes would be on you.

Ricky didn't like the idea of all those eyes on him.

So each day he would walk to the end of Concroft Avenue, turn right and walk another two blocks to the bus stop. There he caught the bus to school with a crowd of other kids including a couple of his cronies, Tommy Barretta and Phil Mendick. Ricky caught the bus every day.

Not today, though.

Today Ricky hadn't reached the end of Concroft Avenue when a car rolled up behind him and a window hummed down.

As he saw Amy Cowan leaning out and smiling at him Ricky had a sudden flash of déjà vu. A beautiful blonde leaning out of a car window.

'Hello Ricky,' she said and Ricky was momentarily lost in the pleasure of looking into her lovely face, enjoying the strange ebbing sensation of déjà vu in his head. He hardly noticed the man in the car with her. It was his sister's history teacher, some guy called Retour.

Amy's smile faded and her face suddenly turned serious. 'Ricky, could you get in the car with us. I'm afraid we have some bad news for you.'

'Isn't there some sort of Buddhist injunction against being a Peeping Tom?'

The Buddhist monk was so startled by the sudden sound of Mrs McCracken's voice that he would have jumped in the air.

But he was already in the air, hanging on to one of the window-sills at the back of the McIlveen house. The shaven-headed young monk had lifted himself up on to the sill as if he was doing a chin-up and now he was hanging there in athletic fashion, with no apparent sign of strain.

His body twitched with surprise at Mrs McCracken's voice and then the young monk turned to look at her.

'You look very silly hanging there in your orange robe.'

'Well, I feel pretty stupid.'

'So let go,' said Lesley McCracken.

The monk let go of his hold and dropped. Immediately below the window was a patch of roses but he managed to land clear of them, alighting sure-footedly on the springy green turf of the lawn. Mrs McCracken was wearing her mirrored sunglasses which, at the best of times, gave her the look of a predatory insect. Now as she glowered at the monk in front of her she looked formidably menacing.

'What are you doing skulking around in Justine's roses, young man?'

A window scraped open above them.

'That isn't a young man. It's the Young Master.'

Cynthia McIlveen and Lysette McCracken were leaning out of the window of Cynthia's bedroom. Mrs McCracken scowled up at the girls.

'He teaches us Comparative Anthropology,' they said.

'And he seems to be doing some fieldwork,' said Mrs McCracken. 'Like peering in your back windows.'

'I need to see Justine,' said the monk.

'You certainly do. I think you'd better come in and explain yourself to the lady of the house immediately, baldy.'

Mrs McCracken led the young man inside the house, doing everything short of dragging him by his ear. They walked through sunny pale rooms into the kitchen where Justine was stirring pancake batter in a large green porcelain bowl.

'Good Lord, isn't there an appliance that can do that for you? Justine, I found this young man skulking in your shrubbery.'

'I wasn't skulking, I was trying to ascertain who was in the house before I announced my presence.'

Mrs McCracken removed her insectoid sunglasses, exposing her eyes for the first time. They were unexpectedly pleasant.

'Actually you announced your presence with your bony knees,' she smiled. 'If one stands at Justine's front door and stares through a certain window at a certain angle, one can see right through the house.'

'And Lesley always makes sure that she's standing at just the right angle,' said Justine

'Damned right. I could see right through the house to another window out the back. And I saw our visitor's bony knees waving in the air as he clambered up one of your back windows.'

'I needed to speak to you urgently, Justine.'

'Is there some Buddhist thing about not using the phone?' asked Mrs McCracken.

'Well, you might as well sit down,' said Justine, setting aside her bowl of pancake batter and fetching a jug of orange juice from the refrigerator.

'Here, let me do that, dear. It had better be freshly squeezed.' Mrs McCracken poured tall glasses for all of them. 'I don't suppose anybody would join me if I cracked open a bottle of vodka? No, not a very good idea I suppose, considering I still have to drive both of our little angels to school.'

The monk had been standing tensely and now he accepted a glass of orange juice but immediately set it aside.

'That's what I've come about. Your children. It's a matter of their safety.'

Both of the women were staring at him now, their eyes suddenly cold with suspicion.

'I'm not explaining this very well. The Doctor sent me, Justine. He said do you remember the time you left your house early one morning? You lived in a house by the river in London and you got up early, to run away from him?'

The suspicion faded from Justine's eyes. She turned away and sat down at the kitchen table. 'Yes, I remember,' she said. And she remembered what had happened in Canterbury afterwards. The thing Vincent had done. Justine didn't want to think of what had happened in Canterbury. The enormity of it would overwhelm her. So now she fought off the rush of memories and focused on the bald young man standing in her kitchen. Mrs McCracken still eyed him suspiciously, protective of her friend.

'The Doctor sent you?'

'Yes.'

'Who are you then?'

'My name is Christopher Cwej. I'm not really a Buddhist monk.'

'No kidding,' said Lesley McCracken.

'The Doctor has sent me to help you.'

'Help me in what way?'

The shaven-headed young man called Chris sighed, as if he didn't know where to start. His confusion made him look even younger, giving him a boyish appeal that called out to the women in the kitchen, both of them mothers.

'Sit down and drink your juice,' ordered Mrs McCracken, and Chris sat down opposite Justine.

'It's all very complex,' he said. 'And I'm afraid you'll find it somewhat disorientating.'

'You said something about my kids. That sounds pretty basic.'

'Yes, right. Well let me explain. There are, in the world, people with strange talents. People who attract the wrong kind of attention. People who have abilities they try to hide from the world.'

'What are you blathering about?' said Mrs McCracken.

'Quiet please, Lesley.' Justine was staring at the shaven-headed young man as if she understood exactly what he meant.

'These people try to hide their abilities. Or when they're young, their parents do the hiding,' he said.

'What is he talking about, Justine?'

'Ricky.'

'Ricky?'

'He's always had a gift. Haven't you noticed?'

'Well, I've noticed that the kids seem to follow him around. And one day I imagine he'll have a real knack for attracting the girls. But I can't say –'

Chris interrupted. 'Ever seen him with a large group?'

'No,' said Mrs McCracken. 'Unless your family counts as a large group.'

'Well, he's right,' said Justine. 'Ricky has some very remarkable power. But he doesn't have any idea how to use it.'

'Not just Ricky,' said the young man. 'All of your children have been under surveillance.'

Justine's eyes widened in shock. 'What do you mean? Since when?'

'I warned you this would be disorientating. You have been under the observation of a clandestine government agency for years.'

Justine laughed. 'This is all some kind of mistake. I appreciate the Doctor's concern but there's been some confusion.' She glanced at Mrs McCracken.

'Do you want me to leave the room or something?' said the older woman, reaching for her sunglasses. 'You have the look of someone who is about to disclose something highly confidential.'

'She is about to tell me that her husband himself works for a clandestine government organisation,' said the shaven-headed young man.

Justine stared at him in fury, unable to believe what he'd said. Chris shrugged apologetically. 'It's too late for secrets. We know your husband works for the Agency, Justine. Mrs McCracken might as well learn that now. But it isn't the Agency that has been keeping you under surveillance.' Chris's smooth bald forehead creased. He knotted his long fingers together and frowned at them with concentration, as though he was studying a puzzle. 'At least, it's not the Agency per se. But Creed's job has certainly made it all the easier for your family to be watched. Essentially one secret arm of the government is spying on another. One secret agency subverting another. The very things that made you secure, the protection of the Agency, has actually made you vulnerable. You've been in an ideal situation to be watched.'

'But watched for what? Who are these people?'

'Weapons research.'

'This is crazy.'

'On the contrary. They see your children as potential weapons.'

'What is he talking about?' said Mrs McCracken. But Justine ignored her. She looked like a woman piecing a puzzle together, juxtaposing the confusing fragments, and discovering that it all made a frightening kind of sense.

'What is your part in all this? Why are you teaching at the school?'

'The Doctor's gradually become aware of what was happening. So he sent me here. Planted me to keep an eye on things. But events are moving much more swiftly than we imagined possible. The opposition is about to make their move, after years of watching.'

Justine stared at Chris. 'But who is there who would go to that much trouble? We're not that important to anyone. Who would . . .'

Mrs McCracken and Chris both saw the terrible realization dawning behind her eyes.

'Oh, my God,' she said quietly. 'He's back.'

At that moment there was a faint sound from outside the kitchen door.

A tiny creaking sound in the hallway.

They all heard it at the same instant, and registered the fact that someone was outside. They shared the same sinking feeling as they realized that someone had been outside, listening all along.

Chris was the first to react, dropping into a martial arts stance and sweeping a long sharp kitchen knife out of its rack.

But it was Mrs McCracken who marched out of the kitchen and dragged the two teenage girls in by the scruff of the neck. 'These are our two darling daughters,' she said. 'Lysette, for whom I'm to blame. And Cynthia who is Justine's personal cross to bear.' She released the girls, letting them slink to a low bench in a corner of the kitchen; they perched there, looking sheepish.

'But you know that, don't you?' said Mrs McCracken, sitting at the table with the other grown-ups. 'Since you teach them Comparative something-or-other.'

'Anthropology,' said Chris absently. 'Where is Ricky? Is he upstairs?'

'No, he's gone.'

'Gone?' Chris had sat down again and relaxed after he saw the girls, but now he was sitting tensely on the edge of his chair. 'He's gone?'

'Yes. He's left for school.'

Chris was up on his feet instantly, his robes rippling smoothly around him. 'But I didn't see him go.'

Mrs McCracken was looking up at Chris with an expression of approval. She'd been agreeably surprised by the swift fluid athleticism of his move. 'He was going out of the front,' she said, 'while you were trying to climb in the back.'

'I didn't hear a car.'

'He gets a bus to school.'

The shaven-headed young man was hurrying out of the kitchen, heading for the front door. He called back as he ran. 'Which way is he headed?'

'Here, let me drive you,' said Mrs McCracken, scooping her sunglasses and car keys off the table and dashing out after him.

'What about our lift to school?' called Cynthia, only letting out the scandalized cry an instant before her friend.

'Keep them both at home,' bellowed Chris from the front of the house.

The girls stared at Justine and she shrugged. 'No school today, I guess.'

The door slammed a moment later as Mrs McCracken followed Chris out.

He was hovering by the passenger door of the Corvette.

'It's open,' said Mrs McCracken as she scrambled into the driver's seat and jabbed the keys in to start the engine. As Chris climbed in beside her she gunned the ignition, getting into the spirit of things.

The powerful old car burned rubber as they squealed out into Concroft Avenue.

They were in luck.

The school bus was running late that morning thanks to a traffic snarl-up down-town. The kids at the bus stop were all still waiting. Tommy Barretta was there. Phil Mendick was there.

But there was no sign of Ricky. None of the kids had seen him.

'It's too late,' said Chris. 'They got to him.'

It was unsettling, and oddly unpleasant, to see someone else sitting behind Mr Pangbourne's desk.

But Ricky decided he wouldn't like this guy Retour even if he hadn't taken over the principal's office. Not that the man had given any reason to be disliked. He was being nice to Ricky, polite and considerate.

Too nice in fact; it seemed Retour was always trying to catch Ricky's eye and shoot him a warm look of approval. Encouragement. It was almost creepy. Ricky would have wondered if the guy was queer for him and if this was some kind of set-up.

But Amy's presence squashed that theory. And then of course there was the news that they'd given him. Ricky could feel the presence of that news in the back of his mind, naggingly present, too tender to touch, like a bruise of information.

Amy sat in the other chair opposite Pangbourne's desk. Ricky still thought of it as Pangbourne's desk.

Retour sat behind it and smiled at him. That creepy smile.

'You don't have any choice,' he said.

It was true. 'Did he really ask for me to do this?'

'Yes,' said Retour. 'He recovered consciousness briefly last night. He was very lucid and matter-of-fact. Like he knew he only had a few minutes to arrange his affairs. They say that happens sometimes with brain injuries.'

Ricky felt a lump in his throat. He looked across at Amy but she sat there, saying nothing, not meeting his eye.

'When do I have to do it?' he said.

Retour checked his watch. 'The whole school will have gathered for assembly by now. Any time you're ready.'

Ricky thought, any time I'm ready? That will be never.

He sat there wanting to sink into the chair and vanish. He didn't want to leave the office. But Retour looked at his watch and then he got up and Amy got up too. They opened the office door.

Ricky didn't sink into the chair. He got up and followed them. As he walked down the school corridor he hoped an earthquake would cause the ground to open and swallow him. But the concrete floor remained firm under his feet.

The door to the school hall swung open as Amy and Mr Retour held it for him. It was odd for a couple of teachers to hold a door open for a kid, but Ricky hardly noticed as he stepped into the big hall.

Every kid in the school was there, sitting in chairs on either side of the narrow aisle. Ricky was walking up that aisle. He wanted to turn back. Turn and run. But Retour and Amy were walking behind him. Walking close together. He couldn't break past them. On either side of him were the kids, row after row of them, all looking at him. Every eye on him as he was escorted towards the front of the big hall.

Towards the stage.

There was a single microphone hovering over a small lectern at the centre of the stage, facing the audience. Normally the principal stood there and addressed the assembled school after the national anthem was played in holographic stereo over concealed speakers.

The principal wouldn't be addressing them today.

Ricky had reached the steps at the side of the stage. The whole school was watching him. A wave of surprise had spread across the room when the kids first saw him. They knew that something odd was happening. A kid standing up to address the whole school? What had happened to Mr Pangbourne?

Now the first shock of seeing Ricky had passed; it had been replaced with a greedy, hungry mood. The kids were expectant, eager for spectacle.

At any moment impatience would begin to set in, with throat-clearing and foot-shuffling. But now they were full of attention, spellbound.

Waiting for a show.

As Ricky began to walk up the staircase on to the stage he suddenly realized what he had to do. There was a trick he could use, the same trick that had worked for years.

Stumble. Stumble as he walked up the steps. If he could make himself trip, fumble, look clumsy, then he would be free. The kids would laugh at him and dismiss him. They'd start to talk among themselves. Their attention, all focused on one point – on Ricky – would fragment. And the horrible weight of that attention would be lifted from him.

Ricky willed himself to stumble on the stairs.

Instead he floated up them gracefully in a lithe continuous motion. He moved like a man who had something important to do. A man with a mission.

Instead of easing, the attention of the crowd grew more intense. You could have heard a pin drop as Ricky crossed the stage.

He went and stood at the lectern, staring into the hundreds of faces, all lost in the common identity of the crowd. He was clutching the papers Retour had given him, a short speech to read to the school.

Ricky knew this was his last chance. He could still shatter the attention of the crowd. He could do it by using his voice. He could stutter, or clear his throat loudly into the microphone, or just dry up completely and lose his nerve. Soon the crowd would begin to giggle and stir, waking from the spell he held them in.

Once again he would become someone to laugh at or ignore. Someone harmless. And then their attention would move on to something else and he would be safely anonymous again. All he had to do was screw up now.

It was his last chance. Dry up. Clear your throat. Stutter.

With a final flutter of despair, Ricky realized that he wasn't capable of doing any of these things. He looked at the crowd, opened his mouth and began to speak.

The weight of his words was such that they seemed to pronounce themselves. There was no way he could diminish the importance of what he had to say. So he spoke in a clear serious voice and instead of destroying the attention of the crowd, he increased it.

'Mr Pangbourne is dead,' said Ricky.

It didn't matter what he said after that. He read aloud the short prepared statement about how the doctors had done everything possible but Mr Pangbourne had died in the hospital last night.

But it didn't matter what he said. It was all over for Ricky. There might have been some chance of escape earlier, but once he'd hooked their attention with the shocking news there was no way out for him.

The crowd watched him as if hypnotized. No one even coughed as he read from the prepared statement.

He could have been reading pages at random from the phone book. It wouldn't have mattered. The crowd would have listened with the same rapt attention. He had them. He held them in the palm of his hand. He could feel the strange energy flowing back and forth between himself and the crowd. Like invisible threads binding him to them. Tug on the threads and make the crowd move.

They didn't cough because Ricky didn't let them cough.

Ricky began to sense pockets of variation in the crowd's response, and he realized that he could play on these variations, shifting his attention here and there, altering the tone of his voice. Subtly applying pressure to them. He was like a conductor summoning different responses from different sections of the orchestra. Feeling it respond to his command.

Ricky was shocked by the power of the relationship he felt with the crowd. Every passing second seemed to reveal new secrets to him, to increase his understanding of the phenomenon. And as his understanding increased, so did his power over the crowd.

Luckily it was only a short statement. When he'd finished he turned away and walked across the stage. The toe of his shoe caught a minuscule crack in the stage flooring and for a second he stumbled comically.

The crowd remained silent.

Then Ricky tripped as he began to descend the stairs off the stage. He waggled his arms in a ridiculous fashion as he struggled to recover his balance.

No one laughed.

Ricky felt panicky. It was too late. None of the old tricks worked. It was as if Ricky had lost his belief in them, so the crowd didn't believe the tricks either. Fake clumsiness didn't convince them any more. They weren't going to be thrown off. The tricks wouldn't work.

Ricky realized that they'd probably never work again. Every person in the room watched him as he walked off the stage.

Ricky realized that they would never stop watching him now.

Behind the stage there was a set of fire doors. Descending the stairs it was possible to turn right and go back into the hall or turn left and go through the doors. Ricky turned left and went through them, hurrying out into the corridors of the school.

Running for his life.

Behind him the school bell rang to signal the start of the first lesson of the day. The crowd seemed to give a collective sigh, and began to shake itself awake. The kids stood up and conversations began as they filed out from among the rows of chairs.

Amy stood staring at the fire doors through which Ricky had fled, as if Ricky's presence still lingered there. The man who called himself Retour stood beside her, staring in the same direction.

'That's my boy,' he said, finally.

'That was extraordinary,' sighed Amy.

'It was the boy. He's a natural. We just have to put him in the right situations and let him rip.'

'You're pretty good at coming up with the right situations,' said Amy. Her curiosity was getting the better of her. 'How did you learn about this?'

'Would you believe through extensive studies in the animal kingdom?' The man stared at the door through which Ricky had disappeared, shaking his head happily.

'Just imagine what he'll be like when we get him in front of the cameras.' The man chuckled. 'They'll never want to vote for anyone else.'

Ricky fled through the school. After what had happened in the assembly hall he thought he would run and run, and never stop.

But there was a comforting familiarity to these corridors; his pace gradually slowed and he began to calm down surprisingly quickly.

Ricky had only been at Scopes High a few days, but he had already begun to feel familiar with the place. It was a school. If you've seen one school you've seen them all. And Ricky had seen plenty of them in his young life.

He had already settled into this one. He'd begun to adapt to the particular rhythms of the place and even to feel at home here.

As he'd got to know the school, got to know the mood of it, he'd begun to find places where he could relax, ways he could hide in the anonymity of the institution and the kids who filled it.

Ricky had been working on how to slip by without anyone noticing him. At all his previous schools he'd used something similar. It always worked. He simply became the kind of kid the crowd ignored. He thought of it as his cloak of invisibility.

Now his cloak of invisibility had been torn from him.

The whole mood of the school had changed. It was no longer the same place. Ricky had nowhere to hide any more.

As he hurried down the corridors kids were thronging to their classes, like a river flowing. And Ricky was like a rock in that river, fixed and immovable. Dividing the current. The kids flowed around him, each reacting to him.

Some kids reacted by standing respectfully aside to let him by. Some reacted by deliberately brushing against him. That had always happened to Ricky, people seeming to go out of their way to bump into him.

Before, he would have flinched at such contact. He would have interpreted it as hostility. Now he knew the truth. The ones who bumped into him were hoping some of his special status would rub off on them.

The members of the pack wanted to share in the power of the leader.

Before, Ricky would have been unnerved by the apparent challenge of the contact. Now every bump only seemed to confirm his status as the alpha male. Each collision was a token of respect. And despite himself Ricky grew more confident with every contact, settling comfortably into his inevitable role in the group.

And as his posture reflected his casual dominance, the collisions became less frequent. Other males in the group ceased to challenge him.

So the crowd of kids flowed around Ricky, hurrying to their lessons, like water around a rock in a stream. And, like the rock in that stream, Ricky shaped the flow.

The crowd came at him, flowing in behavioural patterns. Some kids stood aside to let him by. Some girls marched past him, eyes fixed firmly ahead, pretending not to notice him. Others bobbed towards him, clumsily bumped into him, then drifted on, hoping to have picked up some of the strange authority he had.

Ricky stopped at his locker and collected the books for his first class. He stood there leaning on the open door, catching his breath. In the gloom of the locker he could just see a small white shape, seemingly floating in the shadows.

Ricky knew exactly what that shape was. It was an envelope taped to the underside of the top shelf in his locker, the shelf where he stacked his books. The envelope was full of money. All summer Ricky had slaved away at menial jobs to earn that money. His parents had told him he should put it in the bank.

Ricky didn't want to put it in the bank. He wanted it right here where he could put his hands on it immediately, in case things got too much. In case he needed to turn and run. To grab this envelope full of money and turn and run, as far as the money would take him.

Ricky stood leaning on the door of his locker, listening to the kids behind him, streaming busily past on the way to their classes. Ricky had to hurry or he'd be late. But he stood there, staring in at the envelope and thought about not going to his class at all. About tearing the envelope free and heading for the door. Run away from the school and his family, and everything in his old life.

No. Things weren't that bad. Ricky was feeling a lot calmer now. The situation wasn't so bad. Given time the kids would forget. They'd stop reacting to him like this and he could sink safely back into anonymity.

He didn't have to run.

Ricky turned away from the envelope taped to the shelf. He shut the door of the locker behind him and hurried on towards his first class of the day.

Kids still streamed past. Ricky joined the stream, going down the staircase that led towards the school library. It was exciting being in a mass of people.

He couldn't stop himself falling into the rhythm of the moving crowd. The crowd was like a living thing to him, a collective entity. And he understood how this beast behaved.

Ricky moved through the crowd, sensing its inner pulse. He knew its patterns and its mood, and he knew when that mood suddenly changed.

Until now Ricky had been moving through a zone of the school in which everyone's behaviour was affected by his presence. It had been like a powerful current all flowing in the same direction.

But now he was feeling a cool cross-current in his stream. He was feeling the influence of someone else on the crowd. The kids were responding to another dominant individual.

Ricky came around the corner and found himself face to face with Wolf Leemark and the entire Wolf Pack.

They were standing in the alcove outside the library. The alcove was a small brightly lit recess where new books were displayed in a glass case, to give the whole school a chance to inspect them; they were changed each week.

It had been a ritual Mr Pangbourne had insisted on. The old principal had always believed that books were wealth, and that his students should be given a chance to look at the new treasures as they arrived.

Wolf and the Pack weren't looking at the books in the glass case. They were looking at the suntanned girl from the lunch-room standing under the hot alcove lights. Wally Saddler had dared her to take off her panties in front of the Pack.

The suntanned girl was some kind of slumming intellectual from a rich family. She said she was a nihilist – whatever that was – and wore black all the time. She also read weird French poetry. She seemed to think that hanging out with the Wolf Pack was a cool thing to do.

They'd come out of assembly, the Pack and the suntanned girl, all a little shaken up by the big speech about Mr Pangbourne being dead.

And of course Wolf's dad had been the one who killed him. So Wolf was liable to be touchy about the subject. So no one dared say anything for fear of awakening his rage. Wolf was very touchy lately and there was no telling exactly what he would do or how he would react. The only safe topic seemed to be talking about what a little prick that Ricky McIlveen was. The way he made it such a big deal about Pangbourne's death. Talking about it in that impassioned speech that had put tears into the eyes of even the toughest boys.

When he was talking, Ricky seemed to be talking right to you. Right to your heart. Then when he stopped talking and got down off the stage you just sat there for a moment with your feelings all stirred up inside you. And then things gradually went back to normal, thank God.

And so the Wolf Pack had stumbled out of the assembly hall like men waking from a dream, and the suntanned girl had tagged along with them.

They were all feeling a little upset and dazed. It was a weird mood, and it wasn't helped when Wolf insisted on stopping in the little alcove outside the library. The alcove was a funny place because it was sheltered and yet at the same time very public. The bright lights made it feel a little unreal. A separate little zone.

And maybe it was the sense of unreality that gave Wally Saddler the idea. It just popped into his head and he let it pop out of his mouth. He turned to the suntanned girl, standing there in the bright lights of the alcove, and he suggested that she take her panties off.

Wally Saddler thought she might think it was a nihilist sort of thing to do, what ever that meant. And indeed, the suntanned girl had seemed to take the challenge seriously.

She was wearing a skirt instead of jeans today, so the suggestion was perfectly feasible. You could see the thought run through her mind, see that she hadn't decided yet, and that her decision could go either way. That was a very exciting thing to watch.

So the boys were all standing there under the bright alcove lights, staring like they were hypnotized, waiting to see what she would do.

The outcome was still very much in the balance at the moment when Ricky came striding past, irretrievably breaking the mood.

Everyone could see the suntanned girl had changed her mind. In fact she was staring after the McIlveen kid, suddenly looking more interested in him than the Wolf Pack.

The calamitous disappointment was simply too much for one member of the Pack. It was the same kid who had upset Wolf the other day by talking about Amy Cowan, the school shrink.

Now this kid saw the suntanned girl suddenly ditch any notion of panty removal after that long tantalizing wait. And he saw Ricky sweeping past, obviously the cause of this disappointment.

So he lunged out of the alcove and caught up with Ricky in a few swift strides. Ricky wasn't aware of his presence until the kid grabbed his shoulder. Ricky's expression as the kid spun him around was one of surprise rather than fear. The kid was throwing back his arm, getting ready to punch Ricky.

He never got to throw the punch.

Wolf Leemark was on the kid with such brutal speed that the others hardly saw him move. He dragged the kid away from Ricky before he could disturb one hair on Ricky's head. Then he slammed the kid to the ground and began to stomp him savagely. The kid was caught between the bank of lockers and Wolf, rolling back and forth in a desperate effort to avoid Wolf's steel-capped boots. He was clutching his head, trying to protect his face, when the blows suddenly stopped.

Wolf had stopped kicking the kid. He'd stopped because Ricky had gone up to him and placed a hand on his shoulder. So Wolf ceased stomping the kid and turned to look at Ricky. And he gave a little involuntary nod of the head.

No one missed it. It was a tiny gesture but crucial. It was an acknowledgement of leadership.

Everyone was looking at Ricky again.

Wolf and the Wolf Pack were looking at him, like troops waiting for orders from their general.

Ricky felt the mood of the crowd change towards him. Before it had been like a stream with conflicting currents. Wolf Leemark had exerted a behavioural influence of his own. That was gone now. The pecking order of the school had changed. If the kids looked up to Wolf or the Wolf Pack now they would see the gang themselves looking further up the behavioural ladder towards Ricky.

Now the mood of the school was all flowing powerfully in a single direction. Flowing in the direction of Ricky.

Ricky moved away from the library as fast as he could. He avoided eye contact all the way. He turned into the stair-well and went back up the stairs.

Sad Girl was sitting at the top of the stairs as he hurried up them. He tried to avoid looking at her. It wasn't easy. Sad Girl was looking directly at Ricky, all shyness gone.

She was looking right at him and smiling. She had a lovely smile.

Ricky loped up the stairs and back to his locker. He opened it and ripped down the envelope full of money. He grabbed his jacket, slammed the locker and ran.

Ran out of the front door of the school, the muscles of his legs bending with rubbery limberness.

Ricky wondered what Mr Pangbourne would think of him now.

While he'd read the speech he had imagined Mr Pangbourne being proud of him. That was one way he'd got through the ordeal of standing on the stage in front of the whole school.

But what would Pangbourne think now? Ricky was running. He was turning his back on his problems, on his whole life, and simply fleeing. Did this make him a coward? Ricky didn't know. He just knew he couldn't take any more.

It wasn't too bad once he was out of school. Travelling down-town he encountered a few crowds, but nothing like the school when all the kids had been hurrying to their classes. The worst part was when he had to catch the bus.

He boarded the city bus with a group of white-collar

commuters on their way to work. Climbing on to the bus he'd been packed in so densely with them that he felt the crowd begin to respond to him.

The tense commuters had begun to shift uneasily all around him. Lost in the glumness of their routine journey to boring jobs, all they were really aware of was some additional irritant on the crowded bus. The whole bus stirred bad-temperedly, then gradually settled down as Ricky buried himself away on a corner seat and kept his face turned rigidly to stare out of the window for the full journey. His neck ached by the time he disembarked down-town, hurrying to the train terminus.

Ricky bought the most expensive one-way ticket his money would cover. The destination was Galveston, Texas.

Ricky had no idea what it would be like in Galveston, Texas. But he knew it would be a different place and no one would know him there.

The train was already waiting at its platform, sitting patiently for the journey which wouldn't begin for hours. Clutching his ticket, Ricky felt a flutter of anxiety. Should he have gone for maximum speed instead of maximum distance? Perhaps he should have simply jumped on the first train that was leaving.

Too late now. He was committed. He put the ticket carefully into his pocket and climbed up into the shining silver bulk of the waiting train. Inside it was dim and plush, and luxurious. A smoked-glass dome spanned the roof of the train carriage, letting daylight in. Looking at the expensive chromed fittings and the long bar draped with white linen, Ricky realized that he'd wandered into first class.

With a tug of regret, he left the dimly glowing luxury of the carriage and walked further down the train.

He found an unreserved seat in standard class, made a calculation about which way the train would be travelling when it pulled out, and sat down facing in that direction.

The entire coach was empty and Ricky could sprawl comfortably. He'd stopped worrying about what Mr Pangbourne would think of him if he could see him now. Ricky knew he'd done the right thing.

It was as if a great weight had been lifted from his shoulders. For the first time in months he felt he could truly relax. The clean empty space of this second class coach seemed like paradise in the autumn sunlight.

And then the train began to fill up. People began to trickle into the coach and to take up seats near Ricky.

Ricky had thought he'd be the only one to board the train so early, but all the other passengers seemed to have had the same idea. The carriage was filling rapidly and Ricky began to tense up again at the thought of being in a crowd. Even now he could feel himself beginning to have an effect on his fellow passengers. He could detect a certain awareness of him, a subliminal reaction which he himself was only peripherally aware of. Out of the corner of his eye he would see someone tense up and know that they were aware of his presence.

His very anxiety must have been a signal because almost immediately a fat woman came sweeping along, sweating from her struggle to board the train, through the narrow corridor. She had a heavy bag in each hand, and ignored row after row of empty seats to plunk herself directly down opposite Ricky.

Ricky's alarm at her sudden presence so close to him didn't escape the fat lady. She jammed herself into the seat across from him and as much as they both tried to avoid eye contact he couldn't help being aware of her growing hostility to him. And that made him even more aware and her hostility just grew, her resentful eyes peering out from the doughy folds of her face, daring the world to look at her. Daring it to find her ugly. Then her eyes returned to take a quick angry look at Ricky, as if she was sucking at something bitter.

Ricky realized that the fat woman was searching for a hostile reaction in him. She wanted him to find her unattractive, to fuel the familiar resentment she lived by.

But Ricky decided that there was another approach. He couldn't have this woman travelling for thousands of miles sitting opposite him like this. She was reacting to him so strongly that she was like a beacon, attracting attention to herself and, inevitably in turn, to Ricky. The other passengers were sensing the fat angry woman and beginning to register the kid sitting opposite her.

Ricky had to halt the process. So he made his peace with the woman. On some deep behavioural level he simply forgave her for being fat, for being ugly.

He had soon relaxed and forgotten about the fat woman, and sat in calmness and tranquillity. But this didn't last long. Two more passengers sat down near him. One was a business-woman with a computer. She immediately switched it on and began working as soon as she sat down.

The other passenger was a huge brutal-looking man who sat down across from Ricky, and began tensely kneading his big fists between his knees.

Both the business-woman and the brute reacted to Ricky's presence. They didn't know what was going on, but they both sensed some subliminal disturbance and both grew uneasy. The business-woman typed ever more quickly on her keyboard, and the brute restlessly massaged his knuckles, as though itching for a fight.

For a few moments the tension kept growing, but then Ricky realized that it was his own attention that was creating this reaction. So he stopped concentrating on the passengers and tried to forget that they were there.

It worked. The fat woman was the first to react. A look of great happiness and childlike contentment spread across her face.

Soon the business-woman's typing had slowed down and Ricky sneaked a glance at her. She was casually slouched over her computer, the bright colours of a game flashing on its screen.

The brute had also relaxed. He was laboriously working on crossword puzzles in a much-thumbed book that he'd dug out of his pocket.

Soon, like the fat woman, they had sunk into a state of serene calm. They didn't know why, they just felt peaceful and relaxed. Ricky had spent years making everyone around him feel tense. Now he had learned how to do the opposite.

And he discovered that calm could be as infectious as panic. The mood spread through the passengers crowding into the train and soon the whole carriage was quiet and peaceful, a serene little zone. Even people hurrying through noticed it, slowing down in respect for the mood of the carriage, as if they'd blundered into the silent communal prayer of a church-service.

Ricky felt safe and relaxed at last. He let himself slump in his seat. His face pressed against the cool reinforced glass of the window, and he slept.

As soon as he woke up, Ricky knew something had gone badly wrong.

His face ached where it had been pressed against the window. He wiped the sleep from his eyes and peered blearily at his watch. The train should have departed long ago but it was still sitting at the platform. Ricky wondered fuzzily why the other passengers hadn't raised a fuss.

Then he looked around the carriage.

Everyone was asleep. The fat woman snored gently in the seat opposite him, mouth open like a baby bird waiting to be fed. The business-woman and the brute were both collapsed in their seats, their bodies almost intertwined in the lack of inhibition deep sleep had conferred upon them.

The other passengers in the carriage were all in similar states. Ricky saw them as he got up and hurried out. He jogged along the train corridor into first class and found a white-coated barman collapsed at his post, dozing beside a gleaming cocktail shaker and a bowl of melting ice. In the dining car well-dressed men and women were sleeping face down on the tables or slumped upright in their chairs.

Ricky got off the train. People were lying sprawled on the platform. A uniformed porter was unconscious at the wheel of a small electric trolley which had nosed forward into a tall stack of canvas mail-sacks; it was stalled there, engine gently purring.

Ricky ran the whole length of the train and peered through the glass of the driver's cockpit. The man was slumped there at the controls of the train, audibly snoring.

That was when Ricky finally accepted that he wouldn't be going to Galveston, Texas.

He left the platform. He tried running, but soon slowed to a relaxed walking pace. He wanted to flee but somehow it was impossible to move with haste past all these sleeping bodies. It seemed almost sacrilegious.

The entire station had sunk into a deep sleep. It was like an explosion with the train he'd abandoned at its epicentre. Ricky strolled through the eerie stillness feeling lost and helpless. In the ticket hall passengers were asleep on the benches and clerks were slumped behind their windows. A drunk and a security guard both lay asleep on the floor on either side of the revolving doors, neatly placed like symmetrical heraldic figures.

Ricky went out through the revolving doors into the street.

They were waiting for him.

Chapter 35

'Your daddy got stuck in this elevator one Christmas. Just before our office party. Bet you didn't know that.'

'No,' said Eve McIlveen dutifully.

Grown-ups always liked it when you put that dutiful tone in your voice. They didn't seem able to see through the transparent insincerity. Eve knew that sort of behaviour would never fool another child. In the complex and dangerous world of childhood Eve had adapted swiftly. 'I didn't know that,' she said, making her eyes wide.

The man called Buddy Stanmer grinned with satisfaction. He held Eve's tiny four-year-old hand in his powerful hairy fist. Eve was in awe of the man's great size and his almost animal-like hairiness.

She remembered the way he had looked when she met him, fierce and sweating and bulging with muscle. At the gym. And then he had hit her father in the arm and her father had grabbed Stanmer's hand and made him go pale with pain. Eve had felt a fierce surge of satisfaction in her tiny heart when her daddy had done that to the man. He was a nasty man. He'd been trying to bully her daddy.

'Why did you bring me here?' she demanded hotly. She looked up at Stanmer. The big man shrugged.

'It's like this,' he said. 'Because there are some people after Creed. I mean after your dad. Think of them as the bad guys.' Stanmer squeezed Eve's fist in one of his big hands. He was holding his other hand at a funny angle, out of Eve's sight. He was holding something in that hand and he didn't want her to see it.

Eve tried to see what was in his hand, craning her head around. But then Stanmer looked down at her and she had to pretend not to be looking.

'And I'm one of the good guys,' he said. 'I've rescued you. You've been rescued by the good guys.' He looked down at her and smiled, but there was something forced and false about that smile.

'Why?' said Eve to the man who stood so tensely beside her.

'Because we're, well, some bad guys are angry at your daddy. And we're afraid that someone might want to hurt his little girl.'

There was silence in the elevator. It was a long uncomfortable silence. Finally, to break it, Eve decided to restart the conversation. Mr Stanmer obviously wasn't going to say anything so it was up to her to put him at his ease. He seemed very uncomfortable with her. Maybe he wasn't used to kids.

'Is that why you came to get me? Is that why you came into my house without anyone hearing and took me away?'

'That's right, baby. We did it to protect you. We had to get you out of there before the sh–' The man stopped himself before he said the naughty word, and looked all embarrassed, the way that grown-ups always did. 'Before the doodoo hit the fan,' he finished lamely. 'I had to bring you back here to your daddy's office building. So you'll be safe.'

'But why are we going up in this elevator?'

The man called Stanmer suddenly wouldn't meet her gaze. He looked up, instead, at the numbers flashing by. 'Like I said, baby, so you'll be safe. I'm going to put you somewhere very safe.'

Stanmer finally relaxed his hand so that Eve could see what he was holding. It was a gun of course. Like the one her daddy had. Once, Ricky had sneaked it out of the bedroom and shown it to her and Cynthia. A blunt ugly metal thing that grown-ups used to kill each other.

'Why are we going up?' said Eve, with a sudden new urgency in her voice.

Buddy Stanmer sighed with exasperation. 'I told you,' he said.

'But if we go up in this elevator then the bad thing will happen.'

'Nothing bad's going to happen, honey.'

'Yes it is,' said Eve adamantly. 'If we go up there then the bad thing will happen.'

'Stop worrying. We're almost there. Hey!' Stanmer quickly

reached out and grabbed Eve's hand. The little girl was standing up on tiptoe, straining desperately upwards, trying to reach the control panel. Stanmer wrenched her hand back with more force than was necessary.

Eve looked up at him with tearful eyes. 'Please. I know something bad is going to happen.'

'Honey, everything is going to be fine.'

'But I had a dream,' said Eve, speaking quickly, trying not to trip over the words as they poured out of her. 'I had a dream about daddy. About sharp bones in the moonlight. And things with long sharp teeth.'

'Calm down, baby, please.'

'Dogs with long sharp teeth. And they were chasing after daddy in the moonlight. And I woke up crying. Mommy said it was just a dream. But I knew it was true.' Eve looked up at Stanmer, her tearful eyes huge. Her small mouth was drawn tight, giving her face a monkey-look of anxiety. 'Just like I know it's true about the bad thing.'

'Hush now.'

'Don't let the bad thing happen.'

'Hush. We're almost there.'

'Stop the elevator,' begged Eve.

'Sorry baby.'

'Please.'

'Too late,' Stanmer smiled, relaxing. 'We're there, baby.' The elevator had slowed to a halt and now he grabbed Eve's hand as the doors hissed open. He tugged her out and into the big echoing space.

'It's all empty,' said Eve in a small voice.

'Top floor, spare office space,' said Stanmer. He led her along a corridor, past doors that gaped open to reveal empty offices. 'Room for expansion and all that,' said Stanmer. Then he looked at Eve. 'What's wrong?'

The little girl's eyes were wide. Her expression was a rictus of fear. 'Something moved over there.' She pointed down the corridor to the big open room ahead. Stanmer paused and squinted for a moment. There was a flicker of movement ahead of them.

'It's OK,' he said. 'It's just the flag. You can see it moving through the window.' He dragged Eve out of the corridor into the big room. 'See?' he said.

From the big empty room the giant flag attached to the front of the Agency building was clearly visible. It billowed hugely beyond the high windows.

Standing in front of the windows was a slender black woman in a military-style uniform. She had short-cropped hair and she held a gun.

Stanmer froze as soon as he saw her.

The woman stood watching Stanmer and the little girl. She didn't move. After a moment Stanmer recovered from the shock.

'Who are you?' he said.

'Roz Forrester,' said the woman.

'How did you get in here?'

'With the help of a friend' she said.

'Are you Agency personnel?'

'No.'

'Then you have no business here.'

'I wouldn't say that,' said Roz Forrester. She stepped forward, away from the windows. Behind her the flag billowed beyond the glass, like a giant sea-creature undulating lazily in a big aquarium.

'I've come for the little girl.'

'You have, have you?' Stanmer clearly wasn't intimidated by the woman.

'Her father has sent me. Creed sent me. To look after her.'

'That's nice,' said Stanmer. 'In fact, it's kind of a coincidence. Because I'm also here to look after her.'

'Did Creed send you?'

'He didn't have to. The Agency looks after its own. I found out that Creed was in trouble. That he was being stabbed in the back. So I came to help him.' Stanmer backed slowly away from Roz, pulling Eve along with him. He was moving towards one of the open office doors.

'So you thought his little girl might be in danger.'

'Sure, that's right,' said Stanmer. He grinned tensely.

'These people will stop at nothing.'

'These people?'

'Like I said to Eve in the elevator, the bad guys are after her. So the good guys have to protect her.'

'But how do we know who are the good guys and who are the bad guys?'

For such a burly man Stanmer moved with startling speed. He suddenly shoved Eve into the nearest office.

'My point exactly,' he said. 'Of course, we could both be bad guys.'

'Or both be good guys,' said Roz.

Stanmer grinned. 'That's what's known as the infinity-of-mirrors effect. Things can get confusing in the counter-espionage business. So I guess I'd better put my gun down before someone gets hurt.'

But of course instead of putting the gun down, he made his move.

Stanmer suddenly slumped forward, letting his relaxed body drop bonelessly so no muscular tension gave him away. As he fell to the floor he threw himself into a firing stance.

He was aiming at Roz from a low angle and his first shot would have hit her in the head, entering under the chin and channelling up through her nasal cavity, to blow away the top of her skull.

But Roz was ready for him.

She fired first. Just once. The shot echoed through the empty rooms.

There was a moment's silence and then a piercing wailing from the nearest office. Roz rushed to the door and opened it.

Eve was sitting cross-legged on the bare carpeted floor. She looked up at Roz with tears in her eyes.

Roz smiled down at her. 'Are you OK?'

'I told him something bad was going to happen,' said the little girl forlornly.

Chapter 36

'If I start to drive on the wrong side of the road,' said Redmond, 'just give me a sharp rap.'

Jack chuckled. 'And you give me a rap if I stick my head out of the window with my tongue lolling in the breeze.'

He stared delightedly through the windows of the rented car, at the passing streets of the American city. After a while he pulled down the small mirror, which all cars had to indulge the vanity of the passenger. Jack inspected himself.

His long red hair was beginning to look normal again; the years in the life-support tank had turned it into something that looked like dried red seaweed for the first few hours after he'd woken up. He slapped the mirror shut and pressed the button that made the window hum swiftly open.

A pleasant breeze came swelling into the car. The evening smelled good; but compared to the way things had used to smell Jack felt like a blind man feeling the sun on his eyelids and trying to conjure memories of colour.

That didn't matter. He was glad to be back.

'On second thoughts, I might just stick my head out and do some tongue-lolling. Only stop me if I start pissing against lamp-posts again.' Jack smiled as he glanced across at Redmond.

'Forgive me if I still find all that a bit hard to swallow,' said Redmond. 'I mean, a dog.' He glanced sceptically across at Jack. 'You can understand if it's a bit hard to believe.'

'Sure,' said Jack. 'Listen, if somebody could convince me the whole thing was a bad dream I'd be happy. So long as it's a bad dream that's all over.'

'But what about this whole business with Vincent?' said Redmond.

Jack stopped smiling. 'Yeah, well you might say that was

fate.' He stared out of the window at the passing buildings. A man in tattered clothes was standing on a street corner, unashamedly digging into a garbage can as respectable pedestrians streamed past. Jack remembered the rich smell of garbage and the excitement of rooting through it.

'It was fate that brought me and Vincent together.' said Jack. 'Or maybe it was the Doctor. He has a reputation for that sort of thing; for being a nexus. You know, interesting events happen around him. Although interesting isn't quite the word for this.'

'I'll say.' Redmond slowed for a red light, drumming his fingers impatiently on the steering-wheel. 'There's been a lot of blood shed.'

Jack frowned. 'I know. And if I hadn't connected up with Vincent it would never have happened.'

'Sure. And if your grandmother had balls she would have been your grandfather,' said Redmond. 'There's no point in thinking like that. Don't blame yourself.'

'But I gave Vincent his idea.'

'When I meet this Vincent fellow I'm going to put a bullet in his head,' said Redmond. 'He seems to have caused a lot of trouble for everyone.'

'He wants vengeance,' said Jack.

'Tell him to join the line. Half the world wants vengeance.'

'But I showed him how to get it.'

'I thought this Ricky kid was supposed to be the instrument of his vengeance. His son.'

Jack sighed. 'Yes, but he never would have understood his son's gift, or how to manipulate it, if I hadn't shown him.'

'How?'

'Well, you must have seen sheepdogs,' said Jack. 'The way they can manipulate groups of sheep. Basically, they know how to control the dynamics of the crowd. Dogs are naturals for that because they have their own gift for complex pack behaviour. It didn't take me long to work this out. And I realized I could make use of it. I might not have been able to talk to Vincent, or write him a note asking for help. But I could use this to communicate with him. I could manipulate the behaviour of other dogs. I had the brains to work it out and I was in a position that any student of animal behaviour would have sold his soul for. So I just practised and learned, and developed my ability to manipulate the pack.'

'Did it work?'

'No. By trying to communicate I got his interest all right. But all I achieved was getting him to use me for research.'

'You mean as an experimental animal?'

'Well,' said Jack. 'No electrodes or anything like that, thank God. He simply put me into enclosed areas with a lot of other dogs. It wasn't like the lab near Canterbury.' Jack shuddered. 'Compared to that it was a holiday camp. We had a few acres to roam, inside wire-fenced enclosures.'

'It sounds like Vincent got organized.'

'He had a government grant by then. And the security was too damned tight. By trying to communicate I'd just managed to make myself a prisoner. He knew I was something special so he didn't give me a chance to escape. It took me years to get away. By then my body was getting old, slowing down. But that didn't matter, of course. I had perfected the means of manipulating the pack by then. Not just the pack though. Any dog. All dogs. I tried to conceal as much as I could from Vincent. But he learned a great deal from me.'

Redmond checked the map on the car's computer. 'Not far now,' he said. 'Keep talking. Where does Ricky come into it?'

'That's what I meant about fate. When Vincent began to notice the alpha male characteristic in Ricky he knew exactly how to develop it. He had considerable insight into how it operated.' Jack sighed again. 'All I achieved by trying to communicate with him was to give him the means for his vengeance.'

Redmond didn't reply. He was peering ahead with a look of intense concentration. 'What the hell is that?'

Jack couldn't understand what he was talking about, then suddenly he saw it, in the gutter near an intersection.

'A body,' he said as the car swept past. 'Someone lying in the street.'

'Dead or alive?'

'Couldn't tell,' said Jack worriedly.

'There's some more up ahead. Couple of men and a woman.'

Redmond stepped on the accelerator and Jack only got a glimpse of the bodies as they swept forward. He saw a brown bag beside the woman, spilling groceries on to the sidewalk. Eggs had rolled out of a carton and shattered on the pavement.

'How far to the train station?' asked Jack.

'Just around this corner,' said Redmond, his voice so tense it sounded funny. The tyres squealed as he threw the car into the turn.

'I didn't see any blood,' said Jack. 'Not on any of those bodies. Maybe – Jesus Christ!'

Redmond stepped on the brakes and the car shuddered to a screeching halt. For a long moment neither of the men said anything.

The train station was a tall building, wrapped in a big curving art deco façade. Its pocked white walls were turning a dusty pink with the onset of the city evening, as the sun dropped slowly among the angular black shoulders of the skyscrapers.

A crescent of road ran around the rear of the building, allowing buses, taxis and private cars to set down and pick up passengers from the station. Painted lines guided the vehicles to their designated areas.

But now everything was in chaos. Two big buses were jutting across the painted lanes at sharp diagonal angles, forming a jagged V that blocked the whole parking area. Cars were nosed up on to the sidewalk, and one taxi had run all the way up on to the apron of the grand stone staircase that curved around the corner of the building.

There were bodies everywhere, apparently lying where they'd first fallen.

Jack and Redmond got out of the car, slamming the doors. The sound was unnaturally loud in the strange silence. It was the kind of silence one might find in a cathedral at some hushed momentous point during a ceremony.

Jack and Redmond looked at each other, uneasy in the eerie stillness.

'I can smell diesel fumes,' said Redmond. His voice seemed shockingly loud and he dropped it to a whisper. 'I think that's the buses. I think their engines ran for a while and then conked out.' He looked around at the scattered vehicles and the bodies. 'It's like the *Marie Celeste*.'

'Except that the people are still here.'

'Yes,' said Redmond. He went over to the nearest body, a middle-aged woman collapsed on a bench, her purse lying between her feet. Redmond put a gentle hand to her throat, looking for a pulse.

'Jack!' he called excitedly. 'Jack, she's alive.' Redmond moved quickly to the old man, on the bench nearby, who was slumped at an angle still clutching his cane. 'This one, too. He's breathing.' Redmond turned to look for Jack. 'I think they're all alive.'

'What do we do?'

'Get back inside. Let me think for a minute.'

They climbed into the car and Redmond sat, chin on the steering-wheel, peering through the windscreen. 'None of the vehicles show any major damage,' he mused. 'No bullet-holes. No signs of an explosion.' He frowned. 'Gas?' His eyes flickered anxiously at the open window beside Jack.

'No,' said Jack slowly. 'I don't think so. If it was gas it would have hit us by now. Wouldn't you say? I mean, you have experience of these things, don't you?'

Redmond didn't reply. Jack looked across at him and saw that he was slumped in the driver's seat, a buzzing snore beginning to ease from his pursed lips.

'On the other hand . . .' said Jack, and he reached hastily to shut the car window. Suddenly, echoing from the front of the station, he heard two almost simultaneous sounds.

A gunshot and a girl's scream.

They were waiting when Ricky came out of the front entrance of the station.

'I'm sorry,' she said.

Ricky stood and looked down.

His sister was waiting at the bottom of the steps. Ricky walked out of the revolving doors and began to descend towards her. He had to step carefully over sleeping bodies on the way.

As Ricky came down the curving stone steps he could see that a man was standing beside his sister. He held a gun in one hand and in the other a long plastic leash with a lean black dog tethered to it.

'I'm sorry, Ricky,' said his sister.

'It's OK, Cynthia.'

She was staring up at him, eyes dark in her pale round face. She was a teenager straining to be an adult and she hadn't looked like a child for a long time, but now she did.

She looked like Ricky's kid-sister again. He remembered how close they had been before puberty hit; and even now, with the dog-handler pointing a gun at him, Ricky felt a little sadness for their lost childhood. Adolescence had made them enemies.

But now all that was stripped away and Cynthia was just his kid-sister again. She was looking up at him, mutely asking for forgiveness, a scared girl with a pale face and staring eyes.

'They made me come,' she said. She tried to step away from the dog-handler and the man immediately put his arm across her shoulders. It was like the casual possessive gesture of a guy strolling along beside his girlfriend. Except he had a gun dug in under Cynthia's chin.

Ricky's stomach flinched with fear and anger.

'I understand,' he said to Cynthia. He looked at the dog-handler. 'Don't hurt her.'

'Just keep coming down the steps,' said the man. 'Move slowly. Keep your hands in sight.'

'Shouldn't you be asleep?' said Ricky. The dog-handler glanced around for a second at the bodies scattered on the steps and the pavement outside the station.

'They're asleep, huh?' he said. 'We weren't sure if they were dead or what.' The black dog had become bored and now he slumped on the sidewalk at the man's feet, long tongue hanging out.

'You did this, huh?' said the man, gesturing to encompass the whole strange place, the road and the station and the pavement strewn with sleeping bodies.

'That's right,' said Ricky.

'Well, whatever you've got, she's immune to it.' The dog-handler hugged Cynthia closer to him. 'I guess because she's a blood relative.' He moved the gun fractionally so it was pressed against Cynthia's jaw but aimed at Ricky. 'And as long as I stay close to her I'm immune, too.'

'You won't shoot me,' said Ricky. 'I'm too important.'

The man extended his hand so the gun was clear of Cynthia's face. It was still so close that she shrieked at the painful loudness as he fired.

The bullet chipped the stone steps at Ricky's feet. Stinging fragments blasted past his ankles.

'Correction,' said the man. 'I won't kill you. But I'm authorized to blow your leg off and then patch up the femoral artery before you bleed to death.' He kept the gun aimed at Ricky. 'They'll rebuild your leg but you won't ever walk as good.'

'Don't, Ricky,' begged Cynthia. 'Don't try anything. Do whatever they want.' She sounded on the edge of hysteria.

'Poor girl. Ears must be ringing,' said the dog-handler.

'How did you find me?' said Ricky. He asked the question more to give his sister a chance to calm down than because he cared about the answer.

'They tracked you with the bloodhound,' said Cynthia. 'They went to your locker in the school and the bloodhound sniffed your stuff, and then they came after you. They figured you were down town but they didn't know where.'

'He isn't a bloodhound,' said the dog-handler fondly. 'Trotter's one of the Agency's trained narcotics sniffers.' He smiled with a hint of pride. 'Got a nose on him that can find one apple in an orchard. Trained for attack, too. Trotter will rip out your throat on command.'

'I'm a bit disappointed,' said Ricky. He kept talking to give himself time to think. He was almost at the bottom of the steps now. 'They sent just one guy and a dog to get me?'

The man nodded his head towards the station car park. 'There was a van full of us. The others just didn't stay close enough to your sister here, I guess. They're all sleeping on the ground back there.'

Ricky had reached the bottom step and now he stood staring past the man. 'Looks like one of them just woke up.'

The dog-handler chuckled. 'Nice try, kid. I'm supposed to turn around and look, and then you try something, huh?'

'It must be terrible to be so untrusting.'

At the sound of the voice the dog-handler spun around.

A man had come around the corner of the building from the parking lot. He had pale skin and long straggly red hair and he was wearing a baggy suit that was at least two sizes too big for him. He ignored the dog-handler and smiled at the teenage boy.

'Ricky McIlveen, I presume. My name is Jack. I'm pleased to meet you.'

'Why aren't you asleep like the others?' said Ricky. He seemed to have forgotten about the man with the gun. He stared at Jack in fascination.

'Because we're two of a kind, I guess.'

The dog-handler didn't seem to know how to deal with the new situation. He was trying to hold on to Cynthia and at the same time keep his gun on Ricky and the newcomer. But now he came to a decision. The black dog had risen to its feet, tense and alert, as soon as Jack had appeared.

The man slipped the dog free of the leash. He gestured towards Jack. 'Trotter – kill,' he shouted.

The dog trotted swiftly towards Jack and flung itself at his feet. The dog-handler stared in astonishment as the animal lay there, staring soulfully up at the pale smiling man in his baggy suit. 'Kill,' he shouted again.

The dog rolled over on his back like a puppy, exposing his belly to be patted. Jack obliged, kneeling to scratch the dog fondly. He glanced up at the dog-handler and smiled.

'Oh boy, have you got the wrong guy,' he said.

Now the dog-handler shifted his grip on Cynthia, raising his gun and taking aim at Jack. But the instant he did so, something subtle changed in Jack's stance. His body tensed and his smile faded. And the tension seemed to instantly communicate itself to the dog.

The black animal rolled over and surged to its feet in a flying forward run. It was across the pavement and in the air before the dog-handler could fire.

It hit the man solidly, high on the chest, and drove him to the ground, ripping at him. His gun went spinning through the air.

Cynthia broke free and ran to Ricky. The dog handler's gun clattered down on the steps just behind them.

Jack relaxed and smiled again. Instantly the attack-dog stopped tearing at the man. The man stared up in frozen terror as the black animal stood poised on his chest, alternately snarling at him and glancing up at Jack for approval.

'Good dog,' said Jack. 'Good boy.'

Chapter 37

They met at an empty picnic area designed for tourist traffic that wandered off the highway. It was located just off a small loop of country road in the middle of Gaines Woods.

Creed had been waiting there for ten minutes when she arrived in her little yellow Fiat and parked it beside his car, pulled up on the grass, concealed from the main road by a dense screen of trees.

He'd been wondering what he was going to say to her, how he would act towards her, but in the end he didn't even think about it.

He just got out of the car as soon as he saw her; his body acting faster than thought, reaching for the door, stepping through and then across the pitted tarmac towards her.

He was reaching for Amy as she was reaching for him.

They clutched each other for a long minute, their mouths locked together in a bruising wet kiss. By common consent they said nothing to each other until, finally, they had to break the embrace.

Then they went and sat in his car and began to talk, as they knew they had to.

'This is where you had a tree fall on your car,' said Creed. 'And you built your home-made skis.'

'Near here, yes.' Amy hesitated. 'The Agency received a report from London, filed by someone called Norman Peverell. It seems you got caught up in something nasty over there.' She looked at him and Creed saw dark circles of worry under her eyes.

'It's all over now,' he said.

'I'm glad I didn't know about it when it was actually happening,' said Amy. She touched the bandage on his face.

'It was bad enough reading about it. I couldn't stand to think of you being in danger.'

Creed took a deep breath. 'Cut the crap,' he said.

Amy took her hand from his face. She was staring at him in shock.

'I left you looking after my family,' he said.

'Yes, and there's something I have to tell you about Ricky —'

Creed interrupted her. 'I thought you were looking after them, but it turns out you've merely been keeping them under surveillance.'

Amy stared at Creed in silence. He was very close to her in the car and now there was a fierceness in his dark eyes that almost frightened her.

'What's the matter?' she said.

'I have a friend called the Doctor.'

'I know,' said Amy. 'He's the one who sent the message.'

'That's right. He sent the message summoning me to England. Or did he?' Creed's eyes were strange as he looked at Amy.

'What do you mean?'

'Maybe the Doctor never sent a message, maybe someone else sent it. As a diversion. Maybe someone wanted me out of the country. Maybe they were willing to kill somebody to make it look good.' Creed smiled, but it wasn't a very pleasant smile. 'Those are the kind of thoughts you have in a job like this. You begin to think that maybe the people you're working with can't be trusted. Maybe even the people closest to you. You begin to think that they're manipulating you. Separating you from your family at a critical time. Do you have any idea what it's like when you start thinking that way? It's like a classic case of paranoia. But it also might be true. Suspicion. Fear. Everybody you trust might actually be out to get you. Nothing is what it seems. If you're not crazy to start with you begin to get that way. It's like a fire burning in your mind.'

Amy reached up and stroked his forehead, her face twisted with sadness and compassion. 'Your family is all right,' she said. 'Eve was with that madman Stanmer but, thank God, someone apparently got there in time and rescued her.'

'There we go again. Maybe Stanmer was a madman or

maybe he was following orders. Maybe he was on my side or maybe he was on the other side.'

'And whose side is that?'

Creed looked at her. 'Yours,' he said.

'I thought I was on your side,' she said. Her blue-green eyes were misted with sadness.

'So did I,' said Creed. 'How long have you been working for them?'

'There is no them,' said Amy. 'It's just Vincent.'

'Yeah. We know that now.'

'It's his project, Creed. He's been studying Ricky for years. He got government funding and approval from the relevant bodies, but if he isn't successful they'll deny all knowledge. He's basically alone in this.' She gave him a searching look.

'Except that you're working for him. And you have been all along. You're his little helper,' said Creed. 'You came with the funding and the approval.'

'That's not true.'

'Come on Amy. The Doctor did a lot of digging on this situation. He can get in anywhere with his computers. He knows the score and he told me.'

'But he didn't tell you everything,' said Amy quietly.

'He didn't tell you that you started off as my assignment. But then you turned into something else.'

Evening sunlight was slanting into the car, catching the low branches of the nearby trees. There were dark leaf shadows moving across Amy's face. 'That just happened. I can't control my feelings. I wish I could. Life would be much easier for me if I could.'

Now the leaf shadows were stirring across the pale flesh of her breasts as Creed eased her out of her bra and she moved under him, trying to get her blouse the rest of the way off but it got stuck around her wrists and there it stayed, an obstinate flapping knot of cloth that was sometimes above her head, sometimes rubbing the skin of Creed's back as she drew him closer to her, giving a small cry as he entered her.

The windows of the car fogged up as they made love, obscuring the outside world in a pearly blur of leaves and late sunlight.

They moved back and forth in the tiny space, a gently

rocking cradle of joined flesh. Creed felt the cool tiny crescent of her silver earring pressed to his face, and breathed the warm scent of her hair as she writhed and cried out briefly and clung to him.

'You have to trust me,' she said.

Chapter 38

'Hello, Justine,' said the Doctor.

He stood in the shade of the big white porch. In the mellow evening sunlight of Concroft Avenue he looked like a visitor from an earlier, more civilized era. An Edwardian gentleman come to call on a mild Indian summer evening, holding his straw hat politely in his hand. The crickets were just starting to sing in the dark yards up and down the long avenue and the street-lights were coming on in the gathering dusk.

Justine gave the Doctor a tense insincere smile and waved him into the house.

The Doctor followed her, looking for somewhere to hang his hat. 'You'll be pleased to hear that everything is going as planned,' he said. 'Even now my friends have picked up Ricky and Cynthia safely and another friend is looking after your little girl. In fact Eve should be back with you as soon as Roz can get here. She apparently stopped to buy Eve some dinosaur-shaped cookies and then they hit traffic down-town. I told her not to worry. I said everything would be fine here, since you have Chris to look after you. I do hope I'm not being rude. I seem to be doing all the talking.'

A man stepped out of the shadows holding a gun. 'That's because she's basically too scared to open her mouth.' He took Justine by the shoulder and moved her away so that he had a clear line of fire towards the Doctor.

'Hello, Vincent.'

'Very good, Doctor.' Vincent aimed the gun at the Doctor's head. 'You didn't bat an eyelash. Are you going to say that you were expecting me?'

'Not at all. I was hoping to catch up with you at the school. What have you done with Chris?'

'He's fine.'

'Show me.'

Vincent moved towards the living room, waving the gun to indicate that Justine and the Doctor should precede him.

In the living room Vincent seated Justine in a straight-backed chair beside a gleaming grand piano. He swiftly secured her hands and legs with lengths of heavy black electrician's tape, and used a piece of the stuff to seal her mouth. It looked like some strange black clown's lipstick on her pale face. Instead of a neat slice of tape, Vincent used a long messy strip that circled right around and trapped the ends of her hair against her neck. He kept his gun on the Doctor while he worked.

Finally he set the big roll of tape aside and sighed with satisfaction. 'I tried to get the kind that doesn't hurt the hostage's mouth when you pull it back off again,' he said. 'But they were all out of it at the hardware store.'

'What have you done with Chris?' repeated the Doctor patiently.

'Through here.' He led the Doctor into the dining-room. Chris Cwej was on the floor beside the table, lying motionless among the loose-spooled folds of his orange robe.

'I had to leave him in here so as not to disturb Justine's delicate sensibilities.'

The Doctor immediately knelt and checked Chris's pulse. His eyes were closed and there was blood caked on the young man's bald head.

'See, he's fine.'

The Doctor looked up angrily. 'This is hardly fine.'

'Let's not split hairs, Doctor. He's alive. Now let's go back into the living room.' He waved the gun as he led the Doctor back through. 'Sit on the couch if you like. Get comfortable. I was in the middle of something when you rang the doorbell.'

Vincent went over to the piano and sat on the low stool, near Justine. Her eyes flickered fearfully above her taped mouth, trying to keep him in view.

'I was just filling Justine in on what we might call the missing years. The years since we split up.'

Vincent hitched the piano-stool forward, nearer Justine. The room was hot and still in the evening light. There was a heavy smell of flowers and fruit in a fruitbowl was slowly turning from ripeness to rot. 'Doctor,' he said, 'you might remember the strange things I used to do.'

'Of course I remember,' said the Doctor.

'Naturally, you would.' Vincent's eyes had an odd look to them. 'You used me as a weapon, so naturally you remember the powers that lent me to that use. I learned a lot from that experience. In fact, you might say that I've achieved all this.' Vincent waved his gun in a vague gesture to encompass the current situation. Above the wide black gag of tape, Justine's eyes worriedly followed the movement of the pistol. 'You might say that I've only got where I am today with your help.'

'Do you blame me for what happened to you, Vincent?'

'You used me, Doctor. You used me then discarded me. That would be obvious to anyone.'

'You can force that interpretation on to things, I suppose,' said the Doctor, his eyes steely. 'But we all weave our own destinies, Vincent. And this is the one you've chosen for yourself.'

'And I'm as happy as a pig in shit,' said Vincent. He leant back on his piano-stool and lazily stretched his leg out so his foot touched Justine's where it was fastened to the chair. She couldn't avoid his touch. 'That's now, though. It wasn't always like that. For a long time, for years, in fact I wasn't happy at all. Can you imagine that, Justine?' Vincent began to rub his foot playfully against her tethered foot.

'Justine, baby, after what you did to me I was so screwed up I lost the gift. It was like impotence. When you left me I couldn't function any more. It's funny. I'd spent years wishing it would go away so I could lead a normal life. But when it really did go it was like losing my right arm.'

Vincent looked at the Doctor sitting silently on the couch. 'Which was kind of a pity,' said Vincent. 'Because I was counting on my special talent to get me a job with the security services. Imagine my embarrassment. I was once a human weapon they would have killed to get their hands on. But there was no way I could prove it to these government guys.'

Vincent got up, turned to the piano and played a few simple chords. They echoed harmoniously in the warm dim room.

'But the story has a happy ending,' he said. 'It turned out

it didn't matter, they believed me anyway.' He grinned crookedly. 'My fame had preceded me. They already had me on their computers. So that made it easy. They gave me a job, in special weapons development. And I had some pretty good ideas about special weapons.'

He swivelled on the piano-stool to face the Doctor. 'I figured I didn't have the gift any more, but maybe my child had inherited it. My boy. Ricky.' He nodded at Justine. 'You know, when I told Justine what I had in store for her and her family, she . . . How can I put this delicately? She tried to be nice to me. Said if I promised not to hurt her kids she'd do anything for me.

'She seemed to think that maybe she was offering me something I really wanted. Like, maybe, I'd been in love with her for all these years and longing for her. Aching for her. And she was going to offer it to me, upstairs in the old McIlveen marital bed. Just so long as I left the kids alone. You understand what she was doing? She was counting on my love for her. Like she still had a card to play. Like I still loved her. My cow of an ex-wife.'

Justine sat silently, tightly bound in her straight-backed chair, tears dripping from her eyes. The Doctor got up from the couch, took out his handkerchief and crouched beside her, wiping her face.

'Don't try anything,' said Vincent amiably. 'Don't try to untie her or anything.'

'I won't.'

'I trust you, Doctor. I just don't trust that woman. How low could she sink? Trying to play on the love of an ex-husband. You know what I said to her. I said – *get real*.' Vincent shouted the last two words with great violence.

There was silence in the room for a moment. 'You know what else I said to Justine? My former beloved? I said, "Justine do you know just how ex an ex-wife can be?" You might think it's when she leaves you. Runs off with another man. Gets into bed with him. You might think she's reached the ultimate in ex-wife status. But no. How about when she marries the other man? Has she reached the ultimate? No. Not quite.'

Vincent got up and went over to Justine, peering into her eyes.

'No,' said Vincent. 'The ultimate is when she has another man's child.'

'Vincent,' said the Doctor quietly. 'It may not be too late to abandon this course of action.'

'Abandon it? Doctor, you're nuts. I'm holding all the cards. Your people are bringing Ricky to me. They went and saved me the trouble of tracking him down, and now they're bringing him back to me. On top of that, they're also bringing Cynthia and Eve back for a touching reunion. Your people are bringing back the whole damned family for me.' Vincent paused. 'Except for daddy, of course.' He smiled and nodded, as if savouring a thought. 'I sent one of my own people to bring back daddy.'

'What will you do with Ricky?' said the Doctor.

'Use him, of course. Just like his old man, he's got a special talent. And we'll use it.'

'To do what?'

'Completely restructure the government of this country for a start. Then do whatever takes our fancy.'

'Do you really think he'll be your willing tool?' said the Doctor.

'I don't see why not. I'm his real father and he doesn't seem to like it much around here. He obviously isn't getting anywhere with this sad crew.' He sat back down on the piano-stool. He resumed rubbing his foot against Justine's for a moment, then abruptly stopped. There was the sound of a car in the driveway and Vincent quickly got to his feet. He went to the window and lifted the curtain with the barrel of his gun.

'Looks like the party's started,' he said. 'First guests have arrived.'

A second car pulled up in the driveway and a moment later there was the sound of the footsteps of two people on the porch. The front door opened and closed, and Creed came into the living room followed by Amy.

Creed froze, staring at his wife tied up in her chair. Only then did he take in the presence of the Doctor, and Vincent pointing the gun at him.

When Creed saw Vincent his head went up, his chin rising in an unconscious challenge a million years old. As old as the primates.

'Don't try anything, Creed,' said Vincent. 'If I don't nail you my little buddy will. Look behind you. Surprise.'

Creed turned around slowly to where Amy was standing behind him. She was also holding a gun now. Pointing it at Creed.

Vincent smiled. 'Amy's been really useful. Keeping an eye on you, manipulating you. I sent her out today to bring you back here. I even told her to screw you if she had to.'

Creed looked at Amy for a long moment, then he turned back to Vincent. His face was expressionless.

'I hope you enjoyed taking my wife and child away from me,' said Vincent. 'The wife you can keep. But my boy is coming back to me. He's going to work for his old man. Join the family business so to speak. And the family business is going to consist pretty much of running the United States.'

'Ricky's going to spit in your eye,' said Creed.

'Nope. Ricky is going to be a new kind of presidential candidate. By the time he's old enough to run for office this whole country is going to be begging to elect him. I'm going to have the Republicans and the Democrats bidding for his services. And I'm going to strike the deals. And together Ricky and I will run America.'

'Dream on.'

'Ricky has the power, Creed. You're just too blind to see that. You've never appreciated what that kid is capable of achieving. You've stifled him. He's lived in your shadow. He's like a plant that's never had a chance to flourish in the sunlight. Keep your gun on him, Amy. And watch out for the little guy. The Doctor can be tricky.'

After disarming Creed, Vincent secured him using a pair of handcuffs. He locked one steel cuff on Creed's left wrist and the other around the leg of the grand piano. The piano weighed as much as a small car; there was no way Creed could budge it to free himself. Maybe he could break it. Creed tensed his muscles and tried pulling against the cuff attached to the piano leg. Wood could break. But he knew it was hopeless. The old seasoned wood of the piano was as hard as iron.

Now Vincent was looking at him. He sat down on the piano-stool and scooted it back out of Creed's reach. He was very close to Justine. He held the gun in one hand; with the other he reached out and caressed her cheek.

'You know, when my wife left me,' he said, stroking Justine's face, 'when she took my unborn child away from me, I didn't even know if it was a girl or a boy. We had the scans but we asked the hospital not to tell us.'

Vincent took his hand away from Justine's face and spun on the piano-stool to face the Doctor. He shrugged. 'Of course, when she went off with another man, it didn't matter. But imagine my delight when I discovered that I had a son. And he took after me.'

'Took after you?'

It was the Doctor who had spoken. His voice was full of sudden interest. It was as if he'd been sitting here bored all this time and Vincent had finally said something worthy of his full attention.

Creed wondered what the hell the Doctor was doing. There was something subtly insulting in his manner as he spoke to Vincent.

'What do you mean, took after you? It's not even grammatical.'

'My meaning was clear enough. Ricky has my gifts.'

The Doctor leant forward, peering intensely at Vincent. 'But Creed's other kids have gifts too. Who is responsible for those? Not you, certainly.'

Creed saw that Vincent was beginning to sweat. He clearly didn't like the direction the conversation was taking. Creed wished the Doctor would shut up. Vincent still had his gun aimed at Justine's head and he was clearly upset. More than that. He looked like a man who might go over the edge at any moment.

Creed wished the Doctor would shut up but the Doctor persisted.

'Doesn't that suggest anything to you?' he said.

Vincent wouldn't meet the Doctor's eyes. 'Who cares?' he said.

'You should. Ricky's powers have nothing to do with you.'

'Of course they do. I'm his father. He inherited something special from me.'

'Perhaps, Vincent. Or perhaps it was warlock.'

'Warlock?'

'Yes. Justine took the drug when she was pregnant. It could have passed across the placenta and affected Ricky in the womb. Indeed, it could have affected both Creed and Justine in such a way that their genetic material was changed. Hence all their gifted children. Nothing to do with you. Indeed, what about parenting? Do you remember what happened to Creed in that restaurant in London?'

'No.' Vincent turned away from the Doctor, as if he was hoping to stop the conversation. He smiled apologetically at Amy. 'Sorry to bore you with all this talk about old times.'

'I think you do remember, Vincent,' said the Doctor, refusing to let the matter drop.

Vincent kept looking at Amy, as if hoping she would say something and the Doctor would have to shut up and leave him alone. Like trying to get rid of a terrible bore who had attached himself to you at a party.

But the Doctor continued relentlessly. 'I think Justine told you about it and you remember very well.'

'OK. Maybe she mentioned something about it.'

'Creed once walked into a restaurant full of gangsters and destroyed their leader with body language. He made him flinch. He made it clear to everyone that the leader was no longer in charge of the pack. And soon enough the pack tore the old leader apart.' The Doctor's eyes gleamed now, staring unblinkingly at Vincent.

Vincent was twitching. He looked more and more unstable. The gun was pointing at Justine's head. What was the Doctor doing? He was going to send him over the edge.

'You know it's true. Justine told you about it. Creed was assisted by warlock, but he was manifesting exactly the alpha male principle which Ricky seems to display in such abundance. You've thought of that yourself, I can see you have.' The Doctor smiled at Vincent. 'Maybe Ricky hasn't inherited anything from you at all. Maybe he just took after his dad.'

'OK. Enough of the nature versus nurture debate.' Vincent was shaking with rage. 'Like I said, Ricky's a plant who isn't getting enough sunlight.' He rubbed the gun against Justine's head, as if he was caressing her hair with it.

'It's time to do some pruning,' he said quietly. The gun stirred and stirred through Justine's glossy hair. And then it stopped.

'Goodbye, love,' said Vincent cheerfully.

The gunshot was shockingly loud in the hot stillness of the room.

Vincent slowly lowered his hand, withdrawing the gun from Justine's head. He turned away from her, a distasteful expression forming on his face.

He moved in a slow circle, took half a step and then his gun dropped from his lifeless fingers.

He fell to his knees and reached out for the gun, moving in slow-motion like a deep-sea diver.

Amy fired again and this bullet knocked Vincent over on to his back.

He rolled over, looking up and said, clearly and distinctly: 'Justine –'

Then he died.

Justine never forgot that moment, or the great warmth of the relief that followed, as the Doctor unlocked Creed and he came to her. He gently eased the adhesive tape off her, freeing her. There was the sound of cars in the driveway and the others arriving. Ricky and Cynthia, and little Eve. All her children.

She would always remember all of these things. She would never forget the wonderful feeling that she and her family were safe.

But there was one thing that Justine would always remember in particular.

It was just after Amy killed Vincent.

Amy had shot Vincent and removed the threat forever. She stood, looking dazed at what she'd done, still holding the gun. Creed took the gun from her.

And after he took the gun, just for a second he held on to Amy's hand and squeezed it.

That was when Justine knew.

She knew that her family was safe but her marriage was over.

Chapter 39

Justine opened the front door. Mrs McCracken was standing on the porch, wearing sunglasses, cut-off jeans, and a tiny halter over her spectacular breasts. She was carrying a galvanized bucket. It made an icy tinkling sound and Justine could see some kind of red liquid shining in it.

'What's in that?'

'Why, it's a bucket of Bloody Marys, of course,' said Mrs McCracken. 'Lots of vodka and tomato juice but I couldn't find any tabasco. I hope you don't mind.' Ice cubes tinkled in the bucket as she lifted it for Justine's inspection. 'I trust you have some suitably large glasses.'

Justine led her into the kitchen to collect some glasses before continuing out into the sunshine of the backyard.

Eve was sitting in the sand-box behind the garage, contentedly building castles. Justine and Mrs McCracken sat on the grass under the shade of a tree where they could keep an eye on her. Mrs McCracken served the drinks, the glasses cool and rapidly frosting in their hands.

'Creed has moved out, then?'

'Yes,' said Justine. 'He's found an apartment in town and he's moving in with Amy.'

'Blondes are always the worst,' said Mrs McCracken philosophically. 'But don't worry. In a few years she'll be playing volley-ball with those tits. How is Eve taking it?'

Justine glanced over at the sand-box. 'Not too bad. Creed still sees a lot of her. I'm not putting up any obstacles. And, anyway, she seemed to know it was coming.'

'What about Cynthia?'

'You probably have a better idea than I do. She spends most of her time with Lysette these days.'

Mrs McCracken nodded. 'And what about Ricky? I

understand he's not going back to school for a while.'

'Maybe never.'

'Well, he certainly made quite an impression,' said Mrs McCracken. 'Apparently the kids are still asking after him. What is he doing?'

'He's going on a cross-country trip with some friends.'

'The Doctor?'

'Yes, and our friend the Buddhist monk, and Jack.'

'Oh yes,' said Mrs McCracken. 'He's the nice man who can't stand to see a dog tied up.'

'That's right. They're all going to work together with Ricky to try and help him understand and control his power.'

Mrs McCracken peered into the galvanized bucket. 'I'm sorry about this, dear, but the ice seems to be melting with ridiculous speed. You couldn't fetch some more from the kitchen, could you?'

Justine rose and went into the house. She was opening the refrigerator when there was a sound at the front of the house. She left the refrigerator open and trotted to see who it was.

There, silhouetted in the front door, was Creed. And Justine's heart leapt. She hurried forward, smiling. She hurried because she knew that he'd come back. Creed had come back.

He'd come back to her and everything was going to be all right again.

But as Justine left the kitchen the angle of the light changed and she realized that it wasn't Creed at the front door at all.

It was her son Ricky.

Ricky hadn't noticed her and he was on his way out. Justine followed slowly as he closed the door. She walked to the living room window where she could see him step down from the front porch and head towards the driveway.

The Doctor was there, sitting in the back of an open-top car. Beside him was the big man called Jack and in the front, behind the wheel, was Chris wearing a baseball cap to cover the bandages on his shaven head. Ricky joined them, sliding into the front seat.

Justine watched the car as it pulled away. It was a natural mistake, she told herself. Seeing Ricky like that, in the uncertain light of the front door, he looked so much like

Creed; it was something in his stance and posture.

After all, he was his father's son.

Justine went back, got the ice from the refrigerator, and took it out to Mrs McCracken.

Already published:

THE PIT
Neil Penswick

One of the Seven Planets is a nameless giant, quarantined against all intruders. But when the TARDIS materializes, it becomes clear that the planet is far from empty – and the Doctor begins to realize that the planet hides a terrible secret from the Time Lords' past.

ISBN 0 426 20378 X

DECEIT
Peter Darvill-Evans

Ace – three years older, wiser and tougher – is back. She is part of a group of Irregular Auxiliaries on an expedition to the planet Arcadia. They think they are hunting Daleks, but the Doctor knows better. He knows that the paradise planet hides a being far more powerful than the Daleks – and much more dangerous.

ISBN 0 426 20362 3

LUCIFER RISING
Jim Mortimore & Andy Lane

Reunited, the Doctor, Ace and Bernice travel to Lucifer, the site of a scientific expedition that they know will shortly cease to exist. Discovering why involves them in sabotage, murder and the resurrection of eons-old alien powers. Are there Angels on Lucifer? And what does it all have to do with Ace?

ISBN 0 426 20338 7

WHITE DARKNESS
David A. McIntee

The TARDIS crew, hoping for a rest, come to Haiti in 1915. But they find that the island is far from peaceful: revolution is brewing in the city; the dead are walking from the cemeteries; and, far underground, the ancient rulers of the galaxy are stirring in their sleep.

ISBN 0 426 20395 X

ST ANTHONY'S FIRE
Mark Gatiss

The TARDIS crew visit Betrushia, a planet in terrible turmoil. A vicious, genocidal war is raging between the lizard-like natives. With time running out, the Doctor must save the people of Betrushia from their own legacy before St Anthony's fire consumes them all.

ISBN 0 426 20423 9

FALLS THE SHADOW
Daniel O'Mahony

The TARDIS is imprisoned in a house called Shadowfell, where a man is ready to commence the next phase of an experiment that will remake the world. But deep within the house, something evil lingers, observing and influencing events, waiting to take on flesh and emerge.

ISBN 0 426 20427 1

PARASITE
Jim Mortimore

The TARDIS has arrived in the Elysium system, lost colony of distant Earth and site of the Artifact: a world turned inside out, home to a bizarre ecosystem. But now the Artifact appears to be decaying, transforming the humans trapped within into something new and strange.

ISBN 0 426 20425 5

WARLOCK
Andrew Cartmel

On the streets of near-future Earth, a strange new drug is having a devastating impact. It's called warlock, and some call it the creation of the devil. While Benny and Ace try to track down its source, the Doctor begins to uncover the truth about the drug.

ISBN 0 426 20433 6

SET PIECE
Kate Orman

There's a rip in the fabric of space and time. Passenger ships are disappearing from the interstellar traffic lanes. An attempt to investigate goes dangerously wrong, and the TARDIS crew are scattered throughout history – perhaps never to be reunited.

ISBN 0 426 20436 0

INFINITE REQUIEM
Daniel Blythe

Kelzen, Jirenal and Shanstra are Sensopaths, hugely powerful telepaths whose minds are tuned to the collective unconscious. Separated in time,